THE BOOK OF
OLD HOUSES

THE BOOK OF OLD HOUSES

A
Home Repair Is Homicide
Mystery

SARAH GRAVES

BANTAM BOOKS

THE BOOK OF OLD HOUSES
A Bantam Book / January 2008

Published by Bantam Dell
A Division of Random House, Inc.
New York, New York

This is a work of fiction. Names, characters, places, and incidents either are the product of the author's imagination or are used fictitiously. Any resemblance to actual persons, living or dead, events, or locales is entirely coincidental.

Bantam Books is a registered trademark of Random House, Inc., and the colophon is a trademark of Random House, Inc.

Library of Congress Cataloging-in-Publication Data

Graves, Sarah.
The book of old houses / Sarah Graves.
p. cm.
ISBN 978-0-553-80430-0
1. Tiptree, Jacobia (Fictitious character)—Fiction. 2. Women detectives—Maine—Eastport—Fiction. 3. Dwellings—Maintenance and repair—Fiction. 4. Eastport (Me.)—Fiction. I. Title.

PS3557.R2897B66 2008
813'.54—dc22
2007033869

Printed in the United States of America
Published simultaneously in Canada

www.bantamdell.com

10 9 8 7 6 5 4 3 2 1
BVG

THE BOOK OF OLD HOUSES

D riving up I-95 through New Hampshire and on into Maine, Dave DiMaio noticed as if from a distance how anger made the familiar route look alien to him. *The Way Life Should Be,* the sign welcoming visitors to the Pine Tree State proclaimed. But to Dave it was as if he were seeing it all by moonlight, everything bleached by rage.

Once he was nearly overcome by the urge to lean forward onto the steering wheel and howl over the murder of his friend Horace Robotham, whose death Dave had learned of only the night before. But he was speeding along the turnpike, so he couldn't.

He pulled off at a service area to use the restroom and wash his hands. Blinking tourists, kids with dogs straining on leashes, vans and campers with bikes, canoes, and kayaks lashed to their roofs crammed the asphalt parking area. Coming back out into the sunshine with the air faintly tinctured by exhaust fumes and the smell of breakfast sandwiches from a nearby fast-food place, he was tempted to linger, stretch his legs and work the kinks out of his neck.

But Horace's death—murder, Dave reminded himself fiercely, his friend's brutal *murder*—wasn't all that troubled him. The thing he'd tucked into his glove compartment before leaving home seemed to broadcast its evil presence on a special wavelength that only police officers and car thieves could hear. Then he noticed the scrap of paper on his windshield, tucked under the wiper, and the fragments of red plastic littering the pavement at the rear of his car.

During the few minutes he'd been inside, someone had bumped the car's tail light, shattering it. The note on the windshield held an apology and a promise to pay for the repair, along with a name and phone number.

Dave tossed the paper into a trash receptacle and got back on the road. If a smashed light was the worst that came out of this trip, he would count himself lucky.

At Bangor he threaded his way through numerous highway signs and across the Penobscot River bridge toward coastal Route 1A. On the bridge's far side he pulled into a convenience-store parking lot to buy a soft drink.

All around him the midmorning bustle of ordinary people on ordinary midmorning errands continued, just as if Dave's oldest friend had not had his skull savagely crushed in with a rock one recent night while he was out for a walk.

Thinking this, he changed his mind about the soft drink. A lady coming out of the convenience store peered at him before getting into the car next to his, and it took him a moment to understand that there were tears running down his cheeks, the dark well of mingled fury and grief brimming over again without warning.

Wiping a hand hastily across the moisture on his face, he mustered a smile and a weak *It's okay* wave for the lady, whose own hands now touched her lips in an uncertain praying gesture as if she was trying to decide whether or not to get out of her car and come over to him. But at his wave she just nodded minutely instead, her kind, plain face seeming to say that she'd had a few unscripted teary moments of her own over the years.

That it could happen to anyone. She backed out and drove away, and after another moment Dave did too, following the map's directions to a twisty rural road leading to Route 9.

The sudden change from four-lane highway to something that was little more than a paved trail triggered a flashback to a trip Dave had taken years ago with Horace, to New Mexico, where they'd pulled in very late one night to a motel on Route 66.

Once they were in the room Dave had gone to the rear window and pulled the curtain aside, expecting to look out onto another brightly lit commercial strip of gas stations and restaurants. But he had seen only moonlit desert, dark shapes of what he supposed were saguaro trees marching toward distant mountains.

It had startled him then the way civilization could end so abruptly, and he felt just as vulnerable here in Maine. Once you left a city and the thin buffer of suburbia surrounding it, wilderness closed in on you again in earnest.

He and Horace had risen before dawn the next morning, and as they departed the motel's parking lot Dave had happened to glance in the rearview mirror just in time to see the light over their room's door wink out.

Only theirs, none of the others. To Dave it felt ominous, like a message from the darkness that had enclosed them all night. Horace had seen it too, and as they pulled onto Route 66 in the predawn gloom he'd glanced silently at Dave, wearing that funny little smile of his that Dave now remembered so painfully.

Dave hit the gas just as he had all those years ago, roaring out onto Route 9 between a log truck and a highballing eighteen-wheeler, causing his underpowered old Saab 99 to labor briefly. Soon a lane for slower vehicles opened on the right and he pulled into it to give the faster ones a chance to pass.

After that it was smooth sailing, the landscape rising and the road curving up into it with breathtaking swiftness. Dave sped through tiny settlements surrounded by dairy farms, their pastures stone-studded and terraced by plodding hooves.

Next came land so thinly settled that the towns didn't even have names, only numbers, gated access roads, and desolate highway-maintenance yards sited in the clefts of the high hills. The enormous sand-heaps in the yards testified to the shortness of summer here in Maine, and the treacherousness of winter.

Not that this particular highway wasn't an attention-grabber even in August. Dave drove Route 9 for a long time, his anxiety increasing each time an oncoming truck hurtled around a curve straight at him, then roared past without overturning or losing its load as it seemed the massive vehicle surely must do.

He couldn't imagine confronting those huge trucks when it was snowing or the road was slick with sleet, sand-heaps or no. But Horace used to say that if you wanted to experience the real Maine, come when it was cold. Winter, he claimed, was when the sub-zero temperatures squeezed a few scant drops of the milk of human kindness out of even the dourest old Maine coot.

Without warning, a flashing light appeared in Dave's rearview mirror. His heart lurched as the thing in the glove box, half-forgotten in the seeming endlessness of the challenging road, began to give off its evil *Here I am!* vibes again. He located a narrow gravel turnout just ahead and put his signal on.

The blue Ford sedan with the flashing blue light bar on its roof pulled in behind Dave and the trooper got out, wearing a pair of mirrored sunglasses. Dave felt sure the sunglasses were special, law-enforcement-specific ones that would enable the cop to see right through the Saab's dashboard straight into the glove box.

Courage, Horace used to say, *doesn't mean not being afraid.*

The trooper slammed the squad-car door deliberately, looking down briefly at his summons book as he did so.

Courage, Dave's good old murdered, skull-crushed buddy used to say, *means doing it anyway.*

He'd said it back in New Mexico all those years ago once the sun had come up and the errand they'd been on, to a small adobe house at the end of a dirt track in the mountains' shadow, had ended benignly.

As not all of their errands did. Dave hoped Horace's insight about courage was true, partly because of the police officer's presence. But mostly his errand frightened him. While the trooper was still looking down at the summons book, Dave reached forward to open the glove box, sliding the envelope that held his documents out from beneath a dark lump of metal, cold and oily-feeling.

" 'Morning, sir. May I see your license and registration?"

Dave looked up at the trooper, whose practiced eyes were no doubt scanning the car's interior from behind the mirrored sunglasses. The glove box was shut, the requested items out and ready for inspection.

Over the years he and Horace had done things this young cop wouldn't believe. Thinking of them kept Dave's voice level, even though in the past when weapons-handling had been necessary it was Horace who'd always handled them. "You certainly may. May I ask what the trouble is, Officer? I didn't think I was speeding."

Horace said that Dave might be an ivory-tower academic and a pacifist besides, but he still had the coldest blood this side of a reptile cage, when it was necessary.

Used to say. The trooper handed Dave's documents back. All in order, apparently. The sunglasses regarded him. "No, sir. You weren't speeding. D'you know your tail light's broken?"

Dave smiled. "Oh. Yes, it happened just today. I'm going to get it repaired as soon as I get to Eastport. That's where I'm going," he added.

The trooper didn't smile. "Yes, sir. Eastport, you say?"

Dave waved at the map that should be on the passenger seat,

then remembered that in his haste and grief he'd forgotten it, leaving it on the desk in his office. "Old school pal moved there," he explained to the trooper. "I just got the idea I might try looking him up."

He was talking too much. Lying, too, which he knew was even riskier. The man he'd be looking for in Eastport wasn't a pal in any sense of the word. He was a killer.

Dave was certain of it.

The trooper nodded. "Right, then. Be sure to get that light fixed. And have a nice day."

Dave was about to agree that yes, he would certainly have the tail light repaired at the very first opportunity, when the glove box door fell open. The sound and the unexpected flicker of motion from the far side of the car caused the trooper's head to tip mildly with the beginnings of interest.

Don't react. Dave didn't know what the officer could see from where he stood by the driver's side of the car.

Wondering this, he felt his blood chilling down to the temperature of a Maine winter night, the kind of night when the sand trucks were out in force and even the dourest of Horace's beloved old coots could muster up a few thin, bluish drops of the milk of human kindness.

"Thanks, Officer," he said. He slid his registration and insurance card into the open compartment and shut it firmly. "You have a good day, too."

Then he waited to be asked to step out of the car, spread his legs, put his hands on the doorframe, et cetera. But the trooper merely turned away. Dave watched, his hands resting with elaborate casualness on the steering wheel, as the cop got nearly to his own car, then paused and came back again.

"Sir?" The cop leaned down to Dave's window.

"Yes, Officer?" Dave's own face was now reflected in the sunglasses. Fortyish, dark hair, big ears. Not particularly guilty-looking, and why should it be? He wasn't guilty of much.

Yet. The trooper stabbed a finger at Dave. "You go on from here about thirty miles, you'll see a sign. Little side road meets up with 214; it'll knock half an hour off your trip to Eastport."

"Great," said Dave, not yet reaching for the ignition key. "Thanks very much."

He waited until the squad car pulled out ahead of him before starting the Saab. Reptile or not, he'd been certain for a minute that his quest for information in the matter of his old friend's murder was over before it began.

Information and more. Horace said pursuing revenge was like setting a bear trap and sticking your own foot into it.

But not this time. Route 214 turned out to be a winding lane through sweet-smelling fields long abandoned to goldenrod and blackberry brambles. Cicadas whined shrilly in the silence on either side of the cracked pavement.

Not this time.

As the trooper had promised, the shortcut knocked half an hour off Dave's trip.

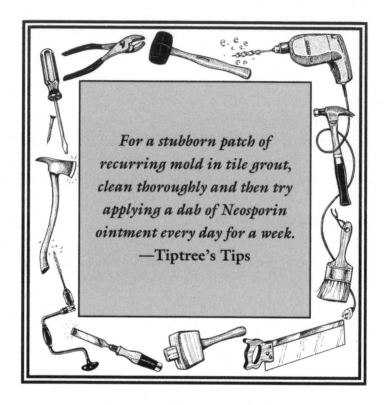

Chapter 2

*For a stubborn patch of
recurring mold in tile grout,
clean thoroughly and then try
applying a dab of Neosporin
ointment every day for a week.*
—Tiptree's Tips

My name is Jacobia Tiptree and when I first came to Maine I took modern bathing facilities for granted. Tubs, showers, sinks with their faucet handles so cleverly and usefully marked *Hot* and *Cold*—

These, I'd believed in the depths of my innocence back then, were the ordinary amenities of life. And when they got broken I thought people could fix them.

Other people, I mean; ones who understood stopped drains, leaky pipes, and shutoff valves that when you turned their knobs—or in my case when you threw all your weight into breaking their rust encrustations—responded by shutting off something.

Instead of just snapping off in your hand, as the handles in my old bathroom did the first time I tried turning them. Next came a moment of stunned horror followed by a geyser so forceful, it hosed all the mildew off the places where the blackish stuff had flourished for decades, way up there on the bathroom ceiling.

And then I called a plumber.

Sadly, even plumbers could do little but stare helplessly when confronted with pipes so anciently decrepit, they belonged in a museum. Probably my bathroom was regarded as the absolute height of modern convenience when the nearly two-hundred-year-old house was modernized. For one thing it eliminated, you should excuse the expression, the backyard privy.

But seventy-plus years later, the bathroom in my old house was not much more than a closet with running water. I finally did find a fellow to replace some of the fittings, so you could take a shower without having to go down in the basement to turn on the hot and cold. But you could still only take a bath if you wanted to fill up the bathtub with a bucket.

And if you wanted to sit in the tub, which I didn't. Call me crazy, but I'm a big fan of bath water that doesn't have other people's personal molecules floating in it, and I especially draw the line at seventy-year-old molecules.

As a result I'd filled that tub repeatedly with enough hot bleach to sterilize a dozen operating rooms. But I still couldn't get comfortable in it, until one day I just went up there and took a sledgehammer to it.

And although I failed spectacularly in my attempt to remove the hideous old fixture—swung hard, the hammer bounced back up off the cast iron with a sound like the ringing of some massive gong, nearly taking my head off on the rebound—may I simply say right here that just trying to destroy an old bathtub with a sledgehammer turned out to be a heartwarming experience.

So I demolished the rest of the bathroom instead. *Wham!* went the cockeyed old wooden shelves, their peeling paint stained by ancient medicaments and scarred from decades of use.

Crash! went the towel racks some long-ago do-it-yourselfer had fastened to the plaster without bothering to find any wooden studs to secure them to first, so anything heavier than a single wet washcloth made them fall down by themselves.

And finally, *kerblooie!* went the pedestal sink, its basin so un-speakably chipped, stained, and rusty that for the last year or so I'd had to close my eyes just to finish brushing my teeth.

"Lovely," said my housekeeper, Bella Diamond, appreciatively, coming in to view the wreckage.

Once, the sounds of mayhem I'd been creating would've made her call an ambulance. But nowadays she knew the score and just came running with the whisk broom, a dustpan, and—this being Bella—a steaming pail of hot, soapy water.

"Yes," I replied, pleased that I'd remembered to shut off the water before smashing the sink. Plaster chunks littered the wooden floor, which someone had coated with a lot of thick, dark varnish about fifty years earlier.

I don't know which I like less in a bathroom, wooden floors or old varnish. "Now we can put a new bathroom in. And we'll open the wall on one side to make it bigger," I said.

Presently we had to stand in the bathtub to get the door closed, and to open the tiny window it was necessary to squooch tightly up against the antique cast-iron radiator and bend into a pretzel shape.

And don't even get me started on the whole idea of big radia-tors in tiny bathrooms. For efficient use of space you might as well put a woodstove in there; then at least you could burn all the old magazines in it.

As for a medicine cabinet, it was a milk crate on the floor, and if you cared to use a hair dryer you were out of luck unless you felt like running an extension cord from the hall; ditto your electric toothbrush.

Not that there was room for one of those, either. But the adjoining room was plenty large enough to nab a few square feet from, partly because, like all the rest of the bedrooms in the old house, it had no closets.

"We can push all the pieces out through the window," I told Bella, "and the junk man can collect them."

To get rid of that sink I was more than willing to bend into a pretzel shape, and to stay that way for months if necessary.

"The tub," I added a bit less cheerfully, "will be something else again. Maybe we can hire a team of fellows to remove it."

I was starting to realize that my fit of sledgehammering might've opened a can of worms. Because besides being hideous, that bathtub was far bigger than the doorway opening.

So no amount of turning or angling had a prayer of getting it out in one piece. Also it probably weighed a ton; the fellows would all have to be related to the Incredible Hulk.

Thoughtfully I raised the balky window sash, tearing only a few of my more important back muscles to do so, and peered down. The sidewalk leading to the back-porch steps lay almost directly beneath. I made a mental note to shout "Look out below!" when the sink parts exited.

But the fact that they would exit at all was encouraging. And I was sure I could find some way of getting that tub removed, too, even if we had to swing a wrecking ball in here and haul it out with a crane.

"A vanity cabinet," I fantasized aloud, turning back to the demolished room and imagining where I would put one of these exotic items.

Pedestal sinks are meant to conserve space but in my opinion consume it; the only way you can put anything beneath a pedestal sink is if you attach one of those awful little gingham skirts to its rim, whereupon it will look spiffy for ten minutes.

"And baseboard heating," I said optimistically. Taking out an old cast-iron radiator is nearly as difficult as bashing up a bathtub. "Plus maybe a towel warmer?"

My arms were still vibrating from the impact of the hammer. Still, I hadn't gone completely crazy; I'd left the commode in place, for instance, figuring I could remove it last and install a new one as an early part of the remodeling process.

Strategy: in a very old house you may think you need books on remodeling, but what you really need is Sun Tzu's *The Art of War*. That radiator might've looked harmless just standing there in the bathroom corner, but I knew it intended to resist its own removal by the heating-system equivalent of nuclear winter.

And speaking of conflict, please don't talk to me about how I was destroying venerable antiques. Because first of all, 1930s plumbing isn't venerable; it's intolerable.

On top of which, do you know how much it costs to get an antique tub out of a house, transported to the place where they promise they will put a brand-new, sort-of-porcelain-ish surface on it, and then get it back in again and up a flight of stairs to your bathroom once more?

Enough to put that disgusting old object on the moon, that's how much. And afterward you can only clean it by wiping it very tenderly with the same kind of extremely soft cloth you're supposed to use for polishing your eyeglasses.

Which never would've worked with Bella around. She was the kind of housekeeper who believed dirt was a manifestation of moral rottenness; her daily cleaning tools included a wire brush and a jug of carbolic acid.

Although at the moment she wasn't cleaning anything at all. Instead, while I caught my breath from my exertions and regarded the mess I'd made, she gazed past me into the mirror on what was left of the wall above where the sink had been.

Amazing, that her reflection didn't break the mirror. Bella was smart, honest, hardworking, and funny as hell. But she was also so ugly, people around town said she probably had to sneak up on a pail of water to get a drink.

Now, in preparation for cleaning that god-awful bathroom one last time, she took her henna-red hair out of its rubber band and twisted it in again, skinning it back even more tightly from her long, pallid-complexioned face.

"All right," she pronounced ominously, brandishing the whisk broom.

Her grin of anticipation exposed big, bad teeth, and the look in her bulging grape-green eyes was one I'd seen once in an old science-fiction movie, just before the team of intergalactic space warriors cranked up their flamethrowers to exterminate the giant radioactive bugs.

"Now, Bella," I said, hoping she wasn't planning to bring a flamethrower in here.

I didn't own one but I did have a heat gun for removing the thick layers of paint that clung to nearly every surface in my old house. And behind all the plaster walls, the ancient wood was so feathery-dry that you could light it with a match.

"Don't go too wild," I cautioned, glancing past her at my own reflection: lean, narrow face, stubborn chin, and large eyes with dark eyebrows that other people called wing-shaped.

Not gorgeous, but at least my looks didn't cause small children to hide behind their mothers. I shoved a dark straggle of plaster-dusted hair behind my ear with a grimy finger.

"Bella, what were you and my dad arguing about down in the kitchen this morning?" Their voices had woken me.

"Your father couldn't find his own backside with both hands and a flashlight."

Which was not exactly an answer. I squinted into the mirror. Bits of sink wreckage clung in my hair with the plaster dust, and the elastic-strapped safety glasses I'd worn while swinging the sledgehammer had left deep grooves in my face.

Also it occurred to me suddenly that I'd just destroyed the

only shower-taking apparatus in the house. Not deliberately, mind you, but a couple of times that sledgehammer had zigged when it should've zagged. If you turned on the water now, the resulting flood would probably drown all the mice in the basement.

"Yes, but..." I began.

My father, an explosives expert and ex-federal-fugitive who was for many years suspected of murdering my mother—he hadn't—lived alone in his own small cottage a few blocks from here on Octagon Street.

But lately he'd been spending most of his time at my place, where he made himself useful at a variety of old-house chores while at the same time alternately annoying Bella and making her laugh so hard that she had to sit down.

"Your father thinks he knows what's best for everybody," spat Bella, wiping furiously at a spot on the old pine beadboard paneling that went halfway up the bathroom walls.

The rest of the walls—what remained of them, anyway—were brightly papered in a long-outdated design featuring silver swans swimming tranquilly on a background of Pepto-Bismol pink.

I didn't have the heart to tell Bella that the beadboard was bound for glory, too, along with the old wallpaper, which I didn't even plan to bother steaming off the rest of the plaster before I got rid of it. Crash, bash, gone in a flash was *my* plan.

But just then a car pulled into the driveway. I left Bella rubbing her knobby hands together in *über*-hygienic glee at the prospect of never having to scour that bathtub again—by the end she'd been employing a product called Kapow! that was so strong, in a pinch you could use it to loosen the mortar between chimney bricks— and went downstairs to find out who the visitor was.

The car in my driveway was an older red Saab I'd never seen before, with Rhode Island plates, a pleasant-looking middle-aged man behind the wheel, and a duffel bag on the backseat. He got out, blinking behind his horn-rims in the bright late-August morning.

His blue button-down shirt was open at the collar, the knot of his striped tie loosened, and his sleeves rolled up over his forearms. Stretching gratefully in the onshore breeze, he brushed thinning brown hair off his forehead with a tired gesture.

"Hello," I said. He looked up, surprised.

"Hello. Are you Jacobia Tiptree?"

Might be, I felt like replying as another car tore by. It was a snazzy red Mazda Miata with a young blonde woman behind the wheel. The blue scarf tied around her head let her pale hair show prettily, and the movie-star-style sunglasses she wore increased the overall impression of glamour.

And money; this was not the kind of person we generally saw a whole lot of around Eastport, even in summer. But she was gone before I could wonder much about her.

My visitor approached the porch steps. If the Miata driver's looks shouted *cash,* his yelled *brains.* And something else; smart, dark eyes, pale skin with a bluish hint of five o'clock shadow, a drawn expression that hinted strongly at grief...

"I'm Dave DiMaio," he said, and at my blank look he went on, "I was a friend of Horace Robotham."

"Oh. Oh, my." I descended the porch steps and took the hand he offered.

"I'm so sorry for your loss," I said. The obituary had been in the *Bangor Daily News.*

He smiled warmly. In his forties, I guessed, but with the lean build some very fortunate men keep throughout their lives. "Thanks. Horace and I corresponded about you before he..."

Horace Robotham had been a Maine-based rare-book expert and I'd sent him a volume my father had unearthed in the cellar of my house. But I hadn't heard much back from him except a few brief notes to say he was working on it, and then he'd died suddenly, murdered by someone who had apparently attacked him while he was out on his evening walk.

A random mugging, the police called it. That had been three weeks earlier.

"I'm very sorry about your friend," I repeated. "Won't you come in? You must have had a long drive."

Not that I knew where he'd come from but getting to Eastport at all—a town of about two thousand on Moose Island in downeast Maine, three hours from Bangor and light-years, it often seemed, from anywhere else—nearly always involved serious travel times.

Dave DiMaio followed me inside to the big old high-ceilinged kitchen with its tall bare windows, pine wainscoting, and hardwood floor. "This is beautiful," he said.

"Thanks," I replied. His gaze took in the built-in pine cabinets, linoleum-topped counters, woodstove-equipped fireplace hearth, and the antique soapstone sink, all bathed in the watery sunlight pouring in through the windows' rippled panes.

From her usual perch atop the refrigerator our cross-eyed Siamese cat, Cat Dancing, opened one piercing blue eye while twitching her tail in irritation, then went to sleep again.

"Sit down, won't you?" I invited. *And tell me why you've come,* I wanted to add.

But the poor man looked exhausted so I gave him a glass of lemonade and set a paper plate of oatmeal lace cookies in front of him instead.

"Oh," he breathed when he'd drunk down half the lemonade in a swig. "Oh, that hits the spot."

He was trying his first cookie when the dogs pelted in, Monday the black Labrador wagging ecstactically at the sight of company, Prill the red Doberman hanging back, her amber eyes alert.

"It's okay, Prill," I said a little nervously.

Prill was a rescue dog with some terrible history that I was better off not knowing. Fine with the family and with anyone else to whom she'd been introduced, she still thought s-t-r-a-n-g-e-r spelled trouble.

Dave DiMaio got up. "Hello, girl," he said conversationally to the dog, crouching before her.

Prill's ears flattened. "Really," I told Dave, trying to keep calm in the face of imminent disaster, "you shouldn't..."

"Hello," he repeated to the unhappy dog, who dropped into a crouch of her own and crept forward, lip curled ominously.

But when she got near enough, DiMaio reached out fearlessly and ruffled her ears, as casually as if she didn't weigh over a hundred pounds and possess nearly as many teeth. I just stared as under his caress her suspicions melted.

Then she rolled onto her side, her stubby tail tattooing the floor. "Dogs seem to like me," DiMaio explained with a shrug.

Prill yawned happily and let out a whimper of joy.

"Yes, so I see," I said. "This one should've liked you with a little barbeque sauce and maybe a side of fries. How did you *do* that?"

The big red dog got to her feet and wandered unconcernedly away into the dining room where I heard her drop into her doggy bed with a soft thump. Monday followed.

"I don't know. Good vibes?" DiMaio smiled briefly as he straightened. "But listen, I'm sorry to barge in here. I've obviously interrupted you in a project."

Bathroom wreckage, I realized with embarrassment, remained in my hair, and although I'd washed my hands before putting out the refreshments, the rest of me looked fit for digging ditches.

Meanwhile Bella was still upstairs, dropping big chunks of sink into, apparently, a metal bucket: *clunk! clank! thunk!*

"I have been a little busy," I admitted, all at once keenly aware of my costume: tattered jeans, a paint-smeared shirt, loafers with most of the stitching torn out.

But then I managed a smile of my own as something about this guy—the set of his jaw, or the odd, brooding darkness that lurked behind the friendliness in his eyes—suggested he'd seen worse.

Much worse. "Have you by any chance brought me back the book your friend had?" I asked.

After reading in the paper about Horace Robotham's death I'd tried writing to the address I had for him, hoping someone might be clearing up the rare-book dealer's affairs. But I'd gotten no answer. I'd just about decided I might have to drive to Orono, Maine, where he'd lived and had an old-book business, to try locating my volume.

DiMaio shook his head. "No. I'm sorry to say I don't know where your book is. Horace's partner, Lang Cabell, looked for it. But it wasn't there. I just talked to Lang last night," he added. "I'd been . . . away."

The light dawned suddenly: my old book, a sudden death, and now this stranger, arriving without warning. . . .

"So that's why you're here," I said. "You want it, too. You've just found out he died, and that the book is gone. And you think maybe someone—"

"No, no," he interrupted, putting his hands up in a warding-off gesture. "Nothing like that. Really, I don't know there's any connection at all between . . ."

Protesting too much. And at my skeptical look he gave in. "All right. It's your book, after all. I guess you've got a right to a few answers. The few I have."

He let his hands fall to his sides. "Long story, though. Do you want to take a walk with me while I tell it?"

What popped into my mind immediately was a walk-and-talk, the kind of stroll people take to discuss something confidential when they suspect their current location might be bugged. Back in the big city where I worked as a money manager to the rich and dreadful, many of my clients were so paranoid about eavesdropping that the only place I ever saw them was out on the street.

But DiMaio's explanation was less paranoid. "I started out before daybreak this morning from Providence, Rhode Island," he told me. "I teach at a small college you've never heard of, special topics in late-nineteenth-century American literature."

"Really," I said evenly. Heard about a death just last night and hopped into his car bright and early; fascinating.

"Anyway," he added, "I've been on the road for hours, and I want some exercise if I can get it."

He wanted more than that, I felt certain. But by now I was curious, and it *was* a beautiful day. Pausing only to brush a few larger shards of pedestal sink out of my hair, I grabbed the dogs' collars from their hook in the hall, which brought them running.

"You're on," I told Dave DiMaio. "I'll give you the fifty-cent Eastport tour and while we're out, you can also explain to me why my old book's so important to you," I said, bending to leash the animals.

Still assuming that the book was the only thing behind his visit. But when we got outside, DiMaio paused. "Um, listen," he began, with an uncertain glance back at his car.

"What?" I asked, peering up at the window through which the entire bathroom would soon be exiting. Once that was finished, we were in for approximately the same amount of construction that it took to complete the Brooklyn Bridge.

And bathroom work wasn't the only thing I had on my plate this fine August morning. The quarrel between Bella and my dad had sounded serious, and her remarks weren't reassuring.

A rift between those two could throw all of our reasonably tranquil domestic arrangements into a cocked hat, so I supposed I would have to do something about it.

Also my just-past-teenaged son, Sam, had recently returned from alcohol rehab. And while I'd realized at last that it wasn't my job to keep him sober, I still couldn't help trying.

There was something else, too, that I ought to remember but couldn't, I thought distractedly. I knew one thing, though: I had no intention of getting involved with murder.

If that was even what it was; if Horace Robotham's death wasn't just a mugging gone tragically wrong, as the police seemed to believe.

"Well," Dave began, "I just wondered if in your house—"

"Yes?" The dogs yanked mercilessly, Prill west and Monday east.

"In your house," Dave DiMaio said seriously to me, "would there by any chance be a good place to hide a gun?"

Half an hour after he pulled into my driveway we'd stashed Dave DiMaio's horrid little firearm in the cellar lockbox where I kept my own collection of weaponry.

The best of the bunch was the Bisley six-shot revolver my husband, Wade Sorenson, had given me before we got married. With its long, blued steel barrel, checkered walnut grip, and general air of being able to stop anything including a charging rhinoceros, the Italian reproduction of the gun that won the West was my favorite, even aside from the sentimental attachment I felt for it.

With the Bisley was a small, gray .38 Police Special, the carrying of which I tried hard to avoid, since if I did it meant I was in way more trouble than I could handle. High among its virtues, though, was the fact that the Police Special was concealable, a big plus in any situation whose successful outcome depends at least in part on your looking like a dumb-bunny.

An appearance, by the way, that I am able to achieve with no difficulty whatsoever. But back to the lockbox and my third gun, a .22 Beretta Model 87 target pistol with an extended barrel.

Dave looked uneasy. "You struck me more as the anti-gun type," he said as I examined the target gun, then locked the box again after putting his weapon into it.

"Mm. Watch out for first impressions," I replied.

The gun he'd handed me was a .22 revolver. It was a cheap,

evil-looking piece of junk perfect for dropping down a sewer grate after you'd used it in a convenience-store robbery, but not for much else.

"My husband repairs high-quality firearms when he's not out being a harbor pilot, and he's a good shot," I told DiMaio.

Which was putting it mildly. Wade guided freighters into our harbor, through the wild tides, vicious currents, and treacherous granite outcroppings with which our local waters were plentifully furnished. Also, he could stand flat-footed and shoot the eye out of a gnat.

"He taught me to shoot," I added, "and I discovered I liked it."

Back then I'd thought guns were for guys with broken washing machines on their porches and mean dogs tied in their yards. But to get closer to Wade I'd have fixed all the washing machines and made friends with every one of those dogs, and after quite a while of his slow, patient instruction I found out that shooting was fun.

Plus, a couple of hours on the target range can make nearly any problem look manageable, since if worse comes to worst you can always just blast the daylights out of it.

I wasn't hands-on familiar with Dave's gun but unloading a revolver is no big brainteaser and I'd accomplished it without embarrassing myself, swinging the cylinder out and dumping its contents into my pocket. I'd have gone on to tell Dave that the Beretta 87 would've been a lot better choice for him than the ghastly little item he carried. For one thing, the Beretta's extended barrel made sighting easier for a beginner. But he'd already lost interest.

"This cellar's amazing," he murmured, gazing at the hand-adzed beams, worn granite foundation, and the arched brickwork in the doorways to the small side-rooms where in the old days they hung meat.

Not to mention bushels of potatoes, rows of quart jars full of fruit, jams, relishes, and pickled eggs, boxes of salt pork and dried fish, sacks of pebble-hard peas, beans, and corn kernels ... "Cellars got a lot of serious use in the 1800s," I replied. "In those days, they weren't just catch-alls."

Like this one now: bottles, cans, newspapers for recycling, Sam's snow skis and his snowmobile-riding gear, cans of paint and plastic buckets of plaster-patching compound ... overall, the place looked like a hurricane had washed a lot of miscellaneous flotsam and jetsam into my basement.

But the big iron hooks remained bolted to the walls and ceiling beams; tufts of deer hide, grayish with age and nailed to door-frames, still testified to the success of long-ago hunting trips.

"That's where the book came out of the wall." I pointed to the corner behind the furnace where a forgotten water main had burst, flooding the place. The hole it had created was now filled with new concrete blocks and mortar, courtesy of my father.

Dave peered at the spot. "Nice repair. So the book was in the wall? Or in the soil on the other side of it?"

"Unclear. My dad took out the stones to get at the pipe, saw a wooden box that the book turned out to be in, and grabbed it before the water got at it. But as for how far in it was ..."

Dave nodded with slow thoughtfulness. "And the foundation was built when? Eighteen twenty-three?"

So he and Horace Robotham had discussed more than the book's mere existence. Either that, or DiMaio had done some old-house research on his own. Again, I wondered what he was really doing here.

"Yes. The foundation's original. So we think the box went in when the granite did," I answered.

"Huh. That would make the book itself nearly two centuries old," he mused. "Interesting."

No kidding, especially since my own name was written in it, along with those of every other previous owner of the house since it was built, all 185 years' worth of us. And how had *that* happened?

The mystery had been what made me send the volume to

Horace Robotham in the first place. That and the fact that to my untutored eye, it looked as if the names were written in...

I put the lockbox back on its shelf. "Dave, did Horace give you any idea what he thought? I mean about how my name got in the book, or..."

Dave jerked back from wherever he'd been woolgathering. "Horace had theories. So did I. But let's go outside, shall we?"

He followed me upstairs. "I'll still need to find a place to stay and get settled," he said.

The dogs had gone to sleep, all fantasies of a walk abandoned when we'd left them to lock away Dave's gun. I let them lie. "I thought I'd stick around a few days," Dave added casually as we reached the front sidewalk.

Stick around? With a weapon? Oh, fantastic. "I see. Well then," I told him, "I'm sorry I can't invite you to—"

"Stay with you? Oh, no, that's very kind of you, but..."

On the street he paused to snug his tie back up under his collar and check his tie pin, silver in the shape of a quill pen with a tiny drop of ink at the tip.

Or I assumed it was ink. Then he turned to regard my old house, a big white clapboard Federal with three full stories, a two-story ell, three tall red-brick chimneys, and forty-eight old double-hung windows each equipped with a pair of forest-green shutters.

"It must have taken a lot of servants to keep this place running back in the nineteenth century," he remarked, changing the subject. "Wood for all the fireplaces, hauling the ashes, maintaining all the candles and lamps. And then the cooking, cleaning, and laundry, of course."

"Yes," I agreed. "Hired help. Young ones, a lot of them. I've been told they needed so many, they sometimes imported girls from cities in the Canadian Maritimes. Halifax, and even abroad."

Not for the first time I imagined the feelings of a young girl arriving here, friendless and alone, carrying only a small bag of her belongings and possibly a Bible.

On the other hand, she wouldn't have had to deal with an-tique shutters. Mine needed repainting again—*scraper, sander, paint, paint sprayer,* I thought—and the flashing around one of the chim-neys looked as if another coat of tar wouldn't hurt it.

Probably that was why a stain shaped like Brazil had appeared on one of the bedroom walls. *Ladder,* I listed mentally. *Tar brush and tar bucket.*

Plus someone to climb the ladder while carrying the tar brush and tar bucket. The whole place needed new screens and storm windows, too, to replace the cheap, flimsy aluminum ones some-one had installed years ago.

"Anyway, on trips like this I generally need plenty of time alone," Dave DiMaio told me. "So I'll be staying at a motel."

Trips like this? But before I could ask him how many friends of his died while researching strange old books, he spoke again.

"That place is lovely." He pointed down Key Street to a Queen Anne Victorian with an ornate porch, bay windows, and multiple gables opening like wooden sails.

Too bad the mansion across from it wasn't kept up equally well. Boarded-up windows and nailed-shut doors scarred its bat-tered, mansard-roofed facade. Generations of pigeons nested be-hind its fascia, staining its clapboards, and its carved trim sagged sadly to mingle with its wooden gutters in a hodgepodge of rot.

We walked on toward Passamaquoddy Bay, blue and breezily whitecapped on this day of abundant sun. The old houses lining this part of Key Street were smaller than mine but just as venera-ble. Their white-painted picket fences enclosed gardens overflow-ing with green hydrangeas, dahlias with blooms the size of saucers, and masses of black-eyed Susans.

At the corner, a crew of tree cutters in goggles and ear protec-tors were cutting and hauling the remains of an ancient elm. "So do you know a lot about old houses?" Dave asked me.

"Probably not the way you mean. I haven't studied them or anything." Isolated on the island, the trees had escaped Dutch elm disease until recently, but now every year there were fewer of the old behemoths canopying the streets.

"But I am slowly rehabilitating my own place, and when you fix something, often you have to start by taking it apart," I told him. "So yes, I've learned a bit about the inner workings of old houses."

With a snarl, the tree-workers' industrial-sized chipper began devouring branches. By tomorrow there'd be only a scattering of sawdust to show that the elm had been here at all.

And it really didn't take long to get used to their absence, I'd discovered by noticing the suddenly denuded yards of other people. The human eye adjusted quickly.

But watching them go still wasn't pleasant. "It must take patience," said Dave. "Working on such old materials."

I smiled. "Yes. And a lot of help from my friends." Many of whom I'd begun hiring professionally, since small- or medium-sized repairs were one thing, but you don't just fall off the turnip truck and start doing the really big rehab projects successfully.

Moments earlier, for example, while surveying the shutters I'd noticed that one of those chimneys needed not just reflashing, but also rebuilding. It would take the extra-long ladders of a roofing or painting crew to get the shutters down, and when the chimney got rebuilt I supposed I ought also to have it relined.

And an aluminum downspout had come loose from its rivets by the front gable. So besides the plumber and electrician I'd be needing to help me redo the bath, before winter there'd be people crawling over the place like ants.

"Why did you bring a gun?" I asked.

"Oh, just predawn jitters. When I left home early this morning things looked awfully dark to me," Dave replied casually.

His eyes widened as more of the harbor came into view. At this time of year, yawls and ketches, motorized pleasure cruisers, and fishing vessels of all sizes from two-man dories to fifty-foot diesel work boats bobbed in the boat basin.

"But now," he added, taking in the flags snapping briskly at the Coast Guard station and the tourists with their hands full of cameras and souvenirs, "now, not so much."

I kicked through a small pile of the last leaves that old elm would ever unfurl, remembering bees massed and buzzing in its branches earlier that summer. With an ear-splitting roar the tree-crew's grinder started up.

"Uh-huh," I said, unconvinced. Not that it wasn't lovely; salt air, sparkling waves, gulls wheeling overhead. It's paradise here if you can manage to forget February. But I really couldn't remember the last time a nice day had persuaded me out of needing a deadly weapon.

I was so sure he was lying to me, in fact, that as we passed the town bandstand, still draped in bright bunting from the Fourth of July, I decided not to let him get his hands on the thing again.

First of all it was so shoddily made, it would probably explode if he tried firing it. And second, I'd have bet any money that he'd never actually used a gun in his life.

I would hide the thing more thoroughly when I got home, I decided.

Chapter 3

To fix a loose hammer head,
pound a nail into the wooden
handle where it sticks through
the metal head. (Yes, with a
different hammer!)
—Tiptree's Tips

At the foot of Key Street I turned with Dave DiMaio onto Water Street, past Eastport's Peavey Memorial Library. It was a massive old heap of rust-colored brick with a green-painted cupola, copper weathervane, arched windows, and an elderly cannon with wooden-spoked iron wheels bolted to a concrete pad on the front lawn.

Once upon a time that cannon's job had been to help protect

Eastport from British invasion, a task it never even got a shot at when British men-of-war poured menacingly into Passamaquoddy Bay one terrible morning two years into the War of 1812.

Faced with enough firepower to reduce the whole city to rubble in minutes, the 75 soldiers at Fort Sullivan put down their weapons. Soon thereafter, British officers began garrisoning men and setting up headquarters in the best houses in town, which is why a few old Eastporters still call the bags of manure they use for garden fertilizer "English tea."

Today the library environs were more peaceful, if you can call a dozen romping, stomping two- to four-year-olds peaceful. Among them was my friend Ellie White, collecting her daughter, Leonora, from the story hour the librarians put on in summer.

"Hi!" Ellie rose with her usual lithe grace from the blanket she'd spread near the cannon.

Across the street an orange dump truck pulled up with a load of gravel for a pothole. The truck raised its bed with a loud grinding sound and the gravel began flowing; it was a *deep* hole.

Dave stared at Ellie. With a long, lean body, a face that would've looked just right on a storybook princess, and a lively, unthreatening manner, she could pretty much charm the argyles off any man within hailing distance, anytime she liked.

The truck finished dumping gravel. As the bed lowered, its tailgate fell shut with a *bang!*

Dave didn't even flinch. "Hello," he said shyly to Ellie.

"Hello, yourself." She met his gaze frankly, sizing him up the way a child might.

Today she was wearing a pink smock with red cherries printed on it over a green long-sleeved T-shirt, orange leggings, and leather sandals. Her auburn hair had sprinkles of glitter in it, her earrings were purple beach-glass pieces, and her toenails were painted the same vivid lime green as the wing on a tropical parrot.

None of which was any surprise to me; walking around looking like an explosion at the Crayola factory had long been her habit. But DiMaio was taking his time absorbing it.

"So what time should we start tomorrow?" Ellie asked me.

"Start . . . ?" I searched my mind. Nothing occurred to me. But she was looking at me as if the answer ought to be obvious.

"The anniversary party," she prodded gently. "Getting ready for it. Cake. Punch. And . . ."

The light dawned, hideously. "Ohhh," I breathed, horrified.

The party was for Merrie Fargeorge, an elderly lady of great Eastport renown, to celebrate the fiftieth anniversary of that worthy person's entry into the teaching profession. Such was her fame and the affection ex-Eastport schoolchildren still felt for her that the planned gala stood to rival the one for Queen Elizabeth on *her* fiftieth.

And in a moment of madness—some say more than a moment—I'd agreed to have the celebration at my house.

And *that's* what I'd forgotten. "B-but . . ." I managed.

Ellie looked hard at me. Twinkles of suspicion glinted in her remarkable eyes. Fortunately, the suspicion was as usual mingled with mirth.

"What?" she inquired gently. "What's wrong?"

Because with me, it could be anything from a collapsed foundation to an absent roof. "Well," I began evenly, "just this morning when I went upstairs to look at that bathtub—"

"Yes?" she said encouragingly.

I felt a flush creeping up my neck. "Well. It suddenly came over me, I mean, really, how much better it would be if only . . ."

She waited patiently. "If only it weren't there," I said. "So I tried a sledgehammer, and when that didn't work . . ."

"Oh," said Ellie. She eyed me judiciously. "That's *sink* in your hair, isn't it? Busted-up sink bits and . . . plaster dust. Oh, Jake. You didn't."

I nodded miserably. "Right through the old walls. And if I'd had a pry bar handy, I'd have taken the floor up, too."

Oh, what an idiot I felt like. If I'd thought about Merrie's bash before I started in with the bashing—but I hadn't. "I'm sorry, Ellie. I know how important the party is, but I completely..."

Luckily, Ellie was the most forgiving friend this side of a Bible story. She sighed. "All right, Jake."

I swear if it weren't for her I'd have probably thrown myself off my own roof a hundred times by now, just out of dismay at my own stupidity.

"I mean, they're not going to want to bathe," she went on pragmatically, then added, "You didn't smash the flush, too, did you?"

The little bathroom downstairs, she meant. "No," I said, thinking, *guest towels. Lots of them.* "You're right, it'll all still be okay."

Assuming that we could also find a place downstairs to put the ladies' summer wraps, flowered hats, and beaded, embroidered, or otherwise elaborately decorated formal gloves. Because as Ellie and I both knew, the big event would be attended by many female personages who were nearly as locally eminent and well-respected as Merrie herself, and they all wore their dressy garments with great flair and considerable dignity right along with their rouge and face powder.

And they were going to be at *my* house in...oh, dear. Less than thirty-six hours.

Unfortunately there were no accessible rooftops handy, but there was an impatient toddler standing eagerly by to rescue me from thoughts of airborne-ness.

"Blah blah black sheets," insisted two-year-old Leonora. Ellie's daughter gazed up urgently at me. "Heddlepenny bull?"

She was a sturdy child dressed in a red shirt, denim overalls, and tiny sneakers. Barrettes shaped like sailboats held back her strawberry-blonde hair; in one hand she clutched a purse with a lot of pink sequins sewn onto it.

"Jack an' *Jill*!" she shouted, tugging at my sleeve.

"We've been reading nursery rhymes," Ellie explained to Dave and me, "but so far she likes the sound better than the sense."

Dave laughed. "Just as well. Some of those things in nursery rhymes are pretty gruesome." Introducing himself, he stuck his hand out a little shyly.

Ellie took it. Her confidential manner was so natural and friendly that in the getting-drenched-with-her-charm department, it was like standing in front of a firehose.

"They've all got some horrible event in them," she agreed with mock seriousness, as her daughter toddled off, singing to herself. "The characters getting thrown downstairs, or having their skulls cracked open."

Silence greeted this comment. "Oh," said Ellie into the awkward pause, looking from Dave's abruptly closed face to my stricken one. "I've said something wrong, haven't I?"

"Dave is Horace Robotham's friend," I explained. Ellie knew about the old book and how I'd asked Horace to look into it.

"Was," Dave corrected without emphasis. The stillness around him was so sudden and complete it was as if a glass bell had been dropped over him.

Still and purposeful. He was humoring me, I realized all at once. This walk, his apparent interest in old houses...

"That's all right," Dave told Ellie. "It's just that I only found out about Horace yesterday. And it came as a shock."

"Of course it did," said Ellie. "My sympathies on your loss. Good heavens," she added, sprinting away suddenly.

Leonora had scrambled onto the old cannon and was attempting to ride it like a horsie, increasing by one the number of cracked skulls we were likely to have around here any minute. Ellie snatched the child in mid-giddyap and carried her back to the blanket where she began gathering up the various toys and snack items required for even the shortest of Lee's outings.

"I think it's time for all of us cowpokes to head on home for our naps and—"

"Dave has a gun," I interrupted. "He drove all the way here

from Rhode Island this morning. He thinks there's a connection between that old book my father found in the cellar and Horace's death."

Ellie looked up from dropping an empty juice box into a quilted satchel. "Oh, really?" Her green eyes narrowed faintly. "Well, isn't that interesting?"

Meanwhile, Dave had turned to regard me with the same sort of surprised appreciation he might have shown if one of my dogs had sat up and started speaking English.

It was my summary of his situation that instantly changed his opinion of me, I felt sure. Until then, and despite all the firearms I had in my basement, he must've believed I was just another this-old-house hobbyist with plaster dust in my pores and chunks of old porcelain pedestal sink still clinging in my hair.

Which only goes to show that appearances really aren't everything—a sage old saying I should've paid a lot more attention to when it came to figuring out Dave DiMaio himself.

Silently cursing himself, Dave left the two women standing together on the library lawn. He would return later for his car, he'd promised, adding that instead of a guided Eastport tour he'd as soon be on his own for a little while.

The truth was, he needed time to gather his thoughts. Giving the gun to someone—mostly so he wouldn't be tempted to do anything hasty with it, should the opportunity arise—had probably been prudent. Still, at the moment he wished heartily that he hadn't entrusted it to Jacobia Tiptree.

She was smarter than he'd expected; perceptive, too. Horace had always said that people were quicker on the uptake than Dave tended to give them credit for, and over the years in several notable instances Horace had been spectacularly right.

Dave hoped sincerely that this wasn't going to turn out to be another of those instances. But what he'd done was now spilt milk, and soon the simple beauty of the place he had come to distracted him temporarily.

Gray-and-white gulls floated over the paintbox-blue waves of Passamaquoddy Bay, their outstretched wings nearly motionless as if suspended on invisible wires. Beyond, islands loomed out of a channel that led, Dave supposed, to the North Atlantic. Pine-studded and wild, the islands emerged from pale lingering fog banks like wrappings of spun glass.

Downtown he found a double row of two- or three-story brick commercial buildings with big front windows facing one another across the main street. On the bay side, an asphalt lot led onto a wooden pier with two tugboats tied to it.

At the pier's entrance, a statue of a fisherman in slicker and sou'wester grinned from a tall concrete pedestal. Next came a hardware store, a soda fountain, antique shops...

At the street's far end stood a huge granite-block building that from its shape and barred street-level windows must once have been a customs house. Beyond that, a sprawling Coast Guard station with a red-tiled roof stood sentry over the marina.

He paused before a small bakery with a pretty cast-iron filigree sign that read *Mimi's* in flowing script. The delicate-looking pastries in the glass display cases were attractive.

But the girl behind the counter couldn't have been more than sixteen, and that wasn't the kind of conversation he wanted, so he walked on to the corner. There in the Moose Island General Store—*Beer, Ice, Maine-made treats,* proclaimed the placard nailed to the clapboard exterior—he bought a doughnut from a big glass jar of them on the counter.

Out on the store's rear deck, the onshore breeze smelled of fish and diesel fuel from the boats lined up at the finger piers in the boat basin below. It was low tide and the forty-foot wooden pilings under the dock dripped brine, the water pale green and so clear that he could see all the way to the bottom of it, the starfish and spiny urchins clinging to the rocks and the sea grass swaying.

On the dock, men and women dressed in jeans and sweatshirts cast heavy lines out, reeling in big glittering fish and dropping them into plastic buckets. Lawn chairs and Styrofoam coolers crowded the spaces between their trucks and cars.

"Mackerel," said the storekeeper without being asked, coming out onto the deck with coffee and a cigarette. His immaculately clean white apron, worn over jeans and a flannel shirt—even in high summer it was cool here, Dave noted—said *Kiss the Cook.*

"Good eating?" Dave asked. The people who were fishing down there seemed to be catching plenty of whatever it was, multiple hooks on the chunky lures coming up loaded each time they were reeled in.

The storekeeper twitched a bushy eyebrow. "It depends," he said, "on how hungry you are. Smaller ones're better. Not so much fat. Plenty of bones, though."

He dragged on the cigarette. "My grandmother used to clean 'em, cut the heads and tails off, put 'em in brown paper bags from the grocery store and bake 'em in the oven. Myself, I'd rather eat the paper bag." The storekeeper stuck the cigarette butt into a coffee can half full of sand.

Dave smiled, finishing his doughnut, which was delicious, and crumpling his napkin. "Listen, I'm new here—" he began.

The storekeeper gave him a look, the substance of which was a polite but unmistakable *No shit, Sherlock.*

"And I'm looking for somebody." Down in the boat basin a guy tossed a black golf bag and a pair of shoes into an open boat and untied the vessel, then hopped in and motored away.

The storekeeper didn't comment. *Here we go,* thought Dave, remembering what Horace used to say about the famously taciturn Maine natives. But he decided to give it a try anyway.

"Fellow about my age, medium height, medium build . . ."

The storekeeper was giving him another flat *give me a break* look. *Oh, what the hell,* Dave thought.

"Merkle's his name. Bert Merkle."

Because it wasn't as if Merkle wouldn't have figured out that Dave would be coming. Merkle had a gift for knowing what other people would do, especially if it might inconvenience him.

I'll inconvenience him, Dave thought with another sudden burst of bleak rage. How much else had Merkle figured out, though?

That was the real question. That, and exactly how Dave was going to manage to get his gun back and shoot Bert Merkle with it. He regretted again having handed it over, even though his hot rush of emotion right now only validated the decision.

He'd never been good at feeling one way and acting another, he reminded himself. Besides, what if Merkle came sniffing and searching for the weapon before Dave could use it?

Finding it, maybe, too. Which Bert could, and there was no sense pretending otherwise.

The storekeeper frowned. "Merkle? That crackpot?"

Just then the bell over the shop door jingled summoningly and the aproned man went inside, returning moments later with two coffees.

"Don't know why anyone would want to go looking for that guy," he went on as if the conversation hadn't been interrupted. He handed one of the coffees to Dave. "On the house. Welcome to Eastport."

Dave sipped, expecting the equivalent of crank-case oil. "I had to throw him out of here, he kept bothering all the customers with his foolishness," the storekeeper went on.

The coffee was good. "What kind of foolishness?"

"Objects," the storekeeper answered. "Unidentified flying ones," he added. His tone suggested that it was the flying part he found especially irksome.

"Guy swears he sees 'em. They land in his backyard, the little green men get out and talk to him. So *he* says." The storekeeper turned to Dave. "Your friend's a few pecans short of a pie."

"Uh-huh," Dave agreed. Merkle always had liked the air of harmlessness created by his I'm-so-crazy act.

Extraterrestrials, though; that was a new wrinkle. "Did he," Dave asked, "ever mention to you what the little green men say?"

The storekeeper looked scornful. In the boat basin, a spry-looking old gentleman in a navy peacoat was urging a small black dog to jump from a pier into a wooden dory.

"Nope," said the storekeeper, lighting another smoke. "'Take me to your leader,' I guess. What else?"

The dog jumped; the man followed. As the man settled himself and began to row, the dog sat in the bow, barking.

"Wears tinfoil hats," the storekeeper went on sorrowfully of Merkle, as if reciting the bad habits of a troublesome relative. "Been around here twenty years, started out no more crazy than any of the rest of us."

Something about the way the storekeeper said it made Dave think personality quirks were pretty common in Eastport, and that a live-and-let-live attitude might be fairly widespread, too, as a result.

And that Bert's recent behavior was stretching even this elastic standard. The storekeeper's next words seemed to confirm the idea. "I mean, a lot of folks here, they'll..."

The man thought a moment, considering how to put it, then went on. "Let's just say conformity's not an absolute requirement for bein' a well-respected member of this community, you just manage to take a shower, brush your teeth, an' put on some clean clothes oftener'n once in a blue moon, you get me? This guy, though. Takes his individuality seriously." And when Dave tipped his head inquisitively:

"Gets up on his soapbox down here right across from the post office every Saturday morning," the storekeeper said. "Shouting about how the aliens are going to get us."

Shaking his head, he went on. "He's got all the gory details down pat, too, Bert does. How the worst ones're already here and they're going to come up out of the bay one fine day, all black and dripping."

He turned to Dave. "With tentacles, like, growing out of their heads. And gills. And about how we're related to 'em, some of us, only we don't even know it."

"That's pretty wild, all right," Dave said, not letting his voice betray any emotion. He wondered what else Bert Merkle had decided to shout from the rooftops.

"Don't happen to know where he lives, do you?" he asked, as if the answer weren't very important to him.

Unfooled, the storekeeper shot Dave a sideways look. "Not a cop, are you? Or the tax man? 'Cause I'm no fan of Merkle but I'm also not in the habit of turning in my neighbors."

He stuck his second cigarette butt into the sand. "Fellow wants to tell stories, his own business, way I see it."

Dave finished his coffee. "No," he replied easily, "I'm not either of those. I went to school with Bert. A friend of ours has died, one of our classmates, and I came to talk to Bert about it. That's all."

"No kidding. Hey, sorry about that." The bell rang again and the storekeeper went inside, then returned.

"School buddies, huh? Funny, I'd of thought Bert was a lot older'n you. Guess seein' little green men must age a person."

Not green, Dave thought. *Black. And dripping.* "Guess so," he agreed, and listened carefully as the storekeeper told him how to find Bert Merkle's place.

"Not a house, really," he said. "More like sort of a trailer that's been built-onto every which-a-way. Back from the street, a lot of old overgrown bushes all tangled up around it."

Inside, Dave tried to pay but the storekeeper wouldn't hear of it. "Can't miss the yard, though," he went on. "Junk right out to the lot-lines, sheet metal, cardboard, bottles and cans, scrap wood, you name it."

A couple of kids ran in, bought sodas, and ran back out. *I was like them, once,* Dave thought, watching them go.

"I hear Merkle even got a summons from the code-enforcement guy, telling him to clean up that yard of his or else. Merkle went to the hearing, told them he's got to have all that stuff. Said it shields his energy, makes it hard for his enemies to find him," the store-keeper said.

Dave thought Merkle had better get himself some more junk. "Guess it doesn't work on little men, though," the storekeeper added. "Or for that matter on you."

"Thanks," Dave said. "And thanks again for the coffee." The bell jingled as he exited.

Out on the sidewalk he decided to retrieve the Saab from Jacobia Tiptree before doing anything else. The longer the car sat, the more interesting he might become to her and that friend of hers, Ellie White.

And that he *didn't* want. That the two women were something other than run-of-the-mill Eastport housewives he'd figured out too late. Also the swift, decisive way in which his gun had been taken from him had felt a bit too much like confiscation for his comfort.

But the box opened with a key. And over the years Horace had taught Dave a few smatterings of the lock-picker's art. So he could get the weapon back one way or another.

He couldn't help wondering whether the women themselves would pose problems, however. He hoped not. They were both rather likable, he thought as he retraced his steps along Water Street.

He entered the water-company office with its windows full of healthy-looking potted plants; Horace always said the ability to grow good houseplants was a sign of a well-ordered soul. There he asked questions about Eastport people's families, houses, and ancestors, explaining his interest by saying he was an amateur historian.

He did the same at the soda fountain, Wadsworth's Hardware, and a pizza place in which the aroma of spiced tomato sauce hung tantalizingly. But his thoughts never strayed very far from the two women, Jacobia Tiptree and Ellie White.

Quite likable indeed, he decided, picturing again the lean, dark-haired one with the faint aura of violence hanging around her like an invisible cloud. Beside her the red-haired young mother with the amazing pale-green eyes and penetrating glance had resembled a colored illustration from some old children's book about fairies and sprites.

Remarkable, really, each in her own way. Horace would have liked them.

Dave hoped they would both turn out to be smart enough to mind their own business.

Back at my house I stomped up the porch steps, let the dogs out, then waited for them to dash back in again before slamming the screen door so hard behind us all that it nearly fell off its hinges.

Nobody home, I thought; Bella must've gone to the store.

"God *bless* it!" I shouted into the empty house. "I swear if *one more thing* happens around here that *I do not want to happen,* I'm going to get one of those damn guns out of the cellar and *shoot* myself with it!"

But someone *was* home; my son, Sam, popped his head out of the parlor. Tall and handsome with dark, curly hair, long eyelashes, and a lantern jaw, he was living here at least temporarily after returning from the alcohol-treatment place.

"Mom?" he said, scanning my face anxiously.

"Oh, hush up," I told him, annoyed. "Can't a person blow off a little steam without a witness around, making shocked faces?"

Which I suppose was not a particularly kind thing to say to a recuperating person, and especially not one who was working as hard at it as Sam was. But oh, I was so cheesed off, and mostly at myself.

Angrily I strode down the hall and upstairs to see if just possibly the whole bathroom fiasco had merely been what my son would've called a Fig Newton of my imagination.

But no such luck. The room was all just the way I'd left it, which is to say I had about as much chance of repairing it by to-morrow as an ice cube had, stuck on one of the tines of Satan's pitchfork. On the other hand, I reminded myself grimly, even the worst home-repair massacre in Eastport was a day at the beach compared to the kind of foolishness I used to endure on a regular basis.

Because back in the old days, before I bought a big antique house on an island in Maine and began pouring pretty much every single drop of my blood into it, not to mention any dollars that weren't firmly nailed down, I lived with my then-husband and son in Manhattan, where I was a freelance money-manager to . . .

Well, let's not get too specific about it. But among my clients were the absolute cream of New York mobster society, guys whose funds were so dirty that when they brought me cash I sent the manila envelopes stuffed full of greenbacks through a nearby com-mercial laundry's steam-cleaning apparatus before opening them.

After that I found ways of investing the cash that would not set off alarm bells down at the Federal Building, where photos of many of my clients—labeled with nicknames like Bloody Eddie, Fast Al, and Tommy "Eyeballs" McGown—were prominently posted.

And at home things were even more interesting. We lived on the Upper East Side in a building so exclusive that it should've had an alligator-filled moat. My neighbors wore diamonds as big as gumdrops to the meetings of their charity organizations, while their husbands got whisked off each morning in limos to jobs that apparently involved guarding the safety of the Free World, or at any rate of all the advertising accounts in it.

Their nannies dressed better than I did. Meanwhile in my own apartment we were apparently holding a contest to see who could break me first:

1. My husband, Victor, the eminent brain surgeon, whose eye for the ladies around the hospital where he worked was so leg-endary that they'd started calling him the Sperminator, or

2. My not-yet-teenaged son, who while still in eighth grade

was already addicted to so many substances that once when we were picking a friend up at LaGuardia, his physical presence ruined a major drug bust by distracting every contraband-sniffing dog in the terminal. Luckily Sam didn't actually have anything illegal on him; it was just that his whole system was so saturated.

One night not long after that memorable incident, I came home from a hard day of transforming half a million dollars in mob money into certificates of deposit so clean that even a forensic accountant wouldn't be able to find anything wrong with them.

Which was the whole point. Dirty money leaves a slime trail. But I'd eliminated it, and earned a hefty commission for myself.

So I poured a glass of wine to celebrate, which was when I noticed that two of the good wineglasses were already missing from the sideboard. One was in the sink, and the other, I learned when I turned from discovering the first, was in the hand of an extremely pretty young woman who did not have much clothing on.

None, actually. She stood in the kitchen doorway between the eight-burner professional gas range and the Sub-Zero refrigerator with built-in icemaker and water dispenser.

On the shelves to one side of her stood the world's priciest Cuisinart, a top-of-the-line juicer, a breadmaker so elaborate you could set it to toast the stuff and spread peanut butter on it for you, a blender I'd bought for making strawberry daiquiris and never used because by that point diluting the liquor just seemed silly, and eight very lovely little shrimp-shaped chartreuse sushi plates with matching sauce bowls that I never used, either.

For one thing, nobody ate much around here anymore. Mostly we drank, and Sam snorted or shot up.

"Hi," the naked girl said blearily. Apparently those wineglasses had gotten a workout.

"Scram," I replied, and something in my voice must've clued her, or possibly it was the great big butcher knife I looked down and suddenly discovered I was gripping.

"Now," I said, whereupon she appeared to remember where the apartment door was located, and scampered away to put it hastily between her towel-wrapped self and the knife.

Which I thought was a wise move. Still, it left her in the hallway without any clothes on except for a borrowed bath towel, and after a few moments I heard her weeping out there.

Serves you right, I thought bitterly at her, stomping into the bedroom to strip the sheets off the bed.

I knew what had happened, of course. Stunned by wine and my husband's take-no-prisoners approach to the art of lovemaking—Victor's other nickname around the hospital was Vlad the Impaler—the girl had fallen asleep.

Gulping from my own glass of wine with one hand, I stuffed sheets furiously into the hamper with the other. Once the deed was done he'd been called back urgently to the hospital, I could only suppose, and after that he had forgotten all about her.

Which sounds unlikely until you recall that he was a brain surgeon, and thus utterly unfamiliar with the mundane realities of life. Only where his patients were concerned was he as focused as a ruby laser.

The girl in the hall wept wretchedly. I grabbed her clothes off the bedroom floor and strode to the apartment door with them, intending to shove them at her.

It was hard enough to get a cab around here at this hour even when you were dressed. Also, if Sam came home all lit up like a Christmas tree and found a nude girl in the hallway, I didn't know what he might do.

"Here," I snarled, yanking the door open to thrust the blue scrub shirt and pants out.

A surgical nurse, I gathered from the clothes I was throwing at her; I tossed a pair of white sneakers out after the scrub suit. But I also made the mistake of looking at her.

Tear-stained and sorrowful, blonde hair tangled and makeup melted into a sad pair of raccoon eyes, she snatched up the shirt and pants and began yanking them on without even looking at me.

She was shivering, partly from cold but mostly, I supposed, from distress. "Oh, get in here," I snapped.

"Go to hell," she replied, and peered around the hall carpet miserably. "I can't ... Where are my damned socks?"

I went to find them, leaving the apartment door open. When I returned with a pair of white knee-highs, she was standing inside.

"Thank you," she muttered when I handed them to her. "I'm so sorry. Victor didn't tell me he was ..."

Married. Of course not. Probably he'd forgotten that, too; I told myself he must have. With Victor, it was not impossible.

She put the socks on, and after that I told her to wash her face while I made coffee and called a cab. While we waited for the doorman to buzz from downstairs, she drank some of the coffee and told me again that she was sorry, she was new at the hospital and hadn't known, and I told her the truth:

That it wasn't her fault, that it didn't really matter, and as far as I was concerned, she hadn't even done anything wrong.

That she should just chalk it up to experience. "It was the shock of seeing you there, mostly," I said.

"No kidding," she replied, and started to laugh, then saw my face and decided to shut up.

After she'd gone Sam came home and slammed into his room, locking the door and turning his music up so brain-thumpingly loud that even if I'd wanted to talk to him, I couldn't.

I never even mentioned the girl to Victor. And it was months afterward that I drove to New Brunswick, Canada, for a stockholders' meeting of a company I'd set up to launder more extortion money.

But on the way home through Maine I took a side trip to a little place called Eastport, on a tiny scrap of rock called Moose Island. And the very first thing that happened was that halfway across the causeway I felt all the stored-up anger, betrayal, and grief draining from me, as if the sparkling blue salt water on both sides of the curving road were sucking it out of me by osmosis.

Next, on the island itself I found a quaint seaside village with city amenities—streetlights, sidewalks, a public library, and even a Mexican restaurant—yet so far from the madding crowd that by eight in the evening you could roll a bowling ball down the main drag and not hit anyone.

Also, Eastport having long ago been a boom town but being one no longer, it contained a lot of big old vacant houses, many of them in shattering states of disrepair, whose windows once blazed with domestic light but now gazed emptily, yearning only for someone to love and care for them again.

Here, I thought, staring at the biggest, most ramshackle one of all. In particular, I thought the antique wooden shutters flanking the forty-eight old double-hung windows would be simple to take down and paint.

They weren't.

Chapter 4

M y father was a lean, clean old man in faded overalls, a flannel shirt, and battered work boots, who wore his long gray hair tied back into a ponytail with a leather thong. A red stone that I was pretty sure was a real ruby gleamed in his earlobe.

"You know, when you decide to do something so drastic to an important thing like a bathroom, it's good to have a plan," he observed, already knee-deep in porcelain shards and plaster rubble.

I had no plan other than to bash a big hole in the side of the house with a wrecking ball and have Bad Bathtub hauled out through it. But from the look on my dad's face now, I guessed I'd better revamp that part of the program, too.

"You start," he added severely, "by finding out which way the beams run." He gestured overhead.

Uh-oh. I hadn't done that, either. "Because?"

"Because if you don't, and you knock out a supporting wall, the house comes down on your head."

Well, well, I thought. *In the old-house fix-up department, you learn something new every day.*

Or to put it more bluntly, *Ye gods.*

Standing amidst the wreckage, my dad looked like a cross between an aging hippie and the kind of self-taught explosives expert who ends up having to go on the run for thirty years. Both of which he was, because when your wife—my mother—dies in a bomb blast and you—an actual self-taught explosives expert—drop out of sight at the exact same moment, it doesn't take a rocket scientist—which he also looked like, especially around the eyes—to figure out whodunnit.

Or who the cops will think dunnit, anyway; local, state, *and* federal.

"Oh," I said softly, noticing that besides pulling down what remained of the plaster—*Sayonara, swans,* I thought, glimpsing the silvery bits of them still swimming in Pepto pink—he'd also taken down the antique wooden lath behind the plaster.

Which I didn't understand at all. Because when you redo a wall, you smoosh the first layer of new plaster in between the lath strips, so when it dries it hangs securely there like a key sticking out of a lock. Then you add the next layer, and the next, and...

"No more plaster, huh?" I said. That had to be the answer: Sheetrock. Meanwhile, I noticed also that the wall the bathtub butted up against looked very solid indeed, even without plaster.

And there was a beam running across the top of it. My dad looked up from scooping the last shreds of swan out of the tub.

"Don't get ahead of yourself. Plaster's the least of your problems, Jake. And forget about the Sheetrock, too."

Double uh-oh. "Okay. Um, maybe concrete board?"

Because of course behind the new tub and shower, we'd want to put in something that wouldn't (a) soak up lots of water and (b) transfer it directly and without impediment to the rooms below.

My father rolled his eyes. "Now, I can see you've got your heart set on expanding this room."

Correct. And due to the shape of my old house, there was no other way to do it unless we wanted to start taking showers on a platform sticking out over the street.

"But," my father said, "that tub's not your problem."

Oh goodie, I thought, *whose problem is it?*

"The problem is how to hold up the ceiling once the wall's gone. See, that beam isn't there for decoration. That beam..."

Just then Bella appeared in the doorway. Or what was left of it; in retrospect, even I thought maybe I'd gone a little too far with the sledgehammer.

The first swing I'd taken, actually, might've been the too-far one.

"Oh," Bella said, seeing my father. "I didn't know you were still here." She gave the *you* a faint, unwelcoming emphasis.

"Yes," he replied evenly. "Well, now you do know."

The look she shot him could've scoured the rest of the old porcelain off the bathtub, peeled the paint off the woodwork, and sanded the floor clean of old varnish all in one swell foop, as Sam would've put it; on top of everything else my son was also quite severely dyslexic.

My father pulled out a tape measure and applied it to the beam over the tub as Bella turned to me. "Missus, could you come downstairs? We need to discuss something."

Yes, we surely did. Up until this morning, my father and my housekeeper had been the sort of sweethearts who think no one else notices that they are flat-out crazy about each other.

Now, though, a chill more appropriate to the Arctic Circle had descended between these two. And I intended to find out why, if only to keep Bella from getting into a cleaning bout so frenzied, it could reduce the place to toothpicks.

But there was one more thing I needed to check out with my father, first. "Dad?" I said.

He straightened, tucking the tape measure into his pocket. Looking at him, it struck me that there aren't too many men who can carry off a ruby stud in the earlobe, senior citizen or no.

"Yes, Jacobia?" His voice, tinged with the wry, long-suffering humor that I imagined kept him sane for all those years as a fugitive, also held the kind of stolid patience that a man whose daughter demolished bathrooms without warning can develop.

Must develop, actually, unless he wants to go on the run again. Meanwhile through the now trimless and sill-less bathroom window I could see Dave DiMaio's red Saab still in the driveway.

And it was making me nervous. "Listen, if a stranger shows up at your house..."

He looked up, his eyes suddenly displaying lazy alertness; see *years as a fugitive*, above. "Uh-huh," he said.

"And the stranger has a gun."

"You've taken it away from him, though."

He knew my opinion: the only handgun I feel safe around is the one in my own hand, or in my husband Wade's.

"So what's the problem?" asked my father.

"The problem is that when people with weapons show up here, I always feel like it's the beginning of something."

"That," said my father, "is because it so often is."

"Mm. He has information about the old book," I added.

His bushy eyebrows rose. "Does he, now? So he's associated with the fellow who got murdered?"

Horace Robotham, my father meant. He'd hadn't believed the tragic mugging story for a minute.

I nodded unhappily. "Friends. Good friends, I'd say."

"I see," my father said thoughtfully. "You're wondering what the firearm's the beginning *of,* then."

"Exactly. I've locked his gun in the lockbox. So he can't *do* anything with it even if he wanted to, but—"

But in my experience people who bring a gun into a situation are different in a single, very important way from the people who don't: they've accepted the idea of using one. And it's that internal notion, not the presence or absence of the actual weapon itself, that ends up making them dangerous.

"So anyway, I just thought I'd run it by you," I finished.

"Mm-hmm." Head tilted back as if praying to some gods of old-house carpentry that only he knew about—and considering the amount of damage I'd done, I hoped that was true—he studied the exposed beam once more.

"You know," I told him, beginning to feel guilty—

When he wasn't working on my house, he was the kind of mason who had a long waiting list of paying customers wanting work from him.

—"I should be doing this, myself."

The bathroom, I meant. Because even as a do-it-yourself home-fix-it enthusiast—buying a huge old house without being one of these is like buying a rocket launcher and then leaving the fuse-lighting to somebody else; sooner or later you end up wanting your own pack of matches—bashing out walls was the kind of thing I'd always said I'd leave to the people who knew how. But that old bathroom had overwhelmed my better judgment.

Such as it was. And I thought it was only right that I should deal with the result. But my father didn't.

"You going to do the wiring?" my dad asked. "Snake the conduits down through the walls, put a new circuit in the system, down in the circuit box?"

"Well, no," I replied uncertainly. "But I—"

"How about the plumbing? Pull out the old lead stuff, solder in the copper where you need it." He eyed the floor. "Going to have to move that drain, too, I guess. You going to do all that?"

"Oh, of course not," I replied a little impatiently. "I'm not a plumber or an electrician. But I see no reason why I couldn't do the rest of the tear-out, and—"

"Jacobia." My dad put a hand on my shoulder. "That's fine, but if I don't find a way to do what that beam is doing"—in order to make it do it about five feet to the south of where the beam was located now, he meant—"then you're going to have to put this wall back again." He gestured at the torn-down lath, demolished plaster, and tattered swans now heaped in the tub.

"Right where it was," he added. "My point is, just *wanting* to do it yourself isn't going to cut it in the holding-the-house-up department. For that you need engineering."

"Oh," I said. "You mean like how big a beam is, and how far it has to span, and—"

I'd heard of the mathematics and so on that architects use when specifying what size the building materials for any project will need to be, and what exactly they're made of.

Wooden beams, for instance, versus steel. But the bathroom was so small I hadn't thought I'd need to worry about any of that.

"Right," he said. By which he meant I'd been wrong. "The longer the beam is, the bigger around you've got to have it, unless you support it at intervals."

He looked at me. "Specific," he emphasized, "intervals."

In other words you couldn't just wing it; damn.

I took a deep breath. "So maybe I could take the rest of the plaster down, though?" I ventured. "Since even if we have to put the room back the way it was—"

Ghastly thought; I plunged on. "—I still want to replace the bathtub. So I could get *that* out of here, and—"

My father sighed. "All right," he said finally. "If you got the tub removed, it would make it easier to—"

"Excellent," I interrupted. "I'll get a bunch of guys to do it right away."

My son, Sam, for instance, was always looking to earn money; probably his friends would pitch in as well. Some of them were even reasonably Hulk-like.

"If I had better access, then maybe I could run a couple of shorties out perpendicular," my father mused aloud.

"But," he cautioned, "if you can't get a crew, *don't* try to take that tub out yourself."

I assured him that despite my rash starting of an enormous, complex project that I didn't know how to finish—how was I to know that adding twenty-five square feet to a bathroom could bring a three-thousand-square-foot two-hundred-year-old house down on my head?—I promised that I would absolutely not try to haul a huge, million-pound bathtub down a flight of stairs all by myself.

Heck, now that I thought about it, just getting it unhooked from the outflow drain might be an interesting trick.

Finally I left him there figuring out how to keep the attic from falling annoyingly onto bathers, assuming we were ever even able to bathe again in the house at all. But as I reached the hall stairs he spoke.

"Jacobia?"

I paused on the landing. "Yes?"

"Don't give that guy his gun back."

A couple of hours later when Bella had begun making curried crab for dinner, starting with crabmeat so fresh the tiny claws could practically hop from their container and pinch you, Ellie arrived.

"Oh! Curried crab," she breathed happily, coming in just as I was beginning to toast a blueberry scone.

So I put one in for her, too. "I see Dave DiMaio's car is still sitting outside in the driveway," she said.

"So?" She hadn't mentioned Merrie Fargeorge's party again. But her voice had that *better pay attention* sound that I'd learned never to ignore. Suddenly I was all ears.

"He was still downtown when I walked home from the library with Lee," Ellie went on.

At the stove, Bella stirred flour into the butter-and-onion mixture. I set the toasted scones on the table; Ellie got up and snagged
some butter from Bella for hers.

Ellie was so slender that she could've applied butter directly to
her hips every day for a year without visible effect. I had mine
plain.

"When I saw him he was coming out of Wadsworth's," she
continued.

The hardware store, she meant. "And?"

A small crumb of scone fell to the tablecloth; I plucked it
up and ate it while Bella poured milk into the bubbling flour-
and-butter mixture. Meanwhile over our heads my father's footsteps moved with a metallic grating sound; he was standing in
the tub.

"And I wondered what he was up to," said Ellie. "So I went
into the Moose Island General Store and started a conversation
with Skippy. He says DiMaio was asking all kinds of questions.
About," Ellie added meaningfully, "Bert Merkle."

Bella turned. "*That* crackpot," she uttered disdainfully.

"Really?" I began. But just then Sam came in with a fishing
rod over his shoulder and a pailful of freshly caught mackerel in
his hand. He stood the rod in the hall and set the pail of fish on the
kitchen table.

"Look!" he said triumphantly. "We can have them for . . ."

Dinner, he would've finished, only Bella had already grabbed
the pail, hustled it out onto the back porch, and returned with an
outraged expression.

"Fish come into this kitchen already cleaned, or they don't
come in at all," she instructed him, but then her face softened.

"Nice mess o' mackerel," she allowed. "Go cut the heads an'
tails off, take the insides out, and wash 'em with the hose."

Being in the same room with Sam had a tendency to make all
women's faces soften, not to mention their hearts; he was his father's son.

"I don't know, Bella," he said, dropping an arm around her. "If I do all that work, are you going to cook them?"

" 'Course I will," she promised stoutly. She was a sucker for his crooked grin. "Go on with you, now," she added with a hint of tenderness, "you're spoiling my sauce."

He let Bella shoo him good-humoredly out of the kitchen and when he was gone she spoke again. " 'Course I'll cook 'em. Fresh mackerel makes excellent cat food."

Cat Dancing purred loudly in response from her customary perch on top of the refrigerator. But then a *ka-klunk!* from upstairs must've reminded Bella of my father and a scowl creased her face.

Fortunately she wasn't looking directly at the sauce at the time; curdled crab is not so delicious. I turned back to Ellie. "So, what else about Bert Merkle?"

Intent on her saucepan once more, Bella made a rude noise. "No more sense than one o' them fish," she commented, but whether she meant Merkle or my father, I couldn't tell.

"Skippy says Dave DiMaio told him that Bert and Dave went to school together," Ellie reported. "Dave wanted to know where Bert lives, as if he intended to go visit his old friend."

Suddenly my decision to hide the lockbox a lot better felt urgent. "If he really is a friend," I remarked.

Ellie dabbed butter from her lip with a napkin. "You know, I think maybe we'd better keep an eye on him."

Bella added salt, pepper, lemon juice, and grated cheese to the sauce she was creating, then took the two slices of homemade white bread she'd turned into breadcrumbs and stirred them with enough melted butter to moisten them.

"Oh, I don't know," I objected. Between the demolished bathroom and a few other home-repair projects that I'd been neglecting lately—and, I reminded myself with a despairing pang, Merrie Fargeorge's party preparations—I didn't need anything else on my to-do list. Cat Dancing gazed down with cross-eyed interest at the container of crabmeat.

"Don't even dream about it," Bella said without looking up at the cat.

"Dave will be coming to get his car soon," I said. "Probably he'll be staying at the Motel East, or one of the bed-and-breakfasts."

That was one good side effect of swinging a sledgehammer around your only bathroom; no overnight guests.

Ellie ate her last scone bit. "Good. Near enough for us to stay reasonably well-informed about his activities, but with no obvious close connection to either one of us."

Right, because such an impertinently inquisitive person-from-away wouldn't quite bring out the tar and feathers, in Eastport.

Not quite. "He seems like a nice enough guy, though," I added, not quite knowing why I was defending him; his recent bereavement, maybe.

"Except for the gun he brought with him," Ellie replied.

Right. Except for that.

Bella stirred more cheese into the sauce. "I don't know why people can't let well enough alone," she said, frowning into the pan.

For a minute I thought she meant DiMaio, but then I looked up and saw my father standing forlornly in the kitchen doorway. "Going home for lunch," he said finally.

No response from Bella. Ordinarily by now they'd have been eating their grilled-cheese sandwiches companionably.

"Do not," my father reminded me severely, "try moving that bathtub."

I was about as likely to run out and try shifting the Rock of Gibraltar a few inches to the left.

"You have plenty of other more manageable projects to finish around this place," he added.

For instance, in my workroom on the third floor a very old attic window awaited me: rotten, paint-peeled, and with most of its antique, wavery-glass panes ready to fall out.

That is, the ones that hadn't done so already. I'd begun repairs, but completion on the window was urgently needed; in winter the wind muscled frigidly in through it, making a mockery of any plan I might have for house-heating efficiency.

Although actually the whole house made a mockery of that. And since it was now late August, I calculated that winter would be here in approximately twenty minutes.

"Right," I told my father as he went out, thinking, *Scraper, chisel, belt sander, paint.*

And glazing compound, lots and lots of glazing compound for putting in each and every one of the five-by-eight-inch panes of glass that needed replacing. Just thinking about it made me want to go shove a bathtub out a window, but if I didn't get those panes in soon I might just as well pump heating oil out through it instead.

Paintbrush, glazing pins... and some extra glass panes, I decided, since even after all the glazing I'd done since moving in here, I still had about a one-in-six breakage rate.

"Now, about the party," Ellie said.

"Listen, Ellie," I said hastily. "Maybe I was a little too optimistic about my hostess abilities when I offered to..."

Cake, punch, napkins, glasses. Real ones, mind you, not the plastic variety, and a pox on paper plates. We'd need a big tea maker, and a coffee urn, and with all that crystal and china on the table I guessed we'd better transfer the cream and sugar into something besides old Tupperware containers.

And the good teacups, wrapped in yellowing newspaper, were in a box in the hall closet. Bella stirred curry powder into the sauce, whereupon a sweet, complex perfume wafted from it, like something being concocted in an expensive restaurant.

"You'll be fine," Ellie reassured me. "I'll just run down to the IGA and get you some spray starch, so it'll be easier for you to iron the linen napkins."

"But... but..." I sounded like an old outboard engine.

"Jake." She eyed me amusedly. "Come on, now, it'll be fine. You've done this before and it worked out very well, so what's the problem?"

Right, I had: ten years earlier, when Eastport ladies were still generously taking pity on me on account of my just-got-here status. So they'd forgiven me my many faux pas including the very large picture of Elvis Presley painted on black velvet that I'd fastened up at the last minute to cover the big hole in the dining-room wall.

But this time would be different. No hole in the dining-room wall, for one thing. And no allowances made, for another.

This time, in the are-you-or-aren't-you-a-real-Eastport-lady department, it was put up or shut up.

"I've got to go. Lee's fast asleep. But George is with her," Ellie added. "So that won't last."

George Valentine was Ellie's husband and a fine, responsible babysitter, but he did have one bad habit: he adored that child so much that anytime she fell asleep, he woke her up again so he could play with her. As a result Lee had learned to take power naps lasting about fifteen minutes, after which she hung on her crib rail and howled.

"Good luck," I said as Ellie departed; when he was small Sam had done the same thing for a while and I'd been puzzled—though I must admit, pleased—when the habit ended suddenly. Later I found out that my then-husband had begun dosing him with tincture of opium, to quiet him.

Ellie stuck her head back in. "Listen—don't forget what I said about DiMaio. The gun means that guy's up to something, I'm sure of it."

Oh, great. "Wait here," I told Bella when Ellie had gone. "I mean it, don't move an inch."

Because if I didn't say it, in the mood she was in she might decide to push that old bathtub out the window herself, and after that it could be bombs away with all the rest of the upstairs furniture.

Leaving her in the kitchen I descended once more the set of narrow, curving steps that led to the cellar, remembering to duck as I passed under some low-hanging pipes and step fast to the left to avoid falling into the square hole where the wood-burning furnace used to be.

The ancient coal chute gaped darkly at me—with only a few additions my cellar could be a museum dedicated to the history of home heating—as did the doorway to the old meat room. In the far corner, past the paint cans, ladders, power sprayer, varnish tins, primer buckets, tarps, and all the other equipment so necessary to the painting of even a single wall in a very old house, there was a loose brick.

I knew, because I'd loosened it with a hammer and chisel. I'd wanted a secure hiding place, somewhere to put things so even the cleverest thief wouldn't find them.

Ten thousand dollars in twenties and tens, for instance; emergency money. Plus the extra key to the lockbox; I took the box down from the shelf where I'd put it when Dave was here, then crossed to the opposite corner of the cellar and pulled the brick out.

The cash was still in there; key, too. I shoved the money to the back to make room. The original tiny brass key to the lockbox hung as always on a gold chain around my neck, along with a gold heart charm that Wade had given me.

I pulled the chain over my head and put the key into the lock. It turned oddly, which was my first hint that something was wrong, with a soft, not-quite-stuck feeling, as if a pin or some other slim object had bent the lock's innards.

"Missus?" Bella called down the cellar stairs.

"Just a minute," I called back. "I'll be right..."

On the far side of the cellar, the door to the steps leading up and out to the backyard stood ajar as it often did in summer, admitting a long thin triangle of light.

Next, through one of the broken cellar windows—and yes, I did know that I ought to replace these immediately if not sooner— I heard a car start up in my driveway.

The car backed into the street, its sound briefly louder and then diminishing. As it faded, I peered dumbly into the lockbox again, still unable to believe my eyes.

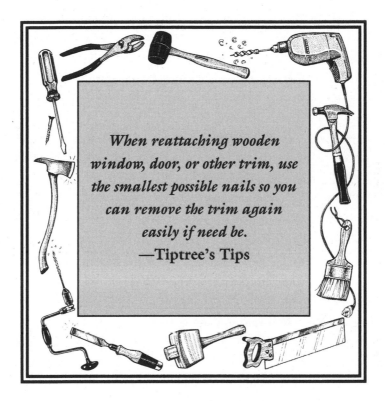

Chapter 5

*When reattaching wooden
window, door, or other trim, use
the smallest possible nails so you
can remove the trim again
easily if need be.*
—Tiptree's Tips

B ella, speak," I commanded twenty minutes later. But she
wouldn't.

We were up on the third floor, in the big unfinished room with
the tall, south-facing windows. Once upon a time, when the house
was new and the family in it had so many servants that they
hardly knew where to put them all, maids and scullery girls slept
up here in narrow beds with only candles to say their prayers by.

Later came stoves, gaslights, and finally the massive old cast-iron radiators. Over the years I'd stripped off the stained wallpaper, patterned in grapevines that must have been green and fresh-looking all those decades ago.

I'd patched up the plaster and put a coat of white primer on it, too, so that now the room was like an artist's studio, airy and full of light. It made an excellent place to repair windows.

"Come on, Bella," I urged. "I can see you're unhappy. But how can I help if you won't say what's wrong? Did my father hurt your feelings?"

For all her exterior toughness, Bella's insides were about as resilient as your average marshmallow. "Don't need help," she uttered stubbornly, but her lower lip was trembling.

"Please," I said, opening the plastic container of glazing compound, "tell me what happened."

Before me, supported by four milk crates on a plastic tarp, lay a tall, rectangular exterior window. I'd already scraped and sanded it, filled the holes with plastic wood, and sanded that. So I just needed to put the glass back in and apply paint.

"Old fool," Bella said, meaning my father.

She sat on an extra milk crate while I dug glazing compound out of the container with a putty knife. The stuff was soft and claylike, pale gray with the faint, pleasant scent of turpentine; the smell increased the artist's-studio feeling.

"He wants to get married," Bella announced.

I paused in the act of rolling the glazing compound between my hands to warm and soften it. "You're kidding!"

Not very tactful, maybe. But she understood. That the two of them were good friends was one thing.

Marriage, though. My mother's ghost seemed to shift uneasily up there where it floated, always a little sorrowful, at the back of my mind.

"Nope. I'm not kidding, and he wasn't, either." Bella looked around as if she'd never seen the third floor before.

"I've always liked it up here," she remarked, as if having confided in me she now wanted to get away from the subject, fast.

"The light," she said, "is clearer. And all the other little rooms up here could be made over real pretty, too."

The chambers adjoining the main room, once home to the small army of girls who in their early teens were already expert at slops-carrying, potato-peeling, and ash-sweeping, offered plenty of space for a bathroom, bedroom, and galley kitchen, plus a small study. I'd often thought that if I ever ran really short of money I would fix it all up and rent it out.

"I'm still not sure I understand," I told Bella. "My father proposed? To you?"

"Yup." Her lips tightened at the memory while her work-roughened fingers twisted the corner of her apron.

"What's he want with me, anyway?" she asked plaintively. "Sure, I know how to work hard, and I'm a halfway decent cook, I guess."

"Uh-huh." Whenever we sat down to eat one of Bella's meals, angels gathered and began singing over the dining-room table. But she'd been married once already and it hadn't been a success. In fact, when her then-husband turned suddenly from a live one into a dead one, she'd been the prime suspect.

Ellie and I had gotten her out of that debacle, but since then the expression radiating from every plain, unyielding molecule of her face was a mixture of harsh skepticism and grim determination, only occasionally leavened with a pinch of simple affection.

"Says he wants more *togetherness*," she scoffed. "But can you imagine? The two of us fallin' all over each other, tryin' to keep out of each other's way in that tiny house of mine. Or," she added with a shudder, *"his."*

Both their small cottages together would've fit easily in my house. And there would be room for a couple of tennis courts, besides.

"Well," I said, "if you don't want to, you don't have to."

But another problem worried me even more than Bella's marriage plans or the absence of them. Pondering it, I pressed a thin band of glazing compound onto the wooden ledge of the sash opening where a pane of glass would sit, then removed the excess with the putty knife.

"Hmph," said Bella. "Maybe. But your father is a persistent old fool."

Dropping a pane into its place and pressing firmly to settle it on the glazing compound, for a moment I imagined Dave DiMaio as one of those mild-mannered superheroes with x-ray eyes.

But that was silly. Life in my old house was indeed like a comic book, sometimes, but in it the main character was always dangling precariously from a ladder, upending a paint bucket, or smacking her thumb so painfully hard with a hammer that imaginary tweety-birds flew chirping around her head.

In short, around here when people could see through walls it was because I'd knocked holes into them. So on that late-summer morning in Eastport, Maine, when everything still seemed okay—except for the demolished bathroom, of course, and Bella, and Sam, who was not yet drinking again, and the party for Merrie Fargeorge with its terrifying requirements of crystal and china and the bar set so high in the hostessing-skills department that just thinking about it threatened to give me a nosebleed—in the midst of it all, I really knew only one thing. The gun I'd taken from DiMaio . . .

Cheap and greasy-feeling; loaded, too. I'd checked, before putting it where I knew no one could find it.

So what had happened was ridiculous.

Impossible, really. Like seeing through walls.

The Bisley and the .38 Special were still in the lockbox. The target gun, also.

But Dave DiMaio's awful little weapon was gone.

.   .   .

Driving the Saab away from the Tiptree house, Dave felt a twinge of guilt. But not for long; the fury that had threatened to overwhelm him upon hearing of Horace's murder now seized him again.

Bert Merkle was here in Eastport; well, Dave had known that. So he would find Bert. And then ... the matter would come to an end.

He drove downhill a few blocks to the Motel East, a brown two-story building on a bluff overlooking the ancient wreckage of a huge wharf.

Rotted stumps of old wooden pilings stuck out of the water like broken teeth, but in their place in his mind's eye rose the steam packet's cavernous terminal building, carts piled high with baggage outside amid the bustle and excitement of an imminent voyage to Boston or beyond.

He pulled into the motel parking lot and entered the office, whose desk was crammed with literature about tourist attractions: Reversing Falls, the Tides Institute, sails for whale-watching and fishing. The woman behind the desk smiled pleasantly as she handed him the room key, and wished him an enjoyable stay.

Enjoyable, he repeated to himself as he collected his bag from the Saab's backseat.

Maybe not, he thought as he opened the door to a large, bright room with two king-sized beds, a tidy kitchenette, and a million-dollar view of the bay.

Satisfying, though. He put his bag down on one of the big beds.

Yes. Definitely that.

"Jacobia!" said a female voice very sharply, inches from my ear. Hearing it, I wished intensely that I'd gone straight home instead of stopping at the IGA.

Or that I'd simply stayed outdoors. As soon as she dropped

Lee off at her play date, Ellie had returned to my house, meaning to dive at once into heavy-duty party preparations. But when she saw my state of mind she'd taken me on an expedition, instead.

Moose Island still held wild areas where in summer brambly treasure-troves of blackberries grew, hidden by old apple trees and thickets of beach roses. In a secret one that only Ellie knew, we filled the quart-sized baskets her husband, George, wove out of ash strips as a hobby during the winter.

"The gun was Dave's, he wanted it back, and he took it," she said of my empty-lockbox discovery, having lured me out with the promise of berry cobbler for dessert.

"Rude, sneaky, and technically illegal." All of which, her tone said clearly, confirmed her original opinion of him.

"But look at it this way, Jake. Now that he has it, he has no reason to come back. I mean," she added, "since it seems you've decided to wash your hands of him."

Her look said she still thought I might be sorry about that later, but she didn't push it. "As for the party, you're being silly. The ladies like you. They'll be delighted by anything you do," she reassured me again.

Right, the way all audiences are delighted by banana-peel pratfalls and grins dripping whipped-cream pie. My inability to entertain properly in Eastport—ladies! teacups! face powder!—was exceeded only by my growing terror of trying and failing at it.

But there were still those berries and that cobbler, so after we filled the baskets, Ellie had returned home and I'd come here to the IGA to get butter, flour, and Maine's superior answer to traditional baking powder: Bakewell Cream.

And it was while I was standing in the produce aisle trying to decide whether or not also to buy a particularly good-looking avocado—Bella loved them, and I thought it might help cheer her up—that I learned just how tricky and difficult a problem Dave DiMaio might actually turn out to be, gun or no gun.

"Jacobia," Merrie Fargeorge repeated briskly. "Look alive!"

I dropped the avocado. Crouching quickly, Merrie popped nimbly up again and gave it to me.

"Standing there woolgathering," she tut-tutted.

People glanced at us, hiding smiles; they'd been students of Merrie's, most of them. Under her gaze I felt like a schoolchild, too, being scolded in front of the class.

And I didn't like it; still, you had to hand it to her. For a person of her age and build—late sixties, round as a cookie jar, wearing a white shirt and denim jumper over white stockings and blue leather clogs—the woman was astonishingly fast and flexible.

"Jacobia," the retired educator went on to admonish me, "you have to do something about him."

"Who?" I asked, trying to take refuge in the thought of all the other things I should probably pick up while I was here, and that I wouldn't remember until I got home. Or I could just start living on pastries from the new bakery downtown—Mimi's, it was called—and dwelling under a rock.

That way maybe Merrie wouldn't be able to find me. "Your new guest, that's who," she replied tartly.

Her hair was pure white, thick and springing from her head in a natural wave like wire coils erupting out of a box; any minute she was going to demand that I conjugate a verb.

"But he's not," I protested, looking around hopelessly as she went on frowning in clear disapproval at me.

Because that was the thing about Merrie, and the real reason I was so worried about her party. Her friends liked me, as Ellie had said. But Merrie didn't, and I couldn't make her; I didn't amuse her, and there was nothing she wanted or needed from me.

Or from anyone, actually. Because in Eastport, Merrie Fargeorge was the real deal, the owner of the most valuable thing a person around here could possibly have: two centuries of Eastport ancestry, traceable all the way back to a fellow who arrived here with an axe, a mule, and a dream sometime way back in the late 1700s. And that, in downeast Maine, was the very definition of royalty.

"His car was in your driveway," she pointed out. "Everyone saw it."

The morning after the first night my then-not-yet-husband Wade Sorenson's pickup truck spent in my driveway, four different neighbors happened to stop by for a visit, eager for details and their feelings a little wounded, I could tell, when I refused to share.

"Oh," I said now. "But, Merrie, he was only—"

"Never mind." She brushed off my objection crisply. "He's all over town prying. Nose a mile long, that one has, and he's sticking it everywhere. Heavens, I would think a friend of yours would have better manners."

Obviously she didn't think so. "But Merrie, he's *not a—*"

Her ice-blue eyes flashed annoyance as she ignored my attempt at a comment. For one thing, of course, I hadn't raised my hand.

"How old's your house? Who lived in it before you? Where'd the folks who built it come from? And what did they do?" Merrie went on with an affronted sniff.

"People don't care to put their whole family history out on display for some stranger with no local connections, you know, Jacobia," she said.

But DiMaio was asking them to do so and it was obviously my fault. Meanwhile, suddenly I understood the real reason why I'd said I'd host the party at all.

And that it was hopeless. Oh, I'd still do it; I'd promised Ellie, whose own house was too small, while the church halls and other usable gathering-rooms in Eastport were already booked at this time of the year, months or even years in advance.

But as for gaining Merrie's approval, I could entertain at the White House and not get that. Decades of confronting rowdy schoolchildren had made her about as personally vulnerable as a cargo freighter, and about as likely to change course easily.

And she'd already formed her opinion of me. Which on the plus side meant that now I knew just what to say to her, too.

"Merrie, I can't help you. As I told you, I don't know Dave DiMaio personally, and I have no reason to pursue an acquaintance with him."

Other than the old book, I remembered, but I had little expectation he'd be able to come up with that. I met Merrie's gaze.

"So if you've got something to say to him, you're just going to have to find him and tell him about it, yourself," I added, offering a polite if not particularly friendly smile as an olive branch. Whether she took it or not was her affair.

She didn't. "Oh, yes, you can do something," she retorted, not backing down. "And you should. When you're as old as I am, Jacobia, you'll realize it's much better to be *proactive* about these things."

Punctuating this with a look that could've sizzled all the paint off my old woodwork, she gave her grocery cart a shove and hurried away from me.

Criminy, I thought with a sinking heart, watching her go; never mind his dratted gun. Dave DiMaio was apparently quite capable of wreaking havoc just with his mouth.

"Why do people even care?" I wondered aloud when I got home.

"Because their past is all they've got, some of them," Bella replied.

True enough; nowadays ownership of a big old house was more likely to mean you were poor than the opposite, what with taxes, heat, insurance, and—a huge, echoing crash came from the bathroom above, followed by a string of curses—maintenance. "Or the history they do have isn't what they want on display for the world to see," Bella added.

Also true; Eastport's past was so full of spies, smugglers, traitors, pirates, and—more recently—clients of the federal government's witness-protection program, it was a wonder any of the locals ever spoke to anyone outside their immediate families.

Which some didn't. "Anyway, Merrie is the closest thing Eastport has to an opinion-maker," my housekeeper added. "If she says he's causing you trouble around town, then he is."

She stopped scrubbing the oven just long enough to accept the biscuit ingredients I'd brought home. The grim set of her jaw as she put them away in the cupboard suggested she'd had yet another talk with my father, and that it hadn't gone well.

Just then he came downstairs, covered with plaster dust. "I got the tub loosened up off the floor," he reported, wiping his face on the blue paisley bandanna he kept stuffed in his overalls pocket.

Bella stuck her head in the oven. From her scowl I gathered she wished it were full of gas.

"Coupla' days, I can gather up enough help to haul it out of there," my father said, ignoring her.

"Fine," I said resignedly. "In the meantime Wade can take his shower at the terminal building before he comes home, and—"

"Hey, Mom!" Sam interrupted, bursting in through the back door. "Mom, do we have somebody staying here who's an FBI guy? Or homeland security? Because I was just downtown and I heard..."

The dogs jumped up to greet him. "No, we don't have anyone staying here," I said. "As of now, we don't even have a working bathroom, so I don't see how we *could* have anyone—"

My father went out, the screen door slamming hard. Bella straightened and shot a look after him; my heart fell at the sight of it.

Then the phone rang and it was Nina from Wadsworth's hardware store calling to say my houseguest was quite the conversationalist, wasn't he, and did I know just how inquisitive he was being? Since sometimes people got off on the wrong foot in Eastport, she said gently.

As if I didn't know. When I first got here I'd tried paying a bird-hunting neighbor who brought me a brace of partridges, their breast feathers darkly bloodstained and heads lolling helplessly. Surely I could give him something for the birds, I'd said, pulling money from my wallet while attempting unsuccessfully to conceal my revulsion, and it took weeks to recover my credibility with that one guy alone, never mind all the other people he told about it.

After Nina's call the phone rang again several times more, and it was the volunteer in the historical-society gift shop, the clerk at the soda shop, the billing-department lady at the water company, and somebody from the pizza place.

Finally I heard from the guy at the Mobil station who always took good care of me when I went in there, asking if I wanted him to go ahead and service the red Saab that Dave DiMaio had driven into town—it needed a new tail light—or should the service-station fellow just let all the air out of the tires? The latter, he confided, was his inclination.

"Man's a worse snoop than you," the gas-station guy added.

Ignoring this, I thanked him, and requested that he please not harm Dave DiMaio's car in any way, since Dave might be a pain but I saw no reason to take it out on an innocent vehicle. Besides, he'd need the car to get out of town, I pointed out.

When I hung up, Sam had finished heaping the laundry basket with, apparently, every clothing item he owned, and was rummaging the kitchen cabinets for, apparently, every food item I owned.

"See ya," he called, carrying a plate piled high with Oreos, gingersnaps, cake slices, sweet pickles, a bottle of apple juice, and a bag of grapes into the parlor, where I heard the television go on.

His evening shift at the fish-packing plant started soon—being a drunk had ruined his other job opportunities in Eastport—and since eight hours per night of fish-innards removal (not counting those mackerel) was enough to spoil even his appetite, he needed to eat early.

I didn't think the heavy-on-the-sugar part of my son's diet was necessarily a good sign, but at least it wasn't heavy on bourbon. Bella, meanwhile, had finished returning the oven to a state that was cleaner than new and begun on the kitchen woodwork, which was already so spotless, it glowed in the dark.

"Togetherness," she muttered while she rubbed it. "Highly overrated, *if* you ask me. *Which* of course no one has."

And I understood perfectly, because it suddenly occurred to me that no one had asked me, either: I mean, whether I wanted a mysterious gun-stealing visitor, an obsessive-compulsive house-keeper trying to repel a persistent suitor who happened to be my father, a newly recovering (I hoped) alcoholic son with a sugar addiction, a demolished bathroom that wouldn't have been if I hadn't taken such a wild notion, or an imminent party for a highly esteemed Eastport lady who apparently enjoyed my company almost as thoroughly as I did hers.

That is, not. So while Bella washed woodwork with a sponge soaked in bleach-water and Sam devoured Oreos while watching a ball game and the dogs snored beside him on the best chairs in the parlor, I called Ellie. I told her that if she cared about my welfare even a little bit she'd stop whatever she was doing and come right back over here again, pronto.

And she arrived in about three minutes; I met her out on the porch.

"So all I'm saying is, whatever DiMaio's doing, maybe we should try getting out in front of it, that's all. Don't you agree? And afterward we don't have to—"

Ellie tactfully refrained from remarking that this was exactly what she'd suggested only a few hours ago. "Why do you suppose he wants to know about Eastport history?" she wondered. "People's families, houses, and ancestors and so on."

Because what could that have to do with Horace Robotham's

death? "Well, the history stuff could be book-related somehow," I guessed. "But if that's why he's here—"

"Precisely." Her green eyes narrowed. "If it's the book and not the death that interests him, why bring a *gun*?"

From the maple tree in the yard a single leaf twirled down innocently onto the lawn; the first of many. Soon we wouldn't only be wanting to take showers; we'd be wanting *hot* showers.

"On the other hand, if you go somewhere meaning to use a gun, why advertise that you've got one?" she went on. "That whole business of him wanting you to lock it up..."

"Maybe it was just his way of letting me know he had it," I mused aloud. "Some kind of warning, maybe. But in that case why *give* it to me? *He* was the one who suggested..."

Sam spoke suddenly from the other side of the screen door. "I used to put cherry brandy in bottles of cherry Coke."

"As a cover-up," Ellie said instantly, turning to him. She was quick on the uptake.

"Uh-huh. Funny thing was," Sam said, "it didn't fool anyone else. But it did me. I actually got so I could pretend there wasn't any booze in it at all."

"Your point being?" I asked, bewildered.

Don't coddle him, all the counselors at the rehab place had instructed me. *Don't condescend.*

He squinted through the screen at us. "My point is, when I drank it, it was like I really *didn't* know what I was doing."

He took a breath. "So maybe this guy doesn't know what he's doing, either. Maybe the one he's really trying to fool is..."

"Himself," concluded Ellie. "Half the time he does want to do something with the gun, and the other half..."

"Thanks, Sam," I said as he went back to deal with more of his laundry. Since coming home he added detergent with the studious care of someone measuring out substances in a chemistry laboratory.

"What do you think?" I asked Ellie when he was gone. "If

Dave DiMaio just found out about his friend's death last night, he might still be too upset to think clearly."

"Mmm, so Sam could be right about a confusion factor. Maybe even DiMaio doesn't know for sure what he's doing, yet. Maybe he just got in the car and..."

"And bringing the gun along could be a part of that," I said.

But I didn't really think so. Our visitor's mild-mannered, absent-minded-professor act was convincing for the most part. Still, something about him reminded me of another guy I'd known, back in the city. The way, for instance, that Dave DiMaio hadn't flinched when that dump-truck tailgate banged shut.

The guy I'd known hadn't flinched, either, at dump trucks or anything else. Whistler, everyone who knew him called him, and mostly he was the nicest fellow you'd ever want to meet: polite, well-spoken, and punctual.

Especially if you owed him money, and even then he'd give you thirty days to pay up. But on day thirty-one he'd shoot you, cut your body into manageable pieces, and wrap the pieces in butcher paper for storage in the walk-in freezer in his basement.

Whistling while he worked. And if Dave DiMaio was feeling like that even half the time, we were in trouble.

Chapter 6

S

o tell me, Dave, how do you know for sure if an old book's really written in blood?" Ellie asked at dinner that night after we'd all had our plates filled with curried crab.

There were seven of us at the table: me, Wade, my father, Ellie and George, Dave, and Sam, whose shift at the fish plant had been canceled due to a fellow with more seniority showing up for work unexpectedly.

Such was life when you'd spent a couple of years viewing the world through the bottom of a glass. I hadn't been sure Dave DiMaio would agree to come, either, but when I'd called him at the Motel East he accepted without hesitation.

Now he thought over his reply with apparent seriousness while he passed a china platter of fresh sliced garden tomatoes across the table to my father.

"Well," he began, pausing again for a sip of the really quite lovely nonalcoholic wine he'd brought; I gathered mine was one of the many Eastport families he'd learned a lot about on his fact-finding mission along Water Street.

On the other hand, it could also have been that Dave didn't drink. Not that I'd ask him about that. I'd decided not to ask him about the gun, either, at least for the time being.

Never ask a question you don't know the answer to is a piece of advice that works badly when applied to old-house repair. But I thought it might be handy for dealing with mysterious strangers. And since his gun wasn't loaded—by now, the bullets I'd taken from it reposed in my top dresser drawer—I figured I had time.

"The best way," he replied at last, "is laser spectrometry."

He ate some curried crab on rice, pantomimed fainting in gastronomic delight, and continued.

"You pass a laser light through whatever you're testing. The light turns color. Each substance has its own color."

He thought again. "So if you see a certain color, you know what substance is producing it. Doing it's not quite so simple as that, of course," he added. "For one thing, you need a laser."

He ate more casserole, drank some faux wine, dabbed with his napkin. Outside the dining-room windows long shafts of golden light slanted onto the flower beds Ellie had planted earlier that year, turning the zinnia blooms to blazing red gems.

"But the result is simple," he went on. "Dating an old book, though," he said, shaking his head. "Finding out its age, that's—"

"A corpse of a different color," said Sam, mangling his metaphors as usual. As a child his speech and even his thoughts were all so bass-ackwards, as he'd have put it, that for a long time he thought we were supposed to pray to dogs.

Dave shot him a wry smile and I remembered he'd said he was a university professor somewhere. His look at Sam made me think he was probably good at it.

"Exactly," he agreed kindly. Then, to the rest of us: "Books are made of many different substances; even so, it's possible to learn what they are. But what if they're all different ages?"

My father listened carefully. "Old paper, new binding. Or some such combination?"

Dave nodded. "Forgers go to great lengths to make their own creations appear genuine."

Which I didn't like at all; it was the first time anyone had even hinted that my old book might not be the real thing.

"Like the Greenland map," said Ellie's husband, George Valentine, unexpectedly. He was a compactly built man with dark hair, milky-white skin, and a bluish five o'clock shadow always present on his stubborn jaw.

"Yes," Dave said, again looking gratified.

Around here, George was your man if you needed a trench dug, a skunk trapped, a chimney repaired, or crows discouraged from having a noisy confab outside your bedroom window at the crack of dawn every morning.

But nothing about his looks suggested that he might also be interested in antique manuscripts; I glanced at him, surprised.

"The Greenland map," Dave explained for the benefit of the rest of us, "purported to demonstrate that the Vikings reached our shores from Europe, decades before Columbus."

"They did," said George, his jaw jutting out stubbornly. "A whole settlement of 'em. In Newfoundland."

"Indeed," replied Dave energetically. His enthusiasm was clearly rising now that he'd identified a fellow history buff. "But that doesn't authenticate the map. In fact..."

While the two argued amiably I stole looks at Sam, still eating his dinner. He wanted a drink, I could tell by his face, which wore the expression of a man crossing a river by creeping along an extremely slippery log. He caught me watching and in reply gave me the first fully adult look of comprehension I'd ever seen on him.

"... so that in the end, the Greenland map did indeed turn out to be ancient parchment," Dave DiMaio was saying.

He, too, was watching Sam. "But with a modern surface put on it," he continued, casually meeting my own gaze.

"Someone had acquired parchment from Viking times. You can't buy it on eBay, but it's not that hard to get hold of if you know how to look for it," he added. "They took off the old surface. You don't write directly on parchment, you see. And they put a fake map onto a new surface. Not a particularly difficult trick, either, if you know how."

George looked reluctantly convinced; facts trump feelings, he always maintained, which was why he believed that not only my old bathroom but also the whole inside of my house ought to be torn out and Sheetrocked, and all the windows replaced. But it made him a fine handyman, that lack of sentimentality.

Meanwhile my husband, Wade Sorenson, put his fork down, murmuring thanks to Bella for filling his coffee cup. He was a tall, solidly built man with blue eyes in a square-jawed face, brush-cut blond hair, and the kind of easy smile that when I first saw it, I thought I couldn't possibly be so lucky.

But I had been. We'd been married for a couple of years, now.

"How'd you know Horace Robotham didn't have Jake's old book anymore?" Wade asked.

A shadow crossed Dave's face. "Well, it's like this. When I got home last night, there was a call on my machine. I'd been out of touch for a couple of weeks after the summer term," he added with another glance at Sam, whose answering look was unreadable.

Bella filled the rest of the cups and brought out the cobbler. She was wearing a flowered housedress, a frilly apron, and an enormous amount of natural dignity, her usual ensemble when we had guests.

"Lovely," I whispered to her, and her lips twitched in a tiny smile of domestic pride. But the smile vanished as her gaze fell on my father, who studied his hands.

"The call was from Horace's longtime partner, Lang Cabell," Dave DiMaio explained. "Lang's in Minnesota now, caring for some elderly aunts of his. He and Horace had been extremely close to them for years—it's all the family either of them had."

"So Lang Cabell told you the book had been stolen?" Ellie asked.

Sam excused himself and took his plate to the kitchen, where I heard him bantering with Bella. But I hadn't missed his wordless glance at DiMaio as he went.

Later, it said, and DiMaio had nodded in reply. I turned back to what he was saying now.

"...not clear the book *was* stolen. Lang says he thinks it was in the house the night Horace died. But in the confusion, the police and so many other people going in and out..."

DiMaio spread his hands helplessly. "Or maybe it wasn't. I know Horace had letters from someone, asking to see the book, and he'd refused. I wish he'd kept them."

Ellie's eyes met mine: *Who?* I moved my shoulders minutely: *No idea.*

"The book was your property," Dave told me, "so Horace didn't think it was right to show it nonprofessionally. But if he sent it out to another laboratory or some other consultant before he died, I'm not aware of it. And Horace usually kept me up-to-date on things like that."

He looked around the table. "You see, in our younger days Horace and I were old-book-hunters together."

The candles flickered briefly. "But not just any old books," Dave added. "We were after the bad ones, ones that shouldn't be out contaminating decent literature."

Uh-oh. Our new pal was about to reveal himself as an even worse crackpot than Bert Merkle. A gun-carrying crackpot...

Dave glanced at me and seemed to read my thought, or part of it. "Oh, no," he assured me. "Not that kind of book. I'm no fan of book-banning. We were looking for ones that are hundreds of years old, most of them. Or older; books of evil spells, recipes for magical potions, incantations to summon the devil...or worse."

He actually sounded serious. I had a moment to consider simply demanding that he give me the gun back. Or telephoning Eastport's police chief, Bob Arnold, to come and do it for me.

But then my father spoke. "I've seen books like that. Ones I've run into were usually for bomb-making. Nine times out of ten a guy tries following the recipe, blows himself up. Sometimes," he added with a look at me, "right along with the whole neighborhood."

It was what had happened to my mother all those years ago.

"Correct," Dave said, nodding. "Just enough information to be dangerous," he added, and seemed about to say more.

By now the candles had burned to nubbins, though; George and Ellie got up reluctantly. They'd managed to get Leonora settled with a nonparent babysitter long enough to come out for dinner.

But a second cup of coffee was pushing it. "I'm not sure what all that has to do with Jake's book," said Ellie.

Carrying plates and cups, George went on out to join Sam and Bella in the kitchen. His opinion of magic was that it was all well and good for sitting around scaring yourself with, late in the evening. But if you really wanted to know whether or not something worked, try cleaning a sewer pipe with it.

"Probably nothing," DiMaio said in answer to Ellie's question. "Because I'm sorry to have to say that most likely your old volume is a forgery of some kind, Jake," he went on, turning to me. "Not a deliberate hoax, maybe, but like the Greenland map the result of coincidences that ended up producing the same effect."

I must've looked puzzled; he went on. "Scholars now think the map was created by a European monk, for his own amusement.

In World War II the Nazis looted his monastery, stole anything that looked valuable."

"The Greenland map would've been a big prize," said George, looking in from the doorway.

"Exactly. To the Nazis," Dave said, "it seemed to show that their ancestors—they fancied they were descended from Vikings, remember—well. The map said *they'd* been the first Europeans to reach the Americas. That gave them the perfect excuse to claim Canada, the U.S., all the way to the Pacific—for themselves."

He went on, "You see, it had been at the monastery a long time by then. And that's one of the things experts look for when beginning to assess a volume's possible authenticity."

"Like mine was," I said. "In the cellar for two centuries."

"Yes," he replied. "If in fact it *was* there all that time."

As we got up from the table the candles guttered out, leaving only the fire's red glow until Wade reached over to turn on the sideboard lamps. In that instant of darkness it was on the tip of my tongue again to ask about the weapon. Only the memory of the many times I'd learned more by keeping my mouth shut than by opening it restrained me.

When the light returned, DiMaio stood just inches from me. I drew in a startled breath; something about his story, finished by leaping firelight in a two-hundred-year-old room, had unexpectedly unnerved me.

That and what he hadn't said. "But if it was? If it's *not* a forgery?" I asked quietly as the others went on into the kitchen.

"My old book," I said to DiMaio. "What if it's not a fake? What if it's as old as the house, and written in—"

I stopped, swallowing hard. Somehow in the dim-lit old room with the fire glowing red and the candles dead stubs, the idea seemed much worse than it had in the daylight.

Worse, and more possible. "Written in blood?" Dave DiMaio finished for me.

He continued. "Horace had already sent it out to several

places. As I said, a laser spectrometer isn't the kind of tool he kept in his own old-book-and-manuscript shop."

What about guns, I wanted to ask, *did he keep those?*

But before I could, Dave was speaking again. "Horace had reports on the ink, paper, and the threads used for sewing the pages. The ink," he told me gently, "was indeed blood."

He was looking levelly at me, the low light throwing his eyes into shadow and the fire's flames reflecting in them. "Human blood," he added tactfully as if informing me of a disease I'd unfortunately gotten.

"Oh." My mouth went dry. "And what about the binding? Oh, please tell me it's not..."

As I spoke I could practically feel the book's smooth old leather cover under my fingers. Too smooth, as if...

A book written in blood, I thought. *Why shouldn't it also be covered in—*

"No," he said firmly, and I let my breath out. "Ordinary cowhide. Very fine, but nothing else."

Nothing worse, he meant, and that knowledge should have been a comfort. But his face said more.

His face expressed doubt, as if perhaps he weren't quite as sure as he'd sounded about the thing being a forgery. And if it wasn't a forgery—

If it wasn't, Dave DiMaio's expression said clearly, then even without human skin for a cover the old book was bad enough.

Later that night, upstairs with Wade in our big bed in the dark: "Of course it's fake," I declared, wide awake. "How could it not be?"

Wade nodded in silent assent.

"A book of names, listing all the people who would live in this house," I said. "How could it be anything but a trick of some kind?"

"Uh-huh. Speaking of tricks, why didn't you ask him about his?" Wade inquired.

The gun, he meant. But before I could answer he drew me down and wrapped his arms around me, smelling like toothpaste, fresh air, and harsh soap from his shower at the freighter terminal.

His breath when he spoke again was warm in my ear. "Jake?"

"I don't know," I replied. "I guess because it's his. I don't like the way he went about it one bit, and I still intend to call him on that, once I've found out a little more about what's going on. But much as I wish it were, it's not up to me to decide who gets to have a gun at all."

I went up on one elbow. "Did you see the fuss Prill made over him, though?"

In the end I'd had to shoo both dogs from underfoot. Even Cat Dancing, wonder of all wonders, had let DiMaio reach up to smooth two fingers between her ears without taking advantage of the tender wrist-flesh he exposed by doing so.

"And it's empty," I added. "I unloaded it when I had it."

This, however, didn't convince my husband. "You bring a gun, you're not going to bring extra ammunition?" he asked.

Of course I would. Which didn't guarantee that Dave had, but the possibility meant maybe I'd better rethink this whole washing-my-hands-of-the-matter idea yet again.

Across the room, the curtains shone white in the moonlight. On August nights in Eastport it was warm enough to keep the bedroom windows wide open, cool enough to snuggle together under blankets.

Wade pulled me back down beside him, tucked ours in snugly around my shoulder, and wrapped the other side around himself.

"I didn't want him to know *I* knew he took it," I persisted. "He might let on more about what he's up to, if he doesn't realize I think he's . . ."

He's what? I wasn't sure. "Maybe he thinks Bert Merkle killed Robotham?" I fretted. "Maybe he's here to do something about that? And about...I don't know. Other things."

"Other things?" Wade's lips grazed the side of my face, his whiskers prickling pleasantly on my neck. I let my eyes close.

"Mm-hmm. Like maybe even get the book back. Because you know, I didn't believe him when he said he didn't know where it...oh."

I bit my lip hard. "Don't move," Wade whispered.

So I didn't, nor make a sound, either, even when at last I turned joyfully into my husband's embrace.

An hour later Wade slept peacefully. But I was awake again, standing by the window-opening in the ruined bathroom, wondering what in the world had possessed me to smash it apart.

Certainly there were times when fixing up an old house meant eliminating what had gone before. But this...

Gleams of streetlight peeked between the maple leaves whose faint rustling was the only sound. A skunk in no particular hurry made his bumbling way from one patch of shadow to the next.

Somebody's wind chimes tinkled. A bird chirped sleepily and fell silent. I turned to go back to bed. But then:

"So where were you?" It was Sam's voice, coming up from the back porch through the window opening.

"What do you mean?" Dave DiMaio asked.

Sam had been waiting for a chance to talk to DiMaio. Now I guessed they must have encountered each other somewhere— since coming home, Sam had become a regular late-night walker— and had ended up back here.

"Come on," Sam said. "I'm just out of the hospital myself, so don't try to kid me. I know the look."

I went on standing there; eavesdropping, but I couldn't help it.

They'd told me to let go, let Sam make his mistakes, fall if he had to. They'd told me I wasn't alone in it anymore, that there would be others ready to help him if he slipped. But when it's your kid who's in trouble, that's far easier said than done.

Small chuckle from DiMaio. "Silver Hill. Needed a tune-up."

"Fancy," Sam remarked.

Silver Hill was a private facility in Connecticut, very expensive and good. Sam had gone to an upstate New York place, cheaper.

The mother in me was glad somebody's son had the resources. But another side of me wondered who'd paid for Silver Hill. Not the pocketbook of an obscure English professor, surely. And insurance companies didn't choose luxury treatment facilities for their policyholders, if they paid for rehab at all.

"Did the job," DiMaio answered. "I just picked a bad time for it. As if there's ever a good time."

A wry note of resignation crept into his voice. I stood processing the information that Dave DiMaio was a recovering substance abuser, too, sober again only a few weeks.

"Your friend died while you were gone?" Sam asked.

"Yup." A world of grief and guilt hung in the syllable. *Horace and I were old-book-hunters together.*

"Listen, do you know anything about a fellow who lives in Eastport, name of Bert Merkle? You don't," DiMaio added, "have to tell anyone I asked."

Sam's reply was inaudible, but the alarm bells ringing in my head weren't. Suddenly Dave's curiosity about old Eastport houses and families made more sense. So did his attempts up and down Water Street to make people think that was the reason for his visit.

Except in the Moose Island General Store, that is. Once Dave had the answers from there that he was looking for, he'd floated his cover story everywhere else, hoping it was the one that would get remembered instead of the real one.

And then he'd invaded my cellar. The sudden impulse to

march downstairs and confront DiMaio seized me. I could demand to know just exactly what he thought he was doing here in Eastport.

And why. But for one thing it would've meant admitting I'd been listening in on Sam's private conversation, which I didn't want to do. Issues of trust were the tiniest bit tricky between us, at the moment.

Besides, I was beginning to believe even more strongly that any fact I knew—and that DiMaio didn't know I possessed—might come in handy sooner or later.

And there seemed to be precious few of them so I decided for the moment to hang on to the ones I had. On the porch a lawn chair creaked as someone got up.

"G'night," Sam said. The screen door squeaked as he came in; footsteps descended the porch steps. I moved closer to the window, trying to catch a glimpse of DiMaio.

At first he was an indistinct shape in the gloom. But as he reached the street and stepped into the glow of the streetlight, he raised a hand in farewell, not looking back.

Not to Sam, who'd already come inside, the back door closing and locking sturdily with a recognizable *clunk-click*.

But to me, as if Dave DiMaio had known all along that I was standing there listening.

Dave DiMaio walked away down Key Street into the silence of an Eastport night. The dinner had been excellent, the company pleasant, and the walk afterward refreshing.

Sam Tiptree, especially, seemed decent. Dave hoped the kid made it through the early post-rehab stage, which Dave knew could be bumpy. He wished he'd had some advice to offer, not the least because the kid's mother seemed worried about him; she must not know, he thought, how that porch roof amplified the sound of footsteps overhead.

But Horace was always the one with good advice. Had been the one. Dave walked on. Overhead, bright celestial objects formed a glimmering net anchored here and there by the moon, the planets, and some of the larger stars.

On Water Street he spied a large feral cat loping along atop the granite riprap by the fishing pier, then another and another. That wasn't unusual; wild cats often infested seaside districts on account of all the rats.

But seeing them reminded Dave of a story Horace had told once, about a Maine island town many miles from the mainland and long before the time of air travel or instant communication.

The town had experienced a single freakishly high tide just before the onset of winter, Horace had said. Next came a blizzard and after that three months of fierce Atlantic storms, and by the time anyone got out from the mainland to check on the inhabitants of the island they found all were dead of what turned out to be bubonic plague.

All the rats were dead, too; thousands of them, more than could be explained. But no cats, though they found food bowls labeled Fluffy or Muffy, cat food in the household pantries, all the trappings of feline-keeping.

Just—no cats. And as far as Dave knew no one had ever been able to explain that, either.

Brushing aside a mental picture of cats fleeing en masse into the sea, he reached the Motel East.

He climbed the open stairs to the second floor, unlocked the door. Switching on the light inside, he paused out of habit in case he got some sense that anyone else had been in here in his absence.

But it seemed no one had been. Crossing the room he pulled the heavy curtains aside, opened the sliding-glass door a crack. Salt air gushed through. But walking away from the window he felt the curtain billowing behind him, and that made him feel uneasy, so he returned to the window and closed it, then took his shoes off and lay down on the bed.

He liked motel rooms, their bland imprintlessness and the light, unencumbered feeling that came from not owning anything in them. Sometimes when he was in one, he turned on the television and watched the late-night shows, a pastime he never indulged at school, where he didn't even own a set.

At school, he was content with faded drapes and shabby furniture inherited from some previous inhabitant. He took most meals in Commons; an amazing luxury, he'd thought when he'd first arrived there as a student, and his opinion hadn't changed.

In those days he'd never even been in a motel. But then he began traveling with Horace, first as a porter, later secretary and transcriptionist; Horace's notes were so hen-scratchingly cryptic that they had to be copied within hours of his writing them or he might forget what they meant.

Horace had asked Dave once if he minded the menial nature of the work. Horace always mapped out their objectives and plans for achieving them, never Dave.

But Dave had replied honestly that he preferred it. Putting his hand to a simple task, especially a dumb, repetitive one like carrying bags or copying notes, felt to Dave like what little he understood of the act of praying.

Thinking this he got up from the bed, slipped his feet back into his shoes, and pulled on his jacket. Outside, he walked away from the downtown area, then turned downhill toward a tidal inlet that was filled in now, but must once have been bridged. Old foundations jutting from the earth above the current street level told him that the bridge had been replaced with a road set on truckloads of hauled-in earth. The bay was as black as onyx and the tide had turned, water rushing in with a trickling sound.

The air smelled of fish and roses, creosote and salt. Ice-cold salt; the water here even in summer was only about fifty-five degrees, he'd read in one of the motel's flyers. Dave wondered how long it would take a body to decompose in the frigid water.

Too long, probably. Striding briskly, he started uphill again until he was looking south over a 180-degree view of night sky, starlit water, and small islands humped like dark animals.

Nothing moved. Dave resumed walking and soon saw the trash-strewn yard and a tiny trailer hunkered at its rear amid heaps of junk. Flattened cans, old wooden pallets, a satellite dish with odd metal projections soldered clumsily to it...

Merkle's place, he thought, as darkly chaotic as the man himself. A dim yellowish light burned behind ancient venetian blinds in the tiny window.

Walk away. Horace's voice spoke calmly inside Dave's head. *Just turn your back, the other cheek, a new leaf.*

Get out of here.

While you still can.

Only Merkle hadn't let Horace Robotham turn *his* back, had he? Instead he'd gotten wind somehow of an old book, realized what it might be, and learned that Horace had it.

And then he'd murdered Horace, making it look as if a mugging had gone wrong, and then—

Then Merkle had stolen the book. It was the kind of thing Merkle had always collected.

Grimoires, mostly; books of spells, many of which he'd tried using. Or so rumor had it; back in their college days, terrible aromas and odd sounds had emanated from Merkle's rooms late at night, rooms to which he'd admitted no one.

Spellbooks weren't all Merkle wanted, though. Most were filled with nonsense. Once in a blue moon one might contain some scrap of usable lore; even then, the trick was not so much in following as in deciphering it. But the Tiptree woman's book was different.

If genuine, the thing was not an instruction manual. This book didn't purport to provide tools—the recipes, spells, or god forbid, incantations—of what naive devotees called the magickal arts. Instead it held a list that, if authentic, could only have been compiled *by means of* magic.

In other words, it was proof. And for that, Merkle would have murdered a hundred Horaces, or a thousand.

The rank smell of kerosene burning in a badly vented stove stank up the neighborhood around Merkle's grim little dwelling. Horace had always said you needed to take plenty of time, not only for planning, but so that you felt confident, when your plan went into action.

Or in case your plan changed, as Dave's was already doing. He'd come to avenge his friend, but so much talk about the old book had reminded him of what Horace would've wanted, instead: The book itself. Dave imagined it lurking somewhere, a patch of darkness swallowing up the light.

Not so bad on its own, maybe. But when you put one patch of darkness with another, and then another...

Standing there, unwilling to leave what he already thought of as the scene of the crime, Dave let his mind drift back yet again to the adobe hut in New Mexico. It had turned out to house only a wizened, half-blind old woman, brewing up useless potions over a smoke-hole mesquite fire and muttering obscenities in Spanish.

The few vile oaths she remembered would never harm anyone, and the book she'd been said to possess didn't exist. But Dave and Horace had returned to Albuquerque afterward, and with Horace in the lead had walked straight out into the desert behind the motel, half a mile or so until Horace said they should stop.

A few round stones peeking up through the sand turned out to be the top of a cairn; under it lay old papers that Horace barely glanced at before burning them. He wouldn't even tell Dave what was on them, nor what the old woman had said about them.

Dave still remembered the care with which Horace had touched the match to those yellowed pages, the relief they'd both felt when each page was turned to ash and the ashes scattered.

And now it was Dave's turn. With a last glance for the tiny, repulsive trailer in which Bert Merkle hunkered, Dave headed back to his room for the night.

He'd never asked Horace if those hidden papers actually belonged to the old woman. By then, he'd known what Horace would answer:

That papers like the ones they'd destroyed didn't belong to anyone. People belonged to *them*.

So when the time came he still intended to avenge his old friend's murder. But first he meant to locate Jacobia Tiptree's book and find out if, like the papers in the desert long ago, it might have the potential to join with other small, widely scattered fragments—

—a howl here, a smothered shriek there...

Enough darkness, finally, to swallow up all the light.

Chapter 7

Quick fix for a too-large (worn-out or stripped) screw hole: Pack it with wooden toothpicks or matchsticks.
—Tiptree's Tips

I woke way too early the next morning with thoughts of Merrie Fargeorge's party rattling in my skull like skeletons trying to fight their way out of a closet.

Today. The party was today.

So even though it was an hour before dawn I slid out of bed, grabbed up some clothes, and slipped downstairs where I started the coffee, dressed hastily in the early-morning chill, then took the dogs out for a quick walk.

Eastport in the darkness before sunrise was damp and chilly, silent except for the pigeons muttering sleepily in the eaves of the old houses. As we came back around the block, the sky changed from black to gray. Trees and roofs appeared suddenly against it like a photograph developing.

A breeze sprang up. A blue jay called raucously. A car went by, its windshield still half-fogged and headlights on. The dogs climbed the porch steps sedately, signaling their intention to go back to bed.

Inside, Cat Dancing was still asleep, but she twitched her tail at me from her throne atop the refrigerator just to show me that even while snoozing she could make a snarky remark.

No Bella yet. While the dogs settled I filled a thermos and carried it with me up to the third floor, stepping carefully to avoid the squeaky tread—*finishing nails,* I thought; *hammer and white glue*—at the fifth step from the top.

In the workroom, mindful of Wade still sleeping below, I took my shoes off. I padded silently across the tarp-covered plank floor in my stocking feet. Paint flakes, sawdust, and wood splinters littered the tarp.

There was a time in my life when I'd have thought a room like this all to myself was heaven, another during which I'd have regarded that bare light bulb with horror; what, no chandelier?

I wouldn't have realized the meaning of stove-thimbles set into the chimneys: that in the iron-cold Maine winters the young women who worked here heated their rooms with tiny wood-burners, carefully parceling out their meager allowances of fuel and budgeting their candles.

Because to a shivering young servant girl in those days, a candle was like gold.

The windows brightened, looking out onto a scene like a

watercolor painting: pale-blue sky with the light pouring upward into it, pearlescent bay with swirling current-lines hinting at the turbulence below, trees with their upper boughs sunny and trunks still heavily shadowed.

After a moment of luxuriating in it I turned away, knowing I shouldn't be here at all. With so much to do, if I started this minute I still wouldn't be ready for the party in time.

And of course if I weren't working on it I should at least be planning for it. But I so much didn't want to; Merrie Fargeorge's belief that she could scold me as if I were a young student had made me feel as fractious as one.

Rebellious, too; the idea of a teacher loved for strictness was one I'd always found more convincing in fiction than in fact.

So instead of getting out the dusty teacups to begin washing them, I crouched by the window sash laid on the milk crates, re-opened the glazing-compound container, and dug a chunk the size of a Ping-Pong ball out of it with the putty knife.

I only had to insert fifteen more eight-by-eleven-inch pieces of glass, pin them with the sharp steel triangles called glazing pins, and smooth on the glazing compound without injuring the glass or—glazing pins being wicked sharp, as are glass windowpanes, whether broken or unbroken—myself.

This for a single glass piece does not sound very difficult, and it wasn't: one pane, zip-zip, zop-zop. Fifteen of them is a chore, though. Finally I sat back on my heels and opened the thermos, to assess what I'd done so far. But as soon as I wasn't actively working on the window, other thoughts flooded in.

Bella, my father, Sam, the old bathtub, the party, and Dave DiMaio all began capering in my head once more, the latter most troublingly. Dave and his dratted missing gun and what was I going to do about them?

Because I could still say it was none of my business. *But that's never stopped you before,* a little voice in my head remarked snidely.

On top of which, now that I'd come up with a theory about just which act he might be thinking of committing with his gun and specifically upon whom, his having the thing at all seemed a lot more worrisome to me.

By now it was full day outside, gulls sailing serenely past the windows and cars moving down in the street. A faucet went on and then off suddenly in the kitchen, triggering a bout of water-hammering that shook every pipe in the house.

Pipe wrench, I thought, shaking the glazing pins from their small cardboard carton into my palm. Then I laid in another old windowpane and began pushing the pins' sharp points in with the putty knife, pinning the pane down snugly.

If he hurts someone, and you could've stopped him . . .

Now came the hardest part: the actual glazing. I'd watched experts do this so fast you could hardly see their hands move, but my way was a little different. After warming and softening another ball of glazing compound, I laid a thickish strand of it along a pane's edge. Next, I drew the knife's angled blade firmly all the way around the pane, pressing the compound in tight and smoothing its top surface, trying not to stop or even slow down around inside corners and maintaining even knife-pressure.

Which no matter how many times I did it was always either (a) mind-bogglingly easy or (b) like patting yourself on the head while chewing gum, walking a tightrope, and whistling "Dixie" all at the same time.

This time it was (b); you have to press *hard* on the putty knife, and my second try was a mess, too, because if you press too hard, the glass breaks. But by the third attempt I began achieving something like the swift, satisfying efficiency that is implied by the phrase *zip, zop.*

Light poured convincingly through the windows as I snapped the top back onto the compound's container, wiped the knife, and dropped the leftover pins into their box. When I finally straightened,

I still didn't know what to do about a lot of things. But as for DiMaio, his weapon, and my suspicion that his presence here was related to a murder *and* to the old book we'd found in my cellar...

Making my way downstairs to the smell of fresh coffee and the *clickety-click* of dog toenails as they danced around the door urging Wade to let them out again—

"G'morning," my husband said, planting a kiss on my neck.

"G'morning, yourself," I replied, planting one back.

—as for *that* situation, I now had a plan.

"Something for you in the dining room," said Wade. "Found a present for you, forgot to tell you about it last night."

"For me? Well, aren't you a wonderful man."

He was, too, if recent memory served. Sipping my hot coffee I went in where he pointed and found a small box. In it, reposing on a bed of cotton batting, was a new pair of pliers.

A *soft-jawed* pair of pliers. "Wade, these are great," I told him, returning to the kitchen to wrap my arms around him.

"Glad you like 'em." He was already dressed, ready to leave: white cobblecloth long-underwear shirt, navy hooded sweatshirt, heavy khaki pants, and a pair of Carhartt boots. He was going out this morning to fix a bell buoy in the channel, and with the breeze still rising it was going to be cold out there on the water.

"See, with these pliers," I told Bella, "you can fix—oh, let's say a faucet, without putting a lot of ugly marks on it. Because of the plastic instead of metal, you see, in the gripping parts."

"Good," said Bella. "You can start with that one." She pointed at the kitchen sink. "Water company flushed the mains, put so much grit in the system that the faucet screen's clogged up," she added.

So I did, and with the new pliers I made quick work of it. Off with the metal collar at the end of the faucet spout, then a fast finger poke to get the wire screen out of the collar, taking care not to lose the washer and putting it in right-side-up again when I'd finished.

Presto, on with the collar again and the job was done; good old Wade, he really knew what a girl wanted. And a good thing, too, since without plenty of water in the kitchen I shuddered to think what the rest of the day would be like.

"Here," said Bella when I returned from putting the new tool in the toolbox. But she wasn't talking to me; instead she thrust a trayful of freshly washed glasses into the hands of a large, very serious-looking lady I'd never seen before.

The lady wore black, thick-soled orthopedic shoes, old-fashioned beige nylon stockings rolled down to midcalf, and a housedress with a border cross-stitched in purple thread on the skirt. She was somewhere between fifty and seventy.

"Hello," I said, and she gave me an affronted look as if to ask me what I thought I was doing here, then took the tray on into the dining room.

"Hired 'er," Bella said before I could ask. "For the party. Daisy Dawton. Her boy, too. He don't talk much, Jericho doesn't. But between 'em they don't have two dimes to rub together nor a pot to—Oh, hello, Jericho." She broke off abruptly as yet another complete stranger strolled in as if he owned the place.

Daisy Dawton's boy turned out to be a smallish fellow with a mop of pale-yellow hair, plus a huge coffee urn under one arm and a half-dozen folding chairs under the other.

"There," instructed Bella, pointing to where his mother had gone, and he hustled in that direction before I could get much more of a look at him.

"And they're both hard workers," Bella added when he was out of earshot again.

She didn't ask me if it was all right that she'd hired them, since (a) she knew perfectly well that it was; she had free rein around here in domestic matters, and (b) what choice did I have? The party was in—oh, dear god—only a few more hours.

From three to five this very afternoon, to be exact, and the closer it got the more I thought I'd rather have dental surgery. Still, Bella seemed to have everything under control—

Well, everything but the lemon bars, gingersnaps, brownies, dream bars, deviled eggs, shrimp puffs, and pepper crackers with curried eggplant dip, all of which Ellie and the other ex-Merrie-students of Eastport had promised to provide, plus sherbet and ginger ale for the punch.

Next, not quite staggering under its weight, Jericho Dawton muscled the biggest glass punch bowl I'd ever seen in through my back door, angled it expertly as he made his way down the hall in order to avoid smashing it into a radiator, then set it down as gently as if it were a bomb at the center of the dining-room table.

From my earlier glimpse at his straight, pale hair, boyish build, and the knobby wrists jutting from his too-short sleeves, I'd made him out to be about twelve. Only when he turned did I realize from his stubbled jaw that Daisy's "boy" was at least thirty-five, and possibly forty.

And that Daisy was watching carefully for my reaction to her son's presence. "All right, then," I said, turning away.

Because in Daisy Dawton's look I'd spied the kind of downeast pride that will cut its own nose off to spite its face, and poverty be damned. And anyway I didn't want to mess up my housekeeper's first try at subcontracting, which was such a good idea I wished I'd thought of it, myself.

In the kitchen, Bella got out cake plates, tossed linen napkins into the washing machine, and polished silver teaspoons so fast that in her hands they were little more than a brilliant blur.

"Let me handle this," she said when I tried helping. Daisy trudged heavily in and went out again, struggling with the coffee urn.

"Here, Ma," said Jericho, taking it from her. "Ain't it what you brought me for, heavy things like that?"

Whereupon Daisy grumbled something ungrateful, but in reply her son turned upon her a look of such melting sweetness that I knew these two were going to work out just fine. Bella, I thought as they went on companionably helping one another, could probably use extra hands for the heavy cleaning when springtime rolled around again, too.

And with so many people working on it, even the party might turn out all right. That is, if I could manage Merrie Fargeorge's disagreeable presence.

Before I dealt with her, though, there was yet another small matter to be handled, and like most unpleasant confrontations I knew the sooner I got it over with, the better.

Carrying my cup to the phone alcove, I dialed the Motel East and asked for Dave DiMaio. He answered on the first ring, sounding as if he, too, had been up for hours.

"Listen, Dave, you know that little gun I hid away for you in the lockbox in my cellar?"

Because if he meant to use it and then claim he didn't have it—implying that someone *else* must've taken it and done a bad deed with it—well, let's just say that as my first serious act of the new day I intended to pound a stake through the heart of that little notion *toot sweet,* as Sam would've put it.

"Ye-es," DiMaio answered slowly.

"Dave, why didn't you just tell me you'd had second thoughts about the gun? And you wanted it back? I'd have given it to you."

In a pig's eye. I'd have come up with some excuse. But:

"You didn't have to sneak in and take it. Which," I added, "my housekeeper saw you do, so there's no sense denying it."

Liar, liar; this last part was so untrue I could practically smell the smoke rising from my pants. But if he thought he'd been seen taking the gun, he'd be more likely to admit it promptly.

Instead of a confession, however, there was only a long silence, so long that for a moment I thought he'd hung up.

Then he spoke again, sounding displeased but calm, as if a piece of bad news that he'd been waiting for had finally arrived.

"Jacobia, I'm afraid I have not the least idea what you are talking about," Dave DiMaio said.

"What do you mean, you want me to check up on him? You just told me you believe him," Eastport police chief Bob Arnold said fifteen minutes later.

We were sitting at a booth in the Waco Diner, a long, low building with a blue-and-white awning out front and a brand-new pressure-treated deck overlooking the bay at the rear. Located at the south end of the downtown waterfront, the place was a magnet for tourists at mealtimes, and a popular hangout for the rest of us at all other hours of the day and evening.

Right now the counter and red leatherette booths were mostly occupied by working men in boots, jeans, and sweatshirts. Some— the ones who'd gotten up even earlier than I had—were crumbling crackers into steaming white-china bowls of fish chowder, while others supercharged their first break of the day with fat wedges of blueberry pie.

All had coffee in thick mugs. "He *sounds* believable. But I didn't say I *completely* believed him," I told Bob.

"Mmmph," he commented as the waitress set his breakfast in front of him. "Thanks, Rita."

He was decked out as usual in full cop regalia: clean, pressed uniform, shiny black shoes, belt loaded with law-enforcement gear including cuffs, radio, baton, and pepper-spray canister.

Plus of course his weapon, a .45-caliber semi-auto with enough stopping power to put down a moose, which around here was not exactly beyond the realm of possibility.

"You don't think he took it, though," Bob said. "The gun." He tucked a bite of syrupy pancake between his lips. "And you'd unloaded it, anyway."

"Well, that's just it," I said. "Yes, I unloaded it. But—"

I repeated what Wade had said about extra ammunition. "And

I could be wrong about him," I finished. "That's why I'd like it so much if you'd just—"

In or out of uniform Bob was an unlikely-looking cop, with a round body that nevertheless was able to move very fast, a soft-looking pink face whose deceptively mild expression had been the surprise downfall of many a crook, and unemphatic blue eyes that failed to hint at the sharp mental machinery behind them.

I'd already summarized what I knew about DiMaio's visit so far, including his hunt for Bert Merkle and his attempts to cover it with a story about wanting to learn Eastport history.

"Or anyway it's what we think he's been doing," I told Bob. "The trouble is, he's so darned slippery. Polite, pleasant, even believable, like I said. And yet—"

Scowling, Bob washed another mouthful of pancake down with orange juice, then chased it with a bite of sausage. His wife and two kids were visiting her mother for a week in Kennebunkport, so he had to get his vitamins where he could.

"Where's Wade? Why can't he scope out your mysterious visitor?"

"He has, but he was eating dinner with him at the time, not cross-examining him. And Wade's working nonstop while the boats are so busy, you know that."

"Mmm," Bob said darkly. "Yes, I do know. Few fellas around here, I could wish they weren't so flush with pocket money. They start spendin' it in the bars, I end up defendin' all their wives and girlfriends. But for most of 'em it's a good thing," he finished by conceding.

It certainly was for Wade, whose current stint of making hay in the sunshine had been preceded by a spell of less comfortable financial weather. "So you and Ellie think this DiMaio guy's here on account of the Orono thing?" Bob asked me. "Mugging gone bad, guy got bonked with a . . ."

"Rock," I finished for him. "Or something. Yes, that's the one. Horace Robotham."

The waitress came by to heat up our coffees; I waited before going on. "Someone apparently sneaked up on him from behind, in the dark."

At the counter a friendly controversy erupted over who would win the pennant this year, the Yanks or the Sox.

Sawx. "Bob, how many muggings were there in Orono last year? I mean, we're not exactly the crime capital of the world."

"Zero." He nodded, made an O shape with thumb and forefinger. "Same for murders, armed robberies, and any rapes that didn't turn out to be date rapes."

I opened my mouth to object; he answered before I could. "I know, rape is rape. I'm not denying that." He drained his juice glass. "But stranger-attackers tend to progress to a whole lot worse, Jake, and you know it."

Yeah, yeah; Bob and I had been through this argument before. But the point now was, getting mugged in Orono was like getting tagged with a random act of kindness in New York City: possible, sure, but not what the place was famous for.

"Anyone look into that, that you know of?" I asked Bob. "I mean, the whole rarity aspect of it?"

In Orono, if a stranger approached you at night he did not want to bonk you over the head and take your valuables. He wanted directions, or to ask if you'd seen his lost dog, or just to say good evening.

Meanwhile, Bob really might know if the crime had made Orono cops curious. He kept his law-enforcement contacts all polished up and ready to use, and himself well-informed on what cooked from the cities to the remotest locations, downeast Maine for some reason being a favorite destination for on-the-lammers from other jurisdictions.

Like maybe we wouldn't notice them here, where local faces were so familiar they might as well have been carved into Mount Rushmore and every stranger wore an invisible sandwich board.

Watch Me, said the front sign; *Talk about Me,* said the back.

Bob shook his head, mopped the rest of the maple syrup from his plate with the last chunk of sausage and ate it.

"Nope. No future in anybody digging into the Robotham case. That much was obvious right from the git-go."

He drank some coffee, touched his rosebud lips with his napkin, and crumpled it, signaling that he was finished.

"Victim had no enemies that anyone knew of. Lived with another guy. He was so broken up over the whole thing, ended up in the hospital, coupla nights. I've got a buddy over there, we talked about it when it happened," he added.

"I wondered if the housemate came under any suspicion," I said.

"That guy?" Bob shook his head. "Nah. Can't fake grief like that, fellow I talked to said. You can tell right away, usually, somebody's putting on a show for you."

The waitress brought the check. "I heard a rare book went AWOL around the same time, though," Bob added.

My ears pricked up; this also confirmed what DiMaio said. "From the vic's book business," Bob went on. "The roommate said he figured someone came back while the place was empty, stole it."

Beyond the booth's window a pair of seals played tag in the shallows around the rocks. Watching them, I thought about telling Bob it was my book that was missing.

Because why not? But he was speaking again. "No sign of any break-in, though. And nothing else taken."

Laying a pair of dollar bills by his plate, he got up. "The theory's still that it probably was just an ordinary mugging, some jerk passing through, found a target of opportunity, now the jerk's long gone."

When I slid out of the booth I got a view into the dining room with its sliding-glass doors out to the deck and its built-in gas fireplace burning low to dispel the night's chill.

In it, sitting alone eating a muffin, was Bert Merkle. Tall, balding, and unshaven, he wore gray painter's pants and a once-white dress shirt over an undershirt that looked unclean, plus black socks and leather sandals.

Looking up from the newspaper he was reading while he ate his breakfast, he met my gaze and held it for a chilly, unsmiling moment.

Bob was already at the cash register. Catching his eye, I angled my head down the aisle between the counter and the booths toward Merkle. Because just moments earlier I'd finished telling Bob who I thought Dave DiMaio was looking for in Eastport.

Not realizing that Merkle himself sat right around the corner. Too far away to eavesdrop, I thought, unless he had ears like a bat.

But maybe he did. Bob stepped outside and I followed.

"No tinfoil hat this morning," Bob observed.

"Not good manners to wear one in a public dining establishment," I replied.

"Never been big on manners, that I heard of. Merkle's been summonsed so often to clean up his place, I can't count 'em all. Anyway," he changed the subject, "about your pal DiMaio."

"He's not my..."

"Whatever." We crossed the street toward his squad car, an elderly Crown Victoria with Eastport's blue-and-orange sunrise decal on the front doors.

"I think I'll have a word with DiMaio about that firearm you mentioned. Whether or not he has it now, he had it when he got here."

Out on the water in a stiff onshore breeze, the schooner *Sylvina W. Beal* hoisted her red sails and came gracefully around in the channel, loaded with tourists and headed out for a morning of whale-watching in the waters off Grand Manan.

Even from shore you could tell which of the passengers had been out before: long pants, sweaters, and even a few down vests on the experienced ones, shorts and T-shirts on the not. Luckily for these latter unfortunates, the *Sylvina* carried blankets.

"Don't know just how it is where he comes from, but around here folks're generally required to have a permit for that sort of thing," Bob remarked.

In Maine, if you could buy a gun legally—that is, if you were over eighteen and not a convicted felon—you could apply for and get a carry permit for the firearm, too, about as easily as you could get a fishing license. After that you could carry the gun loaded anywhere except on school grounds, inside a courthouse, or at the site of a labor dispute. When the weapon was unloaded, you were allowed to transport it in your vehicle.

But you still had to *have* the permit, which gave Bob a good way to find out more about what was what. "And," he added, "it *could* be our UFO-chasing buddy needs *his* chain rattled, also." He glanced back at the Waco. Merkle hadn't emerged. "But I can't be the one to do it."

"Why not? Wouldn't you be the obvious one to—?"

But he was already shaking his head. "Merkle's got his back up about all the times I've been out there at his place lately, citing him for his mess. Fire hazard, public nuisance, violation of zoning regulations—the neighbors are up in arms. But he insists he's being harassed."

Bob got into his squad car. "So he's doing what?" I asked. "Talking about suing?"

I'd been to Merkle's place once on another matter, and the neighbors had plenty to complain about. It looked as if the guy never got rid of so much as a used tissue.

But the inside of his trailer was even weirder than the outside: tracts, pamphlets, self-published books written by the kinds of people who thought eyeballs were growing from the ends of their fingertips, and who secretly kind of liked the idea. . . .

"Yeah," Bob said. "Suing the city. Ain't that a pip? An' the city council has researched the idea; it turns out Merkel could maybe win. And you know there's always some lawyer, take a case where there might be big money damages."

He settled himself in the squad's front seat, moving his body around to get halfway comfortable on the torn upholstery and busted springs. The door of the glove box was held on with hinges fashioned of silver duct tape, which around these parts was known as downeast chrome.

"Merkle's got a friend, though," he said. "You want to know any more about him, you could talk to a local kid, name of Jason Riverton."

By now tourists were streaming from the Motel East, freshly showered and looking for breakfast. I watched a woman in white shorts, a sleeveless shirt, and running shoes get all the way to the edge of the motel's freshly blacktopped parking lot before turning tail and dashing back to her room.

"You know this because..." I prodded Bob as the woman came out again wearing a heavy sweater; August here is still summer in the meteorological sense. Just not in the sleeveless sense.

"Jason's mom complained to me not that long ago about her kid spending time with Merkle," Bob replied. "Or vice versa, far as the complaint went."

"Really? You're kidding. Merkle and boys? I've never heard anything about that." And around here, of course, the chances were excellent I would have.

If there was anything to it. Bob's expression said there wasn't. "I had a talk with Jason, satisfied myself there was no funny stuff going on, reported back to Mom," he recited. "I came down pretty heavy on the kid, actually, made sure he wasn't just trying to hide something from me."

He paused, watching the tourist woman button her sweater up. "But I don't think he was. Or at least not in that regard," Bob finished, frowning.

And not looking *entirely* satisfied. I got the strong feeling that there was more to the whole Jason story than Bob was saying, even without Bert Merkle being somehow in the mix.

"Hey, no law against having friends," the police chief said.

"And that kid, you ask me, he could definitely use a few. Although I probably wouldn't put Merkle at the top of the list, I happened to be the one doin' the choosing. Poor woman," Bob added, and then shut up on the subject.

"I see," I said, even though I didn't. Bob knew a lot of things about a lot of people, naturally, and if he didn't want to reveal them, then there was no way I'd be able to make him.

And probably most of them weren't pertinent to my situation, anyway. "But now you'd like me to pick this kid's brains again on the topic of Merkle," I said. "And the kid will cooperate with me in this because...?"

A sputter of static came out of the squad's radio, followed by some garbled talk I couldn't decipher.

But Bob could. Grimacing, he fired up the vehicle's big engine, wincing as it pinged on account of not getting premium fuel. As the condition of his squad car showed, budgets around Eastport were tight even without Bert Merkle threatening any big-money-damages lawsuits.

"I'm not saying the boy will cooperate," Bob replied. "Matter of fact I predict he won't. He's not exactly Mr. Personality, Jason isn't. But there's something more than meets the eye going on over there, and I sure wouldn't mind if somebody besides me went and—"

His radio sputtered again, more urgently this time. He threw the vehicle into reverse. A heavy *clunk!* came from under the hood; the car jerked back.

"Bring Ellie, too, she's good at that kind of thing, Jake. And you could talk to the kid's old schoolteacher, Merrie Fargeorge. She spent a lot of time with him, I hear." Setting a blue rotating beacon on the dashboard, he roared off.

Leaving me standing alone in front of the Waco with about a dozen more questions.

None of which were going to get answered. Instead Bob hoped I'd be able to find things out and report back to him; in fact I got

the strong feeling that without anybody quite saying so, we'd just
made a deal: I talk to Jason, Bob talked to DiMaio.

Great, I thought. My big lead so far in a case of murder that (a)
might not even exist and (b) that I didn't want anything to do with
anyway was (c) a teenager who probably wasn't going to want to
talk to me at all, followed by his teacher with whom I was already
about as popular as a piece of chewing gum.

If the chewing gum happened to be stuck to her shoe, that is.
For a minute it all made me wish I had Dave DiMaio's missing
handgun, so cheap you could use it to blow a hole in someone,
then toss it down a sewer and never miss it.

But I didn't have Dave's awful little gun anymore, did I?

Nope.

Somebody else did.

Chapter 8

W hen I got home I headed immediately for the phone again, intending to call Ellie so we could visit Jason Riverton together and get it over with. But as I reached for the handset I heard pitiful whimpering coming from upstairs, and when I got to the hall I saw a white thing on the stairway landing.

Halfway around the corner, wedged against the banister on one side and the wall on the other, it was a bathtub-shaped white thing with a pair of mournful brown eyes peering worriedly from the far side of it at me.

Dog eyes. "Okay, girl," I said reassuringly, starting up the stairs. "Stay right there, now. I'm coming to get you, so don't you move an inch."

Seeing me, Monday the Labrador retriever began wriggling and whining even more urgently. "Okay, baby," I said, trying to calm her. "Okay, now."

Because in her excitement she kept bumping against the tub, and if it let go and began sliding down the stairs, guess who it would mash? But as I neared the thing, I saw there was little chance of that.

While I'd been out, someone—my father, almost certainly—had dismantled the bathroom door. He'd also disconnected the plumbing, removed the faucet handles and the spout, and then levered that monstrous old bathtub up with three enormous iron crowbars, now lying in the bathtub.

Next, that same someone had placed four long pieces of iron pipe under the tub, to use as rollers. And finally, this genius of mechanical engineering had put a chain on the tub by running it up through the drain, then through the hole where the spout had been.

A *big* chain. Held taut by...I squinted past the tub to where the chain snaked into the bathroom, then out the window. Monday whined pitifully.

"Just hold on a second," I told the anxious dog. Probably she'd slept through the noise of getting the tub out here, then woken to find herself imprisoned.

I'd seen my father's old pickup in the driveway on my way in here, and noticed the chain hooked to the towing ball on the rear bumper. But I'd paid no attention; he always had projects going on, and the less I knew about many of them the better. Besides, in my wildest dreams I'd never have imagined this.

Monday barked sharply, overcome by impatience and readying herself to leap. "No!" I said, putting my hand up in the *halt* gesture she'd learned as a pup.

Learned what it meant, that is; not necessarily to obey it. "Wait!" I said; see *not necessarily,* above.

If she jumped, she could break a leg or worse, because Monday was young at heart but on the outside she was an old dog, white-throated and brittle-boned.

Reluctantly, she complied while I surveyed the situation further. From the looks of it, my father had rolled the tub to the stairway, gotten it over to the landing, and hitched it to the chain so the tub wouldn't get away from him.

But then it got stuck—very solidly stuck, it seemed to me—as it was going around the corner.

No wonder he'd made himself scarce. And as if that weren't bad enough, Monday began howling her deeply felt objections to her predicament just as somebody rapped sharply on the back door downstairs, and then the phone rang.

"Bella," I called out, climbing into the tub.

No answer from the kitchen or from anywhere else, and no one answered the phone. Maybe she was out buying dynamite to blast the crusted bits of last night's crab casserole out of the oven.

The Dawtons weren't anywhere in evidence, either. Daisy and Jericho had probably finished their prep work, and wouldn't be back until later this afternoon when the party actually began.

The tub shifted slightly under my weight. The chain it was hitched to made a creaking sound, tightening further. I put my hands on the tub's sides, steadying it and trying to stay in the middle.

Perched there, I couldn't have felt any more precarious if I'd been floating in the bay, bobbing along behind the *Sylvina*. Meanwhile the knock on the back door grew more insistent. The telephone quit ringing, then immediately started up again.

"All *right*!" I shouted in exasperation, "I'm . . . oops, sorry, girl," I finished as the dog cringed away from me.

Gingerly, I climbed out of the tub again and reached for her. I could just barely manage to touch her if I stretched to where I nearly dislocated my shoulder.

My fingertips grazed her fur. "Come on, now, girlie, let's get you past this. . . . Damn it, Monday, come back here."

But she still wasn't having any, and as she scrambled away I understood why. She'd been fine until she realized I was trying to get her into the tub. Which of course led to the idea that what I really intended was to give her a—horrors!—*bath*.

Now from the sound of it she was hiding in the guest room, snuffling and panting and trying to shove her seventy-five-pound body into the very tiny amount of space under the bed.

So I climbed back into the tub once more—biting my tongue as I did so, since we really didn't need two of us howling in frustration around here—and then out of it again, this time by grabbing the chain fixed to it and hauling until I was upright.

Staggering into the bedroom I grabbed the elderly dog by her really very unwilling hindquarters. Backpedaling madly, she resisted every step of the trip back to the stairwell, toenails scritching as her toes scrabbled anxiously on the hardwood.

And then just as I was about to force her, she hopped nimbly into the tub and out of it again, and scampered downstairs.

"Oh," I said softly, heart in my throat. But she made it to the bottom all right and vanished around the corner; I was the one who turned out not to be so nimble.

With the phone still ringing and stopping again every thirty seconds or so, I clambered yet once more into the ghastly old porcelain object—once you get them out into the light of day, believe me, they're *lots* worse than you realized—got one leg over the rim and then the other, and made my way down after the dog.

But by then she was nowhere to be found and the knocking on the back door had become hammering, while the phone's intermittent ringing was like the alarm bell in an old firehouse, shrilly insistent.

"I'm coming, I'm coming, just a—Oh, for heaven's sakes, what do you *want*?" I yelled, yanking open the back door.

And then I nearly slammed it again because on the other side stood Ann Talbert, a frustrated local writer and as far as I'd ever been able to tell also the pushiest person on the planet.

"I want to talk to you," she announced, marching past me and in the process letting both dogs out.

They drilled for this secretly, I was convinced as the two of them blasted by, practically spinning Ann around in their wake.

They got up in the dead of night, the big black dog and the big red one together, to practice their doggy escapes.

Fortunately at the foot of the porch steps Monday and Prill turned and made a beeline for the fenced-in part of the yard instead of the street. I hurried after them to shut the gate so they couldn't stray farther, and they settled happily to a session of burying things that shouldn't be buried (the leafy portions of a half-dozen Martha Washington geraniums) and digging up things that shouldn't be dug up (the geranium-plant roots).

Prill also looked around hopefully for an opportunity to chew things she shouldn't, which in her case included most of the human race. From the strength and height of the chain-link fence I'd installed around the dog run, you'd think I raised Tasmanian devils.

And now that they were out, of course I had to refresh the buckets of dog water, haul up the canvas shade because it was getting on for the middle of the morning, and find a bunch of dog toys to toss into the dog run with them, as part of my ongoing but ultimately doomed attempt to salvage at least one of those Martha Washingtons.

So that by the time I finished caring for the animals, I was hot, cross, sweaty, dirty, and out of sorts. Also it had not at all escaped my attention that by this afternoon, I would have to be clean, decently dressed, and (ideally) calm enough to greet guests.

None of which I was now. Unbelievably, it was still only nine-thirty in the morning and already I felt as if I'd been working hard all day at pulling the pins on hand grenades.

And when I got inside the phone was still ringing. "Ann, I'm afraid this is not a good time for me to—"

She'd been waiting for me in the hall but now she strode on into the kitchen ahead of me, yanked out a chair, and plopped herself down in it while I grabbed the phone. With any luck it would be the Department of Homeland Security, I thought, telling me to evacuate.

"Jake—" Ellie began.

"Oh, thank goodness," I said. "Can you come over here?"

I glanced back into the kitchen where Ann sat fuming at the table, tapping her long red nails on the tablecloth and shooting evil looks in my direction from under her mop of short, spiky-cut black hair.

"On my way," Ellie replied briskly, hearing the quaver in my voice that meant I was about to commit mayhem, and hung up.

"Thanks," I said into the dead phone. It made me feel much better, knowing she would soon arrive.

But returning to the kitchen I still found myself wishing that I had a whip to go with the chairs out there, because Ann was only five feet tall and maybe ninety pounds drenched, but she was well known to be a tiger when she wanted something and boy, did she ever.

"The book," she declared as soon as I got within verbal clawing range. "I want that old book, Jacobia."

I want a million dollars and your absence, not necessarily in that order, I thought, then realized suddenly who must've been pestering Horace Robotham with letters.

"Ann," I said patiently. It would've been just like her. "Ann, I've told you before several times, I don't have the book. As you know, I sent it away to an expert."

She huffed out an impatient breath. In addition to the jet-black hair, she wore huge hoop earrings, bright red lipstick, and an all-black outfit: boots, pants, short-sleeved cotton sweater.

"Yes, I do know, Jacobia," she retorted in tones of strained patience. "But the *expert* you sent it to is *dead.*"

She made it sound as if this were my fault. "So now you can get it back and let *me* look at it." She spoke as if instructing a three-year-old.

"Which you *should* have done in the *first* place," she added as Ellie came in carrying a white bag with a red *M* printed on it, that looked as if it might contain pastries. Setting the bag on the counter she got a load of what Ann was saying and rolled her eyes.

"Experts," Ann scoffed haughtily. The hoop earrings were so heavy, they made the corners of her eyes slant down.

"What do *they* know?" she went on theatrically. "Dusty little academics have no *idea*. But I have been writing for *years* so I'm *extremely* well-versed in the Market for Literature Today."

She said it as if it were the title of a college course but I happened to know that she'd gotten it out of a magazine whose entire reason for existing was as follows: *f u cn rd ths u cn b a riter & mk bg $!*

"Based on that book, *which* you are going to supply to me at your earliest convenience—you do realize that, don't you, Jacobia? As I am the only one who can truly appreciate and utilize it—"

Utilize, I thought. If I'd had the book right now, I'd have utilized it as an assault weapon.

"—I intend to craft a modern masterpiece the whole world will clamor to read," she intoned loftily.

Craft. In Ann's favorite magazine, people were encouraged to craft things, not merely write them. "In translation," I said.

"What?" Her eyes narrowed suspiciously at me. Apparently an eighth of an inch of black eyeliner was required not only to match her outfit, but also to complete the writerly look.

"Well, most of the world doesn't read English," I said, "so for them all to clamor to read it, it would have to be in—"

"Oh, pooh." She waved away my comment, her red nails slicing dangerously through the air. I tried to imagine her typing with those things, couldn't.

"That's what agents are for," she said disdainfully. "And editors. My job is to write the thing, to express myself. Not to worry about the piddly details."

Fixing her gaze on some unseen distant horizon, she put a little trill into *express myself,* rolling the *r* as if the phrase were Spanish.

I'd seen a few samples of Ann's writing, and as far as I could tell she thought spelling and punctuation were piddly details. Oh, and paragraphing, too. And maybe the parts in all capital letters were supposed to be dialogue.

She got up, putting her hands on her black-jeans-clad hips and fixing me in what I'm sure she believed was a gimlet gaze. "I want that book. I just know it's filled with colorful material."

Right, if you liked the color of blood. Also, the only thing in that old book was a list; I'd told her that before, too, but I got the strong sense she didn't believe it.

"And from it," she went on, "I'll craft an erotic paranormal historical-fiction novel with grippingly suspenseful romantic overtones and cutting-edge science-fiction subplots, told from the point of view of Mary Magdalene."

She took a breath while I stared at her.

"*Who* as you may know was an important Biblical figure, and *who* I happen to be related to on my mother's side, and *who*–"

She sounded like an owl. Also it occurred to me for the first time in our acquaintance that she didn't sound quite sane. Until now she'd just been annoying, although with Ann it was a mega, economy-size annoyingness.

But this ridiculous new Biblical-pedigree claim—or was it a mama-gree?—seemed to me to be a dead giveaway that her mental status was getting iffy. The tiny spit droplets that flew out of her mouth whenever she pronounced a *p* only emphasized this.

"You know where it is," she grated out accusingly. "You sent it to the man in Orono when I *asked* you not to. That Hobgoblin or whatever his name is."

She hadn't asked; she'd *ordered* me not to send the old book away. I'd thought at the time that she was nervy but harmless and done it anyway, never giving her objections much thought.

"Robotham," I corrected her.

When my father first found the book, I'd been excited and had unwisely told a few people here in Eastport about it; that's how Ann had learned of it. And she'd been an intolerable pain in the tail about it ever since.

"Whatever," she sneered. "Just don't think you're fooling anybody with that story about him losing it, or letting it get stolen, or whatever."

Another breath; fascinating, I thought. From the lengths of her usually disagreeable monologues, until now I'd thought she must take in oxygen via hidden gills.

"Probably," she added snidely, "that *boyfriend* of his killed him."

Years in the money business had taught me not to take other people's idiocies personally. But at her words, a hot little flame of outrage sprang up in my heart.

I hadn't known Horace. But neither had Ann. Luckily, Ellie stepped in.

"Time to go," she said, advancing on Ann in a purposeful way that made Ann's tiny shape back toward the door even as her big red mouth kept moving.

"Want... me... *mine,*" she spluttered urgently, as Ellie went on mercilessly invading her personal space. "I have a *right...* because *I'm...*"

"Good-bye," Ellie said sweetly, and didn't quite give Ann a shove when they reached the hallway.

"...an *artist!*" Ann wailed as Ellie forced her out the door, then followed her onto the porch. I heard their voices out there, Ann's outraged and Ellie's determined, before Ellie came in again. She slammed the door and sagged against it.

"You never told me she was so *insistent,*" she managed, and after a moment I had to smile too, not at Ann but at Ellie, whose delicate exterior concealed, apparently, a Sherman tank.

"Thanks." I sank into a chair. Outside the kitchen window, late-summer sweet peas twined elegantly against the chain-link of the dog run.

"This time I thought I'd never get rid of her," I said. "But was it you who kept...?"

Calling, I meant to finish. But instead Bella's voice rose from the front hall, shrill with alarm. "Missus?"

She'd come in the front door to avoid Ann Talbert at the rear, I gathered; good move. "Jake," I corrected automatically, as I always did.

She ignored this as she always did. "Missus, there's a—"

"Tub on the stairs," I said. "I know, Bella. My father put it there. He's got it chained very securely, though, and I'm sure he'll be back soon to lower it down."

If he can get it unstuck, I added silently. That had to be the plan. "If the dogs want in, just let them in. And if they go upstairs don't worry about it," I called out to Bella.

If white-faced old Monday could handle the tub then surely Prill would be able to. "Just yell at them to come down and if they don't," I added, "I'll deal with it when I come home."

Probably Bella hadn't been out getting dynamite, I realized. Probably she already had some.

And with any luck she'd have detonated all of it by the time I got back.

"Let's get out of here," I told Ellie a little desperately.

The pastries could wait.

Jason Riverton lived on Water Street halfway to Dog Island, which was not really an island but a long, grassy peninsula overlooking a sand beach and the Old Sow whirlpool, at the north end of town.

Here the houses alternated between sweeping, well-maintained Victorians and smaller white Capes or bungalows with odd-sized windows and unwieldy-looking dormers, fronted by patches of grass.

"Ann Talbert was in Orono the night Horace Robotham was killed," Ellie said as we walked toward the Riverton house.

Out on the water, the tide was running and the whirlpool in

it swirled furiously, its paisley-shaped outer curls and dark, treacherous-looking blue sinkholes whitecapped.

"She was?" I asked, surprised. "You mean you've already checked? When? And why?"

Ellie looked nonchalant. "I started wondering about her right after it happened. Horace's death, I mean. Because," she explained, "I knew Ann really, really wanted the book."

"And you thought—?"

"Well, no," Ellie admitted. "I can't say my thinking rose to the level of an actual suspicion. Because you know, at that point nobody was even talking about that kind of a murder. Not even us."

We crossed Clark Street, passing between more small houses on our left and the old abandoned gas plant on our right, its tall brick chimney looking as if a stiff breeze would topple it.

But it had looked that way for years. "Only, when somebody wants something," Ellie continued, "and then the person who has it gets his head bonked, I just always wonder . . ."

Yeah. Other people's first words were usually "Mama" or "Dada." I'm pretty sure Ellie's was "Whodunnit."

"So why was she there?" I asked. "Do you know that, too?"

Ellie nodded matter-of-factly. "Writers'-group meeting. On the U. Maine campus, every other week."

"And you discovered all this by . . ."

"Asking her. Just now, when I pushed her out your back door. Like I say, I'd been wondering. So, once I got her out on the porch, I asked."

And ye shall receive, I thought; good old Ellie. "As in, 'Where were you on the night of . . .' "

"Exactly like that," Ellie agreed. "*That* stopped her in her tracks," she added, clearly enjoying the memory. Ellie hadn't had very much use for Ann Talbert even before Ann became the Writer from Hell.

"She was so shocked, she just kind of coughed up the answer before she thought much about it," Ellie reported.

"So you think she could have killed Robotham, then stolen the book? In which case her demands for it now would be..."

"Camouflage," Ellie supplied. "And no, I still don't, really. Ann isn't *that* nuts."

She paused thoughtfully. "Or I don't *think* she is. But if all we want is to muddy the waters a little for Dave DiMaio, she makes a good start."

I glanced at her. "Muddy the waters?"

"Make him believe somebody other than Merkle might've killed Robotham," she explained cheerfully. "Because other than the book—which by the way he doesn't really seem to be looking for, so maybe he thinks Merkle has that, too? Anyway, why else would he be here?"

"Huh. Good plan," I said. Clearly we were thinking alike; if Dave did believe Bert Merkle had killed his friend, and Dave was here in town to get revenge, producing one or more other suspects for him might slow him down. "So *that's* why you..."

"Called this morning? Yep. To get us onto the same page in case we weren't."

Which of course we had been; sometimes I thought Ellie and I had been separated at birth. "Saving you from Ann Talbert—*and* finding out where she was that night—those were just nifty side effects." She grinned winningly at me. "But my question is, what're we doing *here*?"

We were approaching the Rivertons' house.

"Bob Arnold suggested it." A tall, asphalt-shingle-sided dwelling on a tiny lot, it had a ramshackle shed out back and a pair of warped two-by-fours laid loosely atop stacked concrete blocks serving as the front step. Empty flower boxes at dull windows whose curtains looked sadly unlaundered, a broken hinge on the rusty mailbox, and a patchy, dandelion-studded lawn badly needing a mower all suggested that a caring hand had been absent from it for quite a while.

"Bob thinks Jason Riverton might have something useful to say about Merkle," I added. "But he also wants our sense of what kind of weird stuff, if any, is going on in the Riverton house."

We started up the front walk, cracked and pierced through by clumps of yellow-blooming chamomile. "Seems Merkle's made a pal of Jason, and Bob can't figure out why. And in return," I added, "Bob might have some information about DiMaio for us, too."

We climbed the concrete-block step. "Sam doing okay?" Ellie asked.

"Yeah. So far, so fine." But she understood as clearly as I did that if at any moment Sam stopped being that way, Bob might find out about it first.

And that I intended to be next, yet another excellent reason for staying in Bob's good graces.

Ellie knocked. Moments later we were let into the house by Jason Riverton's mother. She was a small, stoop-shouldered woman with a watery gaze that wandered over our faces without quite focusing on either of us.

After that, it took maybe another ten seconds or so to turn Mrs. Riverton's darling boy into a real, honest-to-gosh murder suspect.

Chapter 9

*Need an emergency leaky-pipe
repair? Wrap the hole with a
"blanket" of rubber (cut from a
rubber glove works fine) and
tighten a sleeve clamp (from
the hardware store) onto it.*
—Tiptree's Tips

I'll be here if you need anything," Mrs. Riverton said as
heavy footsteps thudded down the stairs toward us.

Turning away she went back to the dim front parlor and the
rocking chair in front of the big TV. When we knocked she'd
been watching *The Price Is Right*.

On the TV tray was a paper plate with the remains of a prune
pastry on it. A paper napkin with an elaborate red *M* printed on it

lay by the plate; it seemed Ellie wasn't the only local fan of Mimi's new bakery.

Seating herself, Mrs. Riverton resumed her knitting; I couldn't see what was on the needles. In the narrow front hall, her son looked from Ellie to me and back again.

Jason Riverton was six feet tall and a hundred and thirty-five pounds or so, with intensely hostile dark-brown eyes and a sour expression. A wispy moustache struggled on his soft, damp-looking upper lip. His head was shaved. A gold stud pierced his right nostril. "Yeah?" he demanded.

He wore baggy jeans with a pair of black suspenders and an old black T-shirt with a screen-print of a zombie being pierced by a lightning bolt on it, and maybe it was just the effect of the nose piercing, but I got the strong impression that for some reason he'd forgotten how not to breathe through his mouth.

"Jason, if you don't mind, we've got ourselves a problem and we hoped you could help us out by answering a couple of questions for us," Ellie said after she'd introduced us both.

He shrugged carelessly in reply, then turned and tramped back up the narrow stairs; we followed. Each step was covered with a grit-choked brown rubber mat worn nearly to shreds, and the paint on the walls wasn't much lighter.

Where there still was any paint at all. Over the years the comings and goings of a teenaged boy had gouged the flimsy wallboard and hatchmarked the shaky, paint-peeling banister bolted to it.

Just at first glance I could see a dozen other things I'd have fixed immediately, too: a missing light-switch cover, a flap of loose carpet at the top of the stairs, a doorknob dangling at half-mast from a closet door, and a diagonal crack in the hallway plaster that unless I missed my guess meant the whole foundation was sinking....

But none of it prepared me for the inside of Jason's room, which *had* been recently painted: flat black.

Black—walls, floor, ceiling...And then there were the clippings.

Newspaper clippings, all recent and all on one subject: the death of Horace Robotham. Ellie and I glanced at each other as Jason sank into a chair in front of a computer.

The *Bangor Daily News* had run more than Horace Robotham's obituary, of course. His death had been big news for a few days in a place where serious crime was so rare, and it had been a subject with a lot of angles.

Neighborhood safety, tips on how not to become a victim, effective policing, comments from local residents, town-gown relationships—as Ellie had reminded me, Orono was home to the University of Maine's flagship campus—Jason had them all, snipped neatly out of the paper and pinned to a corkboard on the black wall behind his desk.

A cold, prickly feeling came over me, gazing at them. Why hadn't it occurred to me earlier that looking for more murder suspects also meant possibly finding one right here?

But it hadn't, until now. Without a word, Jason resumed the computer game he'd been playing: blasting wraiths, zombies, and skeletons to gory bits whenever they sprang up in the software-generated dungeon he was navigating with a handheld device.

"So, Jason," I began, perhaps a bit too heartily. "I've got a son only a few years older than you are, went to Shead High. What class are you in?"

A strawberry Slurpee with a stained straw sticking out of it stood on his desk, which was made out of a hollow-core door and two filing cabinets. Unblinking, he drank automatically from the cup, reaching out with a spiderishly thin, pale hand to grasp it as unseeingly as one of the monsters in his computer game might.

From the number of points he'd put into the flashing score panel on the screen, it seemed he was a pretty good shot. But not much of a conversationalist.

"Just graduated high school," he uttered finally. "Got into a construction job. Got hurt. Got on disability."

And now here he was, only a couple of months later, having

said good-bye to the stresses and strains of the workaday world. Efficient young fellow, our Jason.

"I'm sorry about that," I replied. "Too bad, hitting such lousy luck right off the bat." Although his injury, whatever it was, didn't hinder him from manipulating the game controller or reaching the Slurpee cup.

No pastry crumbs, I noticed without surprise. Mimi's creations were meant for grown-up taste buds, and what I'd seen so far of Jason suggested that he was more your basic Little Debbie type of snack consumer.

The rest of the room's decor consisted of a black bedspread on a black-sheeted, wooden-framed bed, militarily neat. Stacked milk crates identical to the ones I used in my workroom held his clothes, mostly jeans and T-shirts like the ones he was wearing.

Plank-and-concrete-block bookshelves lined the opposite wall, the shelves crammed with paperbacks some of whose titles were familiar; Sam had read all the Conan the Barbarian books. Lovecraft, Bloch, and James Branch Cabell—that last name jumped familiarly out at me—were heavily represented, also.

Down at one corner of the lowest shelf a half-dozen titles that didn't seem to belong with the rest were shoved together like outcasts: a high-school grammar text, old hardcover copies of *The Deerslayer, The Last of the Mohicans, Moby-Dick,* and a few more from the you-really-should-read-it department of English literature.

I'd have bet any money Jason hadn't. Someone else had put those books there, trying I supposed to be a good influence on a young man's reading habits. I wondered who it had been; Bert Merkle, maybe?

But second only to the newspaper clippings he'd pinned up, it was the weapons collection ranged out along the top of the longest bookshelf that fascinated me the most: brass knuckles, spiked leather wristlets, a wooden truncheon with a black-leather strap looped through a hole in its stout handle...

Jason apparently shopped in the hand-to-hand-combat aisle,

and not only for the modern stuff. "Where's the mace?" I asked, without thinking.

His slender thumbs paused momentarily in their battering of the computer-game controller.

"What?" His gaze stayed locked on the screen as the score rose up and the creatures fell down, writhing and screaming. But I thought he looked annoyed. Maybe I'd pointed out something he hadn't noticed before.

"Come on, Jason, that's quite a nice collection of medieval weaponry you've got there."

Hey, I watch as much public television as anyone. And there had been a special on war in the Middle Ages a few weeks earlier.

I'd clicked past, then gone back to see the program because it reminded me so much of my first marriage. The correct term for a crossbow, I'd learned, was *arbalest*.

"So?" Jason asked sullenly.

"So it seems funny to me that you've got all those others but no mace," I persisted. "Makes me wonder. How come you're missing such an important one?"

Jason's weapons were reproductions, surely, but still it was a decent-looking collection. He'd even made little labels for each weapon, which to me meant he didn't spend all his time in front of the computer.

Just most of it. Meanwhile according to the program I'd seen, a mace was a heavy metal ball, toothed or smooth, fixed to a thick handle similar to the way an axe-head tops an axe.

"Bert warned me." Jason avoided my question in a voice so flat it could've been machine-generated. "He said somebody'd be around hassling me sooner or later."

A mace would've been a good tool for bashing in the skull of Horace Robotham. The dent it made could've looked as if it were put there by a rock.

"Why?" asked Ellie. "Why would Bert warn you about that?"

Jason finished his Slurpee. "Ma!" he bellowed, ignoring her question, too.

"Coming, dear," Jason's mother called quaveringly.

Soon she appeared carrying a full cup of sweet refreshment, holding it out the way you might put a bit of meat through the bars of a lion's cage. She didn't look straight at him, either, any more than she had at us when we came in.

He grabbed the cup, didn't say thanks. Smiling eerily, eyes fixed on nothing, Jason's very odd mother didn't quite press her hands together and bow as she backed from the room.

But it was close. "Because people just want to get us in trouble," he declared when she'd gone out. "Me and Bert."

He mowed down an onslaught of red-eyed, slavering demons, got a *Congratulations!* screen that asked if he wanted to record his high score, and declined the offer with a keystroke.

"But me, mostly," he finished.

By now I'd had just about enough of Mr. Supernatural Space Slaughterer, or whoever this kid thought he was. His sullen attitude was tiring in the extreme, and I thought the clippings and weapons were doing a plenty good job of getting him in trouble without any help from me.

None of it was evidence. But I still found myself wondering where Jason Riverton had been on the night of Horace's death. As if reading my thought, he turned slowly.

"I was at Bert's that night," he said, following my gaze to the corkboard. "He gave me all these clippings. He doesn't have room for them at his place. He didn't like that guy."

"Is that so?" I replied, thinking, *How convenient. They are each other's alibi.* And whose idea was that?

Not Jason's, I was willing to wager. He sucked up a third of the Slurpee his mom had brought him, leaned back in his chair, and belched.

"Did Bert Merkle say why he didn't like Horace Robotham?" I asked.

Jason shook his shaven head. "Just said if anyone ever started thinking the guy was murdered, Bert'd be the one they thought did it. And I'd get asked questions, too, because Bert and I are friends."

And because Jason was no Hulk Hogan but he was tall enough to hit a fellow over the head with a rock. Or with a mace. The whole point of one of those weapons was that you didn't need to be a muscleman to make a blow with one of them fatal.

"Why?" Ellie asked. "I mean, Bert's a whole lot older than you. I wouldn't think the two of you had very much in common at all. So why are you such good friends with him?"

And what does Bert want with you? I added silently. It would have been Bob Arnold's question, too, when he'd questioned Jason. But Bob had been looking for only one specific variety of slime-toad behavior.

And I already had a feeling we'd need to dredge the whole scummy pond, to come up with Merkle's motivation for this strange friendship. Jason shrugged, picked up his cup again.

As more of the sweet drink glugged down the boy's gullet, it suddenly struck me that like the first one it was a real Slurpee, a forty-ouncer in the trademark gigantic plastic cup with a domed top. And the nearest 7-Eleven store, home of the authentic beverage, was a three-hour drive from here, in Augusta.

I knew because it was one of the things Sam complained about when we'd moved to Eastport, the absence of the equivalent of a pantryful of junk food on every corner. Jason's mom must've stocked up on them, maybe even kept a freezer full for him.

"Jason?" Ellie prodded him. "I asked why you and Bert are friends."

Again he shrugged in reply—at least his shoulders got regular workouts, I thought meanly, but gosh, his sullenness was exasperating—then angled his head at the bookshelves.

A chessboard was set up on one of them, with a book of chess problems lying open alongside it. "Bert gives me books to read. Plays chess, too."

I nodded at Ellie; that much at least sounded right. Even my dad had played the game fairly regularly with Merkle for a while. He'd given it up only when Merkle started trying to pick his brain on the topic of high explosives.

"Bert talks to me like I'm smart. He treats me like a human being. Which is more," Jason added with a further touch of hostility, "than most people do."

He eyed me. "And before you get started, there's no weird crap going on. That's what that cop wanted to know. But Bert's no Chester the Molester, so don't get all panicky about that."

I nodded again. "Right. That's what Bob Arnold told me, too."

But that only deepened the question of why Bert Merkle was interested in the youth, who seemed a deeply unrewarding sort of pal for a past-middle-age man.

Or for anyone, really. But maybe I was being too hard on him. Several major-league baseball caps that hung on hooks on the back of his bedroom door said he had at least one fresh-air interest.

Or maybe he just needed something to keep the sun off that shaved head. "Okay," I said, "you and Bert talk about books and you play chess. But if he ever needed help, you'd help him, right?"

Jason's flat expression didn't change. "I would if he asked. But he never has. Bert's never wanted a single thing from me. He doesn't need my help."

"Oh, come on, Jason," Ellie put in. "He asked you to keep those clippings for him, didn't he? Put them all up on that corkboard, there? That's help."

The boy scowled, whether at the contradiction or something else I couldn't tell.

"So Bert didn't ask you to get something from Mr. Robotham, in Orono?" I persisted. "An old book, maybe? He didn't ask you to go down there and..."

Slow shake of the gleaming head. "Don't go to Orono. Go to Augusta. Drive my mom there every couple of weeks to her doctors' appointments."

And to buy mass quantities of strawberry Slurpees, no doubt. He finished the second one; too bad they didn't deliver the stuff in tanker trucks.

"So we drive to the doctor's, I wait, we eat lunch and go to the mall," he recited in a near monotone.

As he spoke he was playing the game once more, spattering the extremely realistic-appearing insides of red-eyed goblins all over the walls of a tunnel lit by torches.

"Then we come home," he added. Goblins died en masse. Their tinny shrieks echoed from the computer's speakers. Only now he wasn't shooting them.

He'd switched weapons. He was clubbing them to death. The sound effects weren't pleasant; with a keyboard click he made the noises louder, then louder still.

"Jason," I tried, raising my voice to be heard over the din. "If I ask your mother whether or not you were here on the night Mr. Robotham was attacked, what will she say?"

He shrugged. "Nothing." His rudeness was deliberate, I realized. There was more in that hairless head of his than he wanted to let on, I could tell by the books and the chessboard.

And from the look in his eyes. I mean, it's pretty obvious when nobody's home in there, usually. And Jason's mental rooms seemed fully furnished and inhabited to me; just not with anyone you'd want to meet on a dark street late at night.

"Come on, Jason, her chair's right by the front door. Are you trying to tell me she doesn't see you going in or out?"

Even Ann Talbert with her hysterical ambitions and her wild expectation that everyone else would just march to her drummer wasn't actually . . . well, *creepy* was the only word for Jason. Still, his ex-teacher Merrie Fargeorge must've seen something worthwhile in him. Hadn't Bob Arnold reported she'd spent time trying to help him?

See, I was trying to like him; I really was. After all, he was just a kid, and without knowing any details I could tell his home situation was unfortunate. So I was trying to cut him some slack.

But he didn't make it easy. "Correct," he replied flatly. The question seemed to amuse him somehow, provoking a smirky, *I know something you don't know* expression.

Frustrated, I went to the only window, needing relief from the dark, depressing atmosphere and the sweet reek of gloppy pink syrup.

Toward the back of the house was a rickety old wooden shed about the size of a one-car garage, built of gray, rotten wood and ancient, disintegrating wooden shingles with a few new boards peeking whitely through the gaps between the old ones.

Just enough to keep the whole structure from falling down entirely, I supposed. "Okay, I'll bite," I said finally.

I turned to him again. "You say your mom wouldn't notice, I'll believe you. Hey, you know her better than I do. But like I said, I've got a son your age, too, and I would notice. So why wouldn't she?"

"She just wouldn't, that's all."

He stared at the screen, his thumbs moving fast on the game controller. It was obvious he'd come to the end of his attention span as far as we were concerned.

The only reason he'd let us up here at all, I realized, was that it was the path of least resistance. Somebody knocks, you open the door. Wants to talk, you let them talk. Wait them out, sooner or later they'll go away.

I got a feeling that path was a very familiar one to Jason Riverton. And that someone, possibly Merkle, had taken advantage of it. But I still didn't know how. And something about Jason's manner still bugged me, like he had a secret he wasn't telling.

But finally after a few more insolent, one-syllable answers from the skinny teenager we left.

" 'Bye, Jason." No answer. In the living room his mother's fingers moved on whatever she was knitting, as relentlessly as her son's did on his game device.

On the TV screen, Bob Barker was reminding everyone to have their pets spayed and neutered. Something was strange about that, too, though, it seemed to me, and then I remembered.

It was the same thing he'd been saying when we came in.

"Mrs. Riverton?" I stepped into the room. With the shades pulled down and no lights turned on, it was cavelike but for the TV's garish glow.

"Yes, dear?" But her gaze didn't shift when I moved in front of her. And the show on the TV screen wasn't being broadcast.

It was recorded on a VCR tape. The same show, over and over. "Ellie and I are leaving now, Mrs. Riverton."

"Fine, dear." Like a statue, except for the fingers. A bad thought struck me. In the gloom I peered closely at her hands, pale in the screen's light.

Fingers moving. Knitting needles in the fingers. But no yarn on the needles. On the TV screen a hysterically happy woman flung her arms around a white-haired Bob Barker.

But Mrs. Riverton didn't see it. Her milky-blue eyes stared sightlessly at the screen. Something wrong with her, I realized.

I mean, besides the fact that she was blind.

"Whew," Ellie breathed when we got outside. "That was weird. But Jake—if he'd done it, wouldn't someone have seen him?"

Two minds with but a single thought, again: the idea that Jason's gratitude for Merkle's friendship might have led the boy to do something awful.

"So tall, the black clothes and shaved head," Ellie went on.

So recognizable, she meant. "It was dark," I pointed out. "He could have hunched down to look shorter, worn one of those ball caps on his head."

Besides, Horace Robotham had already been dead awhile when he was found by a late-night dog-walker, sprawled across the sidewalk on the quiet Orono street where he'd lived.

Ahead, Merrie Fargeorge's picturesque saltwater farm lay on a long, gentle slope of sandy grassland overlooking Passamaquoddy Bay, at the very end of Dog Island.

"Are you sure this is such a good idea?" I asked Ellie as we headed toward it. Leaving the Rivertons' house I'd expected to be returning home.

But Ellie had other plans, and I had to admit that after the dim, depressing situation we'd just escaped I was glad not to be hurrying back indoors anywhere. Brisk salt air and a high, head-clearing blue sky were just what the doctor ordered after that experience.

"At least she has someone to drive her places," said Ellie, meaning Mrs. Riverton. "And yes," she added, "I'm sure."

We walked on; at length Ellie mused, "If Bert Merkle somehow got Jason to commit—"

Murder. Simple as that. "Yeah. If he did, the both of them are pretty much getting away with it," I agreed. "They're each other's alibi, not that anyone's asked either of them for one."

We walked fast, trying to shake off the atmosphere of the Rivertons' house. "On top of which," I went on, "if Bert can just *finger* people and Jason will do his bidding—"

"Uh-huh. Then who's next? Bob Arnold for hassling Bert about his yard? A city-council member for directing Bob to do it?"

Or—me, for some reason that made sense only in his tinfoil-capped head? And why would Merkle be so interested in my old book, anyway?

Its oh-so-coincidental disappearance right around the time of Robotham's death apparently hadn't meant much to the cops. But to me it had begun seeming more and more like the motive for Robotham's murder.

Still, I reminded myself firmly, we didn't really know Jason Riverton *or* Bert Merkle had done anything wrong at all.

"I checked on him, too, by the way," said Ellie. "DiMaio, that is. I got on the computer at home and Googled him nine ways from Sunday," she told me.

Besides her many other good qualities, she was the suspicious type; gosh, I just loved that about her. "And?"

"And as far as I can tell, DiMaio's what he says he is. College professor. Small school in Providence, funny old buildings. From the pictures and course listings it seems pretty old-fashioned. Greek and Latin and so on. Scholarly. But it's for real. I called the number on the website and a person answered, said Professor DiMaio's on leave until the autumn session."

She turned her face into the late-morning sunshine. Merrie Fargeorge's farm grew steadily nearer.

"Anyway, we might just as well get this over with," she added, meaning an interview with the old educator. "Maybe a talk with you now will take the edge off her mood later. Make the party a little less awkward."

Oof, the party. At her words the full misery of the prospect crashed over me again.

Bad enough to have only the tiny quarter-bath downstairs for guests' use; an old tub lurking on the stairwell was guaranteed to scandalize an Eastport lady of Merrie's refinement, even aside from her annoyance about DiMaio. And the sight of her ancestral home place, as prettily composed and beautifully balanced as a Currier & Ives print, didn't make me feel any better:

House, barn, garden, shed, all laid out on the sunwashed, grassy slope like a model of eighteenth-century domestic economy. "How does she do it?" I wondered aloud.

Because it wasn't just lovely to look at; this was a working New England saltwater farm, with emphasis on the *working*. The raspberry bushes and asparagus bed bore bountifully, I saw as we entered the rail-fenced drive, and the sweet peas colorfully and muscularly climbing a trellis by her back door made mine look like runts.

Beehives clustered at one edge of the garden; beans thatched the curved-bamboo-pole tipis at the other. But most amazing of all was an excavation—a pit, really—that spread about twenty feet square in the soil beyond the garden plot.

Terraced in a series of steps, it was about eight feet deep, its walls horizontally ribboned with the layers of earth—black, brown, moss green, and the pale tan of the surface sand—that had been dug through to create it.

Merrie Fargeorge stood in the middle of it, leaning on her spade, wearing boots, coveralls, and a wide-brimmed straw hat. Holding a trowel in one gloved hand and a small, soft-bristled brush in the other, she looked up at our approach.

"Hello, Merrie," called Ellie. The ex-teacher put her tools down on a tarp as her little dog, a bright, bouncy mutt with a cocked ear and a black-ringed left eye, danced out to greet us. *Caspar,* the tag on his collar read.

"Hi, Caspar. How're you doing, buddy?" I said. At least the dog didn't bite.

"Good morning, ladies," Merrie trilled, removing her spectacles to peer at us. Close up, the excavation looked even bigger. "To what do I owe the honor of your visit today?"

"Why, the pleasure of your company, Miss Fargeorge," Ellie replied gallantly. "May I help you?" she added, reaching out a hand as the older woman got to the excavation's crumbly top step.

Miss Fargeorge twinkled at Ellie's flattery, but she didn't look the least bit fooled—I got the feeling that the last time she'd been fooled was about fifty years earlier—and she didn't want any assistance, either.

Instead, she took the final step up to ground level as easily as the half-dozen before. "Oh," she said, her tone cooling noticeably as she caught clear sight of me. "Hello, Jacobia."

Clearly I was still in the doghouse, and not a nice one like Caspar's with clean straw and a fresh bowl of water.

"Merrie," I began placatingly, "I do think there's been a minor misunderstanding..."

Set out on the tarp at the bottom of the excavation were her other tools: a shovel, a small pickaxe, a large pickaxe, and a long, hollow, tubelike device with a stout wooden handle at one end and wickedly pointed serrations cut into the heavy steel at the other.

"It's a sampling tool," she said, seeing my curiosity. "You push it into the earth by turning the handle, to capture a core sample. Then you pull the tool out and the sample comes with it. From it you may learn whether it is worthwhile digging farther," she added in a lecturing tone.

Her smile had ice in it, as if I'd neglected to hand in my homework and was now attempting to distract her from that criminal failure.

"And there's no misunderstanding," she added. "None at all, minor or otherwise."

Spryly striding away from us over the uneven ground, she started toward the house, the navy-blue ribbon on her straw hat streaming behind her and her dog at her heels.

"But come along, both of you," she called back at us as she went. "Caspar needs his biscuit and it's time for my cup of tea."

Step into my parlor, I thought, feeling like the fly. But after a glance at Ellie, who'd already started along down the grassy path, I followed Merrie, too.

Chapter 10

Writh Caspar frolicking behind, we let Merrie Fargeorge lead us on a grassy path beaten down by many passages of her booted feet. Past a dusty, well-used-looking Honda Civic in the drive we proceeded to the screened porch where our hostess took her boots off, exchanging them for soft moosehide slippers. Caspar darted in ahead of us, skidded around a corner, and vanished, his cheerful yaps echoing.

"Little devil," Merrie remarked. "Can you believe that he's terrified of thunderstorms? Otherwise, he's utterly fearless."

Inside, the house was cool and clean, as neat and airy as a well-kept museum. As full of relics, too; glass cases displayed clay pipes, antique marbles, fine-featured dolls' heads, tools, and dozens of other items that Merrie had dug from her excavation site, which for decades had been the family trash heap.

She explained this as we admired the artifacts and she made

tea in her kitchen, where the slow ticking of an antique banjo clock emphasized the otherwise silent orderliness of the place. Bella would've loved it, but around so much delicate and probably valuable stuff, I felt like the bull in the china shop.

And not a very popular bull, either; Merrie's coolness to me continued as she bustled about the kitchen.

Trying to ignore it—why had Ellie thought this would be a good idea, anyway? I examined the calendar posted on the front of the refrigerator. From it, I gathered why the car in the driveway looked so heavily used:

Merrie Fargeorge was not just a retired schoolteacher with a historical hobby. She was a recognized expert on downeast history and practical archeology, with meetings, talks, and seminars scheduled at historical societies all over the state, at least three days a week and often more.

Also, she was a gourmet cook. Perusing the calendar I suddenly became aware of the delicious fragrance wafting from the stove. Meat and onions, pungent spices, garlic and bay leaf . . .

"Beef bourguignon," Merrie said, seeing me sniffing with appreciation. Soon the citrusy scent of Constant Comment tea joined the other delightful aromas.

"It's a pet peeve of mine," she continued briskly, "these portions-for-one frozen foods. Hideous stuff, all of it. Singles, and especially seniors, should enjoy life too, don't you feel?"

From the notes on the shopping list posted by the back door tomorrow's dinner would be coq au vin, the next night's garlic shrimp in champagne sauce; enjoyable indeed.

"Now," she said, not waiting for a reply as she guided us into the sitting room. Here cooking aromas were replaced by light perfumes of lavender, cedar, and lemon oil, floating together in the still air of the pristine room.

"What can I do for you two this morning?" she asked, placing thin china cups of steaming liquid before us and setting out a plate of raspberry shortbreads.

From Mimi's, I guessed; apparently the new bakery was taking Eastport by storm. Merrie eyed us wisely from behind her spectacles.

"When people come to see me, it's often because they have some kind of historical question," she prompted.

"And generally, Merrie knows the answer," said Ellie, taking her cue.

Aha, I thought; so this was the part where I redeemed myself by listening with appreciation. And I could get behind that, as Sam would've put it. I sat back and sipped my tea, then tried one of the fruited shortbreads, which was excellent, while the banjo clock ticked distantly and Ellie spoke.

According to her, the Fargeorge farm had been in Merrie's family since 1789 when Simon Fargeorge arrived. Soon he became a well-to-do farmer and victualer, supplying meat and vegetables to the ships, military and commercial, that came into the harbor, and to the soldiers at Fort Sullivan.

Since then, generations of Fargeorges had grown up here; most had gone away. But not Merrie; as the last local descendant of one of Eastport's most revered founding citizens, she had her own float in the parade each Fourth of July, a front pew in the Congregational church was dedicated to her family by a bronze plaque—she sat in the pew each Sunday—and when the ladies of Eastport decided to fete someone, Merrie was the obvious choice.

With, this time, unfortunate results for me. Not that I was about to interrupt Ellie's history lesson by mentioning this; the party was supposed to be a surprise. So for once I kept my lip zipped.

That is, until we got to the real point of our visit. "It's about Jason Riverton," Ellie told Merrie.

The tea had begun cooling. "We realize this may sound like a strange question. But we want to know if you think he's capable of committing murder."

The Rivertons had a car, though I hadn't seen it, and Jason

could've made it to Orono and back in four hours, plus maybe an hour for evil doings. And I believed him now about his mother not noticing his absence.

And I *didn't* believe he'd refuse Bert Merkle a favor, maybe a violent favor. But I still wondered if the venerable Miss Fargeorge would blacken the name of a former pupil, even if he deserved it.

So it surprised me that she didn't even ask why we wanted to know such a thing. And her answer surprised me more.

"Jason was the most unrewarding student I ever taught," she announced, putting her teacup down. "And with a good deal less excuse than most. I think his poor mother was at least half the reason why I stayed involved, even after he graduated."

She frowned, remembering. "Although they didn't always seem unfortunate, any of them. Before his father was killed in a hunting accident and his mother became ill, the family appeared solid."

I glanced at Ellie. We really didn't have much time; back at my house there were ever so many chores still to be completed in preparation for this afternoon. But:

Patience, my friend's answering glance instructed. So I nibbled the last shortbread and tried to obey.

"Although," Merrie added, "I suppose we never really do know what goes on behind closed doors, do we?" She sipped tea. "And at any rate that changed later, their . . . normalcy."

I looked questioningly at her. "The accident, of course," she explained, although as before, the word *accident* got an odd little twist as it came out of her mouth.

"Jason was only ten," she went on with her story. "He and his father were out in the woods, in October I think it was, with a pair of rifles."

Her lips tightened briefly. "Deer hunting," she added. "They will take the boys young, around here. Mostly I suppose it works out all right."

"But that time it didn't," I guessed, and she nodded slowly at me. For an instant the atmosphere in the Riverton house closed around me again, dim and strange with a layer of sour, sorrowful dampness overlaying everything.

It had felt like the kind of hidden, unpleasant place where if you wanted to, you could grow your own mushrooms. But now I wondered if what I'd sensed instead was a crop of bad memories.

"No," Merrie answered, "it didn't go well at all."

She considered a moment. Maybe she was wondering how much of her old student's privacy she was betraying, then decided to go on nevertheless.

"They found Jason crying, covered in blood and holding one of the guns, alone on one of the old logging roads. He'd been out there all night, that's why they sent a search party."

"So they'd gone missing," I began; she stopped me with a look.

"Indeed. But the search party knew the general area they'd been in. And when the searchers followed a hiking trail into the woods, they found the father.

"Richard Riverton," Merrie said grimly. "Well-known. Not," she added judiciously, "well-liked."

She looked back and forth at the two of us. "In fact his death, or rather the manner of it," she refined her comment carefully, "was one of the very few things that ever got hushed up effectively around here."

Which at first I found hard to believe, even with downeast-history expert Miss Merrie Fargeorge testifying to it. In Eastport if you get a hangnail at nine-fifteen, people start waving pairs of fingernail clippers at you by nine-thirty at the latest.

"People liked Margot Riverton, you see," Merrie said, seeming to understand my skepticism. "And her health was so shaky, even then...no one quite knew what might happen to her if word got out that her son might've murdered his father."

The words hung starkly. "I never heard anything like that," murmured Ellie after a brief, shocked silence.

Merrie glanced coolly at her. "No, dear, of course not. They made a pact, all the men from that day, that they wouldn't talk. Not about what happened, and not about the end of the story."

The clock in the kitchen chimed the hour; a fresh bout of impatience seized me. But I had to hear the end of the story.

"One of them was my student," said Merrie. "Arlo Bonnet. Arlo was a soft-hearted fellow, always had been. And it bothered him, you see, what had happened. He *needed* to tell someone."

"If the father was dead and the boy had a gun, what 'rest of it' was there?" I asked. "And what did Jason say had happened?"

"Accident," Merrie replied tersely. "That's all Jason told them. But Arlo told me when they went down the logging road searching, they saw the boy before he heard them."

"And that was because?" I pressed.

"Crying too hard, Arlo said, to notice anything."

Merrie paused, recalling it. "Arlo told me," she said, "that it looked to them all as if Jason was trying to get the gun barrel into his own mouth, to reach down and pull the trigger."

"To kill himself." Ellie said it softly. "A ten-year-old boy. Out of . . . fear? Or grief?"

Merrie looked disapproving, as if someone had failed to work up to grade level. "Guilt," she corrected sharply. "I'm certain of it. Arlo said it was obvious, from what else they found. Only Jason couldn't do it. Couldn't reach the trigger, because his arms were too short."

Maybe so, but the story still didn't make sense to me. And neither did the way Merrie was telling it, as if there were no question at all that Jason Riverton had murdered his own father.

"I don't understand," I said. "Without witnesses, how can anyone be sure it wasn't an accident? He'd still feel guilt about it, and if he was frightened enough—"

"Think about it," Merrie interrupted.

Another silence. I spoke first. "Maybe," I said, "the father was shot in the back? Or even . . . the back of the head?"

In other words, way too high. Accidental hunting deaths are almost always body shots, I'd learned after spending nearly a decade's worth of hunting seasons in Maine. That's because the chest on an adult male human being is just about shoulder-high on your average white-tailed deer.

Which is what the accidental shooter usually thinks he's shooting.

The old schoolteacher nodded slowly again, her look grave. "They couldn't be certain. But the medical examiner said he believed it was the back of Mr. Riverton's head, yes."

The medical uncertainty, I thought, was interesting in a nightmarish sort of way. But Ellie picked up on a different angle of the story.

"But that's outrageous," she said. "People've known it all this time . . . *you've* known what happened? How . . . how could you?"

Keep the secret, she meant. Obstruct justice, cover up a murder, let a kid loose who ought to have been in detention, or worse. But Merrie Fargeorge had an answer for that, too.

"Nobody *knows* what happened," she said coldly. "All we knew for sure was that if Jason was prosecuted and found guilty, Margot would be alone. And we knew her well enough to know she wouldn't be able to take it."

She got up to clear the cups and biscuit plates. "What was done, was done. Mr. Riverton was gone. He couldn't be brought back. And whatever the reason was, we knew it wouldn't happen again. Or," she added, "we thought we did."

"Why was that?" I got up, too, following her and Ellie back to the kitchen with its placidly ticking clock and smells of good cooking. Merrie pulled an apron on and began rinsing the cups at the sink.

"Well, isn't it obvious?" Her back was to me as she replied. "A boy only has one father. And what that father did to provoke a ten-year-old boy to murder, we didn't know."

She turned, wiping her hands on a linen towel monogrammed in red. "Margot often had bruises. A cut lip, a black eye . . . she *said* it was because her sight was failing."

The dog, Caspar, pranced to the door, wagging to be let out. Merrie complied, looking past the animal to the excavation site where we'd interrupted her.

"We were so sure nothing like Jason's 'accident' would ever happen again," she said. "But now . . ."

The towel's red monogrammed *F* seemed to drip from her hands as she turned back to Ellie and me.

"Maybe we were wrong," she finished, hanging the towel on its hook.

"Okay, so I guess now we know the reason for Jason's guilty look," I said as Ellie and I walked back down Water Street toward my house.

"Uh-huh," she said distractedly. From the expression on her face I could see she was considering what Merrie Fargeorge had said.

And not liking something about it. "*And* I think we know why Merrie doesn't like Dave DiMaio going around Eastport asking questions," I went on. "She and some of her contemporaries covered up Jason's dad's possible murder. She doesn't want Dave stirring all that stuff up again."

"Maybe," Ellie replied. "Maybe that's it. But it doesn't quite make sense as far as DiMaio's actual interests go, does it? Because you know, he wasn't asking people about the *recent* past."

We climbed Adams Street toward the high school, past wood-framed houses whose tiny fenced yards were wedged into crevices in the granite hill; halfway up I turned to look out over the blue water below. Loaded with sightseers wielding cameras and binoculars, the Deer Island ferry was chugging back from Canada into the cove; near the landing two uniformed U.S. Customs officers got ready to check the passengers' IDs.

"Did it strike you as odd, though, that Merrie didn't even ask why we wanted to know about Jason?" I asked Ellie. "I mean, talk about your loaded question..." But Merrie hadn't flinched.

"Mmm," Ellie agreed. "As if she's just been waiting for someone to come along and ask. Which doesn't fit with wanting to cover it up, either, does it? The way she spilled the beans so fast."

The hill wasn't a shortcut to my house, distance-wise, and it certainly wasn't an easier way to get there, exertion-wise. But this route at least avoided downtown Water Street, where we would be delayed by enough casual conversation to fill up Merrie Fargeorge's archeology dig.

I thought a minute. "Maybe she's been wanting to unburden herself, too, like her student. D'you suppose Bob Arnold knows?"

It was hard to imagine otherwise. But if he did, why hadn't he done anything about it?

Meanwhile there was still something else going on in Ellie's mind, I could tell by the furrows between the gold-dust freckles on her forehead. "So?" I prompted.

She blurted it out suddenly. "Jake, I'm pretty sure Merrie wasn't telling us everything. Because I never realized it before, but I think my father was in the search party that day."

Ellie's folks were dead now, buried side-by-side in Hillside Cemetery. Eastport old-timers joked it was the only time in fifty years that the two ever lined up in the same direction; Ellie's mother would've spun in her grave, they said, to turn her back on Ellie's dad.

"Really," I commented, and waited for more. Clearly whatever memory Ellie was tiptoeing around wasn't a happy one.

Few in her childhood were. "You know," she asked, "how when a beaver gnaws down a tree, it leaves the stump chewed to a point?"

She was still striding ahead of me. Gasping, I paused to catch my breath at the entrance path to the old Fort Sullivan site. A nice white-pine bench seemed to beckon conveniently to me from alongside the path.

Ellie didn't stop. "Yes, I do know, actually," I said.

Whippy maple and ash saplings had been chopped down around the bench to make a clearing. Personally I thought there should be public oxygen tanks there, too, for people who tried climbing the Adams Street hill behind Ellie.

"But d'you by any chance want to tell me what in the world pointy beaver stumps have to do with anything?" I managed.

A small wooden sign marked the path to the spot from which you could see down the bay to the Narrows, where ships from the south entered our waters. It had been the lookout place back in the old days, too, when Fort Sullivan's establishment had signaled the American desire to hang on to the region.

A desire that got squelched as decisively as a candle's flame being pinched out; now the fort was only a memory, all its keen youthful vigor lying under the saplings and matted grass. Still, I could never pass without thinking about how awful it must have been, that first sight of the British warships in 1814.

"That *is* the point," Ellie said finally. "What I overheard my father telling my mother that night...I didn't understand it. Hey," she added defensively, "I had my own problems."

That was for sure. She sighed, remembering. "And anyway, when I heard it I was half-asleep. But now after what Merrie told us, I think I do."

She paused, half-turning to me. "Understand, that is. What my dad said, down in the kitchen."

Near the top the hill grew even steeper, past the ruin of an old Carpenter Gothic–style house with no windows and hardly any roof left on it. Through the empty front door-hole you could see straight into the parlor to the sodden wallpaper and shredded window-lace, once some Eastport woman's pride and joy.

Somebody had stacked old lumber in there recently. Ahead of me, Ellie resumed walking uphill steadily; I swear that woman had the lungs of a Tibetan sherpa.

"And here's the detail Merrie didn't want to describe but my dad did," she went on again after a while. "When they found Mr. Riverton out there in the woods, he'd fallen face-forward."

I forced my aching legs into brisker action, to keep up. "Face *down*," Ellie elaborated, "right onto the pointed end of a gnawed birch sapling. Impaled, actually. His head . . ." She faltered.

"Yuck," I said as we crested the hill at last. No wonder the medical examiner had been uncertain. Perspiration dripped stickily down my back and my lungs felt seared with exertion.

"Yuck is right," she agreed. "I don't remember Jason's dad too well but he was a large man. His weight brought him down hard and the sapling pierced his skull, my father said, so—"

We turned left on High Street past the grade-school playground. Two hundred years earlier, this table-like area just short of the island's highest point had been home to Fort Sullivan's barracks, munitions storage, and parade areas.

"So the sharp stump went through-and-through," Ellie said. "That's what I heard my father saying that night. Must've been."

The mental picture her words summoned up was so grisly, I understood now why she'd repressed it. But it explained a lot.

"And that," I said, "would've obliterated the bullet's entry and exit holes." We started downhill.

"There'd be nothing to use against Jason even if they wanted to," I went on. "So maybe it wasn't exactly a complete cover-up. More like a judgment call."

Still . . . "But how'd they decide he even might've been shot in the back of the head, then? Did your dad talk about that?"

"Not directly. But from what I recall it was something about the bullet still being in there."

So the medical examiner might've guessed from its position, but couldn't have known for sure; once a bullet gets in a skull, it tends to bounce around in there before coming to a halt. My ex-husband the brain surgeon used to talk about it.

"Gosh, isn't that strange?" Ellie's voice was a little dreamy-sounding. "I remember being in my bed, and my dad and mother talking downstairs. All the gory details...but when I woke up the next morning, it felt like a bad dream."

She shook her head wonderingly. "So I just forgot it. And I haven't thought about it again. Not once in all those years."

"And Jason himself?" I asked. "What'd he have to say about it all back then? Anything more?"

"I don't know. He was much younger than me, of course. So if he did say anything, I wouldn't have heard it. You know how kids are at that age, they think of the littler ones as babies."

We continued downhill past Town Hall, the Methodist church, the bank on the corner, and the funeral home, where the masses of yellow roses climbing the old south wall glowed in the noonday sun. As we crossed Boynton Street, a small private plane powered up out of the Quoddy airfield, barely a mile distant.

It flew overhead, dipping its wings in a wigwag farewell, then soared on out over the ocean, hop-scotching the clouds to who knew where. "Anyway," I told Ellie, "we've gotten what we wanted. Two new suspects to wave under DiMaio's nose."

"Two?"

"Ann Talbert," I reminded her. "You said yourself she was in Orono the night Horace died. And she has been pretty wacko about the book. *And* she knew he had it."

"Oh. Right. I guess in my mind Jason's kind of replaced her. After what we've heard, I really *wouldn't* rule out his clobbering Horace and stealing the book for Merkle, if Merkle asked him to."

Especially, she meant, now that we knew it might not've been the kid's first outing in the bloodletting department.

"Bert might be some kind of a father figure to him?" I theorized.

"Maybe," Ellie said slowly. "Why *would* Bert want your old book, though? Or why would DiMaio think he did?"

As we approached the house, I spotted my own father going in the back door ahead of us, so probably by the time we got there Bella would be in rare form again, too.

I sighed at the thought of it. "Ellie," I said, "I have no idea."

At all the thoughts, actually: bathroom, Bella, book. Fear over Sam's fresh try at substance-abuse recovery; hope that this time he would make it.

Plus pure reluctance at the party plan, so unattractive and inescapable.

And so imminent. Merrie hadn't seemed to warm up to me during our visit to her, either.

To the contrary.

"I'll stop at the motel on my way home and talk to DiMaio, shall I?" Ellie paused at the end of the sidewalk. "We'll need to let him know enough of what we're thinking to keep him from doing anything hasty."

Yeah, like killing Merkle. "And then I'll be back," she promised.

"Really?" It was lunchtime, and when George was on morning duty with Leonora, Ellie took charge of the afternoons.

She beamed at me, the troubled memories vanishing from her face. "Of course. George and I traded times so I can be here for the party. You didn't think I'd make you do it alone, did you?"

Actually, I had.

"How about we invite Dave out for dinner tonight, too? They're having fireworks offshore, we can watch them from the dock at the Lime Tree," she added. "After all the party stuff Bella won't want to cook. And it'll give us another chance to find out what he's up to."

"Good idea," I replied distractedly. The Lime Tree restaurant overlooked the bay and the food was excellent. From inside the house came the voices of Bella and my father.

Not shouting, exactly. But it didn't sound friendly. "Only what if Dave's not at the motel?" I asked.

Ellie was already striding away. "I'll find him," she called over her shoulder as, inside, a door slammed and a plate shattered.

I knew the sounds well from back when my first husband was around. So at the foot of the porch steps I reminded myself: *This is my place. I set the rules here. And if people think they can run around smashing plates in it, they are about to learn differently.*

Then, straightening myself into the same sort of bravely ridiculous posture that I imagined Napoleon must've hoped would do him any good at Waterloo, I marched inside.

Chapter 11

*Cleaning and reorganizing
your tools and supplies is
a worthy home-repair
job all by itself.*
—Tiptree's Tips

I could tell from the stiffness of my dad's flannel-shirted
shoulders as he stomped off down the hall that he didn't want to
talk about what had just happened between him and Bella.

And when he didn't want to talk, his jaw might as well have
been wired shut. So I really had no choice but to begin torturing
Bella about it, instead.

"Oh, yes, you are," I told her in the kitchen about five minutes later. She'd used up most of those minutes insisting she wouldn't discuss it, either.

But Bella never aired anything personal unless I dragged it out of her. And maybe I was wrong, but I suspected that right now she desperately wanted me to.

"You most certainly are going to talk," I said. "To me, immediately. Because if you don't, I've got big news for you: you're fired."

The minute the words were out of my mouth, I wanted to cram them back in again. But too late; Bella's big, green eyes stared at me in horror.

"You wouldn't," she breathed.

"I said it, I meant it, I'm here to represent it," I shot back rashly. Because that was the other thing about her; from somewhere or another she'd gotten the goofy idea that I was smart, determined, and fearless.

That I would stick to my guns. And if I didn't have to fire her, I *wanted* her thinking so, or she would lose all respect for me. After that, the next time I asked her not to scrub out the insides of an old fireplace flue with toothpaste she would do it anyway, with minty-fresh but old-brick-destroying results.

And my father's recent remarks about support beams notwithstanding, I strongly believed the chimneys held up my old house in several important places. The roof, for instance. And all four of the sides.

Bella hesitated, in case I might take the threat back. Meanwhile I calculated the size of the raise I'd be forced to offer if I did.

"Oh, all right," she exhaled at last, bending to pick up pieces of broken plate.

Sorrowfully, she traced the gold rim of a shard with her callused fingertip. "We could glue it back together." Her voice was uncharacteristically soft. "Or I could."

Even if we found all the pieces, I doubted anyone could reassemble them. It was one of the set that had been in the house when Sam and I moved in here, bone china with a scalloped edge and a delicate, hand-painted floral design.

"No. Never mind, just put them in the trash, all right?" I said. "It doesn't matter. Because you know what, Bella?"

Her shoulders sagged. Cautiously, I stepped nearer, slipped a tentative arm around her waist.

To my surprise, she didn't resist. "Things break," I told her simply. "You know, sometimes, they just..."

Her fingers opened; the china shard dropped to the floor and broke into four more pieces, two slowly spinning clockwise and two of them counterclockwise.

We stared down at them in silence together as a door slammed angrily upstairs, followed by a curse.

And then Bella Diamond, the toughest, funniest, most damn-the-torpedoes-and-full-speed-ahead downeast Maine housekeeper you could ever want to meet....

Bella wept.

Right up until nearly modern times, some children in Eastport were sardine-cannery workers as soon as they grew tall enough to stand at a cutting table, whacking the heads and tails off the shiny creatures with knives that often took along a small thumb or finger.

Old photographs from the turn of the century show the boys in short pants and suspenders, boots, and caps. The girls wore dresses, buttoned shoes, and black stockings. Their small hands were often already scarred or freshly missing a digit.

By the time I found Eastport, most of those children had lived long lives and were in their graves. But sitting with Bella always made me think of them, somehow.

"He won't give it up," she told me. "He wants to get married, and he wants to get married *now*. And there's," she finished bleakly, "an end to it. He wants what he wants."

We were stealing a moment on the front steps of her house, a tiny wooden cottage that had once been a cannery-worker's shack a few streets uphill from the ferry landing. Each of us was eating a jelly doughnut from Bella's cupboard and drinking coffee that we had bought on our way over here.

I coughed a doughnut crumb. "You're kidding," I said. Then, realizing this wasn't very tactful, "I mean, not that he wouldn't want to . . . that is, I don't see *why* he shouldn't . . ."

"I do," she said, without the slightest bit of rancor.

Because when it came to self-pity, her attitude was the same as that of those children at the cutting table: it didn't stop the bleeding and you had to keep working anyway.

So you might as well get on with it. She bit half the jelly out of the doughnut, washed it down with some coffee, then set the cup on the step.

"I ain't no oil painting," she pronounced. "Man'd have to be blind not to see that."

But oil paintings don't move, and breathe, and exert their special, individual will upon the world. They don't laugh.

Or weep. Upon reflection I understood exactly why my father wanted to marry Bella Diamond.

But behind us her tiny house sat snugly self-contained, full of her mystery novels and puzzle books, her *TV Guide* marked with the programs she liked, her robe and slippers in their accustomed places and her clean, white teacup on the drainboard.

Once she stopped weeping, I'd invited her out to dinner with us tonight and she'd accepted, but didn't want to go in what she was wearing. She'd offered to let me use her shower, while she changed too, so I'd brought my bath bag and fresh clothes of my own.

Okay, I thought, so when the ladies arrived maybe I wouldn't be Princess Diana. But at least I wouldn't reek.

Too bad that when we arrived, we found that today the water company was flushing the mains on *this* side of town, so that what came out of Bella's tap turned out to be even dirtier than I was.

Which by now was really saying something. "Why," Bella asked plaintively, "ain't things good enough the way they are? Whyever does your father want to try changing what's already workin'?'"

Sun poured through the blackish leaves of the copper beeches. A breeze sprang up, laden with the tantalizing fragrance of meat grilling at Rosie's hot dog stand on the breakwater.

"I live alone and like it," she declared. "I ain't too old, but I am way too selfish an' set in my ways to go turning my life into a social-studies experiment."

As I listened, a wave of impatience at my dad washed over me. You'd think a person who knew how to build a stone wall would know better than to hurl himself headfirst into one.

But apparently not. "Missus," Bella said, "if he don't let up, you won't need to fire me. I'll have to go on my own. I ain't had such good work in I don't know when, but—"

"Bella, think, now. Are you sure it's only because you're used to living alone that you don't want to do it?"

She glared at me. "Now don't *you* start in. I'm just telling you that I ain't..."

Her tone was fierce and her look implacable. But I refused to back down because doing without Bella was one thing.

But being without her... "I'm not starting in," I said. "Obviously you don't have to marry him if you don't want to."

Seeing it again only reinforced my earlier certainty that two adults couldn't live in her house comfortably, and my dad's was not just small; it was also downright primitive. And my place always seemed to be so full of people she would end up with no privacy at all if she married him.

And that was the heart of her objection, I decided, watching a little red sports car whiz by. It was the same red Mazda Miata I'd seen on Key Street around the time DiMaio arrived, I realized distantly, with the same attractive blonde woman driving it.

Bella reached out a bony hand to help me up, and maybe it

was my imagination but I thought she gripped mine a bit longer than necessary before she let go.

"Thank you," I said.

"You're welcome," she replied, and after that we went back together to my house and went on with our day.

Because quite a lot had changed around here since Eastport children stood at the fish-cutting tables. But one thing hadn't:

Get on with it.

When we got home the old tub still squatted at the top of the stairs. And it wouldn't do. Especially after the antique elegance of Merrie Fargeorge's place, it simply wouldn't do to have the tub there when the ladies came. So I was delighted when my dad came in behind me, lugging a coil of rope.

Enormous rope; the kind of stuff they tied the tugboats up with. I gazed happily at it.

"I kept thinking I needed a chain," he said. "But getting the chain to slide smoothly over the edge of the roof turned out to be a problem."

I followed him down the hall. "I can see you're making some progress. Do you want to clue me in on what you plan to . . ."

"But *then* I realized if I nail sheet metal to the edge of the roof," he continued, "and use line instead of chain 'cause it's smoother . . ."

Nimbly he climbed the stairs. But near the landing he paused.

"Hmm," he said, frowning. "You know, though, when I planned this all out I forgot one other thing."

"You mean the part about it being stuck."

He'd already taken the chain off, and in just the little while since then the heavy tub had dug a sizable dent into the plaster. It had also pushed the banister post out of line more than an inch.

"But that's what you're going to do first, right?" I said. "Haul it back up again, pull the bathroom window out, and—"

Lower it, somehow. Winch it out, or something. He scratched his jaw thoughtfully until a new idea occurred to him and he swung into action once more.

"Come on up here," he instructed, limberly traversing the obstacle while waving at the rope coil. "Haul that into the bathroom. Put it under the window."

I hopped in and out, too—bleaghhh—and did as he asked. Coiled up, the rope was heavy enough to sink a battleship; when I staggered back he'd passed its free end through the drain hole, then tied it in a neat bowline.

"Now what?" I asked, beginning to feel hopeful again.

Maybe I really would get the tub out of here before the party. Heck, there was still an hour to go before it began. And once the tub was out, there was a chance of starting in on the bathroom renewal, possibly by tonight.

Walls and floor, window, washstand, maybe even a baseboard heating pipe instead of a radiator...A little song began trilling in my heart.

But it trailed off sourly as I thought of all that had to come before: cups, glasses, cake, little sandwiches, and punch made with ginger ale and rainbow sherbet. The punch would be creamy, foamy, and as thirst-quenching as lukewarm sugar water usually is, but it was expected so we were having it.

"Next step, I tack the sheet metal to the porch roof," my dad said. "But for now I'll just make the line fast to my truck. So if the banister breaks or the wall fractures—"

He waved at the tub again. "—I don't have to worry about it sliding downstairs and killing someone, today or tomorrow."

Today or...oh, no. "But, Dad, you've got it all tied up now. Why not just haul it..."

Back into the bathroom, and out into the huge metal embrace of whatever enormous machine you plan to borrow or rent, I would've finished. But he was already following the line into the bathroom. There he hoisted the coil, then threw it out the window.

A huge thud rose from the yard below. He hurried downstairs again with me following behind, sputtering like the little engine that couldn't.

In the driveway he looped the line around his trailer hitch. "There," he said. "When I get back the day after tomorrow—"

"The day *after*...!" I yelped in dismay.

He ruffled my hair. "Patience, Grasshopper," he intoned.

Phooey. I didn't know which I disliked more, that phrase or the gesture that went with it.

"Rome wasn't unbuilt in a day, you know," he added.

Double phooey. But there was no sense arguing with him.

"Fine," I gave in. "Wherever you're going I suggest you start going there. Much more of that thing on the stairs and I won't answer for the kind of mood I'll be in when you get back." I caught the truck keys he tossed to me. "Where do you have to be that's so important, anyway?"

"Augusta. To get my ID papers straightened out."

When he was on the run all those years after my mother died, he'd had plenty of IDs; just none that really belonged to him.

"I'm taking the bus," he added. "So I can leave the bathtub tied."

I thought about why he might need legitimate ID. Probably it wasn't so he could start paying taxes. "Listen, Dad, I don't know if you've noticed, but Bella doesn't want to—"

Marry you.

He frowned. "Yeah. I know." Then: "Don't touch that line," he ordered. "Unless you need to move the truck, which by the way you are also not to do unless it's an emergency."

Personally I thought a bathtub on the stairs qualified as an emergency, and more so by the minute. "If you have to, untie the line first, and get Wade to tie it again for you afterward," he cautioned.

In a pig's eye. I could tie knots. Maybe not as well as Wade, but...

"See ya," he finished, and strode off downhill toward Water

Street, where within a block or so he would meet someone headed for the bus stop on the mainland, and catch a lift.

"See ya," I repeated, lamely. Then I went back inside where I immediately began plotting how to get rid of the old tub before he returned. It would, I thought, be a surprise.

But as it turned out I was the one who got one.

Ellie walked into the yard as I was starting up the ladder leaning against the back porch. "Hold on to these, will you?" I said, gesturing at the ladder's legs.

What I intended shouldn't take long, I'd told myself while I was still in the preparatory stages: *Line untied from the trailer hitch? Check. Ladder out of the cellar and up against the porch roof? Check.*

But then came the part about me going up the ladder, check, and now I was in my most unfavorite position; i.e., anywhere more than a foot off the ground and with nothing to hold on to because my hands were full.

"But...oh, all right. Are you *sure* you should...?" She came over obediently and gripped the ladder, steadying it.

"Yes," I said. "I am. It's my dad's idea. I'm going forward with the execution, that's all."

"Forgive me for thinking that's a really unfortunate choice of words," Ellie replied.

But she went on holding the ladder steady while I climbed another step and then another. "Hurry up," she said. "Because I don't like this, Jake, I really do not..."

My head rose above gutter level, which is usually about the time when *up* and *down* start feeling interchangeable to me. A crow flapped by, shot me a beady look of disdain, and cawed mockingly.

Okay, now: *Hammer. Nails and sheet metal. Confidence level way out of proportion to my actual experience...*

Well, heck, if I worried about that I'd never have bought the house in the first place. And anyway, how hard could it be to...

"Yikes!" I shoved the hammer under my arm and grabbed the gutter with both hands. "Ellie, what are you—?"

"Sorry. My nose itched." She smiled up at me. "You okay?"

"Other than so scared that I can feel my heart beating in my eyebrows? Fine," I said irritably. "Don't let go again."

The rope needed to come down over the edge of the porch roof just about...there. Carefully I positioned the rectangle of sheet metal atop the shingles where it would serve as a sort of edge guard; otherwise I could imagine the rope with the bathtub's weight on it sawing right through the roof.

I'd punched holes in the sheet metal first with a hammer and nail, too, to make it easier to pound the roofing nails through it. Next with some six-inch PVC pipe meant for a drainage-ditch—in the spring, my driveway resembles an irrigation canal—I made a channel for the line to run in, so it wouldn't slip off the roof's edge at an inopportune moment.

Such as for instance *any* moment; I used the drain holes in the pipe to nail it over the sheet metal. Finally Ellie passed the rope's end up to me—a feat all in itself—and I stood on tiptoe to get it through the pipe's far end.

This, however, turned out to mean crawling out onto the porch roof. "Jake," Ellie warned, "maybe you'd better...Oh!"

Because just then that crow dove at me, grazing my hair with his clawed feet while shouting something unpleasant in crow-ese. Something like *Die, scummy invader of my sky territory!*

Or possibly just *Oops, I thought your head was a nest.*

Either way, I lost my grip. My right hand went one direction, my left hand the other, and the ladder went abruptly from under my feet.

"Ellie!" I cried as the condition of the fasteners holding the gutter to the roof's edge grew interesting. You hardly ever think of gutters as holding much up but rainwater and leaves....

But now one held me. My feet dangled uselessly as my grip on the gutter loosened; also, the gutter was made of aluminum, I suddenly recalled as the thing began bending inexorably.

"Ellie!" I whispered. Nails pulled out one after the other: *cree-e-eak!*

"Here," Ellie said, a dozen feet below me. The ladder clanked as she lifted it.

My sneaker toes touched a ladder rung. But straightening a ladder while someone is already standing on it—or trying to stand on it—is a pretty good trick, too, so it was still quite a while before I reached solid ground again, heart thudding.

"There." Ellie tactfully ignored the fact that I had nearly killed us both. The ladder had missed her head by inches when it fell, and the hammer, when I dropped it, by not much more.

"Now, if you want my opinion," she went on briskly...

I didn't. And I was running out of time.

Inside, the tub still loomed on the stairs, wedged in on one side by a big oaken banister post and on the other side by the cracked plaster.

"What," Ellie inquired sternly, "are you thinking?"

"You'll see," I told her just as Sam came in carrying more laundry.

"Listen," I said to him, "I need you to crawl out on the porch roof. I'll toss you the end of a line, and you feed it through the pipe, okay?"

Years of messing about in sailboats had made Sam so agile, if you saw him climbing around in the rigging of one, you'd just think the local circus had lost its chimpanzee.

Cooperatively, my son put down the laundry, went upstairs, and stuck a leg out the window. I ran outside again. There I grabbed the line from where it had fallen with the hammer and the ladder.

"Okay," I called, tossing it up. Sam caught it acrobatically on the first try and fed it easily through the PVC pipe.

"Want me to tie that for you, too?" he offered, waving at the truck.

"No, thanks. I was the one who taught you how to tie your shoes, remember?"

He shrugged. "Whatever you say."

Then he returned to filling my washing machine with the world's smallest laundry load. Once upon a time, in his opinion, if you could close the machine without standing on it, it wasn't full. But not anymore; caution was his watchword these days even in trivial matters.

Ellie surveyed the scene. "This looks risky."

"Oh, come on. What could be risky about it? It's not as if anyone has to go back up a ladder."

The on-the-roof portion of the program was over. I threw a couple of half hitches confidently onto the towing bar.

"Drat," I said. "We can't pull the tub up; it's just too heavy. Maybe heavy enough to snap even that big rope."

Ellie's expression said the half hitches ought to be thrown around *me*. I had a sudden inspiration. "We can lower it down, though," I said. "Slowly."

"How? It's still stuck in the..."

Stairway. Yes. "If we unstick it enough to get it around the corner and aimed down the stairs," I explained, "we could use the truck to ease it the rest of the way."

"Hmm." Ellie was frowning. "By backing the truck toward the house? Well, maybe. But I still think—"

The back door slammed: Sam, who didn't like sitting around waiting for the washer.

"No more thinking. It's time for action," I declared.

Which was probably just one of the many incredibly stupid things I said that day.

But it was a doozy.

.   .   .

Another fifteen minutes and I'd bashed out a piece of the stairway wall, loosening the tub from the dented place where it was trapped against plaster and lath. Next, Ellie helped check the line tied to my father's truck, and made sure also that it was fastened securely through the tub's plug hole and tied there with more half hitches.

"I don't know about this, Jake," she said for the hundredth time.

"I do," I retorted. "All I need now is to get the banister post loose and pull it out."

Banisters are built to be sturdy. But luckily this one was put together originally like a big wooden puzzle. Once I removed the decorative wooden ball atop the first post and lifted off a length of railing by tapping it from below with a padded hammer, a whole section came out easily, nearly freeing the other side of the tub.

"Do you think one of us should go out and make the line taut before you take the final post away?" Ellie asked. "Because right now it's the only thing holding the..."

Tub up.

"Hmm. Good idea." Even though I thought the tub's weight would keep it from moving until I gave it a hard shove, we might as well get all the preparations over with in advance.

Or so I told myself optimistically. "You go pull the truck forward," I said.

When she had the truck positioned properly so the line was nearly-but-not-quite taut, I'd lean on it. My weight plus the little bit of slack and the broken-out section of plaster would surely give the tub enough room and reason enough to turn on the landing, aligning itself with the stairs.

And then we could back the truck up, lowering the tub in a controlled manner. Of course, I'd still need to get someone to haul it the *rest* of the way outside....

But the worst would be over. Right, sure it would...So anyway, Ellie started the truck while I perched in the window, ready to shout.

That was when I noticed the next problem: a lot of extra rope. A good thick line that long was expensive, so my dad hadn't wanted to cut it. And I'd tied it a little differently than he had; i.e., at the end instead of somewhere in the middle. As a result, yards and yards of it remained when the truck reached the end of the driveway.

Sam returned, sauntering along the sidewalk, and saw what was happening. Amiably he began directing traffic: three cars and a motorcycle cruised by, their drivers gaping at the truck, the line tied to the back of it, and me in the window.

The truck inched forward; so far, so good. But then a sound came from the hall: a faint, crisp *snap!* like someone breaking a toothpick.

A bad thought hit me. The post I'd left in place couldn't be breaking, though. It was so sturdy, there was no *reason* for it to be . . .

Snap! Pop! And then, much to my horror, *CRR-A-A-ACCKK!*

"Ellie!" I yelled out the window. Because if the line didn't get pulled taut right this minute . . . *"Go!"*

Later she insisted she'd heard me shouting "No!" and in response stopped the truck, hauled the emergency brake on, then jumped out to see what was wrong.

I ran for the hall; there were at least thirty feet of loose rope left, more than enough to—

BANG! The banister post broke off violently and flew across the hall. Suddenly freed, the tub swiveled hard on the carpeted step and began slanting downward.

Now it was aimed the way I wanted it, but *my* plan included a restraining force: the rope, which was still slack. Slowly, the tub began sliding, first one inch.

Then two. But it would be all right, I told myself; the tub would crash all the rest of the way down, probably, but I could repair whatever. . . .

And then I saw them: two dogs grinning up at me, one red

and one black, both clearly wondering eagerly what new game this was, and how best they could manage to get in on it.

"Git! Go! Go on now, both of you, get out of—"

"Jake?" Ellie called through the back door.

The tub slid six inches. The animals watched with the kind of keen, unknowing fascination that probably first gave rise to the term *dumb dog*.

And that would soon give rise to the phrase *dead dogs*.

Panicked, I jumped into the tub—bad move, since my weight made it even more unstable—and then out, intending to scramble downstairs, grab the dogs, and shove them out of the way.

But before I could do any of that, the tub itself let go.

I hurtled downstairs ahead of it as the damned thing *raced* at me: *thud-thud-thud-thud*, popping balusters out one after another.

"Jake!" Ellie shouted. "Get—"

Out of the way: You betcha. Six steps left; I soared over them in a Flying Wallenda leap, seized two dog collars in one mighty grab of my left hand and the newel post with my right, and swung all three of us wildly around the corner into the dining room, where the dogs kept going and I fell down.

The tub continued thudding. With the kind of momentum it had, it was going to blast right through the front wall and out onto the lawn.

"Oof!" said Ellie from behind a recliner in the parlor.

I thought she was hiding, which to me made a tremendous amount of sense; just then if I could have gotten into a bomb shelter, I would have.

But then the *recliner* moved. Meanwhile and without any conscious intention on my part at all, my brain began racing through a series of diagnostic routines:

Dogs safe? Check. Move arms and legs? Check. Ellie . . . ?

"Ellie!" She finished shoving the recliner to the foot of the stairs as the tub paused.

For the space of a breath, I even thought the pause might be permanent.

But then it charged again: *thudthudTHUD!!!*

"Ellie..." I flew at her, crossing the tub's path to seize her shoulders; the two of us hurtled past the foot of the stairs with the massive iron thing racing at us, so close now that I could smell the *kapow!* on its breath.

We hit the parlor rug just as the bathtub crashed into the recliner, shoving it all the way across the front hall. The recliner slammed into the front door with a sound like an accordion being dropped off a building; then something deep inside it broke with a loud, metallic *sproing!*

The footrest popped out. I held my breath, looked for the dogs. Both of them obviously thought this was the best exercise they'd ever had, and could we do it again?

"Good...heavens," murmured Ellie, checking herself for injuries and—miraculously—not finding any.

Blinking, Sam peered in. His eyes studied me, the dogs, Ellie, the recliner, the tub, and the stairs, which looked like a meteor had crashed into them. The front door had (a) a jagged hole the size of a bathtub in it, and (b) a bathtub in it.

"I see you got the tub downstairs," he said mildly. "Way to go, Mom."

He bit into the apple he was holding, chewed, swallowed. "I hate to bother you when you're busy, but I can't find Bella. Do you have any more laundry detergent?"

"There was some in the bed of my pickup," said my father.

I hadn't even heard him come in, no doubt because I was busy listening to the equivalent of an atomic bomb going off in my home.

He eyed the destruction. "I had a feeling I shouldn't leave you alone," he remarked. Then: "Where *is* Bella, anyway?"

It struck me that I hadn't seen her for a while, either, and that

she surely would have come running if she'd heard what was going on.

"I don't know," I said. "She was right here a little while ago.
Anyway, I thought you were—"

He shook his head. "Changed my mind. First things first."

Opening his hand he revealed a small gold object: a ring.

"I'll find her," he said. And it was only by means of extreme
daughterly begging that I persuaded him to haul the old tub the
rest of the way out the broken front door, instead.

That took care of the immediate present. And I'd be able to
keep Bella busy and my father out of her way for the rest of the
day, I was sure of it. But I could see from his look of calm purpose
that the reprieve was temporary.

Sooner or later, we were in for an explosion bigger than the
one I'd just made.

And I didn't have the faintest idea what to do about it.

For sheer domestic misery, nothing quite beats bathing in a
washtub. A big washtub, but still.

And it didn't help any that the only person I wanted pouring
tepid water over me while I stood naked and shivering had already gone to work. The minute he'd heard about the party, in
fact, Wade had made sure he would be nowhere nearby at any
time during the whole day.

He loved me, he'd said.

But a man had his limits. So I poured the water over myself.

Also, by now the house was full of people—Bella, the Dawtons,
who'd returned to be kitchen staff for the event, and who knew
who else coming in unannounced from the library or the school
board or the PTA, with yet another tray of party refreshments.

As a result, it was not only a washtub I bathed in; it was
a washtub in the cellar, with Bella delivering kettles at regular

intervals. Although not regular enough; the best, most efficient way to cool heated water quickly, I learned that afternoon to my sorrow, is to pour it into a washtub.

At least there was a drain in the cellar floor, put there by my father right after the pipe burst and washed the old book out. I'd thought he might have trouble finding an outflow pipe downhill enough to hook the drain to, seeing as the cellar floor was considerably below ground level and the drain had to be lower than that.

Because of gravity, and so on. But as it turned out, the water main that had burst needed afterward to be dug up all the way to the street. And when the backhoe opened the trench, the sewer pipe turned out to be there, too, only about a foot deeper.

So he'd put the drain in; now I watched soapy water swirl down it as I tried and failed to raise the kettle (a) high enough and (b) angled enough to (c) rinse the shampoo out of my hair without (d) spilling too much.

Also I was cold, wet, covered in goosebumps and bruises, and shivering so vigorously I could barely hold on to the kettle at all. If my teeth didn't quit chattering soon I'd be able to hire myself out as the accompanist to a flamenco dancer.

Now I understood why in the old days, people only did this kind of thing once a week whether they needed it or not. As far as I could tell, a bath in a washtub was the surest way to catch your death short of actually injecting yourself with pneumonia germs.

But it was still better than going upstairs. From the patter of feet above my head, it was obvious that the party preparations were accelerating and that the ladies would soon be arriving.

I poured another kettle over my head and shivered.

Bert Merkle grinned knowingly at Dave DiMaio.

Standing at the end of the Eastport IGA checkout counter

while Merkle's purchases were totaled up and bagged, Dave gazed expressionlessly back. He wasn't sure why, but now that he was actually here, his brooding fear of the other man had evaporated completely.

Although not his anger. He'd been following Merkle around most of the day, not bothering to try hiding his interest. For his part, Merkle seemed to accept Dave's dogged shadowing without protest.

He'd recognized Dave instantly, of course. And to Dave's relief there had been no fake surprise, insincere smile, or hideously false *Hey, how are ya?* from his old college classmate.

Only silence, and a long, somehow disconcerting look of calm gratification. It was as if Dave's sudden appearance early that morning outside his trailer was merely what Merkle had been expecting.

Horace used to say Bert Merkle had a nose for news, especially bad news.

Merkle paid the clerk. He lifted the two white plastic bags containing his groceries. Then to Dave's surprise, he turned and spoke: "Don't put it in the microwave."

Merkle gestured at Dave's own purchases, now being totaled by the cashier. They consisted of a roll of aluminum foil, an apple, some cookies, and two slices of already-baked pizza from the delicatessen.

"The aluminum foil," Bert warned. "Don't microwave it."

"Oh." Belatedly Dave realized: Merkle either knew or assumed Dave was staying at the Motel East. Also, that Merkle must be familiar with the rooms there, and the furnishings in them.

With the microwaves in the kitchenettes, specifically. The appliances were not allowed in the residences at the school; they drew too much power from the old wiring, some of which had not been updated in a long time.

A very long time, and Merkle would know that, too. Being a virtual outcast in his student days hadn't lessened his later interest in the place, as his infrequent but always well-informed notes to the alumni magazine made clear.

So Merkle might've reasoned Dave might not be familiar with the "no-metal" rule pertaining to microwaves.

Thus Merkle's remark made sense. It also gave Dave another hint that perhaps all might not quite be as he'd believed with regard to Merkle.

But it was what Merkle said next that astonished Dave. "Not to interrupt your vendetta," Bert continued matter-of-factly, "but there's a kid here in town you might want to meet."

Dave blinked. What new mischief was this?

"Difficult past, unpromising on the surface," Merkle went on. "But he has possibilities. Interests. In my humble opinion," he added.

He mentioned a name; then with an ironic little bow in Dave's direction as Dave paid for his things, Merkle proceeded to the parking lot, where he transferred his bags' contents to the rusty wire baskets mounted saddlebag-style on his bicycle.

It was an old red balloon-tired Schwinn with a flashlight taped to the front fender and a reflector tied with string to the seat-back. Merkle swung a leg over the bike, then paused again.

"How's the book hunt going?"

"What?" But of course Bert would know about that, too. Back at school Bert had always understood other people's motives, sometimes even before they fully understood them, themselves.

Now without waiting for a reply he finished mounting the bicycle and pedaled away slowly, his front wheel wobbling precariously. Dave got into his car and followed.

Bank, post office, library, gas station—the balloon tires had taken a squirt of air front and rear, Dave noted. Now, with his errands seemingly done, Merkle aimed the bike toward his home.

Driving behind, Dave stayed well back, slowing when Merkle

approached an intersection, careful not to give any excuse for complaint. For now he just wanted to know more about Merkle's routine.

If Merkle still had the old book—and Dave felt certain that Merkle did, that whatever his odd remarks might have meant, the book had been the reason for Horace's death—there would be time to find out.

That Bert might have winkled Dave's gun out of Jacobia Tiptree's cellar somehow was at least possible, Dave decided. More probable was the notion that she didn't want him to have the gun, and had come up with a story—however unbelievable—simply to avoid having to give it back to him. But whatever the reason, Dave now regarded his weaponless status as a stroke of luck.

With the gun in his possession, Dave might have done something hasty. Better to wait. To get, as Horace would've put it, the lay of the land.

Abruptly, Dave turned back toward the Motel East. Let Merkle wonder for a while where he might've gone, Dave thought.

In his room he arranged his groceries in the kitchenette, which besides the microwave contained a small refrigerator and a coffeemaker. A writing desk, color television, upholstered chairs, and a round kitchen-style dining table with two straight chairs completed the room's furnishings.

Dave ran a glass of water, took off his shoes, and lay down on the bed, letting his head fall back onto the pillow. Horace used to say you should take your comforts where you found them, however mundane. There would be slings and arrows to contend with eventually; no sense adding to them or hurrying them.

Turning his head toward the kitchenette area, Dave realized he'd begun to feel hungry and considered making a meal of the pizza. It was an idea that Horace, with his passion for good food, would surely have vetoed. But Horace was dead, and so could not be relied upon to object very strenuously.

Dave had another moment to think about this before the phone on the credenza rang. Wondering superstitiously whether his good old friend might be playing some sort of very Horace-like trick on him, he got up and answered.

Chapter 12

I should have known right from the start the identity of the sole possible culprit. She was, after all, the only one who could have gotten away with it.

Or if she didn't, she was the only one who could be certain of being forgiven. At first, though, there wasn't even any evidence that anything had been done.

It was a little over an hour after I'd completed my washtub experience. The party was in full swing, ladies laughing and chatting in my dining room and in the front parlor. The curtains Bella had lavished so much care on hung gorgeously in the freshly polished windows, asters and chrysanthemums from Ellie's garden bedecked the mantel and tables, and trays of scrumptious finger foods with delicate white paper doilies peeping from under them were on their way to being demolished.

There was even a selection of Mimi's pastries, or had been. I took the last one, a combination of crisp phyllo, ricotta, and raisins that could've lured cherubs down off the Sistine Chapel's ceiling, then peeked anxiously into the kitchen.

But there I needn't have worried, either. Bella and the Dawtons had the party's life-support system running like a fine machine: out with old coffee grounds, in with the new; napkins fresh where napkins used had briefly languished; and finger bowls.

They had actually put out finger bowls. Not only that, but Ellie had stitched up a floor-length banner whose appliqued blue-and-gold letters spelled out CONGRATULATIONS MERRIE FARGEORGE.

Once we managed to duct-tape its top edge to the top of the door frame, the banner even hid the hole the bathtub had made. We'd cobbled the banister back together well enough to camouflage that mess, too. A bouquet of tattered ostrich feathers nabbed from the lobby of the Eastport Hotel Museum blocked the stairs and hid the plaster disaster.

And to my vast relief, the ladies loved it. "Jacobia, how clever of you to keep this dining room the way it was in the old days," said Hermione Flamme.

Hermione was sixtyish, with short white hair curled in a tight permanent wave and a red-lipsticked smile over a gold front tooth. "So many people buy an old house and the first thing they do is something wrongheaded," she lamented.

"Add some utterly wrong modern element like a sunroom. Can you imagine? But you've kept it pure," she added enthusiastically.

"Thank you," I said, swallowing the last of my pastry, then looking around for a napkin and finding one practically at my fingertips; *Gracias,* Dawtons. "I'm glad you like it."

It did look good, I realized with a tingle of pride; the heavy green draperies with cream shades, the reddish-brown paint, and the cream trim formed a fitting backdrop for the cranberry-glass table lamps, cherry-veneer corner hutches, and half-round marquetry tables with tatted doilies on them that I'd found over the years at tag sales.

The restored tiled fireplace and carefully repaired maple floor looked decent, too, and for a wonder the discount-store Oriental rug I'd put down didn't shout *discount,* or not very loudly.

The effect overall was supposed to be that Thomas Jefferson or Abigail Adams might've dined here without feeling too out of place; well, except for the electric lights, of course. And as I looked at it now with people in it happily eating, drinking, and so-cializing, it seemed to me that after all I hadn't missed the mark too widely.

So I didn't tell Hermione that a couple of months from now, when winter days grew so short that they went by like lightning flashes and sun-deprivation put me in such a foul mood that I mostly just wanted to murder everyone, if somebody offered me a sunroom I'd be delighted to drive a bulldozer through the dining-room wall myself.

Instead, I wandered over to the mahogany breakfront where Izzy Hill and Bridey O'Dell, elderly twin sisters who'd taught dri-ver's education to Eastport fifteen-year-olds for forty years, were finishing off the last shrimp puffs.

"Oh! Jacobia. Such a triumph," said Bridey, munching. She and Izzy had brought oatmeal lace cookies, crisp, buttery-gold confections so light and tasty, they floated into your mouth. "You've positively outdone yourself," she added.

"And Merrie is delighted," agreed Isabelle, waving her teacup at the guest of honor, who caught her gesture and smiled at all three of us, dignified as a queen.

She'd arrived late for her own party, as royalty is wont to do. But she was making up for it now and clearly she was pleased. "And this is Key Street in the old days—" Her voice carried over the chatter. She'd brought along a shoebox full of snapshots and was showing them around.

"Oh, my," Ellie marveled, head bent over the photographs.

"Look at all the elm trees! It's so sad most of them are gone. And— look at that one! It's right outside this very window."

The ladies turned as one to reflect upon the absence of the massive old elms, one of which I gathered had been practically in my dining room.

"I never realized..." Ellie began; then her voice dissolved again in the pleasant general murmur.

She had, I thought, been right to make me do this. "And, Jacobia, we were just remarking on how well your household help has worked out, too," said Bridey.

As if to prove it, Jericho Dawton strode through the room gathering up used plates, dispensing fresh cream pitchers, and re- plenishing trays of goodies which by now looked as if locusts had been at them.

"Not," Izzy added with a meaningful glance at her sister, "like some."

But I didn't know what her meaningfulness meant, or even if I was supposed to. "Ones so bad people still talk about them?" I asked.

Bridey swallowed the shrimp puff. "You hadn't heard?"

Her tone suggested I must be the only one. "About the awful servant girl who came here, cast her spell on the oldest son, and the next thing anyone knew, everyone else in the family was—"

"Bridey," said Merrie Fargeorge, appearing at my elbow. Her tone was perhaps crisper than she'd intended; Izzy gasped.

"Now, dear," Merrie continued. *Dee-yah,* the Maine way of say- ing it. "You know perfectly well nobody needs to hear that foolish old story again."

Bridey coughed startledly and sipped tea as Merrie went on, "I'm right, aren't I?"

Her lips pressed together as she smiled at Isabelle, who I thought had actually gone a shade pale, and then at Bridey again.

"Besides, it's not fair you two girls spinning such romantic tales about that old house of yours. Not everyone's has such an interesting history, you know."

Isabelle blinked. Bridey looked mystified and a little put out. "But, Merrie, we weren't—"

"Never mind," Merrie interrupted. She placed a confiding hand on Bridey's arm. "And anyway you must let me express my gratitude to Jacobia, now, for her hospitality."

Then, turning to me: "My dear," she enthused, "it's positively splendid, and I thank you from the bottom of my heart."

"You're welcome," I replied. "It's been a real pleasure," I added, although in truth the emotion washing over me was more like relief. Meanwhile, Isabelle O'Dell's parchment cheeks had developed pink spots, and her eyes were like a couple of agates.

"So nice to see you again, Merrie," she uttered flatly, then turned away quickly with her sister, leaving me with the impression that although appearances must be kept up, there was no love lost between the twins and Merrie Fargeorge.

Some snub or insult long ago, I imagined, had never been healed, and after that I thought very little more of it as the party began winding down. Eventually I spotted Ellie by the punch bowl and made my way through the thinning crowd to her.

"Congratulations," she said, looking tired but happy. "You pulled it off."

"Not me. You, and everyone else." Because as she'd promised, when it came right down to it, I'd hardly had to do anything.

Besides, the ladies seemed remarkably ready to be pleased, if not when they first walked in, then very soon thereafter. Even now bursts of laughter, some of it quite raucous, came from the small groups lingering in the parlor and out in the hall.

Their faces, I decided, were quite naturally flushed with the pleasure of an old-fashioned afternoon social in one of the big old houses they all remembered from their childhoods.

"Maybe I'll even do it again," I said. "Because really, with enough help it wasn't even all that—"

"Mm-hmm. You should have some of this," said Ellie, raising her punch cup. The stuff looked even less appetizing now that all the sherbet had melted to pastel foam.

"Here, try some." She held the cup out to me.

I knew from experience that it would be like drinking cotton candy. "No, that's okay."

She pressed the cup into my hands. An odd smile curved her lips. "Try it," she insisted.

I sipped reluctantly. "There, are you—?"

Satisfied, I'd meant to finish. But instead I took another, larger sip of the punch, which was strangely tasty. In fact, I was sure I'd had the same thing once in a New York City bar, while waiting for a client who never showed up for our appointment.

Or for any other appointment ever again, for that matter, but that's another story.

Anyway, the punch was heavily spiked. White wine, I thought, or Champagne... Anxiety pierced me. "Sam's not here anywhere, is he?"

It would be just like him to glug down a whole glassful of the stuff without realizing what was in it.

Ellie shook her head. "George asked Sam to ride along with him today, to help amuse Lee while George buys tires."

By now most of the ladies had departed. But across the room the guest of honor, Merrie Fargeorge, still stood watching me.

When she had my attention, she dropped her gaze to the punch cup in her own hands, then raised it minutely in a toast.

And winked.

As it turned out, Dave DiMaio hadn't been at the motel when Ellie stopped by, so I ended up calling him myself and he agreed to come out for dinner with us that night.

"Did you tell him? About the other ones?" Ellie slid onto a stool beside me, in the downstairs cocktail lounge at the Lime Tree restaurant.

Other suspects besides Merkle, she meant. It was 6:05; Ellie had left the party a little early once she saw no further disaster arising, and the last lingering ladies had toddled home tipsily soon thereafter.

Dinner wasn't scheduled until 7:30. But by 5:25 I'd been on the phone with Ellie again, asking her to meet me early.

"Yes, I told him," I said.

The restaurant was on a wharf with a dock extending over the water behind it. From where I sat I could see all the way to the end of the dock, where Ellie's husband, George, was helping to load crates of explosives onto a barge.

Fireworks tonight; the Fourth of July had been too foggy. I took another sip of my dry martini, which the way I felt now I'd have preferred to have injected.

Into my brain. "I told DiMaio that *if* Horace was murdered, there are at least two other people besides Merkle who might've had a reason to do it," I said.

I ate my olive. "But now there's a new wrinkle."

Ellie ordered a Jameson on the rocks, sipped delicately. "And the wrinkle would be?"

"That Jason Riverton is dead," I uttered, and just barely resisted the strong impulse to order another drink.

Instead I thought about the sullen, black-clad kid who had been so unrewarding when we'd visited him, remembering his tiny room with its many books, his violent video games, and all the newspaper clippings about Horace Robotham's death.

And his poor mother, of course, blind and a little addled. I wondered what would happen to her, now. I wondered what Jason might've grown up into, what kind of man he might've been once the storms of adolescence had passed.

As now they never would. From the somber look on Ellie's face, I knew her thoughts were like mine.

"Bob Arnold phoned just after you left my house," I told her finally. "He wants us to meet him over there at the Rivertons' place in a few minutes."

That's why I'd called her and asked her to join me, so we could put our heads together in relative privacy before going to a murder scene.

Or I assumed it was one. So much for bathrooms, parties, marriage plans, or the lack of them. Or anything else that might possibly be on my own personal agenda, such as a few minutes' worth of peace and quiet, for heaven's sake.

"Everything all right with that?" I asked Ellie, nodding at the dock, where George was just now hefting the final crate of explosives. My dad was down there, too; he liked being around the bright stuff, as he called it, for old times' sake.

"Mmm," Ellie said, swallowing more Jamesons, turning what I'd said over in her mind. Because whatever was going on around here, it was clearly even worse than we'd thought.

Way worse. She finished her drink and got up; I followed. "So what happened?" she asked as we stepped outside. "To Jason?"

The parking lot was filling up fast as people gathered for the last big public event of the summer season. I spotted several of the women from the party being let off at the eatery's door, Merrie Fargeorge among them.

Catching sight of me, she waved gaily; I had indeed been rehabilitated in her eyes, it seemed, as Ellie had predicted.

"Bob says he thinks poison," I replied. "State cops are on their way, and the mobile crime lab, too, from Augusta. But since we were the last ones to see Jason alive—"

"Maybe," Ellie said.

"*Maybe* we were the last to see him," I amended. "Anyway, Bob wants us to look at his room, see what's different about it from when we were there. If anything."

Bob Arnold's aging Crown Vic with the blue-and-orange sunrise logo on the door panel idled in the Rivertons' driveway. Mrs. Riverton sat in the front seat with a blue cop sweater around her shoulders. Her sightless eyes stared ahead.

Inside, her son, Jason, lay sprawled on the scarred, gritty floor of the upstairs hall where it seemed he'd gone down all at once like a tree falling. As he collapsed, he'd reached out for the newel post at the top of the stairs, breaking it off at its base.

"I guess his mom heard him fall?" I asked, stepping over to him. I swallowed hard.

"Uh-huh." Bob hitched up his belt, moved his shoulders under his blue uniform shirt, uncomfortable in the dim, stuffy confines of the small house.

Through the doorway to Jason's room I could see his computer's screen saver flickering, white stars endlessly wheeling on an ocean of solid black. Walking into the cramped space, I accidentally bumped against the desk; the screen snapped instantly to a word-processing document.

Two big capital letters had been typed on it: DD.

Bob looked over my shoulder. "Initials. Maybe Dungeons and Dragons? I know he was big on the computer games all the young guys seem to like."

But I knew about computer games, too, because Sam had been a fan. "No. D and D is a role-playing game. Multiple players. Jason was into the kind called first-person shooters."

The irony of that hadn't struck me before. But after hearing what Merrie Fargeorge had said about him and his father, now it did. Because Jason really knew what it was like to be a first-person shooter, didn't he?

Or at least some people thought so. "What's the difference?" Bob asked.

"Isolation," I answered. At first Ellie had stayed outside with Mrs. Riverton, but now I heard her footsteps pass through the living room and go into the kitchen.

I scanned the musty chamber Jason had lived in. The science-fiction novels, reproductions of old weaponry, and empty cups in the stuffed-full wastebasket were no more enlightening than they'd been hours earlier.

But now there was a bottle of red wine, unopened, on the shelf among the weapons. And a new book stood on the shelf below that: *Poisons and Antidotes, A Practical Guide for Clinicians.*

A medical text. My ex-husband had owned a copy. I pointed it out to Bob.

"That why you think poison?" A half-empty forty-ounce Slurpee cup still stood by the computer.

Bob sighed. "It helps. Book on poison, kid falls dead."

He kept looking at Jason as if one of these times, he'd see something that would give him another chance to keep an eye on the youth, alive.

A better eye. "Besides, take a look at that cup. No, not the half-full one. The one in the trash, there."

There were a half-dozen of them. I pointed. "This one?"

He nodded. "Don't touch it," he added hastily as I reached for the big drink container. "Just look kind of sideways at it."

I angled my head obediently. "Anyway, what were you saying about games?" he asked as I bent to peer closer.

The clear-plastic domed top had come off. A rainbow-hued iridescence overlaid with green, the color of a soap bubble, lay on the drops of liquid remaining in the cup. I'd seen that iridescence before, when I lived in the city and especially in winter here in Eastport, in places where cars got parked regularly.

"You need other people," I said, "for a game of D and D. Jason played the kind of game where you're the only hero and you move through a maze, slaying dragons or zombies, or even other humans. And—perfect for Jason's personality—you do it alone."

Which he had. Died alone, too, with his blind mother right downstairs having no idea what was going on. As I straightened, I wondered what would happen to Mrs. Riverton now.

"That's antifreeze in the cup," I said.

Again, Bob nodded. When I asked where he thought it might have come from or if he thought the boy might've administered it to himself—don't, by the way; it's a lousy way to die—he shrugged.

"That's for the state guys to figure out," he said. "So what *do* you think the letters mean?"

The screen saver had popped back up; this time we left it alone. I shook my head. "Could be a lot of things."

The memory of Jason kept replaying itself in my mind: sullen speech, seemingly dull thoughts. More pronounced neurological symptoms such as delirium and hallucinations would've come later.

And after that, the heart and lungs would've failed. I knew because when Sam was a toddler, he tasted anything he got near. So in addition to clearing our apartment of poisons I'd read up on a laundry list of harmful substances, from arsenic to zeuterium.

So why had I missed the signs in Jason? Because his unlovely appearance and general air of being a sullen numbskull had prejudiced me. Instead of clear warnings, I'd thought his symptoms were a normal part of his personality.

I should've made something of the difference between his apparent dull-wittedness and all those books in his shelves. And the chess set.

But I hadn't. So now, I accused myself bitterly as I stared down at his body once more, who was the numbskull?

From downstairs came the sound of someone stepping on the kitchen garbage pail's lid-pedal, then letting it fall: *squeak-clink*.

Next, Ellie's footsteps crossed the living room again and started up the stairs toward us.

"I don't know if that particular cup was in the trash when I was here earlier," I told Bob Arnold.

From the way other cups were piled on top of the offending one, and from the rate at which Jason had seemed to empty them, I guessed the fatal beverage might've been consumed first thing that morning.

But a guess was all it was. The book and wine bottle hadn't been present earlier, I was certain. As Ellie reached the top of the stairs I bumped the desk again, deliberately; the computer screen snapped from black starscape to black letters once more.

"Huh," she said when she saw them. She shot a look at me.

Right; Dave DiMaio's initials. "There's something downstairs that you both might want to see," she told us.

The kitchen was a 1940s-ish room with an old red-and-black splatter-patterned linoleum floor. Dingy white curtains hung sadly at the windows; a round-shouldered old Frigidaire wheezed in the corner.

No clutter, though. Everything in its place, as it would have to be for a blind woman to function in it. This time between the curtains I spotted what I figured must be their car, behind the old shed; it was an aging blue subcompact that looked, as my dad would've put it, as if it had been ridden hard and put away wet, too many times.

Ellie stepped on the trash can's pedal again. Atop the eggshells, coffee grounds, and a white, *M*-emblazoned bag from Mimi's bakery lay a yellow quart-sized plastic jug.

NoFrost, the black-and-white label read. "Antifreeze," Bob Arnold said flatly.

Ellie looked thoughtful. "Who found him, anyway?"

"What kind of killer puts the murder weapon in the household trash?" Bob mused aloud.

"I don't know. But you can buy this stuff anywhere around

here. The IGA, the hardware store, or it could have been sitting in someone's garage since last winter," I said.

Ellie let the garbage-pail lid fall shut as Bob spoke again. "I found him. His mom kept calling upstairs to him, didn't get an answer." He shook his head regretfully. "Scared to go find out what'd happened, she said. Pushed 911 on the speed-dial 'cause that's what she and Jason had agreed she would do, anytime she had a problem."

As we returned to the living room, two vehicles pulled in outside behind Bob's squad car: a blue Maine State Police sedan with a blue light bar on the roof and an oversized radio wand curved over the chassis, and the big white boxy Mobile Crime Lab van from Augusta. Ellie went out to speak with Mrs. Riverton in case she might be frightened by the strangers.

I stayed with Bob. "I wonder what Bert Merkle will have to say about this."

He nodded grimly, readying himself to deal with the state guys, who would want to nitpick everything he'd done so far. "Ayuh. I wish now I'd pressed him harder on why he hung out with the kid. But you know, there was nothing illegal about it. And hell, the kid didn't have any other friends."

We moved toward the front door, the initials on the computer screen still clear in my mind's eye. Had Jason realized too late what was happening? Had he tried to leave a clue? Or had someone else left the initials, along with the wine and the poison handbook?

If the latter, then they were part of a cruel joke that at the moment only I was getting. Because back in the bad old days—right after my mother's death and long before my life with Sam and my ex-husband in the big city—I'd been a country kid up in the remote hills where people made still moonshine.

Often they made it in car radiators liberated from wrecks at the local junkyard. The risk was, it's difficult to get all the antifreeze out of the radiator.

Fortunately, booze itself is an effective antidote to antifreeze poisoning, so fatalities were rare. "How long's it take?" Bob asked.

"What? Oh." To die of ethylene glycol poisoning, he meant. Bob didn't know my childhood history; he just thought because my ex-husband had been a doctor I knew about medical things.

And in this instance I did. "It varies," I said. "Depends on the size of the dose versus the size of your body. Enough of it, you can be comatose in a few hours."

The stuff tasted sweet; you might not notice it in a soft drink, for example. Or a Slurpee.

"Early intervention, if you're young, healthy, and lucky, you've got a chance," I said. "Otherwise, not."

Bob nodded slowly, watching through the window as one of the state cops bent to the open passenger-side window of Bob's squad car, talking to Jason's mother. Introducing himself, I supposed; her hand moved to her lips in dismay.

"Well," Bob said glumly, "time to face the music. Do the old second-guess two-step."

As he went out, both state cops turned to him. I glanced at my watch; we weren't due to meet Dave at the Lime Tree for another half hour. So I went home, called him at the Motel East, and told him to show up in five minutes. Standing there in the phone alcove with the empty house shimmeringly silent around me, I didn't give him any time to argue or ask questions.

"Just be there," I said. When the phone rang again as I hung up, I thought it was him calling back to argue about it.

But it wasn't. "Jacobia?" It was Merrie Fargeorge and she sounded upset. "Jacobia, I just heard about Jason Riverton."

Of course she had. Eastport's jungle drums probably started beating two minutes after Bob's squad pulled up in front of the Riverton house.

"Yes," I began, "I'm afraid it's—"

"Is it true about his computer screen?" she interrupted. "The initials?"

I hesitated. "How did you know that, Merrie?"

She didn't miss a beat. "Ellie called just now to see if I could go over and help Mrs. Riverton, and of course I will. I'll bring her here to stay with me, if she wants, for as long as she needs to." She rushed on. "Ellie wanted to know if *I* knew anyone *Jason* knew who... oh, my, that's a complicated sentence, isn't it?"

But I understood what she meant.

"... with the initials *DD,* because that's what was on his computer. Written with a word-processing program, Ellie said?"

Well, that answered that. "Yes, Merrie, we wondered if maybe he wrote it and that it might—"

"No," she interrupted again, sharply. "He didn't."

"Beg pardon?" Cat Dancing yawned and twitched her tail from atop the refrigerator. In the parlor the dogs got up, turned in circles, and settled.

"Jacobia," Merrie said impatiently, "I don't know what went on over at that house today, but I can tell you that Jason didn't write any initials using any word-processing program."

"How can you be so sure?"

A huff of annoyance escaped her. "Well! If you knew him, you would be certain, too. I've tried for years to teach that boy to do anything more than play those awful shooting games. Jason was my student at the high school, you know, before I retired. And I've kept in touch since."

"But, Merrie, he might've..."

Learned on his own, I thought. Or Bert Merkle might've taught him.

"Might've, schmight've," she snapped. "I offered that young man a hundred dollars to learn word processing just well enough to bring the program up on the screen and type a few words. That was all I asked, and I told him scout's honor I'd hand the money to him immediately, cash on the barrelhead."

"And?"

"And he couldn't. Apparently he simply couldn't. And if he'd learned between then and now, don't you think he'd have come to me, to collect the reward? I'm telling you, Jacobia, whoever wrote those initials on his computer, it wasn't Jason."

Fascinating, I thought. The bottle, the book . . . and this.

"He couldn't," Merrie said. "He couldn't, and he didn't."

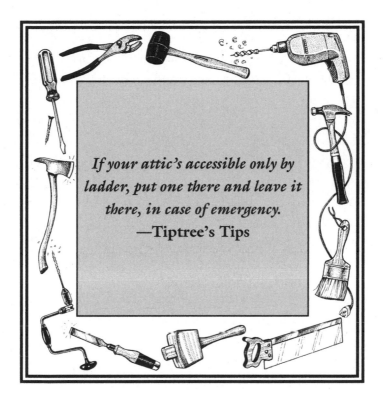

Chapter 13

If your attic's accessible only by ladder, put one there and leave it there, in case of emergency.
—Tiptree's Tips

W ait a minute," Dave DiMaio said indignantly. "You don't think I had anything to do with–"

He was in the bar when I got back to the Lime Tree. It was busier than before, ice cubes clinking and voices mingling in relaxed, end-of-the-day conversation.

I wasn't relaxed, and wasted no time ordering a drink, either. I just sat down and let him have it.

"You show up here, you're carrying a gun, you know where I put it, and then it goes missing. You've got a grudge against Merkle, and now Bert's young buddy, Jason Riverton, is dead. But not of a gunshot wound, which strikes me as a nice way to aim suspicion at someone else—"

He looked confused as I added more details: the antifreeze, the computer with Dave's initials on the screen. "Jason had a car. He idolized Merkle. He might have done what Merkle asked—drive to Orono, try to get my old book back from Horace. Maybe Merkle offered to pay him, or maybe Jason just did it out of some weird idea of friendship."

Or twisted hero worship. "Maybe things went wrong and Jason got mad, lost his temper. Or maybe that was the whole plan all along. Or maybe," I finished hotly, "you just think it was. But now you want revenge."

At the word *revenge,* he winced. "Look," he said, "I met the kid. Earlier today, in fact—Merkle told me about him, said he thought the kid might be right for our school."

Skepticism was a mild term for what my face expressed, in the mirror behind the bar.

"But how would I get antifreeze into his drink?" Dave demanded. "And if I did that somehow, why would I write my own initials on his computer?"

"I don't know." The bartender waved the Beefeater bottle at me and I nodded. "I don't know any of that."

When my drink arrived I took a sip. "But I do know you're angry, and you've been bird-dogging Bert Merkle, I'll bet, too, haven't you?"

That last part was just a guess. A guilty flush said my wild dart had found a sensitive target. It didn't explain how DiMaio could've connected Jason to Horace's death.

But that didn't mean it hadn't happened. He signaled for a refill on his own drink, a lemon soda.

No alcohol; I recalled the conversation I'd eavesdropped on the night before. "It doesn't bother you being in here?" I asked.

"What, a bar?" He smiled ruefully at his fresh glass. "No. Drinking with others has never been my particular difficulty."

As opposed, I guessed he meant, to drinking alone. "So what put you back in rehab?"

I figured I'd let him catch his breath, make him think I'd quit pushing him so hard. Then maybe he'd let drop some careless detail I could pounce on.

"Relapse is just a symptom of the disease," he said. "You get a flare-up, you deal with it and go on. Case closed."

Glancing over at the doorway I spotted the blonde woman I'd seen driving the red Miata earlier, now in a white cocktail dress and with her pale hair pulled into a topknot.

She saw me, too, and something in her eyes made me think she recognized me. It crossed my mind to wonder whether perhaps Bert Merkle wasn't the only one getting followed; that maybe I was. But her look at me had more of curiosity than malice in it, and a moment later she was gone.

"I picked a bad time to fall off the wagon, though," Dave went on ruefully. "Horace died the same night I went into the hospital."

A sports car started up outside. "I already knew Bert Merkle lived in Eastport," he continued. "We went to school together, back when Horace was teaching where I am now. I figured out what kind of guy Bert Merkle was pretty quick—so did everyone at the school—and I've kept tabs on him over the years." He frowned at his glass. "I'd warned Horace to watch out for Bert. I said he might try some sort of maneuver to get his hands on your book."

"Come on, it's been a while since you two were students. Why worry about what Bert's doing now? And why would he want my book, anyway?"

Not that he'd have been the only one with a yen for it. Eastport's most ambitious unpublished author, Ann Talbert, seemed pretty crazy to get her mitts wrapped around the thing also, I recalled. But at least she had a reason, however unrealistic it might seem to me.

"All right," Dave said reluctantly. "I'll tell you. But you're not going to believe a lot of it."

"I'll be the judge of that," I said. And then as if summoned by my thought Ann herself walked in, wearing skinny black jeans, a white silk shirt, and a good leather jacket. On her feet were a pair of high black-leather boots with toes so sharp you could've skewered a shish kebab on them. She'd exchanged her hoop earrings for bright tube-shaped danglers the size of bass-fishing lures, and her red lipstick for orange; otherwise, with that head of black hair gelled into daggerish spikes and eye makeup so exotic that it probably glowed in the dark, it was the same old Ann.

The words *I want* were practically tattooed on her forehead. She at least had manners enough to take a table by herself rather than intrude right away, but I knew by the way her eyes narrowed when she spotted me that I was getting a delayed sentence, not a pardon.

"Go on," I told Dave, "and don't dawdle, please." The rest of our group would be here soon, too.

He nodded. "I've already told you Horace and I used to go on book-hunting trips together. I'd just gotten out of college, and he was . . ."

"Never mind that. Cut to the chase." More people were coming in, gathering at the tables and ordering drinks.

"*Dangerous* old books," Dave said flatly. "Books like that, even fragments of them, are in high demand in certain circles. They contain information that people believe they might use. Or misuse, more to the point."

"You think that's why Bert wants it? The book's collectible, so it's valuable?"

DiMaio shook his head. "Bert's not a collector. I've known

him a long time, and I doubt he's changed much from the kind of fellow he was when we were in school."

"Why, then?" Tapping her foot impatiently, Ann Talbert sat drinking a wine cooler and waiting for her chance at me. The triumphant gleam in her eye didn't bode well.

"Merkle wants your book for the simplest of all reasons," Dave said. "He wants to use it himself."

Oh, please. A mental picture of Merkle dressed in wizard's garb, a pointy hat and a shiny robe with stars on it, maybe, rose in my mind.

"But that doesn't make sense," I objected. "It's just a list of names."

Written in blood, said an unpleasant voice in my head. *Names no one could possibly have known, back when the list was compiled.*

But someone had. "Right," said DiMaio. "But think about it; an object that can't exist. Yet it does. How could such a thing be created?"

He eyed me levelly, waiting for my answer as if he were back at his school once more and I were his student.

"Well," I replied slowly. "Not that I believe in any such thing myself, mind you..."

Oh, no? sniped the voice in my head. "...but *if* it isn't just a clever, complicated hoax...then I suppose it would have to be done by...magic?"

I wanted him to laugh at this idea, but I knew he wouldn't. And he didn't.

"Magic," he repeated. "And given that the ink in the book is exactly what you guessed it must be..."

Human blood. "...I'd say it must be black magic. Wouldn't you?

"So now imagine you're Merkle, who's spent his life trying not to cleanse the earth of evil stuff, but to gather it to himself and use it."

"Oh, please," I began, but his gesture stopped me.

"No, hear me out, Jake. Short of a spellbook that tells how to do it, what else would you want more than an object created by it?" His eyes held mine. "Drenched in the power you covet, *and* whose very existence proves that the power must be real?"

"Oh," I breathed, convinced—for a moment—that everything he'd said was true. No doubt he really was an excellent teacher.

But then I remembered the missing gun, Jason Riverton's poisoned body, and Horace Robotham's crushed skull, none of which had a single damned thing to do with magic.

They had to do with murder. "All right, you had me going there," I told him. "But your explanation fails to cover a few important details."

Dave looked impatient. "Look, I realize it sounds crazy. But I didn't take my gun back. I didn't kill the Riverton boy."

Sure, like he'd have admitted it to me. He went on, "I think there's a good chance Merkle took the book from Horace, with the boy's help or not. I think Bert has it, and he mustn't be allowed to—"

"Wrong," Ann Talbert interrupted. Apparently she'd gotten tired of waiting. "So, Jacobia," she went on, "I hear Jason Riverton's computer had initials typed on the screen. DD," she added to DiMaio, as if daring him to comment.

She was slurring her words a little; that wine cooler, or whatever it was, clearly wasn't her first drink of the evening.

"Good news travels fast," I replied. "Trust you to be tactful and sensitive about the whole thing, though."

Right then if I could have lifted Ann bodily and dumped her over the dock rail outside, I would have. But she didn't care.

"As for the book, I don't know who you were talking about but whoever it is, he doesn't have it. I do," she said.

She smirked, having dropped what she knew was a news bomb. "And," she declared with a wriggle of glee, "I intend to keep it."

. . .

Upstairs from the bar, the Lime Tree dining room was all pale polished wood, white tablecloths, and tall windows running along the water side of the building. Our table sported a lavish bunch of greenish-white hydrangeas as its centerpiece.

By the time we were all seated my complexion was probably pretty green, too, and Dave's was worse. "But..." he'd spluttered at Ann's announcement minutes earlier, then blurted: *"How?"*

"Someone mailed the book to me," she'd said. "Anonymously. Someone who must've known *I* deserve it, *I* appreciate it, *I–*"

"Ai-yi-yi," Ellie murmured to me now at the table; I'd told her about Ann's surprising claim, on our way upstairs.

With us were Bella, Wade, George Valentine, and my father, seated beside Bella Diamond despite her best efforts to shoo him away. At least they weren't openly squabbling; I guessed he must've postponed the ring-presenting project.

And Dave DiMaio was with us, of course, sitting on my left.

Sam had been invited, too, but said that until further notice, he wouldn't be coming to any places that served liquor.

"What's Ann mean, *make use of it?*" Ellie asked, still in a whisper.

Apparently in an effort to raise her annoyance quotient right up to the shriek level, Ann had taken a table near ours. So on top of everything else I got to watch soup getting spooned into her face.

"I don't know," I said. "She went through her usual spiel, all about how she's an *artist* so she has special *feelings* that we all need to *respect.* Only this time, she's loaded."

Ann started on a chef's salad; we had barely put our orders in. I gathered the waitstaff liked her as well as I did, and wanted to get rid of her quickly.

"I'll give her a feeling," I added grimly. "When I told her it belonged to me and she should return it, she practically stuck her tongue out at me."

"Hey. You okay?" Wade looked handsome in good gray slacks, pale-blue broadcloth shirt, and a blazer.

"Now that you're here, I am. Want to beat somebody up for me?"

"Anytime. Twice on Sundays." His mouth formed a quick kiss in my direction; then the waitress returned, and soon we were all eating and chatting cheerfully enough, under the circumstances.

But as the plates were being cleared I began noticing other faces, people leaving their tables and moving out onto the deck to await the fireworks. Bob Arnold was here with the pair of state cops I'd seen earlier; apparently their opinion of his first-on-scene work hadn't been as negative as he expected.

Ann Talbert still lurked nearby, too; any nearer and she could've reached out to take food off my plate. I sort of wished she would, so I could slap her hand away. And I spotted Merrie Fargeorge with two women whom I recognized as Eastport Historical Society members.

"Don't look now," Ellie said quietly. "Table for one, near the kitchen door."

"Criminy." Bert Merkle hunched protectively over his food as if fearing someone might steal it, casting dark glances between forkfuls of bloody prime rib. Catching my eye, he grinned, raised a glass to his grease-stained lips, then resumed devouring rare beef.

"Enough," I snapped, getting up. "He's spoiling my appetite retroactively."

You, too, I felt like telling Ann Talbert. But when I turned to where she'd been sitting, Ann was gone.

A band had set up under the lights near the outdoor bar and begun playing waltzes. Night had fallen; George jumped down onto the fireworks barge, its running lights moving smoothly away into the darkness on the water.

Wade swung me into his arms and onto the dance floor, his

hand between my shoulder blades warming through my skin and into my bones.

As he whirled me around and drew me near again a breathless laugh escaped me. "There's my girl," he said. "I was starting to think I might not hear that laugh today at all."

I can't dance a lick except in Wade's arms. "And that," he added as the fireworks began, "would've been a shame."

A *boom!* shook the dock and a bright-white chrysanthemum erupted over the water. With a whizzing sound, a twisty-purple sizzler with a flaring red tail spiraled up.

"That DiMaio guy giving you problems?" Wade asked. "Because if you want, I can drop-kick him off the end of the pier."

I laughed again, mostly from knowing that if I asked him to, he would. The pleasant feeling didn't last long, though, as over Wade's shoulder I spotted Bert Merkle coming out onto the dock.

With his wolfish profile and a calculating expression on his unshaven face, he looked like a predator casually easing into the henhouse. *Scram,* I thought, then lost sight of him in the crowd as Bob Arnold made his way over to us.

"State guys'd like to talk to you, Jacobia," he told me. "Just routine stuff. How Jason seemed to you and so on. Tomorrow?"

I nodded. He went on to find Ellie, to tell her, I supposed, the same thing. Wade and I moved to the edge of the floor. A barrage of fireworks went off all at once, like fiery confetti overhead.

"Oohh," said the voices of the people on the dock. *"Ahhh."*

Then came the scream, sounding at first like an outburst of hilarity. But when it came again, fainter, an uneasy ripple moved through the crowd.

People quit dancing. The music stopped. The dock lights came on; we all blinked in the sudden glare.

"Somebody fell," a woman said. "Off the dock, someone..."

I counted heads; Ellie, Bella, my father, and Wade were all visible. But where was Dave DiMaio?

Then I spotted him. He'd climbed up onto the dock railing.

"Hey, get down from there!" Bob Arnold roared, trying to see out into the water and to move the anxious crowd back.

Dave's hand shielded his eyes from the overhead lights. From the fireworks barge, a barrage went up, heavy blasts dumping pools of colored illumination onto the black waves.

Another scream came from the water, fainter still. An outboard engine fired up nearby but if they couldn't find her in the dark–it was a woman's voice, I was pretty certain–a boat wouldn't be much help.

I pushed through the crowds to the dock railing. "Where?" Bob Arnold demanded of DiMaio, struggling meanwhile to release an orange life ring from the safety line tied to the rail-post.

"I don't know," DiMaio replied, squinting into the darkness. "I thought I saw something, but..."

Bob pulled a utility knife from the clutch of equipment on his duty belt and freed the life ring. But he still didn't know where to throw it. Just then a fourth scream came, the sound of a last gasp if I ever heard one.

The fireworks barge turned its searchlight on. The fat white beam strobed the water, tipping the waves with its icy glow.

"Wade," I began urgently.

Grimly he eyed the proceedings. "Nothing we can do."

Another low rumble approached from the south, a much bigger beam on the water ahead of it. The Coast Guard, I realized with momentary relief; they practiced this stuff all the time.

But by now, minutes had gone by. And in fifty-degree water, that was time enough.

Still on the rail, Dave DiMaio scanned the waves as the searchlights crosshatched. How he managed to keep his balance up there I had no idea, especially when he began kicking his shoes off.

"No," I whispered, aghast. Because maybe he was a swimmer and maybe he wasn't, but either way he had no idea how strong the currents were here.

Bob Arnold stuck a hand out to snatch the foolhardy would-be rescuer down from his perch. But as he did so, Dave jumped.

And swam straight out. "He's a goner," I heard someone say.

"DiMaio!" Bob shouted. "Stop! Tread water and wait!"

"Attention, you in the water!" came an amplified voice from the Coast Guard's vessel. Its deck lit up brightly, it maneuvered to where DiMaio swam.

"Stand by!" the voice ordered as the crew members took their rescue stations.

DiMaio's face was a tiny, intermittent dot of white in the flood-lit water. Then it vanished. Two Coast Guard rescue swimmers went over the orange craft's side as in the distance the low *whap-whap* of a helicopter's rotor grew louder.

"Where is he?" I whispered to Wade. But I was afraid I knew.

"Come on," Wade said, tightening his arm around my shoulder. "You don't have to see any more of this."

Still I resisted as George Valentine leapt from the docking barge and came toward us. "Why the hell did that idiot jump in?" he demanded. "Didn't he think one drowning was enough?"

Scanning the far side of the dance area, he spotted Ellie and hurried to wrap her in an embrace. Over by the outdoor bar I spotted my father and Bella, she with a hand to her lips and he with an arm around her; for once, she wasn't trying to shake him off.

The helicopter arrived with its own set of lights. Crisscrossing the waves, the beams moved like fingers pointing at nothing. "Who was it?" one of the busboys asked Wade.

"Some woman," answered the band's guitarist, coming out to start packing up his stuff.

Because the party was over. "One guy in the bar said he was right there when it happened. Said he saw her go by on the way up and over, and then she was gone."

He closed the snaps on his guitar case. "Guy said she had on these huge earrings."

A horrid suspicion struck me. "Wade," I began just as Ellie hurried over to me. "You don't suppose..."

"George talked to Bob Arnold," she broke in. "Bob says Ann Talbert's things are still upstairs in the coat room. Jacket with ID in the pocket. And nobody can find her."

The helicopter rose and swung away, then steadied to resume the search. "Tide's turned," Wade observed.

"She wouldn't leave without her things," Ellie said.

"No." I looked out to where the Coast Guard's *Zodiac* had paused in its own search pattern, its strobe motionless. Suddenly a line flew out from the craft, briefly shining.

"Hey!" A shout went up from the local men still clustered at the end of the dock. "They've found someone!"

"I've got to go," said Ellie. "George is picking me up out front."

Her face was pale with anxiety and dampened by mist; her red hair, escaped from the combs she'd pushed into it, clung wetly in tendrils on her white forehead. She gave me a quick hug, her eyes conveying what we both knew: that Dave DiMaio had been there when Ann Talbert bragged to me about having the old book.

And that he'd been out here somewhere when she went over the rail. Not that it couldn't have been an accident. The rail was high and extremely sturdy, as it had to be for the public, but she'd been under the influence. She could've climbed up partway onto it, then leaned over too far. Or maybe somebody helped her, pointing something out to her—something that wasn't there—and giving her a shove.

As Ellie departed, I thought about how easily it could have been done, at night in a crowd with everyone watching fireworks.

"They're pulling someone in. Looks like...alive." Bob Arnold came back with the state cops. One carried a pair of field glasses, peered through them.

Even without the glasses I could make out a motionless shape being hauled over the *Zodiac*'s transom. "I don't know," I began doubtfully. "I can see a person, but..."

But then the shape moved. More of the vessel's deck lamps came on: dark hair. White shirt. And...a striped tie.

Suddenly the figure clambered up, staggered to the rail.

"Dave DiMaio," I said. "You're right, he looks okay."

As for Ann Talbert...*I've got that book...and I'm keeping it.* God, why hadn't she just kept her mouth shut?

"Looks like they've got another one." Bob had taken the field glasses from the state guy. "Black pants, white shirt."

"That's what Ann Talbert was wearing. Is she...?"

"They're doing CPR."

But she'd been in the water half an hour, wearing leather boots too heavy to swim in. They'd have filled up fast and hauled her down like a couple of anchors.

Wade put his arm around me; I leaned against him sorrowfully. As medical first responders, Ann's rescuers couldn't pronounce her dead *or* quit trying to revive her.

Not without a licensed physician's okay. So she couldn't be *officially* drowned until she reached dry land. But then...

Then she would be.

Chapter 14

F ancy meeting you here."

Dave DiMaio looked up, startled by my voice and blinded by the flashlight I aimed at his face. It was just past midnight, and when I surprised him he'd been trying unsuccessfully to remove a window screen from Ann Talbert's Lyon Street house.

"Turn that thing off, will you?" He held one hand up, squinted at me through his fingers. "I've got a killer headache."

"Very funny." I scanned the ground around his feet with the flashlight, then aimed it at his pants pockets. He'd changed clothes, but the dry ones he had on now were all smutched with moss and soil, his shoes and hands grubby.

"I don't have any weapons on me," he said, understanding my scrutiny. "And I didn't do anything to that woman. I didn't even see her after we left the restaurant's dining room."

Lyon Street was a short, tree-lined dead-ender about halfway between downtown and Dog Island, a detour on my way home after finally driving Bella to hers. It had been late by the time we got settled after the upsetting evening, and she'd insisted on being right to hand, as she put it, in case we wanted anything.

All I wanted was a straight answer, such as for instance to the question of whether or not Ann had really had the old book.

She could have been lying. A couple of drinks had perhaps fueled a malicious desire to put the screws to me.

To get back at me, maybe, for not caving in to her demand for the thing in the first place. Or she could've been telling the truth.

Her house was a white cottage with a wraparound porch and a lot of overgrown forsythia bushes mostly shielding it from the street. The porch light was on and a lamp burned low in the front-hall window.

"So what are you doing here?" I asked DiMaio. As I drove by, a tiny white penlight beam had flitted intermittently behind the bushes; not enough, probably, to alert any neighbors.

But it had alerted me. No answer from DiMaio, and anyway I knew. He wanted the book, too.

I took a step closer. Right now Bob Arnold was still busy filling out paperwork on Eastport's second unnatural death in one day—a modern record for us—and the state cops were probably already in their motel rooms, watching the late-night rebroadcast of *SportsCenter* on ESPN.

Yeah, blatant stereotyping; guilty as charged. And what the heck, maybe I was wrong. Maybe they were listening to opera.

Either way, I was alone out here. DiMaio took a jackknife out and unfolded a blade big enough to gut an elk with.

"Hey, hey," I objected as he approached the window screen with it. So much for no weapons. I wondered what he thought might qualify as one, an AK-47? "Don't do that."

Because I wanted in there as well, and I didn't want a lot of break-in evidence left behind. I moved in alongside him, hoping whoever had put modern aluminum storm windows on this old house was just as cheap and careless as whoever had installed mine.

"Hold this," I ordered, handing him the flashlight and craning my neck to examine the window edge. Bingo; the gap I wanted was there between the screen and the frame.

I put my hand out for the knife. "Have you got a pry tool on that?"

Scowling, he folded the elk-eviscerator away and pulled out another gadget, like a Swiss Army knife only larger.

Much larger. Whatever else I might have to say about Dave DiMaio—such as for instance that maybe he was a murderer—he came well-equipped.

Which, I reflected as I struggled with the aluminum screen, could be a good thing or a very bad one depending on how the next few minutes turned out. The window's lower ledge was about chest-high on me, so I had to work with my arms extended fully upward; ouch.

But the tool on the gadget was just right for my purposes. I shoved it in between the screen's edge and the frame. "Hold the flashlight steady. If anyone comes, switch it off."

"Yes, yes," he said, his voice heavy with strained patience. "I've done this kind of thing before."

"Somehow that information doesn't comfort me." I slid the blade up and down. Right along here somewhere should be a . . .

"Got it." The screen's metal edge flexed and so did the frame it was fitted into, due to both being made of a substance just slightly stiffer than your average cardboard.

The tablike trigger that held the screen in its channel moved when I twisted the blade near it. But the screen didn't pop loose. "Wait here a minute," I told DiMaio.

Back at Wade's truck, I groped around in the darkness under the front seat until I found the short iron pry bar he kept there. Returning to the house, I kept the bar's curved end in my hand with the shaft parallel to my arm until I got past the hedge. Just in case anyone did happen to glance out a neighboring window, I didn't need to be seen carrying forced-entry equipment.

Prying the screen out with the pry bar bent it, but I didn't care. "Okay, give me a..."

But he was already down on one knee in the classic proposing-marriage pose, the other knee forming a step.

Or a trap. If I stepped on his knee to get myself up to the window and through it, he'd have time to do something to me. On the other hand, the look of frustration on his face when I showed up—not to mention the dirt on his clothes—told me he'd been here awhile, trying to get in.

No surprise there, either. Ann had been a single woman living alone, so she'd been careful about security. The big Block lock I'd glimpsed on the front door, for instance, screamed *Don't bother* at burglars or other intruders.

Or anyway she was as careful as a person could be and still have those crappy screen windows. She probably hadn't known they were so flimsy.

What it all added up to was that if he wanted to get in, Dave needed me to get in first. Then I could open a door for him from inside.

All this went through my head in a fraction of a second while he crouched there with one knee out, waiting for me to step onto it. "Okay," I said. "I'll need a little bit of a running start."

He frowned questioningly. "To get me up there enough so I can haul myself through," I explained. "I don't have enough upper-body strength to..."

I waved at the window ledge, just high enough to make what I was saying believable. "Get ready," I said. "Just brace yourself a little and I'll do it on the count of three, okay? One..."

On *two,* I took a running step forward onto his knee, grabbed the window ledge, and pulled hard on it while pushing off with my foot. The change in plan startled him enough so I was able to vault over and inside before anything untoward happened.

Such as him grabbing my ankle and then having another knife. Or the gun . . . Quickly, however, I stopped worrying about that and started worrying about my landing.

Luckily, no sharp-edged furniture happened to be in my way. No rug, though, either. Wincing, I got up from the hardwood floor.

"You all right?" he whispered outside.

Like he cared. "Uh-huh. Pass me the screen."

He handed it in. I slid it back into its channels, hammering with my fist on the bent part. But all it had to do now was look good, not work well, so I didn't waste much time on it.

"Go to the back door," I said, and the penlight moved away as I felt around for a lamp and switched it on.

The room it illuminated was an office, a very nice one. Tiled fireplace with a green ceramic woodstove fitted into it, wooden file cabinets, an oak desk with a cushioned swivel chair.

On the desk stood a computer hard drive and a sleek, black screen. Bookshelves lined the room. But my book wasn't in any of them. I yanked the desk drawers out fast, one after another; no.

A manila envelope was in the wastebasket: addressed to Ann, no return address, and the size was right. But I couldn't read the postmark and DiMaio was already knocking impatiently.

In the kitchen my nose wrinkled at smells of rancid milk, old coffee grounds, a sour dish rag. Bella would've had a field day, here. DiMaio knocked again, harder this time; I moved to the back door. But then I paused, noticing a phone on the wall.

Its buttons were lit, and when I checked, it had a dial tone, too. Which meant that on his way around the house, DiMaio hadn't cut the wires. So I could call Bob Arnold, *then* let DiMaio in.

Or I could alert no one, stay, and perhaps learn more about what if anything was in here. So let's see: bail out or find out?

"Hey," DiMaio said urgently. "Where are you?" He rattled the doorknob.

"Coming." Crossing the darkened kitchen I put a hand out,

searching for a table or countertop to balance and locate myself. But instead my fingers found something that was soft, skinlike, and I jerked back, gasping.

She'd left the book right out on the table. Swiftly I grabbed it, stuffed it into the back of my pants, and dropped my shirttail over it.

The door rattled again, harder. When I opened it, DiMaio came in looking angry.

"You know, if you'd stop being so pigheaded and listen, you'd realize..."

"What?" I demanded. "That maybe you poisoned Jason Riverton and pushed Ann Talbert?"

"Don't be stupid. I nearly drowned trying to save her."

"Maybe so. But right now as far as I'm concerned it's a good bet that either Merle killed Jason...or you did."

"Right, and then I typed my own initials—" Suddenly the kitchen's fluorescent overhead light went on, startling us both.

"What in the world are you two doing here?"

It was Ellie, with a house key in her hand.

"Where'd you get that?" I asked, and she made a *you-should-have-brought-me-along, shouldn't-you?* face at me.

"Bob Arnold sent me. Ann's body's at the hospital in Calais and they want to know, is there a next of kin they can notify?"

DiMaio looked disgusted at the appearance of yet more company on what he'd clearly hoped would be a solo visit. "And you just happen to have a key to her house because...?"

"I didn't. Bob did. Ann went to Florida last winter. She gave him one while she was gone. It's been in his office ever since." Her tone turned businesslike. "So now that we're here, let's get to it, shall we? Probably there's a desk somewhere."

"With an address book, maybe," I agreed, wanting to stay off the subject of anything else with pages in it.

Such as the ones stuffed in my pants. But DiMaio didn't move. "Listen, you two, this may be just a game to you, but—"

Ellie turned. "You mean like the one you're playing? You act like you're harmless. And we're supposed to believe it because . . . why was that, again?"

She rushed on, beginning to sound angry. "Oh, I remember now. Because you say so. While you lie and snoop, sneak around and tell tall tales about—"

"But it's all . . ." Dave tried interrupting her. But no dice.

"You, who blew into town one minute and two people were dead the next! Not counting the first one in Orono," she added, raking him with her eyes.

That was Ellie: the iron hand in the gingham glove. "Does he have weapons?" she asked me. "Because if he does have any we should take them, and if not . . ."

She turned back to DiMaio. "Then maybe he should just sit down and shut up."

"You've got it all wrong," he protested. "I keep telling you I didn't take the gun. Or do any of the other things you seem to think I did."

He looked down at his hands. "And . . . keep quiet about Horace, all right? Just . . . you don't know anything about him."

He paused, getting control of his voice. Then: "Horace was the best friend I ever had. I was a skinny, dumb kid with acne, horn-rims, and a drinking problem. All I cared about was bottles and books."

He took a shuddery breath. "Horace taught me and other kids like me that the things we were interested in were valuable. And that so were we. He taught us that books, even the weird, unusual books everyone else said we were wasting our time on—that they were *about* something. And he encouraged us to get out there and find out for ourselves what it was. He gave us—he gave *me*—the whole world. But I never thanked him. I thought—" His voice broke. "I thought there would be time."

"Only there wasn't, was there?" another voice asked.

The woman who appeared in the kitchen doorway was in her

early twenties, slender and deeply tanned with long blonde hair curving smoothly to her shoulders.

"And who," she added unpleasantly, staring at DiMaio, "did *that* work out just fine for, I wonder?"

She wore a blue crew-neck sweater and tan slacks with soft-looking tan leather sandals on otherwise bare feet. "Hello, Dave. Long time, no see."

She laughed softly. "Never, actually." It was the woman who'd been driving the red Miata.

"Nice story," she added, not sympathetically. "I'm Liane Myers," she said. "Horace Robotham's daughter."

DiMaio's mouth dropped open. "And I'm here to give this jerk a run for his money. Literally," she finished.

"I don't intend to make any trouble for you," Liane Myers declared the next morning in my kitchen; yeah, right.

"Fine kettle of fish," Bella had fumed when I told her the story. Well, except for the part about getting back the old book.

Which was now up on the third floor of my house under a floorboard; a nailed-down floorboard, the hiding place disguised with old nails and a newly applied coating of workroom grime.

Because maybe DiMaio had been telling the truth and maybe he hadn't. But the last person who'd gabbed about having that book was lying in a morgue room and I didn't want to become her next-drawer neighbor.

"Seems to me we should put a drawbridge on the causeway," Bella had grumbled as I looked through the mail: bills, several more bills, and to top it all off a couple of bills. The final envelope was full of coupons, none of which were for anything we ever bought.

"We should just make folks state their business before we ever even let 'em onto the island," declared Bella.

Now Liane Myers stole uneasy peeks at my dour housekeeper.

I'd told Liane where my house was the night before and instructed her to be here by eight at the latest, or I'd add her to the
list of topics I intended to discuss with Bob Arnold.

And apparently she hadn't wanted that. "I'm glad to know
you don't mean to cause me problems," I told the young blonde
woman. "Although I don't quite see how you could."

Translation: Don't get too full of yourself, missy. Because the
idea that some pretty young twit in a sports car could come
around here and upset my applecart was—well, maybe when I was
still married to my ex-husband, she could have.

But not anymore. "But I'm confused about why you *are* here,"
I added. "None of us has even met your father, and—"

She turned her pale-blue gaze on me. Today she wore a white
linen blouse, tan woven-silk pants, and a cashmere cardigan. On
her feet were a pair of patent-leather slides with grosgrain bows on
them. In other words, she looked like a million bucks, as she had
the night before.

Just a different million bucks. "I'm not the only one you're
confused about," she said. "Other people might think my dad was
a great guy. But to me, he was a first-class jerk."

Her eyes narrowed with remembered pain. "I wrote to him as
a kid. He never answered one of my letters. I finally gave up."

She straightened her shoulders. "But that's old news. The
point now is he had a will and I'm not in it. But *he* is. That
schemer, Dave DiMaio."

"Really," Bella commented, looking over from the sink.

Suddenly Liane seemed to realize who Bella was and what she
was doing here. Spurred by this brainstorm, she shot my housekeeper one of those snotty little *Why am I talking in front of the help?*
looks, about as subtle as a punch in the nose.

Bella deflected it with a casual twitch, as if she'd found something unpleasant on her sleeve. Then she summed up Liane's difficulty neatly:

"So your father had money but he didn't leave a penny of it to you. He left it to—"

"That little DiMaio geek," Liane agreed venomously, turning back to me.

"As for my dad's *partner*"—she put a mean twist on the word—"he's already *got* money. That Lang Cabell person. A couple of old aunts of his, that he ran off to as soon as my dad died?"

Liane sniffed enviously. "I did a little research on them. They're dripping with it, and at their age what else do they have to spend it on but him? Meanwhile," she added, "*I* haven't got a dime. My *husband*—"

No wedding ring. She saw me looking. "He passed away. After a long, courageous battle with gambling and skirt-chasing."

She smoothed her hair back. "So when I found out what Dad's will says, I decided to make sure DiMaio knows he's not getting anything. To start with, I went to visit that so-called college of his, and do you know what *that* place is like?"

"No," I said, "why don't you tell me?" Because even annoying people can be informative, and she was proving it in spades.

"Well," she replied, gratified at my interest. "It's just a bunch of old brownstone dormitories plus weird wooden houses, so narrow they all look like they're only one-room wide. All kind of leaning together. Or *at* you. It's creepy!"

"Do tell," I murmured as Bella left the room.

"And the students. Pale and skinny. Wispy beards and hollow eyes. All carrying ratty old books around like they were in love with them," Liane added scornfully.

She got up. "Anyway, I asked around there and finally found someone in the grungy old office that he shares. He'd left a map on his desk, with Eastport circled on it. So I came here, too."

"You're contesting Horace's will, then? With a lawsuit?"

"I sure am," she declared as if daring me to do something about it. "Unless DiMaio gives up *his* claim."

Which depending on how much money we were talking about, Dave actually might. As I knew very well from my days as money-manager to the rich and filthy, fighting it out in court over the terms of a will was expensive, and prevailing was anything but a given. You could lose plenty, trying to win.

But Liane Myers must've known that, too. In fact, I got the impression she was counting on it.

"He wouldn't listen last night," she said. "But he's going to. Because I'm going to make him."

She walked around the kitchen as if inspecting it, then peered through the phone alcove into the dining room.

"This is another funny old place," she said dismissively. "Though I guess it could be fixed up. Some wall-to-wall carpet and . . . track lighting, maybe? You know, *modernize* it."

And after that comment of course I didn't haul her by her hair out the back door.

"How'd you know DiMaio would be at Ann's house last night?" I asked.

Liane hadn't been nearby when Ann was talking in the restaurant. She didn't seem to know about the old book at all, in fact.

Or at any rate she hadn't mentioned it. But she was the type who might try to make it part of her father's estate, too, if she learned of it and suspected it had any value. That had been most of the reason I wanted to talk with her, in case she represented some last little book-related loose end I needed to yank into a square knot.

Because let's face it, now that I had my property back, the rest of it was really none of my business.

"I didn't know," she said. "I had been waiting around to get a minute with him. I'd decided to talk to him and figured I might as well just get it over with. Finally he went out on the dock with the rest of you and I thought it was my chance. But then the woman fell and he jumped in."

To try to save Ann.

Or make it look as if he were trying.

"After that of course the cops had to talk to him," Liane continued. "That took a while, and then he had to go dry out, get dry clothes on, and so forth. So I waited around outside his motel and when he came out again, I followed him."

So far, so believable. Except: "You knew he *would* come out again because...?"

She gave me a look. "After what he'd been through, d'you think you'd be able to just lie down on a bed and turn on the TV, read a magazine or whatever? I sure couldn't."

At the back door she paused. "My father could ignore me when he was alive," she said. "I couldn't do much about that. But I'm his only blood relative, so now I've got the upper hand. And I'm going to shake it."

She stalked away toward the Miata; not scared; not stupid. And apparently well-motivated. Where had Liane Myers been on the night of her father's death? I wondered.

As if I'd spoken aloud, she stopped at the car door. "A million," she said.

"What?" The pale morning sun turned her hair to gleaming platinum.

"My dad's estate. Well, more like a million and a half," she amended. "Give or take a few hundred thousand."

Well-motivated, indeed.

Anything worth doing was worth researching thoroughly first, Horace had always said. But the morning after Ann Talbert drowned off the end of the Lime Tree's dock, Dave DiMaio wasn't researching anything.

He'd lost his tie pin and he was hunting for it.

He'd been all over his motel room, and retraced his steps

downtown. He'd missed it just as he was cleaning up to go out to dinner the night before, but he'd been too upset to think of it again until at last he'd returned to his room for the night.

He wanted it; Horace had given it to him. And even though he knew he was being childish about it, learning that Horace had a daughter Dave knew nothing of made the thing seem even more important to him.

As if once he'd found it other things might go back to the way they'd been, too. Mulling this, he drove out Water Street toward Dog Island, intending to start his search there.

A car zoomed up alongside him before he arrived, though, and with an imperious horn-honk, Liane Myers veered her own car hard, forcing Dave's old Saab nearly up onto the sidewalk.

She skidded to a halt and got out, stalking to his window. "You killed my father," she said.

He stared at her. "What are you talking about?"

Her resemblance to Horace was more striking in daylight: pale hair, cleft chin, those eyes, which behind all the hurt and the makeup were so very like Horace's.

At the sight of them, sudden memory assaulted Dave, of the day he'd first met Professor Horace Robotham in his spare, elegant office on the first floor of the old Strange Literature building. Generously donated by the Strange family, of course, Horace would always tell parents and prospective students as he herded them on obligatory campus tours.

Usually prospective students got the joke. Usually—though on occasion one could surprise you—the parents didn't.

"Get out of that car," Horace's daughter ordered now.

Dave did, unsure why he was obeying. Something in the voice, so like his old friend's . . .

Behind her, the bay was pale blue with dark swirls in it. Gulls rose in clouds from the surface of the water and settled again. "You're not getting away with it," she said.

Getting away with what? Did she think he'd been part of a

plot to get Horace to ignore her? But where was the sense in that?

Perhaps if the choices were to be made now, Dave thought, Horace would've done things differently. Still, he must have had reasons.

"He must have thought you'd be okay," Dave ventured.

But that turned out to be the wrong thing to say. "Sure. He was real concerned," she replied, her tone sarcastic.

"I guess now you'll try telling me you don't know anything about his will, either," she added.

Indignation seized him; did she think this was about money? "Of course I don't," he retorted. "And even if I did..."

Then it occurred to him what she must mean. "No. He wouldn't do that. Lang gets it, surely. They'd been together for..."

Well, practically forever. As long as Dave had known Horace, anyway.

"He left it all to you," she said flatly. Challengingly.

He couldn't believe it. But then suddenly he did, and for the barest instant allowed himself to think what it could mean.

In winter he wouldn't have to move all his work over to the library where it was warm. And the Saab needed... well. He could buy a new one, couldn't he?

She spoke again, angrily. "And I'm not okay. I'm living on credit cards... I'll be waitressing in a diner pretty soon, for god's sake."

All at once, a feeling of calm came over him. It was as if instead of an angry woman he was inspecting an old manuscript, an ancient map, or a bit of yellowing parchment. Her deep tan looked recent, artificial. But in the bright outdoor light he could just make out a faint, white ring around her wedding finger.

"You got divorced?" he guessed. Her lips tightened to a thin line. "Or—no, he died, didn't he? That's it."

He watched her face; it said yes. "Your husband died and... his family tossed you out? You've run through whatever he left you—"

She didn't deny any of it.

"—and your own family, your mother and her people, maybe, they won't give you any more, either," Dave finished. "Is that just about the size of it?"

Because maybe she thought he was a harmless little sap whom she could bulldoze right over. Between her take-no-crap attitude and her startling brand of blonde-bombshell beauty, she had a lot of weaponry at her disposal.

But he was getting his wind back now, after the news she'd dropped on him. And he'd never been a sap.

"Then you found out your father died. You knew or hoped he had money, and now you're here. To get it."

"So what?" She looked defiant. "It's mine. I deserve it. After what I've been through..."

Another thought struck him. "Where have you been living?" he asked, interrupting her diatribe: absent fathers; cold, neglectful husbands; the cruel, cruel world.

"What d'you care?"

He gazed past her at the water and the little boats on it. A massive freighter sat on the horizon, its bulk reminding Dave of a large animal nosing its way in among smaller ones.

"I just wondered," he said.

Horace's old-book-and-manuscript business wasn't a money tree. Mostly he'd handled first editions, historical signatures, and hand-colored illustrations, reasonably profitable but in no way windfall-creating. But that merely created a context within which Horace's real work could hide in plain sight.

"I suppose you must've been interested in him," Dave added. "Wanted to meet him. Maybe you even thought of calling or just showing up, but didn't know if you should."

He doubted this girl even had a clue to what Horace had been all about. But if she had somehow learned that her father was wealthy—

Without warning another memory assaulted him, of a wizened

old woman with eyes like coals in a New Mexican desert outpost so remote, he and Horace had needed burros to traverse the last dozen desolate miles. In her adobe dwelling, amidst shrines to the Blessed Virgin and to San Fausto with all the arrows sticking out of him, they'd found an ancient book written in Spanish, wrapped in bright-red coarsely woven cloth and surrounded by its own regiment of burning candles.

Among other things, the relic was supposed to cure boils, a notion Dave had dismissed until he developed his own, on the ride back. Corn tortillas cooking on a smoky fire...Horace had sat on his haunches and conversed with the old woman in her own dialect, a mixture of Spanish and old-native Nahuatl.

Dave bit his lip hard. Sooner or later these sudden attacks of grief would ease.

Wouldn't they? "What did your husband die from?" Dave asked Liane Myers.

She stiffened. "Suicide," she said brusquely. "Pills."

And then, in an aggrieved rush: "But first he wrote a letter accusing me of doing it. So I'd get blamed for it, and the police *believed* it."

Her blue eyes filled with a child's resentment. Dave played along. "That wasn't very nice of him. So there was a trial?"

"Yes. But he was always mean. So the jury believed me when I said he'd written that letter just to hurt me."

Something calculating in her tone, her eyes sneaking a quick peek sideways at Dave as she spoke.

Seeing if he believed it. "That was lucky for you, wasn't it?" Dave asked.

She'd have worn the wedding ring until afterward. The grieving widow would've played better to a jury. He guessed aloud again, more certainly this time. "You didn't happen to be in Orono the night Horace died?"

"No! Why should I—"

Too late, she remembered the credit cards she'd mentioned; he saw it on her face. If she was in Orono overnight she'd have had to use a card to get a room. And credit-card records, as everyone knew, could be checked.

She swallowed hard. "Okay, I was there. I wanted to meet him," she admitted. "I thought if I did, maybe he would—but he got killed instead. Just my luck," she finished bitterly.

"You thought maybe he'd give you money. And when he didn't?" He advanced on her as he spoke.

She backed away. "No! I drove to his house, but I never even got the nerve to go up to the door."

"I see."

Her face darkened like that of the old *bruja* in the adobe dwelling where the firelight had flickered weirdly. "You know what?" the girl asked suddenly. "How do I know *you* didn't do it? You get the money. You knew where he was. I think I'll tell the cops maybe *you* killed my father." With that she slammed into the small red car and roared off, her blonde hair flying.

Dave watched her go, thinking that if ever he was glad he had listened to Horace's research advice, it was now. Liane Myers was angry and penniless, and he thought maybe she really had done away with that husband of hers no matter what she'd conned a jury into thinking about it.

And that, he realized, was where his sudden calm had come from; not the notion of getting money but the feeling of a brand-new fact slotting decisively into its rightful place.

Twenty-four hours earlier, he'd believed the only suspect in Horace's death was Bert Merkle, his motive a strange old book.

But now things looked different.

Completely different.

Again. Dave started the Saab and drove to the end of Water Street where the windswept rolling fields and high, grassy bluffs of Dog Island began. He parked by the side of the road, already scanning the pavement for his tie pin.

Not far off lay Merrie Fargeorge's saltwater farm: fence, barn, house. A little dog frisked in a shaded run near the porch. A shovel stuck up from a pile of earth in the excavation pit; other tools, neatly arranged, lay side-by-side on a tarp.

Dave retraced in his mind his steps of the day before. The tie pin was here somewhere; he was sure of it.

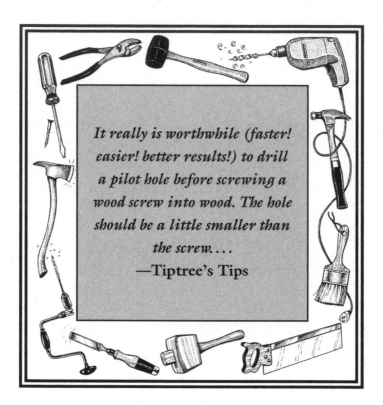

Chapter 15

It really is worthwhile (faster!
easier! better results!) to drill
a pilot hole before screwing a
wood screw into wood. The hole
should be a little smaller than
the screw....
—Tiptree's Tips

Y ou're not going to believe this," said Ellie soon after
Liane Myers drove away from my house.

I was coming out of the post office where I'd sent off one of the
coupons I'd received that morning, in hopes of winning a vacation
in Costa Rica. I would have to inspect time-share condos while I
was there and perhaps even pretend to be able to buy.

But maybe when I got home the bathroom would be fixed up,

Bella and my dad would've eloped, and Sam would've finally landed hard on both feet instead of tentatively on one.

"What?" I asked as Ellie steered me across Water Street.

"The state cops've decided Jason Riverton's death was an accident, that's what."

"You're kidding!" I let myself be led into the Moose Island General Store, past the cooler and the shelves full of local products: smoked salmon, stone-ground mustard, hand-knit woolen socks, and gourmet chocolates. Behind the counter Skippy Fillmore was slicing onions for hero sandwiches; his apron today said *I Brake 4 Margaritas*.

"Nope," Ellie said. With a wave at Skippy she plucked two bottles from the cooler, got cups and a plastic tray.

"Take one blind woman, add a jug of antifreeze, stir with a bottle of strawberry syrup sitting right next to the jug, and . . . well, the plot turns. Or the worm thickens, or whatever."

I followed her out onto the deck. "I don't understand. What strawberry syrup?"

"The Slurpee drinks," she said. "They'd buy a supply of them on their trips to Augusta. But the drinks would thaw out by the time they got them home. The ice in them melted."

"Oh," I breathed, beginning to understand. "So . . ."

Ellie nodded energetically. "So every time she served him one she'd pour some of the diluted stuff out and add a big dollop of strawberry syrup. Jason," she added, "didn't know."

"She kept the syrup in the cabinet under the sink."

"Uh-huh. This is what she told the cops. A great big dollop, half a cup, maybe. Because remember, they were those forty-ouncers."

So they'd take plenty of syrup. Inside, the little bell over the door jingled; Skippy left his onions, wiping his hands on his apron-front as he approached the counter.

"There'll still be an autopsy," Ellie continued. "But under the sink right next to the syrup jug the cops found an empty spot like a footprint, same size and shape as the antifreeze bottle."

We hadn't looked under the sink. "So she might've..."

"Exactly. The stuff in Jason's cup plus Mrs. Riverton's blindness *and* the arrangement in the sink cabinet was diagnostic, in the crime-scene guys' opinion. Barring new evidence, the state cops told Bob Arnold they've just about made up their minds."

"She reaches down, grabs the wrong jug, doesn't notice... But, Ellie, that doesn't work. She had a fifty-fifty chance of getting the real strawberry syrup instead of the antifreeze, didn't she?"

"Not if the syrup wasn't there at the time," said Ellie.

"Oh. Oh, gosh, what a lousy trick. You mean someone could've come back and..."

"Set the stage for the second act, right. First replace the syrup with the antifreeze. Later come back and put the antifreeze jug in the trash, slip the syrup into its usual place. Afterward it would look as if Mrs. Riverton had mixed them up. Which is how it does look," Ellie added. "Just not to us."

"Wow," I said. "I guess that takes care of any illusions I might've had. Like, that maybe somebody else was going to deal with all of this."

Because if the cops thought Jason Riverton's death was accidental then that was the end of it, the opinions of a couple of Eastport housewives notwithstanding. We sat in glum silence at the picnic table on the deck for a while, digesting the situation; then I told Ellie about Liane Myers's visit.

"A real wannabe heiress?" she asked. "The kind who sues? I don't think I've ever met one of those."

But there was something more on Ellie's mind. She pushed an open address book across the table between our cups of Moxie; Ann Talbert's name was written on the first page of the book.

"You got some of her relatives' names out of it, then, for the hospital?" I asked.

She nodded. "When I got home last night I called, gave the cops all the names and numbers that looked likely. But by then

Lee was fussy and George was grumpy—you know how he gets when something bad happens on the water—and I was dead on my feet."

Like many coastal natives, George regarded salt water rather differently from the way tourists saw it. Simply put, he thought the ocean was sitting out there just waiting for you, scheming to kill you even if the day was clear and the waves a calm, serene-appearing blue.

"Like me right now," I said, meaning the dead-on-the-feet thing. As soon as Liane Myers had gone out the door I'd started feeling as if somebody were working me over with a brickbat.

The stairs fiasco, the party for Merrie Fargeorge, and after that the late, thoroughly unpleasant evening…they'd all taken a toll, and my body said pretty soon I'd have to start paying it.

The Bella-and-my-dad problem, too; I knew their truce of the night before was just that. She'd resist, he'd keep insisting—for all I knew she was writing her I-quit note right this minute.

But Moxie, the official soft drink of downeast Maine, tastes enough like medicine to make me feel better even if it isn't. "So?" I said, indicating the address book.

"So this morning I looked it over again," Ellie said. "And this was inside."

She lifted it and a folded sheet fell out, a flyer listing the dates of recent and upcoming meetings of a writers' group. It said Ann was scheduled to read some of her work at an evening meeting at a restaurant in Orono, the night Robotham died.

Which we'd already known, more or less. But now Ellie's look said she'd come up with a new slant on the information.

"Try this idea," she said. "What if Jason did kill Horace to get the book?"

"But then how would Ann have ended up with it?"

She raised a finger. "I'm getting to that. But first back up a lit-tle. Maybe Jason could hit someone over the head and run, and maybe somebody would ask him to. I'm okay that far. But would you send him into a strange house to look for something right afterward, to steal it?"

"He was just a kid. Something unexpected came up, he might lose his head. I'd want someone who could stick to a plan, stay calm, improvise if he had to, and . . . oh."

"If Merkle sent Jason to do the real bad-deed part, and Jason did it, then Merkle couldn't very well leave Jason walking around and able to talk about the whole thing afterward, could he?"

In other words, Merkle might want to eliminate Jason. "But," Ellie added, "what if that's all Jason did? What if Merkle had two people doing his dirty work that night?"

I looked at the flyer again. The writers' meetings lasted from seven-thirty until ten. Say half an hour of schmoozing in the restaurant bar afterward . . .

"Ann would've had time to get there after the so-called mugging and wait for a chance to get in," I said. "No guarantee the house would be empty right away, but–"

But sooner or later there was a good chance that it would be. "They probably asked Lang Cabell to go identify the body at the hospital," Ellie agreed.

"So you could expect he'd at least be gone for that long." In other words, long enough, and Ellie's theory provided a motive for Ann's death, too.

To shut her up, just as Jason had been shut up. "But, Ellie, it means Ann knew in advance that Jason was going to . . ."

"Not necessarily. Who knows what Merkle might have told her? And even if she suspected, people can manage to ignore a lot of things when they're getting what *they* want."

And *want* was Ann's middle name, lately. "The story about someone mailing her the book could've been a lie, then," I said. "And the envelope could've just been window dressing, something she could show in case somebody pressed her on the subject."

Down in the boat basin a couple of teenaged boys hopped into a wooden dory, hauled a cooler off the dock into the boat with them, threw the line off, and rowed away. Moments later they were out past the breakwater, heading for open water. "Coming over to my house to demand it could've been part of the plan, too," I added. "So I'd think she *didn't* have it. But if the idea was for Merkle to get it, then why did she, still? And why brag about it later?"

Ellie looked troubled. "I don't know. Maybe she realized what had really happened, once she learned Horace had died? And with that she had something to hold over Merkle. To make him let her keep it?"

Or so she'd have thought. Until it was too late. The bell over the door tinkled and Merrie Fargeorge entered the store, and spotted us through the sliding-glass doors leading to the deck.

"Good morning, Merrie," I began in my cheeriest tone. Might as well at least try keeping things light, I thought.

But no dice. "Hmmph!" she sniffed. "Maybe for *you*. I want to know when you mean to put a stop to that man's awful snooping!"

So much for the party cheering her up permanently. "Merrie," I began a little less sweetly, "I'm afraid that I'm not the boss of—"

She glared at me. "I don't care. You're the only one with a connection to him at all so you'll have to handle him. Do you," she demanded, "have any idea how difficult it is to get some of these Eastport old-timers to open up and talk to a person?"

I couldn't say I'd ever had difficulty in that regard. My most recent visit notwithstanding, on most days just trying to get through the IGA in a timely manner was like swimming through soft tar, what with all the conversations involved.

But Merrie's research meant learning who'd slept with whom nine months before so-and-so was born way back in 1849, and never mind what baptismal records said. And the way people felt about family stuff around here, a blot on great-great-grandfather so-and-so's honor might as well be branded on their own foreheads.

"He's making people nervous," she insisted. "And I want it *stopped*."

"Really." I kept trying to be polite. But I was suddenly very glad she hadn't been my high-school teacher and she must've sensed it.

Her plump face hardened. "Of course you must do as you think best, Jacobia," she said tightly.

Then she turned on the heel of her orthopedic shoe and tootled away, practically chuffing steam.

"Gosh, what do you suppose brought that on?" I breathed as we disposed of our soda cups on the way out of the store. Skippy waved a plastic spatula at us in farewell.

"No idea. If I had to guess, I'd say she's either seen Dave DiMaio again or heard from someone who has, and that's what's got her all fired up," Ellie replied.

And then, surprisingly, "You know what, though? Maybe it's time we let go of all this." She peered at me. "Because you look beat, and we're just not getting anywhere. Besides, you've got it, haven't you? Your book. Don't deny it, I saw it in your face last night."

I hadn't meant to deny it. And she was right; we weren't winning this one. Not even close.

And not that it would be a big disaster for me if we didn't. If Merkle came after the old book I could call the cops. If that didn't work I could pay him a visit. Bring the Police Special and if *that* didn't work, the Bisley.

Or Wade. And believe me, only a guy with a death wish would ignore Wade. So life would go on.

And Jason Riverton's mother would go on believing that she'd killed her only son.

"Yeah, I've got it," I said. "Has Margot Riverton moved back into their house yet?"

"No. She didn't want to stay at Merrie's, either. Bob told me she said Merrie'd gone to enough trouble trying to help Jason and look how that turned out. So she's in the assisted-living home for now." Ellie sighed. "She can't be on her own and she has no close family. She depended on Jason and from what I hear, she's afraid to live alone."

"Does she have any money?"

"Social security. She had Jason's disability income, but now that'll be gone. And some rental income, I think, some little piece of property she owns somewhere that she's been renting out practically forever. But it's losing Jason's monthly check that's really going to destroy her."

"Great. So there's another life ruined."

I felt furious, suddenly; maybe at Merrie Fargeorge with her imperious demands and air of being entitled to have them met, no questions asked. Maybe at myself, because there was a connecting thread in all this somewhere and I wasn't seeing it.

Or possibly I just understood too well how Jason's mother felt, thinking her son's death was on account of something she did.

Or didn't do. In Sam's case, so far it was a potentially fatal illness and not his actual demise. Still: somebody you were and shouldn't have been, somebody you should've been and weren't.

Something. Let the experts say differently, but go ahead; try not feeling that way in your heart.

"If the cops have already as good as said Jason's death was an accident, I don't suppose they've gone through the house. Not the way we would," I ventured.

Ellie shook her head.

"No one," I went on, "has confronted Bert Merkle about all this, either. As far as we know."

She fell into step beside me. "Nope."

"About killing Jason to keep him from implicating Bert in Horace's murder, sending Ann into Horace's house for the book, killing *her* to keep her quiet about it *and* get the book back..."

It was just past noon and the sun, newly slanting in these last warm days of August, turned the island of Campobello across the water to a gleaming gold bar. Sailboats cavorted in the wind, and on the breakwater an ice-cream truck played the same innocent song over and over.

"Only I got to the book first, which he didn't plan on," I said. "Listen, Ellie, what would you say to one more day? Would George go along with that, do you suppose?"

But both of us knew that if Ellie said she wanted to go to Mars, George would be out renting the rocket ship. "I was going to head home," I said, "try getting some things done in what's left of the afternoon. But instead..."

Instead it was time for a little more breaking and entering.

Emphasis on the *entering* part.

Installed in a cheap wooden hollow-core front door, a keyed doorknob lock keeps you from having to walk around thinking *Darn, I left my door wide open again.*

But unlike the Block-manufactured behemoth Ann Talbert had installed, it doesn't do much else. The Rivertons' front door swung open; I dropped the tiny screwdriver back into my bag.

"What're we looking for?" Ellie whispered.

The front hall smelled musty. A path worn in the rug led to the living room, where the TV remote still perched on the arm of Mrs. Riverton's chair. Grime on the remote, dust on the screen; even though nobody else was in here with us the atmosphere in the house felt heavy with silent sorrow.

"I don't know," I whispered back. Suspecting that someone had crept in and set up a poisoning death made even the ratty old sofa, crocheted afghan, and age-stained drapes seem ominous.

"But if no one's really checked around in here thoroughly, then maybe we should at least look at that computer again. Just in case Jason got e-mail from Merkle, for instance," I said.

"You think he'd have written anything incriminating?"

Mrs. Riverton's ChapStick lay on the table by the chair, beside a half-finished cup of tea. In the kitchen a bundle of laundry stood by the washer; on the counter were a group of small orange plastic pharmacy bottles and a vial of eye drops.

"She didn't take her pills along with her?"

"I imagine they've given her new prescriptions," Ellie said. "After what they think happened they wouldn't want her taking any of these."

Right; in case strawberry syrup wasn't the only thing she'd gotten mixed up. From a tiny screened back porch the tumble-down shed at the rear of the small yard was visible, its sway-backed roofline looking ready to fall at the least excuse.

Behind the shed, a back alley ran along the rear of all the properties on this side of Water Street. The Rivertons' car was still pulled into the yard at an angle from the alley. A couple of well-worn ruts beside it showed where visitors parked.

I opened the cabinet under the sink. Nothing in there looked unusual now; no strawberry syrup, no antifreeze jug.

A phone hung on the kitchen wall. But there was no answering machine and no caller ID so I couldn't check on calls they might have gotten, and the wall calendar held a reminder for a doctor's appointment but nothing more.

Jason and his mother had lived quiet lives. No wonder he'd been open to whatever weird excitement—or even just the plain old variety—that a friendship with Bert Merkle might offer.

I peered into the breadbox, the silverware drawer, and the sugar bowl. Nothing. "Jake?" Ellie called from upstairs. "Um, you want to come look at this?"

I found her in Jason's room. It seemed even smaller and shabbier than it had with him in it. Black walls and woodwork that badly needed repainting, pine-board-and-milk-crate bookcase full of tattered paperbacks, and his desk...

All just the way we'd seen it last, even the wine bottle and the poison handbook. "Cops didn't think these were strange?" I asked.

Ellie sat, turned the computer on. "Bottle's unopened," she pointed out. "And he had a lot of unusual books."

"Uh-huh." I still thought a poisoned kid with a book about poisons and their antidotes on his shelf was interesting. But if anything it bolstered a suicide theory, which they'd discarded.

"Password?" I asked.

Her fingers moved on the keyboard. "No. You can get right into his e-mail. I don't see much except spam, though."

"Maybe he deleted things?" The room smelled like teenaged boy, which is only a pleasant smell when it's your own teenaged boy.

That, and the fruity reek of strawberry Slurpees, which was an aroma I knew I'd never enjoy again. Ellie's fingers flew.

"Nope again. He had a software program on here that he could use to recover deleted things, including e-mail."

We waited. A line appeared on the screen: *Number of Files Recovered = 0.*

"How come you know so much about computers?" She'd looked up Dave DiMaio on the Internet, too, I recalled, which now that I thought about it was also more tech-savvy than I'd have expected of her. Ellie's life consisted of real things, not pixel-images.

Small laugh. "Lee's reading picture books already. Getting curious about chapter books."

That is, with lots more words in them. "So any minute she'll be on the Internet, herself."

She nodded. "To stay ahead of her I need to start now, or I'll be like those other parents who have no clue until the kid runs off with some pervert they met in a chat room."

She hit *return*. Lines began scrolling down the screen; she hit *pause* and leaned back in Jason's chair. "Here's a log of the programs Jason's run recently."

"Those Internet slimebags'll have no chance against you."

"I hope." The screen quit scrolling. "It's a short list," she added. "E-mail, web surfing, music, and the one he used most, for games." She pointed at the screen. "This Shock Jock module had to get loaded each time Jason started a new session of game-playing. By the look of it, he'd leave it running all day, then load it up again the next morning."

"I get it. But help me out, here. Your skill in finding all this is very impressive but I still don't see—"

"It's what you don't see that's interesting," she explained. "Something Merrie Fargeorge told you made me think of it—that Jason had never used a word-processing program in his life."

Not even when Merrie had tried to pay him to do it. "What about the word-processing program itself? Does it show things that got created with it?"

Ellie typed. The screen filled with the two-letter message that had been there when we found his body: *DD*.

More keystrokes. "Only one word-processing document. Created yesterday, two fifty-nine P.M. Could he still even have been conscious when this was written?" she wondered aloud.

"It hardly seems likely, does it? His mom called Bob Arnold about four."

A sound from downstairs interrupted us. Not a loud sound or even a threatening one . . .

Maybe nothing at all. I strode to the hall and looked down. "Someone there?"

No answer. Halfway down the stairs I peered left and right, saw no one and heard nothing, then spotted the TV remote on the carpet where it had slipped from the chair's upholstered arm.

But no one was in the house. When I got back to Jason's room Ellie was shutting down the computer.

"So why'd a kid who never wrote a word in his life struggle out of a fatal coma to fire up his word processor?" I wondered aloud.

She shrugged, moving the computer mouse on a black mousepad whose gold-and-red script read *Shoggoth Lives*.

And who, I wondered irritably, was Shoggoth? "And write," I added, "a message that no one can figure out what it means?"

"Oh, I'm sure someone can," said a voice from behind me, and I just about dropped dead of fright right there, first on account of anybody being behind us to say anything at all; I'd been sure the house was empty.

And second, because it was Bert Merkle. "What are you doing here?" I demanded.

Yeah, pretty lame. But it was all I could think of on such short notice. And besides, I *really* wanted to know the answer.

Dirty fingernails, scruffy thinning hair...to look any more like a Halloween scarecrow the man would have had to have straw sticking out of his cuffs, and as for those teeth—

"I could ask you the same," he pointed out.

But even more than a scarecrow, what he really reminded me of was the fact that there was no other way out of this room.

"I happened to be passing, noticed the front door ajar," he said, his fingertips pressed together so that his curved, unkempt nails resembled the spines on a Venus's-flytrap.

"So I decided to check," he finished. But he was lying. We hadn't left the door ajar. He'd tried it and found it unlocked so he'd come in.

And found us already inside. His eyes were pale gray, like a couple of pickled onions. I totaled up the number of negative factors in this situation: evil guy, scene of a murder, no one knew we were here.

Et cetera. But then Ellie spoke up. "Mrs. Riverton asked me to make sure Jason's computer was shut down properly," she lied smoothly.

"And," she added, "to lock up when we left. Which we are doing." She moved purposefully toward the Merkle-blocked door.

With an ironic leer, he stepped back to let her pass. I followed, holding my breath and tensed for sudden movement on his part.

None came. But on the stairway landing I halted.

"Coming?" I asked. Because from the way he was waiting for us to go, it was clear he didn't intend to.

But eventually he followed us grudgingly downstairs and out the front door, where he ambled away with no farewell while we walked in the opposite direction.

"I wonder what he wanted," I said once he was out of earshot.

"Me, too." Ellie turned abruptly. "But I'm not finished with that place," she declared. "There's still that shed out back, and I want to know what's in it."

"But it's..." *A ruin,* I would've finished. A falling-down ruin that probably wasn't even safe to—

Ellie wasn't listening. "You wanted a day, we're doing one more day," she said. "So let's just do this." She halted before the dilapidated old structure on the Riverton property. "That way, we can at least say we've tried everything we could."

Yeah, including maybe having a roof fall down on our heads, I thought as I surveyed the place uncertainly.

The shed had no visible windows, just nailed-up sheets of plywood where they used to be. Rotting sills and a rotted-plank door gray with age, plus a loose doorknob that practically fell off in her hand, were also among its charms.

"Ellie, come on, it's a wreck. What do you think we're going to find in—"

Ignoring me, she pulled the sagging door open.

"Oh," I said, nonplussed. Because hidden behind the rotting old door was a brand-new one; a steel door with two brass-bright, nearly-new locks—not Blocks, but extremely solid-looking—one tumbler-style and one deadbolt.

Seeing them she turned expectantly to me. "Oh, no," I said, putting my hands up in a warding-off gesture. "Just because I did the flimsy one, that doesn't mean I can..."

Shoving a screwdriver into the first lock had been easy. But on the other hand, no one put locks like these on unimportant things, did they?

"All right, all right," I gave in. "You know, someday your confidence in me is going to be sadly..."

"Good morning." I spun around; Dave DiMaio stood there.

"Don't you have anything useful to do but follow me and Ellie?" I began impatiently. But then I stopped, because he hadn't been following me, of course. Or Ellie, either.

He'd been following Merkle.

"Sturdy," he commented. He eyed the locks.

Correct; like the Grand Canyon's a biggish ditch. "I suppose you want to get in there," he said.

"Yes," I told him. "That was the general plan. But unless you brought dynamite, a bulldozer, or the keys, that's not–"

"Step aside." He removed something from his pocket: a ring of tiny hooks, strips, and other small metal implements.

Moments later the door swung open, which to me meant that DiMaio didn't merely have professional lock-picking tools; he was also good at using them. The Blocks at Ann Talbert's wouldn't have tumbled for him, but...

Flipping a light switch just inside the door, he crossed the threshold... and stopped.

"My god," he said.

Chapter 16

I'd expected a ruined inside to match the battered outside of the Rivertons' shed. But instead we found a science lab.

Or something like it. "Oh, my goodness," Ellie breathed.

"Yeah," I agreed inadequately.

"Well," Dave DiMaio murmured. "This answers one question."

I gazed around. The shed's interior had been rebuilt; not professionally but adequately. The recently leveled floor held up new support beams; same with the ceiling.

It wasn't a bit pretty—unfinished Sheetrock never is—but it was functional. I got a mental picture of Jason Riverton and Bert Merkle working together out here.

Or Merkle alone. Maybe Jason's contribution was just letting Merkle do it and keeping quiet about it. Or—suddenly I recalled the small income that Ellie had said Mrs. Riverton had, from renting out some little place since forever.

This was that little place. "What's all this stuff for?" Ellie wondered aloud.

But I was already beginning to guess that, too. Along one wall was a laboratory bench with a long black-slate work surface punctuated by a brushed-steel double sink, a Bunsen burner, and an electric hot plate. At right angles to the lab bench stood a drawing table with a lamp clipped to it.

The lamp had magnifying lenses that you could rotate to peer onto the lighted surface. Slowly, DiMaio entered the work area.

"I wish Horace could see this. He'd have loved it."

But I'd had just about enough of good old Horace, mostly on account of his being dead and therefore no help to us.

"Dave, d'you by any chance want to tell me what this means? Because otherwise I think I'm just going to call the cops and—"

"Don't do that. And don't *touch* that!" Dave added sharply to Ellie as she reached for something on the workbench.

Her hand jerked back. "You don't know what's been on that bench," he explained. "Some of the chemicals used in this kind of operation can be poisonous, even radioactive."

"Dave. Exactly what kind of operation are we talking about?" I asked.

Sheets of old parchment, yellowing and flaking. Spools of what looked like thread, equally old-appearing. Tiny pots of gold paint, a wickedly sharp-looking curved needle, quill pens with nibs newly cut, an embossing tool, a big iron kettle, which by the smell in here had been used for tanning leather...

"It's a bookbinding shop," said Dave. "A very special one. Bert Merkle's, I can only suppose, where he fakes old books."

Some pieces of leather had sections cut from them; book-shaped sections. The parchment sheets had been similarly used. Dots of gold splotched the work surface under one of the lights; a clipboard with lined sheets of paper on it seemed to chart the progress of various projects.

There were a lot of lined sheets on the clipboard. The earlier ones had gone yellowish and curling with age, the newer ones were fresh.

"He's been doing it," Dave said, "for years."

Back at home I found Bella in the yard beating carpets with a tennis racket.

Bam! A cloud of dust flew up. "Bella?" I asked hesitantly.

She lowered the tennis racket. But from the look on her face I decided getting too close might be a fool's move.

"What?" she demanded warily. "But before you tell me, let me just tell *you* that it better *not* be no message from your father."

Bam! More dust. "I've had my last talk with *him* until he gives up his damn fool notions. I ain't a-marryin' and I ain't a-movin', and that's—"

Bam! "—*final,*" she said.

She wore an old cotton housedress with the sleeves rolled up over her ropy arms. Over it she had on a carpenter's apron with generous front pockets. From one, the spray can of compressed air she used for getting dust out of small crevices peeped.

"He can't come live in my house," she said as she resumed beating the rug, " 'cause there ain't enough room. We'd be at each other's throats."

My father's rough edges among her carefully arranged things; I thought again that it would be like a porcupine trying to get comfy.

"And his ain't no better. Worse, 'cause not only is it small, but let's face it, the man's sixteen years old at heart."

He liked Bella's style and he kept to her rules when he was in my house, but at his own his idea of cleaning was to sweep the dust into a corner so he wouldn't trip over it.

Bam! "And we ain't buyin' bigger. Even together, what we'd raise sellin' our two places wouldn't make the down payment. And don't even think of us takin' a loan for it, neither."

I had been thinking of it, actually, as I walked home from the Riverton place. It made a nice change from thinking about my old book, now unmistakably exposed as a fake.

Suspecting it had been one thing. But having it shown to me—the how, where, even the what-with, as in those parchment bits and vials of fake-old ink—was a whole other bowl of chowder.

Chowdah, as Bella would have put it.

"Not from you, nor anybody else," she went on. "I got this far in life without bein' beholden, and I aim to do the rest the same way."

"All right, Bella," I said. "I understand."

She glanced at me, surprised and I thought disappointed that I wasn't arguing with her. But I already knew arguing with Bella was about as smart as stepping within range of that tennis racket.

"Fine," I told her, then went into the house and straight to the phone. Because maybe everything else was falling to bits, but I clung desperately to the notion that I could still fix one thing.

And on that topic I'd just gotten an idea. "That's right, George, I want you to come over here right away," I said when I got Ellie's husband on the line.

"And bring along anyone you know who's good, reliable, and not already working on some other job," I added.

Through the window I watched Bella viciously attack another rug; any more and my backyard would need a pollution-control device.

"Yes, as soon as possible," I said. "It's a big project, I know, but I will pay the men good wages and overtime, and if you bring along enough of them . . . yes. Yes, I know, George."

Then I listened while he told me that I would need, if not a blueprint, at least a detailed sketch of what I required.

But I disagreed. "George, I'm going to delegate all that to you. The pipes and the wiring are all accessible, and they'll dictate where everything else will be, so you just use your judgment."

There ensued a short silence while he digested the unusual notion of me delegating any such thing. Looking hard at the idea might've made it indigestible to me, too; for instance, George was currently responsible for the faucet handles in the old shower looking like the controls on a nuclear reactor.

He'd bought them cheap from a discount plumbing-supply place and installed them without showing them to me first. But after the shower debacle we'd had a chat about esthetic choices, and I didn't have time to supervise this.

"I need it done, I need it done right, and most of all I need it done soon," I told him. "So can you?"

Whereupon he allowed as though he probably could.

"And, George?" I added, taking a deep breath.

But he seemed to read my thought. "While we're there," he ventured, "we could take care of that other little matter." He cleared his throat. "Few days, it could be done. Because you know," he added kindly, "it's brand-new construction."

He waited, then went on: "What that means is, it won't take near the kind of ingenuity and cleverness you use for fixing the old parts of the house."

Which was the nicest way he could possibly have communicated the fact that, while I was fairly competent at old-house repairs, rebuilding a bathroom in one of them wasn't just another bowl of chowder, it was a whole vat of the stuff.

"Fine, George," I said gratefully. "You do that, too, then, along with my dad. I've got a list of materials, part numbers for the fixtures and tile, the paint colors, and so on. Will that be enough?"

Of my involvement, I meant, and he said it would; we agreed he would start immediately and hire whomever else he needed.

Finally, we hung up. I stood there a moment with my hand on the phone, thinking about Jason Riverton, his unlucky mother, and the fact—sure as shootin', as my father would've put it—that she hadn't accidentally killed him.

And then I went out to catch a murderer, damn it.

.   .   .

It was the girl's soft, bitten-looking lower lip and its tearful quiver, so deliberately calculating, that finished Dave finally.

"I want you to tell me about my father," she said. "I want you to tell me *now*."

She stood blocking his way on the main trail in Shackford Head State Park, a wild, forested area on the island just east of town. He'd come here to clear his head.

So much for that idea. Liane must have followed, scampered up the trail to accost him where they would be alone.

He walked straight at her. When it appeared they were about to collide, she faltered, then fell into step beside him.

"Well?" Liane demanded. "Are you going to tell me about him or not?"

After a small meadow and a wooden boardwalk over a swamp, the trail led uphill between old spruces, maples and pin oaks, and venerable white pines. Blue water peeped through breaks in the trees.

"I'm thinking about it," he replied.

She huffed out an impatient breath. She wore jeans, a tan cotton sweater, and a pair of calf-high laced leather boots that were too delicate for the trail. Once when she stumbled he caught her arm. He released it only when she had steadied herself.

"I'm his daughter, aren't I?" she demanded as the trail took a sudden left turn, diminished to a rock-strewn path for the last few uphill yards.

"Yes." He repressed a smile. Not much doubt of that. She was more like Horace each time he saw her, and the brazen insincerity of her expression when she'd made her demand only increased the resemblance.

Because at heart, Horace had been a man who always got the goods, hadn't he? Whatever it took; that his daughter should be the same didn't surprise Dave a bit.

They climbed to a high, rocky outcropping. A stone bench perched on it, overlooking a nearly 360-degree view of water and islands. Gray lichen crept over the granite where it elbowed up through the thin soil.

They sat. "So why the change of heart?" he asked.

Silence. "First you wanted money," he pressed. "Now you want information. What changed?"

She gnawed her lip. "I want both. Is that so hard for you to figure out? You're still not going to see a dime of my father's money."

He shrugged. "Then neither are you."

Because he'd been thinking about it, and he understood, at last, why Horace had arranged his will the way he had.

She glanced at him rebelliously. "The shape you're in," Dave explained, "if I let you take it your dad would rise up and haunt me for the rest of my life."

Horace must've known Lang Cabell wouldn't fight for the money. And he must have hoped Dave would. "A lot of cash right now would ruin you," he told the girl. "You wouldn't know how to handle it."

Another exasperated sniff. "So you say." But faced with his implacably delivered statement—he wasn't an experienced teacher for nothing, Dave reflected—she seemed to give up the subject.

For now. A fog bank lay motionless to the south behind the skeletal-looking bridge joining the Maine coast to Campobello Island. In a little while she spoke again.

"That's where Benedict Arnold went," she said, surprising Dave. "With his wife. But she didn't like it there, it wasn't fancy enough for her." She glanced at him, caught the look on his face. "What? You don't think I'm smart enough to know a thing like that?"

"No. I can tell that you're smart. I just wondered where you learned it, is all."

She turned back to the glittering water. "I read a tourist

pamphlet," she said flatly. "So, do you still think I killed him for his money? My dad?"

This time he did smile. He couldn't help it; for all her attempted toughness, she was so young. "No. I've changed my mind about that."

"Why not? I thought you were all convinced I'm some kind of awful gold digger."

"Mmm. I was. But I've been trying to imagine you hitting him with a rock, or something. And I can't. Because the idea is completely ridiculous."

For a moment she looked unsure whether she should take this as an insult or a compliment. Then she nodded. "Good. You've figured out what really did happen to him, then?"

"I thought I had. But there's been a new development. I'll have to think some more about it."

"Oh," she replied. She sounded disappointed.

He waited, but she didn't say anything more, and after a few minutes she got up and began walking back down the path away from him. He followed, watching the flimsy boots waver dangerously.

"Wait. I thought you wanted to know about Horace."

She hesitated. "I still don't understand, though," he added when she'd let him catch up. "Won't your mother tell you?"

She was weeping. He shoved a clean handkerchief at her.

"She can't. She died a couple of months ago. That's how I found out my dad had died, too."

She snatched the handkerchief, dabbed her streaming eyes. "I've been staying in her house till it gets sold," she explained. "And a letter came for her from my dad's lawyer. Horace must not've known that she was . . . anyway, I opened it."

"I see." They walked on.

"She always thought that stuff my dad was into was stupid. Whatever it was," she added, stopping again.

Bars of sunlight angled through the trees, illuminating the emerald-colored patches of moss at their gnarled roots. "I don't know what to do," she said wretchedly.

Dave knew the feeling. Wheels within wheels, the events he had set in motion, some of which were now threatening to careen out of his control...all of it fell away, though, in the face of this girl's surprising existence.

Because Horace had possessed a secret, a sad one: that he had a daughter. Why he'd kept that hidden and what he might've meant to do about her had he lived, Dave didn't know; maybe he never would. But she was standing in front of him now.

"Listen," he said, coming to a decision.

"What?" she demanded sullenly. But she started down the trail with him again, this time letting him help her where the footing was iffy.

"It's going to take a while to tell you all about Horace. He was"—Dave hesitated—"a complicated guy."

Liane laughed bitterly, pulling out the handkerchief once more and blowing into it. "Yeah, I guess that's one way of putting it. But so what?"

"So if you wanted to," he offered tentatively, "you could come to the college. I could arrange for you to stay in the women's residence. We could have meetings, I could tell you about your dad. You could see where he worked when he taught there."

"I don't have any money."

Not said manipulatively this time, just a bald statement of fact. "We can find you something. Not waitressing," he added hastily.

At the boardwalk a fat frog plopped into the water. The biggest turtle Dave had ever seen regarded them with unblinking eyes. "What do you mean, 'we'?" she asked when they reached the foot of the trail.

"Well, Lang, of course. He'll want to—"

"Why?" she demanded, whirling on him. Her pretty face was

a wreck; he wished he had a hot washcloth to offer her, and a glass of water. "Why would he want to have anything to do with—"

"Liane," he cut her off, seizing her shoulders. "Don't you get it?"

He let go. She hadn't cringed away from him; not quite. "You're so smart, get this through your head, young woman. You're Horace's daughter. That's why I'm going to help you. And when he finds out about you, Lang's going to feel exactly the same way."

Assuming Lang didn't know, which was another question; one Dave had been avoiding. But now he thought he would handle all that when it began posing practical problems.

If it did. Liane gazed at him wide-eyed, as if what he'd just told her wasn't only new information but represented a new way of thinking entirely.

"Okay," she whispered finally.

He walked her to the little red sports car she liked so much and would probably not be able to keep. But they could deal with that later, too.

"It'll take a few days for me to get back to Providence and arrange things," he said. "You have enough cash until then? And somewhere to go?"

He saw her think about hitting him up for money and decide not to. That encouraged him somewhat, as did the small grin she managed.

"Credit cards're pretty beat, but they still work. Not for very much longer, but..." Shrugging, she added, "I have a sister. Half-sister," she amended. In the fading afternoon the sun made her pale blonde hair look red. "She doesn't want me. But she'll take me," Liane said, "for a little while."

"All right, then." He stood there uncertainly while she got into the car, wondering if she would do any of what they'd talked about. Time would tell. "Go there, and call me in a few days."

He handed her a card with his number and e-mail address on it. "And try..."

Liane nodded. "Yeah. Try not to get in a fight with her, get kicked out. I know the drill."

She looked exhausted. Dave hoped that when she got her wind back, some of what they'd said would stick with her.

"All right," he said again as she started the car. "I'll see you soon. And when I do, I'll tell you..."

From behind the wheel her pink-rimmed eyes remained narrow with habitual suspicion, but he saw the tired gleam of lingering hope in them, too. She was too young to let go of it completely.

"Everything," Dave promised.

"Bob, my old book's not real. It's a fake, Bert Merkle made it in the shed behind the Rivertons' house. He got it into my cellar somehow, I don't quite know yet how he did that, but after I found it and sent it to Horace, Bert must've realized he'd made a mistake, something Horace would see and connect with Bert. So Bert killed Horace to get it back."

I stood in the old Frontier National Bank building on Water Street, now Eastport's police headquarters. The red-brick structure still held the high, glassed-in customer counter, green floral curtains, and the steel-doored vault where Bob kept weapons and ammunition.

"Then he killed Jason Riverton and Ann Talbert because they knew he'd done it, they helped him, and—"

Nowadays Bob's office also sported a row of telephones, a radio console, and *Wanted* posters thumbtacked to the corkboards where the bank used to display rates for savings accounts, CDs, and Christmas Club investments.

Bob eyed me from behind the Xerox machine where he was

copying the paperwork he'd been up all night finishing. I didn't even bother asking him if he'd questioned Dave DiMaio about the little gun yet; I didn't need my head bitten off.

"You don't say," he remarked unenthusiastically. "And you think I'll be able to do what about it, Jacobia?"

His round, plump face looked discouraged. "Or this?" he added, gesturing at the pile of paperwork. "And before you ask, I can't go question Merkle about it. No cause. Kid's death was an accident. The drowning, too. So sayeth the powers that be."

The state police, he meant, and the medical examiner. "Bob," I repeated. "My book's a forgery. And it's the *reason*—"

He kept copying. I took a deep breath. "He must've done it years ago. Probably he started faking them practically as soon as he moved here, just waited to do mine—the one he cared the most about—until he'd gotten really good at it."

No reaction from Bob. I persisted. "Bert hadn't rented the shed at the Rivertons' yet, that's why mine's not on the project list he's got posted over there."

More silence. "But Horace Robotham was the expert on such things. Merkle knew that sooner or later Horace would be asked to give an opinion on it."

Another breath. "And probably sooner," I added, "because Horace was right here in Maine. But in the long run that wouldn't have mattered. In the field of weird-old-book authentication, Horace was the man no matter where the item happened to turn up."

Bob was silent.

"The idea must've been that Horace Robotham would pronounce the thing genuine, and then Merkle would triumphantly reveal it was fake. Thus," I finished, "embarrassing Horace Robotham."

My friend the police chief looked levelly at me. "Okay. Let's say you're right. Merkle fakes the book, gets it to Robotham, and then realizes . . . well, let's leave aside whatever it is he realizes. But back up a little, 'cause your theory's got problems earlier than that."

He held up a finger. "One, *how* did Merkle get the old book into the foundation wall of your cellar, and two, *how* the hell did he expect to get it out again? Because maybe he is just as crooked as you think but I don't believe he could engineer a broken water pipe just by saying *presto*. Do you?"

And a broken water pipe, Bob knew, was what had flooded the old book out. He didn't wait for my answer. "Sorry, Jake. For me to get involved here, you're going to need a little item called *proof*. Plus a better story."

"Okay," I said slowly. "Then how about...?"

I was struggling and he knew it. But this was my only chance. Once Merkle learned we'd found his workshop, he'd know we were a step closer to linking him to Horace's murder.

And by extension, to Jason's and Ann Talbert's. And if that happened, he might run, and that could spell the end of getting to the bottom of any of this, ever.

Or he might try getting rid of me. "Okay, how about fraud?" I suggested. "Faking old books, selling them as the real thing—isn't that a crime?"

Bob perked up at the questions. "Yup."

"So what if we could prove he's been doing that?" I asked. "Say, by establishing that he's been renting that workshop from Mrs. Riverton. Which means the items in the shed belong to him."

"Records? Canceled checks?" Bob asked.

"No." We'd gone back into the Rivertons' house looking for them but hadn't found any. "He'd have paid cash, it would've worked better for him and for her. But there are materials, Bob. Old parchment, old ink ingredients, binding material."

The easiest way to get the materials, according to Dave DiMaio, was by cannibalizing a genuine antique. That might cost you, since even relatively non-rare old volumes could be pricey. Still, to Merkle the investment would've been worth it.

"He's been nursing a grudge for years, ever since Horace picked Dave DiMaio to be his apprentice instead of Bert," I said.

DiMaio had told Ellie and me as much back in the Rivertons' shed, while he'd stared dazedly at Bert's fraud factory.

"The other thing you need is know-how," I went on. "Since constructing an old book at all...well, to make one that fools experts, you need to do it the way old bookbinders did it."

"Which is?"

"The workshop had all the right ingredients and equipment. Antique parchment of the right age, glue, leather and thread, and..."

Bob made a face. "Okay, okay. So he fakes books and sells 'em and if we nab him for it, on that there's a chance of prosecuting him."

"Great. But this has to get done now, Bob, before Bert makes his next move. Possibly against me because now I've got the book back. So my question is: Are you going to help me or not?"

Bob's shoulders sagged under his uniform shirt. His tired gaze strayed to the copies he hadn't finished making, the stack of report sheets still waiting to be filled out, and the cruiser outside in its angled parking spot, waiting to be cruised in.

All were part of the job Eastport citizens paid him to do. My request wasn't, which meant it was time for my trump card.

I held up a small brown paper bag, lightly stained here and there by mayonnaise and butter. The clock said four-thirty and I was betting he hadn't had any lunch.

"What's that?" he asked hopefully.

But at this time of the summer, in that kind of bag, with those kinds of stains on it, there was really only one thing it could be. His eyes brightened. "Did Bella make—"

"Crab rolls," I confirmed. "Crabmeat and homemade mayonnaise on a toasted Pepperidge Farm hot-dog bun. Bella," I added, "says the crabmeat's so fresh it could pinch you."

He looked both sad and happy, the way a man does when being confronted by a temptation he simply cannot resist.

"Two of them," I added shamelessly. "Both yours if you'll

come along with me and Ellie for half an hour, tops. She's waiting outside."

His expression wavered. "Come on, Bob. You can say," I added in a sudden burst of inspiration, "that you went up there to stop *us* from hassling *him*."

Sighing, he switched the copier off and put on his hat.

Bert Merkle's tiny ramshackle trailer, set amid neat small bungalows and trimmed lawns on a patch of trash-strewn ground at the island's south end, was the kind of place that made the local real-estate agents throw their hands up in despair.

"You could break in with a can opener," Ellie murmured as we drove toward it with Bob Arnold following in the squad car.

To search it, she meant. But we weren't going to break into Merkle's hideous dwelling with its piles of cardboard and barrels of tin cans and bins of who knew what else littering the yard.

No, I wanted to confront the man himself. At the corner Bob slowed, letting us go ahead; we didn't want Merkle knowing his audience included the police. We wanted him to *brag*.

Ellie's nose wrinkled fastidiously as we got out of my car; near the trailer stood a burn barrel in which Bert was apparently disposing of rotting fish parts. Through the rank smoke we made our way to the door.

But before we could knock, it opened with a long, agonized-sounding creak. I was instantly reminded of a B movie Sam had brought home recently, about a back-from-the-dead serial killer and his bloody exploits. There'd been the standard scare sequence starring the scantily clad girl who goes unwisely down into the dark basement.

And Bert Merkle's mossy grin provided a similar effect. At the sight of it an old slogan popped into my head: *Is This Trip Really Necessary?*

"Yes, ladies?" he inquired, rubbing his hands together in parody—I hoped—of the aforementioned demented killer.

On the other hand, that was precisely what I thought he was, so maybe the comparison wasn't so far-fetched.

Determinedly I climbed the rotten planks that served him as front steps, Ellie behind me. But Sam had been bringing a lot of movies home, lately, what with his no longer spending most of his evenings in bars.

Now as I stepped inside all I could think of was the cop in *Psycho*. The cop who'd thought he could handle whatever happened, too.

"Come in, come in," Bert went on crooning, and it was all I could do not to look over my shoulder to check for Bob.

But I didn't. If this worked out, no one would know Bob had been here at all until quite a long time later, when he testified to having heard Bert Merkle confess to whatever kind of fraud the district attorney decided was appropriate.

Or—if luck was really with us—to murder. "Listen," I told Bert. "We know what you're up to. We know about the old books."

Inside, the trailer was as trashy and unappetizing as the yard. Dirty dishes in the sink, dirty clothes on the floor, and dirty bedding on the narrow fold-down platform Bert slept on.

I'd been in here once before, on another matter. He'd had books, and a chessboard with a game set up on it. Since then, though, Bert Merkle had gotten loonier. The door closed behind us with a decisive click.

"Oh, really?" he replied. "You know that, do you?" Those teeth were like the "before" picture in an *Illustrated Textbook of Nasty Dental Pathology*.

"Bert," I insisted in what I hoped was a conspiratorial tone. "We need to talk. Because the thing is, Dave DiMaio knows the old book is fake, too. He's seen your forgery lab, in the shed behind Jason's house."

Saying this, I carefully refrained from looking toward the open louvered window. I hoped sound carried well from in here; in fact, I was depending on it.

"I'm not sure," Merkle said unconvincingly, "why you think I'd be interested in that. Or why you think anything at Jason's house is mine, or what it is you really want."

Ellie wandered to the table in the squalid kitchenette. On it lay several squares of sheet tin like the kind you might use to patch a roof, plus a rivet-insertion tool and a power sheet-metal cutter that resembled a pair of battery-powered electric scissors, but a lot heavier.

It looked as if Merkle had graduated from tinfoil hats to a higher level: making them out of real tin.

"We'd like to make a deal with you," Ellie said.

By now Bob Arnold was right outside, I hoped, near enough to the open window to hear us. And to hear Merkle.

"Really," Bert drawled, not yet sounding convinced. "Well, as you can see—"

He waved a mottled hand at his living quarters, crammed with the kind of amateurish pamphlets, cheaply printed booklets, and blurrily illustrated newsletters favored by crackpots everywhere.

"—I'm always open to new ideas."

Uh-huh. "Okay. The thing is, I know you've been faking old books and selling them, probably for years. But now I need my old book to be *real*," I said. "Because I need money. Lots of it. So I meant to get the book authenticated."

Now he was the one watching me. "By Horace Robotham," I prattled on. "Then I meant to sell it, get the money I need. I've heard that it would be valuable to the right kind of collector. And—"

Here was the kicker. "I've got my book back." Gosh, but I was out there on a wing and a prayer. "But DiMaio's knowing about it has messed my whole plan up."

Merkle's lips pursed consideringly. "And do I assume correctly that you'd like to turn the clock back on that little event?"

he asked finally. "Erase," he added, "our friend Dave's brand-new knowledge of your book's being a forgery?"

Oops. I needed Bert thinking someone else knew what *we* did, or he might decide to do something drastic to us before Bob could intervene. But I didn't want Merkle going out after DiMaio, once we were gone from here.

"Not exactly," I said. "I'll take care of Dave."

He turned sharply. "What do you want, then? Come, come," he added, "you wish me to be frank with you. Why should I not demand the same?"

Ellie stepped in, making no effort to sound friendly. "The truth is, we think you killed Horace Robotham, Jason Riverton, and Ann Talbert. Since you also faked that old book, we think the reason you killed them must be to keep the forgery a secret. We want it to remain that way, also."

He smiled, seemingly in appreciation. But behind the smile was a hint of malicious amusement I didn't like one bit.

"Dave said it's key for something like that to have been in place for a long time," I put in. "So it made sense to hide it in the foundation of my cellar."

How he'd managed *that* trick was something I'd have liked discussing with him, too. But we didn't have time; if he thought about this too hard he might figure out what thin ice Ellie and I were skating on.

"But once Horace had the book something happened," I said. "Something that meant your plan to embarrass him wouldn't work, maybe some flaw that he as an expert would surely recognize and link to you."

Merkle listened with seeming interest. "You realized that if that happened your other fakes could get exposed as well. You could," I finished, "go to jail for years."

"Wouldn't I risk the same kind of exposure with my original plan?" he inquired reasonably. "Expose the forgery? Expose my own hand in it?"

"No. The original plan would've revealed the book as a fake, all right. But a fake perpetrated by someone else."

"Go on," he said intently.

"With Horace dead, you thought your problem was solved. Until DiMaio showed up," I said. "And then all kinds of things started going to hell, didn't they?"

Merkle's eyes narrowed. "Continue, please. I'm especially interested in knowing why you think I'd entrust a valuable item of mine to the Talbert woman. Since she did end up with it and in your view that could hardly have been an accident."

"Because you sent her and Jason to steal it from Horace. Whose idea killing him was, yours or theirs, I don't know and it doesn't matter. It happened, that's all," I replied in a rush.

Saying it aloud to him made the cruelty of it all the more real: Horace's pain, Dave's grief and Lang Cabell's. The sudden, violent ending of a quiet, decent life, and for what?

Some damned book, that was all. "Jason would've done anything for you," I said. "But to get Ann to go after the book with him, you must've threatened her, somehow. Or promised her something."

"Maybe that she'd get to keep it," Ellie put in. "Or at least use it."

"Right. For her research," I added, the word sour in my mouth. "You must've believed she'd hold on to it, and keep her mouth shut about it until *you* could steal it from *her*."

"That way even if things went badly," said Ellie, "no one would find such an incriminating piece of evidence in *your* possession."

"Very clever. I'm flattered," Merkle remarked with a touch of sarcasm. He still wasn't admitting anything, though.

"But afterward Ann and Jason were dangerous to you," I said. "Jason was loyal, but who knew how long he'd stay that way? And Ann—well, she started bragging practically right off the bat. So you had to get rid of her, too."

Even as I said it, I wondered *why* she'd bragged. You'd think she'd keep quiet about it. But then, common sense hadn't been her strong point. And in any case, we'd never know, now.

Ellie took up the story. "It was dark and noisy on the dock. People had been drinking. Ann, especially. And it all must've happened so fast. You meant to invade her house and take the book just as *she'd* done at Horace Robotham's after *his* death. But Jake and Dave DiMaio beat you to it."

As she spoke, she picked up the electric snippers from the table and pressed the switch experimentally. The thing whirred; she put it down.

"I might have watched Horace for a few days or even weeks and learned his routine, that he always went out for a walk in the evening," Merkle said as if testing the idea. "Alone."

He looked at me. "Theoretically I might have asked Jason to follow him, strike him with something—a rock, a brick—which he'd have tossed away somewhere later. And you're right, once Horace's house was empty I could've sent the Talbert woman in to take the item I wanted. If," he added, "I'd wanted it."

He joined Ellie by the table, gripped the tin snips, turned them on again. The sharp, serrated edges moved in a blur.

Yeeks. I hoped Bob Arnold really was right outside as he'd promised. Merkle's gaze flickered at me. "As for the rest, that might've worked as you've described, too. But—"

Theory, schmeory. I needed him to say he'd committed fraud, or some other criminal act, so Bob Arnold could grab him up and clap him into handcuffs and deliver him to people who were much better at rattling bad guys' cages than I was. Let *them* work on getting Merkle prosecuted for murder; right now I just wanted the process begun, starting with him in custody.

"Look," I said, interrupting him. "If you'll just fix up the book you faked so I can sell it as authentic, obviously it'll be in my best interests to forget anything else you might've done, and—"

"Right. Me, too," Ellie agreed, nodding energetically just as a loud *thud!* hit the trailer's door.

I jumped. "What was that?"

Another bout of hammering, and then several more in quick succession, rattled the trailer. Merkle frowned, rushing to the door. He grasped the handle, which turned easily enough.

But the door didn't open. Bert yanked on the knob, then put his shoulder to the door; nothing happened, though. And unless I missed my guess nothing would.

Fixing up an old house makes a person pretty familiar with the sound of a hammer. Which is used, of course, to pound nails. Or spikes. Whichever; that door was *shut*.

And now I thought I smelled smoke. "Is there another way out of here?" I asked Merkle, who looked alarmed.

Me, too. "No," he growled. "No, there's only the—"

"Hey!" said Ellie as a grayish wisp of something floated in through the tiny window.

That is, too tiny for us to crawl out of. Her freckled nose twitched unhappily. "What's . . . ?"

But we both knew. It *was* smoke, and not the stuff coming out of Merkle's burn barrel. This was the heavy, acridly oily kind from flaming rags or papers, if they're doused in something.

Say, charcoal-starter fluid. And Merkle's trash wasn't only in his yard; there'd also been plenty shoved under the trailer itself. Suddenly an errand I hadn't bothered telling anyone about because we had Bob Arnold riding shotgun for us didn't look so guaranteed-safe anymore. The opposite, in fact, because come to think of it, where *was* Bob?

I shoved past Merkle and Ellie to the window. "Fire! Help!" But the only reply was the crackle of flames under the trailer. And then I glimpsed it, crumpled in the weeds a dozen yards from the trailer. Something that glittered.

It was Bob Arnold's utility belt, and the shiny thing on it

was his pair of handcuffs reflecting a fire. And the crumpled thing—

That was Bob. I stared as the orange gleam grew brighter and he didn't move.

"Jake," Ellie managed, then stopped as a bout of coughing seized her.

Merkle vanished into the trailer's inner recesses. He came back gripping a fire extinguisher; he aimed it around uncertainly, his eyes streaming.

Uncertainly, because from where we were there was nothing to extinguish. The fire was *beneath* us, not inside, spewing toxic smoke up into the trailer, and the tiny window did little to vent it.

"Jake," Ellie repeated, sounding frightened. "We've got to do something...."

I felt the floor under my feet growing warmer. The fire was now visible through a crack in the linoleum by the door. "Bert," I demanded, "do you have a crowbar, or anything we could use to pry the—"

Coughing convulsively, his eyes streaming with tears, he shook his head. "No," he choked.

I struggled to think clearly. But the fumes made me dizzy, burning my throat and blurring my vision. Ringing in my ears rose to a siren sound I thought might be real, even though the trailer was out of sight of any neighbors.

Someone passing might've seen something and called 911. But when I peered desperately out again no truck or emergency vehicle—no help—was anywhere in view.

And Merkle, damn him, didn't even have a phone. I hurled myself against the door but it didn't budge, then punched the window hard, agony exploding up my arm. Behind me Merkle reeled like a helpless animal, kicking walls, shoving me aside to rattle the doorknob again as the fire's crackle deepened to a rumble, *whoof*ed to a roar.

Ellie's coughing grew uncontrollable; she couldn't speak but I felt her gaze on me, begging me to do something.

Only I couldn't, and moments from now this place would be an inferno. It'd only been a matter of a few seconds but it already seemed we'd been in here forever.

And we'd be here forever, too, I thought in despair, until our blackened bodies or what remained of them got sorted from the charred rubble.

But then . . . blind, deafened by the fire's greedy roar, and terrified out of my wits, I remembered the tin snips lying on the table. The power tool Merkle had been using . . .

Where? Fumblingly I located the table's corner, groped my way across its surface until my fingers closed on the tool. Or tried; a searing bolt of pain jolted from my bruised knuckles, and my fingers wouldn't grip the tool's handle firmly enough to use it no matter how hard I willed them to.

"Bert!" I snarled. Ellie was coughing too hard to help, what breath she had left coming in short, scary-sounding whoops. Any moment she'd be unconscious.

And so would I. "Bert! Where the flooring's loose, over by the door . . ."

He flailed like a wounded beast, but got the snippers into his hands. The spot where I'd first seen the fire's glow was an orange-red triangle, bright licks of flame greedily poking up through it as if sampling a delicious meal to come.

"Cut there!" I gasped. "Then up and away from . . ." A convulsive fit of gagging stopped me, but he half-crouched, half-fell toward the flaming gap.

Because the door's frame was likely made of reinforced steel, but the area nearby was obviously thinner and flimsier. And I'll say one thing for the weird old goofball, he might not have given two figs about us but Bert Merkle had a powerful sense of self-preservation.

Through the smoke and flame I saw the blade tips, black in sil-houette, against the enlarging fire. Hearing the tool's busy whirring I thanked my stars the flames hadn't yet burst through.

But that's all the stars granted; I couldn't see Ellie. Or hear her. *Don't panic,* I told myself, but we were locked in a box and it was on fire; any instant those flames would erupt.

Terror flooded me, drowning me in grief; the roaring in my ears built to a howl, rising and falling, and still the door didn't open.

No air, just a desperate absence of it. Heat, smoke...The flames faded. I hit the floor hard, grasping for some handhold to pull myself up again but not finding one.

The smothering dark closed in, blacking out everything else. I fought for another breath, just one more sweet, precious gulp of fresh air, but there was no air.

There just wasn't any.

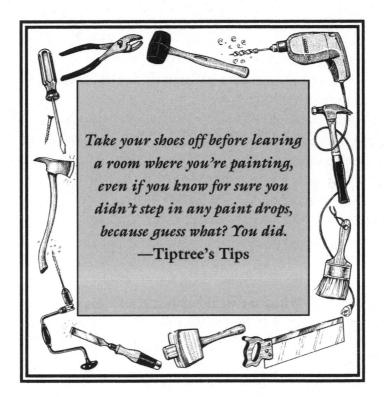

Chapter 17

*Take your shoes off before leaving
a room where you're painting,
even if you know for sure you
didn't step in any paint drops,
because guess what? You did.*
—Tiptree's Tips

J ake? Come on, damn it."

It was Wade, coming out of the darkness at me...the darkness of death, I supposed, because surely this was it.

Fuzziness, flares of light, incomprehensible sounds mingled
strangely with voices of the living....I couldn't find my body and
I guessed this must be what it was like to be a ghost.

Ellie. A wailing ghost, because I'd killed her, too, hadn't I? Brought her along on a damn-fool errand...

"Oh!" I lurched up, fumbling at the cool moisture on my face. Not dead, but if this was living there was one crucial adjustment that needed to be made right this instant...

I ripped the oxygen mask off, leaned sideways, and let my stomach turn itself violently inside-out. "Oh, god..."

"Here, put this back on," Wade said, wiping my face with a damp towel and replacing the mask.

I don't know what else they put in those oxygen tanks, but it tasted like champagne. "Thank you," I murmured, unable to muster the breath for anything more, and fell back on the grass.

My throat was afire, my head felt like tons of wet concrete had been dropped on it and left there to harden, and an elephant sat on my chest.

And that was nothing compared to the way my conscience felt. Bob Arnold, Ellie, and probably Bert Merkle, too...

Gone. "I'm so sorry," I muttered.

Wade bent over me. "Sorry? I don't—"

Somebody pushed him aside: Ellie. Her red hair, fluffed out around her face, resembled a halo.

"Jake? Can you hear me? Oh, my god, she's awake. Oh, Jake, I thought you were dead!"

She crouched and wrapped her arms around my shoulders. "Oh," she wept, "I'm so glad you're alive, I thought—"

I pushed her away just far enough to see her face again; her beautiful, *living* face. "I thought *you* were..."

"Yeah, well, you both almost were. And me, too," growled Bob Arnold, fingering the back of his head. "Somebody must have hit me with a two-by-four or something, knocked me right out cold."

"Merkle?" I whispered. Bob's look turned grave.

"Took him in the ambulance, they were workin' on him when they left. Can't tell, from what I saw, whether he's gonna make it or not. But it didn't look good."

I sat up, still dizzy and nauseated. "Ouch."

Wade was working on my hand, cleaning and taping the places I'd crunched by punching that window with it. Ordinarily it would have been one of the med techs' jobs, but Wade wasn't letting anyone else near me.

"Who?" I grated at him through a throat that felt shredded from the smoke and the screaming. "Have they...?"

He shook his head grimly. My knuckles were very painful but his touch wasn't. Sitting there, I thought that if I could only keep my hand in his forever, I might be all right.

"No," he said, applying a gauze pad. "Whoever hit Bob and started the fire must've been following you. But they got away."

He finished securing the gauze with tape. "You might end up needing an X-ray on that," he said, not meeting my gaze.

He was crying, his breath coming in gasps he was trying hard to control. He kept looking down at my hand, then leaned forward to wrap his arms around me and hold me, his tears leaking down my neck.

"Don't let me lose you," Wade whispered. "Please don't."

By then I was weeping, too, because it had been close, hadn't it? It had been so terribly close, our losing each other. Which of course we would do someday; everyone must.

But not today. "I won't," I whispered, his warm arms wrapped tightly around me feeling like a gift I didn't deserve.

He released me as George's truck skidded to a halt down on the street and George jumped out. Spotting Ellie he ran to her. His embrace nearly knocked her off her feet.

By now it was late in the afternoon, the setting sun a pale disk in the gathering fog. I tried to get up and couldn't; not on the first try.

The medical technicians were gathering their equipment. "Any word on the other fellow?" I asked.

Whispered, actually. Other than my knuckles the worst injury seemed to be to my voice.

If you didn't count my conscience. Because even though no one was dead on account of it—yet—this all still felt like my fault.

The ambulance tech shook her head. "No, we haven't heard."

She might've said more, but Bob Arnold broke in. "When you feel better, Jacobia," he began, his eyes like ice chips. "And by that I mean tonight at the very latest."

I nodded obediently. The gesture only made the whole world tilt a few sickening times. "You want to talk to me," I finished.

Or listen, more likely. Because this wasn't a mugging, or an accidental drowning, or a suicide. This was attempted murder.

Or if Bert Merkle didn't survive, never mind the *attempted* part. "I want to know each and every single solitary thing you and Ellie have done, what you saw and heard, who you talked to and what you told them and what they said back, since this whole mess started. Have you got that?" Bob inquired grimly.

Peering at me not with his friend face on, but with his cop face: no fooling around.

"I've got it, Bob," I replied. A fresh wave of guilt washed over me. Because if I'd let all this alone, who knew what might've happened?

Not this. This wouldn't have happened.

"How'd we get out?" I asked as Wade helped me into the truck.

Through the rear window, Merkle's trailer was a blackened heap of junk. *The neighbors are probably thrilled,* I thought distantly.

"Merkle." He threw the truck into reverse, backed out of the trash-heaped lot.

The fire still crackled in my ears. "But...I don't get it. I thought the smoke..."

"Took him down, right. But he was out, first. He went back in after you and Ellie. That's when it got him. According to the EMT guys, Merkle shoved you two out the hole."

Those snippers...Bert had done what I told him to. "And then he collapsed. EMTs pulled him out," Wade said.

"Oh." It was coming back to me, Merkle and the tin snippers, hands gripping my shoulders in the dark, a hard shove.

"Wade, if Merkle wanted to, he could've left us in there. Besides DiMaio we're the only ones who know..."

"Jake. Maybe you should rest for a while."

Let it rest, he meant. Because Wade was a patient man, and a kind one, and to his mind a fully formed independent spirit was necessary equipment in a wife. He'd married me in part because I was, as Bella would've said, as independent as a hog on ice.

But this was bad. He turned onto Key Street. In the dusk our own house-lights glowed, yellow bars slanting onto the lawn.

We pulled into the driveway. "I can't," I said.

Because Merkle hadn't struck Bob, or started that fire. Or left Ellie and me to die in it; someone else had.

Someone who would try again. "I can't let it rest," I repeated. But Wade was already out of the truck and coming around to open my door, so he didn't hear me.

Inside, I learned that the news of my narrow escape was already all over the island. "That phone," Bella grumbled irritably as it rang again.

"Give it to me," I said as once more she went into her "Missus Tiptree can't be disturbed" speech.

She'd already mouthed *Merrie Fargeorge,* at me, and if I told Merrie the truth maybe that would start setting the gossip-wires humming with facts, instead of the nonsense burning them up now.

That Bert Merkle and I were having an affair I'd tried to end, for instance, or that he and Ellie were having ditto, or in the most extreme version that both Ellie and I were...

You get the idea. "Hello, Merrie," I whispered. My throat felt like steel wool. "I guess you've heard all the excitement."

"I have," she replied crisply. In the background an old cuckoo clock sounded the hour; six o'clock. "I trust that you and Ellie weren't badly injured?"

"We're shaken up," I admitted. Also my hair, skin, clothes, shoes, and the insides of my eyeballs stank of smoke.

Which I'd have taken care of already, but the shower still wasn't working. So I'd been contemplating another washtub bath.

That is, until I heard what Merrie said next.

It took me about two minutes to put together a kit bag of soap, shampoo, towels, and an outfit of fresh clothes. Trying to talk Wade into letting me walk to Merrie's was harder, though, and in the end I gave up.

"Sorry, but you can get your fresh air by rolling the window down, and as for solitude, you're not getting any of that until I know for sure some lousy son of a bitch is behind bars."

He started the truck. "You can call me when you're ready to come home, Jake, and I'll pick you up again," he finished stubbornly.

Well, I couldn't blame him. So with my bath kit on my lap we set off for Merrie's house and more specifically for her tub and shower, which she'd generously offered to let me use.

Downtown we passed the fish pier with the tugboats tied up alongside it, their deck lamps glowing against the darkening sky. Across the water the lights of Campobello gleamed fuzzily through the gathering fog; approaching Dog Island, the fog thickened to a gray curtain.

"Wade, what's that?" Nearly to Merrie's house, a dim light bobbed alongside the road.

I stuck my head out the window. Quiet here; houses set back from the pavement peeped from between ancient lilac bushes, the ghost of their springtime perfume still seeming to linger in the murk.

Then I gasped as a figure suddenly took shape beside me and Dave DiMaio's face loomed out of the fog.

Wade slowed the truck. "I've lost my tie pin," Dave said to me. "Horace gave it to me and I'm looking for it."

"Here? In the dark?"

"Yes. I called your house a little while ago in case by some chance it was there. But it's not, and–"

He must've called right after we left; Bella might even have told him where I was going.

And now here he was. "My tie pin," he uttered, his flashlight beam probing the road's sandy shoulder. "It's got to be here somewhere."

Then the fog swallowed him up. "I think I'll sit out in the truck and wait at Miss Fargeorge's," Wade said as we drove on.

"Fine with me," I replied, suddenly glad I hadn't pulled the girl-in-a-nightgown-goes-into-the-dark-basement trick.

Because it was very dark out here, indeed. And Prill the Doberman might still trust DiMaio, but I didn't.

Not anymore. A foghorn hooted lonesomely. DiMaio was out looking for something; his tie pin, supposedly. But another idea seemed more plausible.

Scarier, too.

Maybe he'd been looking for me.

Merrie, this is so good of you." I set my bag down in her warm, delightfully cozy kitchen.

Inside, Caspar greeted me less effusively than the previous time; first meetings were the animal's specialty, I gathered.

"My dear, I am delighted to do it," Merrie said, bustling from the stove to the kitchen table where she poured me a cup of tea.

Her mood had improved substantially since the last time I'd seen her, and if she noticed the way I kept glancing at the door— one look at my face and the hurried way I entered, as if even in her dooryard some creeping fog-wraiths might be after me, and she'd thrown the bolt with a decisive, fear-banishing *click!*–she didn't mention it. "Old Eastport houses like yours are delightful, filled with history and atmosphere," she went on as she poured her own cup.

A plate of pastries appeared; gratefully, I took one. "But they can be full of other things, too," she added with a touch of asperity.

Right, like busted plumbing parts. Not that Merrie seemed to have any of those, or anything else that was broken, either. On the mantel the clock ticked peacefully. From the hall another one tocked, then suddenly cuckooed.

I jumped, spilling tea. "I'm so sorry," I began.

"Never mind, never mind." She got up and fetched a dishcloth with which she wiped away every drop.

"After what you've been through I can't say I'm surprised. I told people Bert Merkle was a bad man, but nobody listened. And I warned Jason's mother that *she* should put a stop to it. Whatever he was up to over there, it was no good." She sighed, folding the dishcloth. "Not that she *could* put a stop to anything. Or make Jason do anything, either."

"No. Nobody could, I guess."

I didn't add that whoever had started the trailer fire, it hadn't been Jason; instead I suddenly wanted to get my bath taken and go home with Wade, who waited outside as promised.

Merrie Fargeorge's warm kitchen with its good-food smells, beautifully tended houseplants, and shining-clean surfaces still felt like a safe haven. But DiMaio was out there somewhere, too, and I'd already pushed my luck too far once tonight.

She shot me a look of sympathy and it struck me suddenly how judgmental I'd been about her. I made a sudden resolution to be kinder to her, even if at times she could be a bit difficult.

"You poor thing," she said. "You've been having quite a day for yourself, haven't you, Jacobia?"

She patted my shoulder. "You come along, now, and have your nice, hot shower."

Hung in the long carpeted hallway were dozens of old framed photographs, each with a printed slip fitted neatly into a slot in its matting. Ranging from small 1840s-era daguerreotypes to sepia-toned images of the late 1800s, it was a small but complete and possibly even museum-worthy collection.

"Come along, dear," she repeated; I hurried to catch up. "Take your time, don't worry about a thing, and use all the hot water you like," she added, opening a door.

"Oh," I breathed, looking in. Somehow I'd expected yet another old claw-footed tub, possibly with a jerry-built shower apparatus and a drafty plastic curtain. But this—

The room was huge, floored in brown terra-cotta tiles and paneled in cedar, with a tub approximately the size of Noah's Ark if the ark had featured spa jets, set into a tiled surround. A hand-held shower wand perched at the head of it while at the foot a tiled shelf offered gently curved, heel-shaped depressions, so you could put your feet up and soak.

"This is lovely," I said inadequately, taking in yet more: a sky-light over the tub. A small woodstove radiating warmth.

"In the basket there are a few toiletries you might like to try." Merrie indicated a profusion of French-milled soaps, exotic sham-poos, and luxury skin lotions.

Nearby on a hook hung a thick white terry-cloth robe; more shelves held thirsty-looking towels. There was a sea sponge, and a hair dryer with a comb attachment.

"Oh, thank you," I told her sincerely, eager to try bathing in the twenty-first century instead of the nineteenth.

The tub was already full of steaming-hot water, I noticed as she departed. Getting in, I experienced the kind of happiness I'd thought was reserved for children on Christmas morning.

Rub-a-dub. The *sapone* that I chose—it was labeled in Italian and rested in a large, heavy carved-stone soap dish—smelled like heaven and lathered generously. It washed away the smoke and the clinging stink of fear.

Built into the room's cedar-paneled corner was a slate-floored shower with a bright, positively enormous brass shower head. Pink with cleanliness, I pulled the canvas curtain shut around myself and turned on the spray for a final rinse.

She must have a pressure tank, I decided as what felt like all the water on the planet began cascading luxuriously over me. *Nobody gets this much water pressure without a—*

But then through a tiny space between the tiled wall and the shower curtain, I saw it. Out the window, which—I did a little fast mental geography—faced toward the road: the haloed beam of a moving flashlight.

An *approaching* flashlight. But not on Wade's side of the house; from where he waited in the truck he wouldn't be able to see it. Naked and gripping the soap-on-a-rope I'd found hanging in the shower, I rushed to the window and drew the shade aside.

There I found unhappily that the flashlight was a good deal nearer than I'd first thought. Right outside, in fact.

But the side of the house was still blocking it from Wade's view. Merrie's little dog yapped once and fell silent; next came pounding at the door.

The *front* door, drat the luck; still no line of sight from where Wade sat. Merrie's footsteps pattered to answer.

Don't! I thought, but too late. The door opened and slammed hard as Merrie's voice rose briefly.

I scrambled for my clothes, tangled in a heap on the floor. No time for my bag. No time for getting dressed at all, in fact.

Merrie's voice, again, louder; then came a sound that could only be something striking somebody's head, a sickening ripe-cantaloupish thump followed by the crash of glass smashing.

Oh, Merrie, I thought as footsteps approached in the hall. Wildly I scanned for an escape route but found none; *This,* this *is why you shouldn't paint a window shut,* I thought, struggling with it.

But it wouldn't budge, so I couldn't even shout for help. And the bathroom door itself led to the hallway, which ended one way at a blank wall and the other . . .

The intruder was coming the other way, toward me. Slow but sure, step by sneaky step, the stealthy sounds proceeded on floorboards that were themselves oddly silent instead of creaky as they'd been under my unfamiliar tread.

But of course the intruder would be trying very hard not to make any sound on the other side of that closed bathroom door, which in my delight at the deluxe bathing arrangements, I hadn't even bothered to lock.

So there I was, naked and weaponless as the doorknob began turning, leaving me one choice:

Quickly, I hopped back into the shower and cranked it on. As I did so, I pulled the curtain shut and started wrapping the rope from the soap-on-a-rope tightly around both hands, with a length of the rope loose between them.

Because fear, surprise, and whatever weapon the intruder had brought along with him were a formidable combo, to be sure. But a naked lady armed with a strangling-tool made of a soap-on-a-rope was something else again, I thought determinedly.

I just didn't know yet precisely what. Meanwhile from beyond the shower curtain came the soft, unidentifiable yet unmistakable noises that in the movies always mean that the naked lady happily scrubbing herself is at that very moment being snuck up on by a crazed killer.

And that's what they meant now, too, except for the scrubbing part. And the *happily.*

Still, I had to try something. Dave DiMaio might believe he had the upper hand at last but as I stood waiting, shivering and dripping, I decided that at the very least, I was going to wash that bastard's mouth out with the soap.

But then, perhaps stimulated by the vast quantities of fear chemicals coursing through my brain, a blazingly new idea occurred to me. Because after all, here I was in the two-hundred-year-old, historical-artifact-filled home of a woman whose entire life was devoted to Eastport's past.

And yet... dear heaven, I'd missed the obvious and it might be about to kill me, that foolish assumption.

The bathroom door creaked softly.

A hand thrust past the shower curtain at me.

Gripping a big, sharp knife.

Chapter 18

T he hand grew larger and smaller. *Drug,* I thought with what little I suddenly had left of reasoning power, *some kind of . . .*

The shower curtain snapped back. The abrupt change in light and perspective nearly finished me. A gray mist filled my vision and the water's hiss rose to a roar.

Whatever the drug was, it had come on fast; when I could see again, Merrie Fargeorge stood there, her eyes pitiless and her lips flattened into a narrow line of grim purpose.

I'd hoped that when my vision cleared the knife would be gone, that it was some kind of medication-induced delusion. But it wasn't; not even a little bit.

Good steel blade and wooden handle; sharp point.

Extremely sharp, and aimed directly at my bellybutton. Suddenly I knew how the fish in a sushi restaurant feel, just before the guy with the blurry-fast cleaver act goes to work on them.

"Don't," Merrie said grimly, "move an inch." She reached out and unwrapped the soap from my unresisting hands, dropped it.

Actually I was too scared to move even a millimeter, and on top of that I couldn't feel my feet anymore. A warm glow rose up through my chest; when it got to my head it would be all over.

"What did you give me?" *Wha'ygmugh?*

Her eyes narrowed, gauging the extent of my wooziness.

"Caspar's thunderstorm pills," she replied. "They're very strong; did you know that dogs require ten times the amount of tranquilizers that humans do?"

I hadn't, and I can't say the information was very welcome, either.

"Just wait a bit longer. It won't," she added, "hurt."

Well, that's all right, then, I thought in some distant, as-yet-unanesthetized part of my brain; I guess sarcasm is the last to go.

"Fuggoo," I said. Which felt satisfying, but didn't do any good, either.

"You see, that old book of yours," she began, and I knew the idea was to pacify me, to keep me still and not trying to fight until the drug finished its work.

Then she would do whatever it was she intended to do to me. A horrid, ice-water thrill of panic shot through me when I began thinking about that.

So I stopped. Caspar's terror medicine didn't want me to be anxious or upset. *Lamb to the slaughter,* I thought, staring once more at the sharp knife.

"No, dear," she said, noticing my gaze fixed on it. "I'm not going to stab you. Unless you try something," she added coldly.

Gee, what a relief. It seemed the acid-humor part of my mind would actually have to be dipped in acid before it would give up. Meanwhile I kept on trying to think of something, anything to get out of this madwoman's clutches and get out of here.

"That book," she went on, "isn't what you think it is."

Actually, I was pretty sure it wasn't what *she* thought it was. But by now I couldn't say so.

Also I was losing the ability to stand upright; if I opened my mouth again, my jaw's weight might unbalance me, throwing me forward onto that knife.

"It was written by an ancestor of mine," she said.

From the nutball-murderer branch of the family, I thought, but by then couldn't have pronounced for the life of me. Merrie's sweet, round face with its bright pink cheeks and white hair swam in my vision.

Those eyes, though: like a pair of cold steel drill bits. "Her father sent her from Halifax to work as a servant in one of the big houses," Merrie said.

My house, I thought confusedly. *But then why . . . ?*

"As," Merrie went on, "punishment for her activities. Girls didn't read much then, you see, or at any rate not anything but Scripture. And certainly not books on witchcraft. This all came down by word of mouth in my family, you understand," she added by way of explanation.

And it was all completely irrelevant, I thought. But she didn't know that, either.

A sound came from the hall; my heart lifted. But it was only the little dog. "Hard work didn't soften her heart, however," Merrie continued. "The family employing her began noticing things."

I'll just bet they did, I thought woozily.

"The young man of the house fell in love with her, married her against his family's wishes. He was the first to die."

That's what happens when you start letting the servants have the run of the place. The story Izzy and Bridey tried to tell me, I thought.

But then the thought floated away. I couldn't feel my lips.

"Angry, vindictive girl," said Merrie. "She killed the rest off one by one. She was . . ."

Mad, bad, and dangerous to know, I concluded dizzily. But the house hadn't been Merrie's and the book was a fake, so *why* . . .

The shower enclosure turned faster. She smiled unpleasantly. "That's right, dear. It won't be long, now."

Only by standing quite still could I keep my balance, my *precarious* . . .

"Once you're unconscious, I'm going to bash the back of your head against the shower-floor ledge," she informed me, "very hard, so I'm certain that the first blow kills you."

The world suddenly took on a weird, electronic *wah-wah* feel, some psychedelic special effect that made the shower walls expand and contract.

"And later I'll find you, the victim of a tragic accident. Most accidents, you know, do occur in the home."

Correct, I thought. *You murdering bitch.* I made a grab at her wrists. "You *hit* Bob Arnold?" I managed.

Because even with the drug-sludge filling my head, it was an astonishing idea. Bob was so well-liked in Eastport that even the few habitual criminals we had wouldn't hurt him, or even say very many mean things to him while he was arresting them again.

"And . . . the fire?" My mouth was mush but she understood.

"Oh, of course," she agreed. "I was downtown doing errands when I saw you go into Bob's office. So I followed afterward to see what you might be up to, and happened upon my chance."

Right, and the charcoal-starter fluid, or whatever it was, had just jumped into her car all by itself. She sniffed proudly, as if explaining how she'd disciplined unruly schoolchildren.

"I sneaked up behind him. Bob never saw it coming," she said, unable to resist describing it all to the only person who'd never be able to tell anyone else about it.

That is, her next victim. Which would be me. She jerked her wrists easily from my grasp.

"Why?" I whispered. Ann Talbert and Jason, almost certainly

Horace Robotham; Merkle, too, if he didn't survive. And Dave DiMaio...

Wade would've come to the back door, not the front. So it must be Dave out there on the parlor floor unconscious after that awful cantaloupe-thump. Merrie eyed me as if I should know why.

"She married the son. The servant girl did... and they all began to die."

Yeah, yeah, tough to get good help. I was veering in and out of the drunken-humor phase of narcotics-overdose symptoms: *Me smart, everything funny.* Then without noticing the transition I was on the shower floor, water falling around me. Cold...

"Before she killed her young husband she had a son of her own," Merrie said. "Simon Fargeorge's grandson, my great-great-grandfather. It must've been her intention all along, to produce a son." She said it bitterly.

Her eyes bore into mine. "He could inherit, you see, on her behalf. *Her* offspring. The son," she finished, "of a *witch*."

And with that I did understand. All her exalted, colorful-local-character status, the authentic old Eastport bloodline that made Merrie Fargeorge so special, honored and treasured by all...

The witch story was merely a fantasy, of course, a couple of centuries' worth of fireside tales and malicious rumors, likely embroidered over time. No doubt the real servant liked reading and disliked praying. It was, in those days, a damning combination.

But Merrie believed it. And if my old book were pronounced real, it would resurrect the story she'd worked so hard to suppress; in a heartbeat she'd go from living treasure to an object of lurid curiosity, while her treasured ancestors became the characters in a sordid soap opera.

If the book was real. But it wasn't. Relief flooded me; all I had to do was tell her that what she feared wouldn't happen.

"Mhhhh." My lips flapped rubberishly.

Darn. That hadn't worked. I wasn't scared anymore; whatever she'd given me had taken care of that just fine. But it had also disconnected what was left of my brain from my speech apparatus.

She turned the shower off. On the far side of the door the little dog, Caspar, scratched harder, then apparently began hurling himself against it.

But with a murderess looming over me I couldn't spare much thought for her canine companion. And anyway I had no thoughts. They'd gone somewhere; swirled down the shower drain, maybe.

Merrie grabbed handfuls of my hair, one on the right side of my head and one on the left.

"I'm so sorry," she told me, and she probably was, for her own twisted value of *sorry*. "But I'm too old to start over, Jacobia. Once you are gone there'll be only that foolish fellow out there to finish off."

DiMaio. My eyes unfocused, cold spreading through me as if embalming fluid had already been injected in my veins.

She did not, I thought clearly, even realize that Wade was still waiting for me in the driveway.

But it didn't matter. Her hands lifted my head, cruelly gripping my hair. Calmly I waited for the downward thrust, the impact at the back of my skull that would smash my lights out.

"After that," she droned, "I'll get the book. Being as I'm a local-history expert there'll be no trouble about giving it to me once you're gone. And there'll be an end to–"

Then two things happened fast: the door crashed in and came violently off its hinges, one breaking with a deep *crack!* and the other pulling slantwise from the wall with an agonized *creak*.

And she let go of my head. Through the commotion behind her I felt it begin dropping, slowly at first and then faster.

A lot faster. Merrie's round wrinkled face still hung hugely over my own with a look of surprise, anger, and—inexplicably—pain.

Falling and falling, I had a last glimpse of the brass shower head with its dozens of round black holes, each seeming to stare down at me like a wide-open eye.

Finally my head hit the stone edge of the shower enclosure, just as Merrie had intended.

And all the eyes snapped shut.

If you ever find yourself in the unenviable position of wanting to reverse a serious narcotics overdose, there's a dandy little injectable medication called Narcan that will do the trick in a lot less time than it takes to tell about it.

Boom, the stuff runs in through an IV and it's over: heartbeat, pulse, and respiration abruptly restored, blood pressure rising and awareness slam-banging inside your head like someone was crashing together a lot of pots and pans in there.

Which doesn't do much for your mood, combining as it does the opposite situations of (a) being glad you're not dead and (b) wishing you were, if only so your awful headache would stop.

Meanwhile, Merrie Fargeorge hadn't survived her shower-stall encounter with Dave DiMaio. While I was in the ER being revived, she was in the next cubicle being treated unsuccessfully for a blow to the back of her own head. After bursting in, he'd grabbed that stone soap dish I'd admired so much and hit her with it while Wade still waited, all unaware, out in the truck.

All of which was still on my mind ten days later, when my father took me upstairs to unveil with a flourish—*ta-dah!*—the newly remodeled bathroom.

"Oh," I said softly, feeling my throat tighten. "It's just beautiful."

I'd come home only that morning; X-rays they'd taken in the ER just to be safe showed that when my head fell onto the edge of Merrie's shower stall, I'd fractured a small bone in my spinal column near the base of my skull. A specialist operated the next day—someday I'll describe just how much fun that was, three hours on my back in an ambulance to Bangor, wearing a thick foam collar—and reassured me afterward that the damage was fixed.

Or as fixed as he could make it. "You're sure you like it?" my father asked hopefully. "George and his guys helped."

"It's wonderful. Absolutely wonderful."

In the end, he'd decided to have the old tub refinished after all. And he'd had the floor sanded and coated with enough high-gloss polyurethane to waterproof a submarine.

The shower walls were built of special, moisture-resistant concrete board covered with ceramic tile. The pipes had been fixed, the flush replaced, the window weatherized, and the massive old cast-iron radiator sandblasted and enameled a pale cream color.

Next to it stood a brand-new sink set into a cabinet; above that hung a mirror with pinkish lights all around, so when I used it I wouldn't look like Dracula's daughter.

Or not quite so much. Surgery and recovery had definitely given me a bloodless, horror-movie appearance. But there were still a few weeks of fine weather left for the regaining of my normal skin tone, Ellie had assured me cheerfully.

"Oh." Bella sighed when I took her upstairs to see all the improvements; until now my father hadn't been letting anyone in.

"My stars and garters, doesn't that look lovely?" she said.

Peering into the tub, she put an experimental finger on the smooth, stain-resistant surface, so shiny it looked as if it not only repelled all dirt but *ker-whang*ed it into space, molecule by bounced-off molecule.

"I'd of missed the old monstrosity if you'd got rid of it," Bella confessed. "And I'm glad you didn't move the wall."

The bathroom was no bigger but it *looked* bigger; pale paint and smooth surfaces. She avoided my father's gaze.

"No sense changing just for change's sake," she said. "Most things'll do, you leave 'em the way they are."

"Hmm. We'll see," I said. My dad's face gave nothing away. "But while we're up here, Bella, let's look at the third floor."

Because while I was away, George and his team had been working there, too; now we'd see if it had been worth it.

"Right this way," I said, going ahead of her up the stairs. They'd been fixed, and the banisters repaired, as had that tub-battered front door, all while she was gone on a week-long, ordered-by-me vacation.

Peering past me as we approached what had been my work area, she frowned. "What's this? Why's there a lock on that door all of a sudden? It's never been locked before."

Then, turning to look down at my father, who was bringing up the rear: "I suppose *you* had something to do with this, you stubborn old coot."

Inserting the brand-new brass key into the brand-new lock, I opened the door. "Step in," I invited with a smile that I hoped hid my sudden nervousness.

Because she might not approve, even though George and his team had transformed it into a cozy hideaway with a big, well-lit sitting room, a large bedroom with two closets, a galley kitchen, and a bath with a glass shower stall, his-and-hers sinks, and a towel warmer.

So my dad could keep his house. Bella could keep hers. And when they were here ...

Bella's eyes widened. Walking from room to room she put her hand first on the rocker by the woodstove in the sitting room, then on the spotless white surface of the studio-apartment-sized stove. There was even a bottle of Kapow! on the counter.

Not that she'd need it. Everything was new and as easy to maintain as I could arrange. "Like it?"

"Yes," Bella whispered, resting her chin on her clasped hands to keep it from trembling. Hastily she grabbed a corner of her apron and dabbed her eyes with it.

My dad stepped forward cautiously, ready to hop back again; Bella's elbows were sharp and accurate.

"Oh," she breathed again into the apron; then a sob escaped her, and cautious or not, he knew what to do about that.

"There, there, old girl," he said, slinging an arm around her. "Don't cry, now, you'll spoil that pretty face of yours."

A snort burst through the apron. "Hush up, you old fool," she said, seizing the red bandanna he offered. "Something wrong with your eyes," she scolded, "if that's what you—"

Think. But he did. I closed the door on them. Downstairs, Sam was probably already waiting; he'd asked me to go to an AA coffee-klatsch before the meeting with him tonight.

But when I reached the back hall, to my surprise Dave DiMaio was there instead.

"Hey," I said. "I didn't know you were still in town."

He bent to smooth Prill's ears as the big red Doberman gazed adoringly up at him. "I haven't been. I called the hospital to see how you were doing, they told me you'd been sent home. So I came back."

He frowned. "Bert Merkle's ashes were scattered off the Deer Island ferry, today, too. I guess I thought somebody from the school should be there for that."

Bert had died without regaining consciousness. "He'd left—"

"Instructions, yes. For the disposal of his remains. There's a fund for things like that, for alumni."

"Well. It's good of you to handle it, then, after...anyway, I'm glad you're here. I've been wanting to thank you."

"I was in the right place at the right time, is all. Got the tie pin back, too, by the way." He tapped his chest.

It was in his tie; a silver quill with a drop of ink hanging from the tip. Or I supposed it was ink.

"Merrie Fargeorge had it all along," he told me. "Must've found it where I dropped it. And she had Horace's house key," he added, "in that big glass jar she hit me with. When I woke up, there it was, lying in front of my nose."

"You recognized it? Among all the other...?"

"Horace had painted a raised dot of enamel onto it so he'd know it by the feel," Dave explained, "coming home from his walks at night. When I saw the enamel dot, I knew it was his."

"So that's how she got in after she..."

He nodded. "It wouldn't have been like Lang not to lock up the house, no matter how upset he was. She must've taken it off Horace's body after she killed him, and in all the confusion afterward no one ever thought of looking for it."

He paused sadly. "She'd kept the weapon, too. Some kind of reproduction of a medieval tool."

I recalled the one missing from Jason Riverton's collection.

"So we have at least a part of the story of what happened, even though she's not around anymore to tell it," he finished.

But *I* wasn't finished. "How did you know? Walking around out there in the fog that night, how did you—"

The yard lights had been on, so he could have seen me going in. And the house hid Wade's truck from his view as well as from Merrie's. But none of that would have told Dave the most important thing, so what had?

"She never asked." Dave's eyes met mine. "I'd spoken with her, you see, told her I knew Horace, and she knew I'd met you. The obvious connection was the old book and in a town like this I felt sure she knew about that, too. But she never mentioned it. And when I saw you going into her house that night, all at once I knew why."

It was precisely the same thought that had struck me with such force while I stood in her shower: that Merrie was such an avid finder and collector of Eastport artifacts.

But she'd never asked me about this one. Not once, as if by the force of her silence she could erase its very existence.

"But if Merrie's ancestor was a Fargeorge by marriage and took over the Fargeorge homestead," I began, "then why—"

"Why would Merkle decide to hide a fake book in your house instead of hers?" Dave asked. He followed me to the kitchen where I got out cups and began making tea; Sam might want some, too, when he got here.

"I wondered that also, and it turns out there's an answer," he said. From atop the refrigerator Cat Dancing opened a crossed blue eye, yawned, and went back to sleep.

"Do you happen to know two elderly sisters named Izzy and Bridey?" he asked me. "They make," Dave added, "very good cookies."

When I said I did he continued. "They seem to think Merrie's servant-girl ancestor didn't go right to the Fargeorge house from Halifax. They'd heard she worked somewhere else first. Although," he added, "not for long."

Of course. "Here. In my house."

He nodded. "Maybe the original family caught on to her wicked ways and sent her packing. Or maybe they just didn't have a marriageable son."

Dave looked regretful. "Merkle would've known. He'd've made sure to get his history straight before starting his own plan."

The kettle whistled. "I imagine it'll be a mess trying to sort out all Bert's other book forgeries," I said.

DiMaio watched me pour boiling water into a pot. "Yes. Lang Cabell's been hired by some of the dealers Bert sold to, to help identify them. Not that anyone will get any money back, but it's important figuring out what's what."

"And Liane?" I asked. "Is she still suing you? Or trying?" I'd forgotten about the girl, but seeing Dave reminded me of her again.

"For the moment she's given up the idea." His lips pursed judiciously. "We seem to've taken Liane under our wing, Lang and I. We'll see how that works out."

I poured the tea. Outside the kitchen windows, the pointed firs at the edge of the yard cut sharp black outlines on a fading sky.

"So how'd you ever learn to swim like that, anyway?" I asked as he sipped. "Jumping in after Ann Talbert that way."

He shrugged modestly. "The school where I teach has a pool. Water safety," he added cryptically, "is quite a large part of the curriculum."

Probably there was a story behind that, too. But I let it go. Then, getting to the heart of the matter: "Dave, how did you happen to lose the tie pin in the first place? Way out there on Dog Island."

He glanced up alertly. "Well," he began, preparing to lie. But my look must've told him not to bother.

"Did you by any chance hear the story about the Fargeorges' servant girl quite early on?" I asked him. "From Bridey and Izzy, maybe, when you were going around Eastport asking local-history questions?"

He might've met them on the street, or in one of the shops. And his air of being such a nice young fellow not having deserted him even in middle age, he might've engaged them in conversation.

And the girls, as everyone here still called them, did like to talk.

"And what you heard made you feel curious," I said. "So you called Merrie Fargeorge, or . . . no, she called you, didn't she?"

His face said I was right. "Thinking maybe she could charm you somehow into going away," I added.

"Why would she want to do that?"

"Maybe her guilty conscience convinced her your interest in local history was really a cover for something else. Curiosity about the manner of Horace's death, perhaps. But at any rate the conversation didn't develop as she planned, did it?"

I filled two cups. "Because Merrie didn't realize how much you'd already learned. Did the two of you end up swapping war stories? Two experienced teachers like yourselves trading tales out of school? She might've tried that, to soften you up."

He smiled into his tea as I continued. "First she told one, about, say, a kid named Jason Riverton?"

Monday came in, laid her glossy black head on my knee. "She wouldn't have hesitated mentioning Jason to you. Her frustrations with him as a student, even her contempt? In a way, it would have helped divert suspicion, her willingness to express that."

It was the reason behind the wine and the book, I thought: *Here is the antidote, here are the instructions for using it. Too bad you're too stupid to take advantage of them.* The initials on the computer screen, Merrie's insistence that Jason couldn't have typed them—misdirection, I thought, meant only to confuse.

Bottom line, Merrie didn't really care who took the blame as long as the boy's murder aimed any suspicion away from herself. "Then it was your turn to tell a story," I said. "Only it wasn't about a student, was it? It was about a servant girl from long ago."

He waited expressionlessly. "It was a test," I continued. "What Bridey and Izzy told you made you wonder...had Merkle not killed Horace after all? Was there some other reason for Horace's murder?"

Still no response. "You panicked Merrie on purpose. To see what she would do or say. And her reaction confirmed your suspicion."

I waited, thinking how difficult it must've been for her, putting a good face on for the party at my house after killing Jason and talking with DiMaio. Not that she'd kept it up for long; by the next day, she'd been acting like her old, irascible self again.

But what she really must have felt was pure panic.

"Maybe you didn't even mention the Fargeorge girl by name," I said. "Maybe you just hinted. But that was enough to confirm what she feared, that you were indeed a threat. And whatever she said to you in response must've told *you* that, for a woman whose life revolved around the human equivalent of a dog's pedigree, that book was plenty of motive for murder."

Dave's smile had vanished. "Merrie was the one who'd pestered Horace about it, not Ann Talbert," I said. "Maybe she thought if she could get hold of the thing even briefly, she could destroy it."

I put down my cup. "You probably saw her calendar, showing that she traveled all over the state for lectures and meetings. Maybe it said she'd been in Orono that night, I don't recall."

His face said he did recall, and that it had. "So did you, Dave? Was that when you met her? Did you go out there to see her after she called you, and tell her a story, and was that when you lost your tie pin?"

Because if he had, he'd tipped over a final domino, spurring Merrie's fear to even greater intensity and leading eventually to my final encounter with her.

And to his justification in killing her. So that in the end he'd gotten what he came here for, hadn't he? Just not quite all of it; not yet.

I went to the dining room, took the old book from its place on the mantel; while still in the hospital I'd sent Wade upstairs to resurrect it from under the floorboard, before the carpenters could entomb it there forever.

With its soft, skinlike leather and the faint prickle of warmth seeming to rise from it as I held it, it *felt* real, as if some tricky wickedness was still in it. So much so that even now a faint uneasy feeling kept me from opening it.

Instead I returned to the kitchen. "Here," I said, holding it out to Dave.

The look on his face was priceless. "Are...are you sure?"

"Why not? It's just a forgery. And it's not as if it's going to conjure up good memories, so I have no reason to keep it. But it might mean a lot to you, because of Horace's connection to it. So I want you to have it."

As he took it, the back door opened and Sam burst in. "Hey! You'll never believe what I just—"

He held something in his closed hand. "You were right," he told Dave. He uncurled his fingers.

On his palm lay a tiny tinfoil hat. I leaned in for a better look. "You found this where?" I asked.

"Out in front of the house," Sam explained. "Way down deep in the ground where the old tree used to be."

Amazing how fast you can run out of conversational fodder while you're recuperating in a hospital. So I'd told Sam about the tree that once grew in front of the house and about a lot of other things, too; the girl who showed up naked in our apartment in New York City so long ago, for instance.

There was still one subject we hadn't discussed yet, but I wanted to talk with Wade about it once more before I raised that.

"Dave said somebody should dig, just to see," Sam told me. "So I did."

I raised my eyebrows at DiMaio. "Well," he explained, "if the book didn't go into the wall from inside, then it had to be from the outside. And if the earth was soft enough..."

As it would have been, recently filled after the old tree's removal and the soil mixed with wood chips. "Bert could have waited until he knew who was buying the old place," Dave added.

Waited, so my name would be in the book. And then he could simply have come over here one night very late, shortly before I moved in, and dug himself a hole. The old tree's roots might even have loosened a few foundation stones for him: presto, instant book depository.

DiMaio regarded the foil hat bemusedly. "And I guess while Bert had the hole open, he just couldn't resist signing his work."

Out on my back porch, the three of us stood awkwardly for a

moment. Then Dave spoke again. "Say so long to Ellie for me, too, will you, Jake?" He punched Sam lightly on the shoulder. "Take it easy, guy. And if that AA sponsor of yours craps out again, get another one."

He descended the porch steps; I walked with him to his car. "I misjudged you," I said.

He smiled. "Watch out for those first impressions."

Uh-huh. "But you know, it still wasn't reason enough."

Dave paused with his hand on the car door.

"For Merrie to do all those terrible things..." I continued. "It was so out of character. Sure, if the book got declared real it would've been news, and she would've been part of it. Her fine old family name would've gotten a blot on it...but that would have ended, eventually. People would've forgotten."

Dave got into his aging Saab sedan, started it, and rolled down the window.

"She even brought pastries to the boy's mother," I went on, "at the same time as she brought the poison."

Something flickered in his eyes. "No, she didn't. I brought the pastry."

Surprising to the end, our Dave.

"I'd tried to visit Jason that day," he told me. "Bert said I should talk to him, to see if he might be the right kind of student for our school."

"And you believed Bert?"

"Whatever else he was, he was always interested in the place we'd both come from. I thought Horace would've wanted me to find out if...Well. There seemed no harm in trying." He looked embarrassed. "I brought the pastry as a sort of...just something to show my good intentions, I suppose."

"And was he? The right kind of student?"

"I don't know. He wouldn't see me. He wouldn't even answer his mother when she called upstairs to him. Or he couldn't."

There was a brief silence while we thought about that. "But

you're right, I can't fully explain what happened, either. I wish I could. Good-bye, Jake."

From the street he waved but his expression was distant, as if he were already thinking about something else.

Driving away, he didn't look back.

As it turned out I didn't accompany Sam that night. Sam's sponsor canceled so Sam skipped the coffee party and went to his meeting alone, while Wade and I took a ride around the island together.

"Hey," he said as I slid into the truck's cab beside him. "How're you feeling?"

"Okay," I said, although my neck hurt like hell. The doctors had given me some pain pills, but after the dose I'd had out at Merrie Fargeorge's I didn't want to feel drugged again anytime soon.

Wade smelled like lime shaving cream, laundry soap, and the Badger Balm he used to keep his hands from cracking in the cold air when he was out on the water.

"Good enough, anyway," I said.

It was getting on for dark. We crossed County Road past the youth center and continued toward the old factory that extracted pearl essence from clam shells, for iridescent nail polish and so on.

"So did DiMaio want his little popgun back?" Wade asked.

I shook my head. "He didn't even mention it. I think maybe he was glad to be rid of it. Wade, did Sam really believe I might shoot myself with that thing?"

Because that was what had happened; my son had heard me shout out a threat about it, a thoughtless outburst that now I didn't even remember making.

And . . . he'd worried about it. Halfway down the road as it entered a grove of pine trees, Wade cut the engine. We drifted to a grassy verge overlooking the water.

"I'm not sure what Sam thought," Wade said. It hit me then how precarious Sam's situation really was, how unsure he must feel about everything.

"And he opened the box how?" I'd thought keeping the key on a chain around my neck was safe enough. But apparently not.

"Jake, he's known about that loose brick for years," Wade informed me gently. "The spare key, too. And the money."

The ten thousand, which he'd never touched; not even when he was at his worst. And the guns. I had, I suddenly realized, been fortunate in a lot of departments.

"He said the spare key wasn't in very good shape after all those years. He's worried he damaged the lock."

"He did," I said. "I'll need a new box." With, I'd already decided, a digital thumbprint-reader. And a retinal scanner.

Wade glanced at me. "What he said was that he didn't know how much of what he was worrying about was real, and how much was just that drying-out feeling he still gets."

At my puzzled look he added, "His body getting accustomed to the no-booze thing. So he told me he figured he should err on the side of caution, is all."

"Oh. All right. I guess I can understand that. But he left the Bisley and the .38. And the target gun, so I don't see..."

"Yeah. I asked him about that, too." Cars were parked on the verge, engines off and parking lights on.

"Sam told me one thing he did know was that you wouldn't use a gun I'd given you or one you and I had used together," he said.

Which made no sense whatsoever out in the real world. But in our little family, it did. I leaned against Wade.

"Good for him." Across the water the last bit of pink faded from the sky.

"So how come Merrie sent the old book to Ann Talbert?" Wade wanted to know. "That's the part I still don't get."

High on the hillside a hundred yards from the parking area, a white-tailed deer emerged from the trees.

"As soon as Dave came to town, Merrie must've started getting scared. A stranger asking questions wouldn't have spooked an innocent person, but she wasn't an innocent; she'd already murdered Horace. So she did exactly what she'd advised me to do: she got proactive."

"With Jason Riverton as a diversion," Wade said.

"Correct. But at the same time, she also knew the old book linked her to Horace's death, and that if anyone learned she had it, she wouldn't be able to explain it."

Behind the first deer another appeared, and another. The buck's antlers were a bone-colored crown in the dying light. Last came spotted fawns, gangly and feisty, kicking up their heels.

"But I guess she couldn't stand to just bury it somewhere," I said.

Someone got out of one of the cars and threw a lot of apples and carrots into the grass; the deer watched patiently.

"In case somebody else might find it," I continued. "Merrie must've believed Ann Talbert would take care of it *and* keep quiet about it, though, because Ann was nearly as obsessed with it as Merrie was, herself."

A meteor streaked the sky, dripping sparks. A phosphorescent trail on the water mirrored it as the deer munched warily.

"She got rid of the book but kept the house key?"

"Well, she kept it in a big old jar with a few hundred other antique ones that she'd collected. So it didn't exactly stand out."

"Huh. You wouldn't think Merrie Fargeorge could tip a young person like Ann off a railed dock, though," Wade said.

"Not usually," I agreed. "But Ann was a tiny little thing, and she was very drunk. And remember, Merrie had been digging around with a pick and shovel in that yard of hers, most of her life."

So she'd been strong. "If we hadn't showed up at Ann's house so fast, she'd have gotten the book back herself that night. Or tried." I recalled those big Block door locks Ann had.

A gawky fawn stuck its head into the illuminated circle of the cars' parking lights. It grabbed an apple from the few remaining ones and backed out again to savor its prize.

"It turns out that Merrie'd been visiting Mrs. Riverton for years. Mrs. Riverton said so, when Ellie went to tell her how Jason really got poisoned. Apparently she'd been going there just out of the goodness of her heart," I added.

And that to me was still the most perplexing question of all: how a person like Merrie had gone so suddenly—so thoroughly—*bad*.

"She'd been in the house once already that day when Ellie and I went. That's when she must've left the antifreeze jug in the cabinet, in place of the syrup."

Wade started the truck. At County Road he turned right, past the convenience-store gas pumps, surreal in the outdoor lights.

"Later she went back. Put the syrup back under the sink and the jug in the trash, so it would look like Mrs. Riverton had made a tragic mistake. That's also when she left the wine bottle and the poison-remedy book."

"Risky." Wade turned into the elementary-school driveway, followed it all the way around to the rear where the ball field spread out, and parked.

"Not really. You can't see the alley behind the Rivertons' from the street. And she'd parked there so often in the past that probably no one would make anything of seeing her there again."

It was cold-hearted, though. By that time, Jason might have already been unconscious.

We climbed the stony path leading away from the schoolyard. Above, fog moved in ribbony swirls.

"Besides, it was Merrie Fargeorge. Who'd suspect her? Poor Jason, though," I added. "All he ever wanted was someone to like him."

Wade put a hand out to help me. Between my aches and pains, bruises and stitches, and the lingering sense of having been run over by a fleet of eighteen-wheelers, that hill was no piece of cake.

"And all Merkle was after was the use of that shed? Staying in good with Jason . . . that just ensured the boy wouldn't decide maybe he wanted it for himself?" Wade asked.

"Or spill the beans about what Merkle was doing in it, I suppose. He knew Jason was so desperate for a friend, he'd never betray one. So he behaved like a friend . . . sort of."

"Christ," Wade said softly.

"Yeah. Sad, huh? On the other hand, Merkle did save Ellie and me."

Where Bert had found the goodness for it, I couldn't imagine, or the impulse to try to help Jason Riverton, either. But he had; maybe that school of Dave's had done him some good, in spite of himself.

"Yes." Wade's hand tightened on mine. "Yes, he did."

From the top of the hill, the night view stretched from Deer Island past Campobello and the Lubec Narrows, all the way around to Shackford Head and Carryingplace Cove. With the lights far and near glistening wetly it resembled a fairy-tale setting, but the fog that had sat motionless to our south all day long gobbled it steadily now that it was dark.

Finally we drove home. "Ellie's keeping Merrie's dog," I said. "She thinks sending him to a shelter is just too hard-hearted."

Caspar had been sleeping on her lap the last time I'd talked to her, with Lee stroking his ears, and George planned on training the animal to ride shotgun with him in his truck.

"Look," Wade said as we pulled into our driveway, and I followed his wave up to the third floor where for the first time in years domestic light glowed warmly.

"Let's go in," I urged, lonesome suddenly for my own kitchen, the battered tea kettle with its bright summoning whistle, my own chair. And...maybe even a bath.

"A hot toddy?" Wade suggested.

"Yes," I agreed, hurrying alongside him as, with our arms clasped around each other, we went into the big old house together and closed the door firmly behind us.

Chapter 19

Drink water regularly and eat properly when involved in a difficult/lengthy job. You may think you're sick to death of the task, when in fact you're only dehydrated and/or hungry.
—Tiptree's Tips

D riving out Route 190, Dave DiMaio saw the banner hung at the entrance to the Seaview Campground: *Bonfire Tonite!*

He drove in past the putting green and the cottages under the pines, among dozens of travel campers each with its awning, lawn chairs, and barbecue grill. The road wound on past a small general store, downhill to the water.

A long grassy area sloped to the dock where boats were tied up. Dave walked out slowly to the end of the dock, then returned to the Saab and drove all the way to where the road dead-ended at a metal gate.

He sat in the car, looking across the water to where the last light faded. When it grew completely dark and the bonfire's first flames glowed behind the hill, he returned to where a few campers had already gathered, one with a guitar.

"Nice night," said the guitar-playing fellow.

"Yes," Dave agreed as he began tearing parchment pages out of the old book. He had the idea that the fellow sitting across the flames from him knew what he was burning.

But that must be only his own imagination, and besides, it didn't matter. Neither did the absence of any hard proof that the book was precisely the kind of thing Horace Robotham had spent his life eradicating, not a forgery at all.

Merkle's secret workshop and his history of creating shams, even ones good enough to convince professional collectors, had persuaded Dave briefly that this volume, too, was merely another fake among many. What could be more reasonable?

But on the other side of the ledger were five deaths, and the transformation of a harmless old woman into a killer. For Dave it was evidence enough, as it would have been for Horace, who might not have waited even this long before setting the thing alight.

Smoke curled from the parchment pages and vanished until only the binding remained. Dave fed that in, too, pushing it with a stick to be sure every bit reached the fire's heart; at last the final fragment vanished with a sizzling pop.

The guitar guy nodded ponderously. While Dave worked he'd been strumming the instrument quietly. Now he played a sprightly ending-ditty: *shave and a haircut, two bits!*

"All finished?" he asked.

Dave rose stiffly from his haunches and breathed in the gathering fog, letting it quench the hot, painful places in his heart. "Finished," he said.

Back in the Saab he eyed his reflection in the darkened windshield and realized that it was true.

On the car's backseat lay the long, ruggedly slender tool that the Fargeorge woman had used for coring out samples from her backyard archeological dig. The tool was useful, not only for getting things out of the earth, but also for putting them in.

Small things made of tinfoil, for instance. So there was no sense leaving the device where people might get ideas from it.

Doubts, questions; no need, anymore, for any of those. His journey, begun alone in anger and sorrow, had come to its end. It was as if his old friend were with him, in firelight and in the sense of a task completed.

Thinking this, Dave aimed the Saab back toward Providence, to his own funny old college, his bachelor rooms tucked up under the eaves of the ancient residence hall, his students and books.

Someday he might be to one of his pupils what Horace had been to him. His heart moved hopefully at the notion. But now in the darkness of a late-summer Maine evening thick with mist and the shrilling of crickets, there was no hurry.

So that when he came to the small white wooden sign by the side of the road, this time he didn't bother taking the short-cut but instead drove straight on into the unmarked night.

About the Author

SARAH GRAVES lives with her husband in Eastport, Maine, in the 1823 Federal-style house that helped inspire her books. She is currently at work on the twelfth Home Repair Is Homicide mystery, which Bantam will publish in 2009.